Praise for
A Summer All Her Own

"Rosanne Keller's *A Summer All Her Own* is a luxurious trip to Greece where we find not only the azure Aegean Sea and breathtaking landscape, but more important: wise advice about how art and life intertwine to teach us who we were meant to be."

—Patti Callahan Henry

"A luscious book. The descriptions of Crete are pure sensual pleasure, the men she meets are yummy, and tucked among all this are some truly beautiful meditations about loss and love. Best of all are the scenes when Anna is alone, discovering herself as an artist and as a woman connected to the physical world."

—Nancy Thayer, author of the Hot Flash Club novels

"*A Summer All Her Own* is a tenderly romantic and touching story of loss and recovery."

—Hilma Wolitzer, author of *The Doctor's Daughter*

Written by today's freshest new talents and selected by New American Library, NAL Accent novels touch on subjects close to a woman's heart, from friendship to family to finding our place in the world. The Conversation Guides included in each book are intended to enrich the individual reading experience, as well as encourage us to explore these topics together—because books, and life, are meant for sharing.

Visit us online at www.penguin.com.

A Summer All Her Own

Rosanne Keller

NAL ACCENT · NEW AMERICAN LIBRARY

NAL Accent
Published by New American Library, a division of Penguin Group (USA) Inc.,
375 Hudson Street, New York, New York 10014,
USA Penguin Group (Canada), 90 Eglinton Avenue East, Suite 700, Toronto,
Ontario M4P 2Y3, Canada (a division of Pearson Penguin Canada Inc.)
Penguin Books Ltd., 80 Strand, London WC2R 0RL, England
Penguin Ireland, 25 St. Stephen's Green, Dublin 2, Ireland
(a division of Penguin Books Ltd.)
Penguin Group (Australia), 250 Camberwell Road, Camberwell,
Victoria 3124, Australia (a division of Pearson Australia Group Pty. Ltd.)
Penguin Books India Pvt. Ltd., 11 Community Centre, Panchsheel Park,
New Delhi - 110 017, India
Penguin Group (NZ), cnr Airborne and Rosedale Roads, Albany,
Auckland 1310, New Zealand (a division of Pearson New Zealand Ltd.)
Penguin Books (South Africa) (Pty.) Ltd., 24 Sturdee Avenue, Rosebank,
Johannesburg 2196, South Africa

Penguin Books Ltd., Registered Offices:
80 Strand, London WC2R 0RL, England

First published by NAL Accent, an imprint of New American Library,
a division of Penguin Group (USA) Inc.

First Printing, September 2006
1   3   5   7   9   10   8   6   4   2

 REGISTERED TRADEMARK—MARCA REGISTRADA

LIBRARY OF CONGRESS CATALOGING-IN-PUBLICATION DATA:

Keller, Rosanne.
A summer all her own / Rosanne Keller.
p. cm.
ISBN 0-451-21943-0 (pbk.)
1. Widows—Fiction. 2. Crete (Greece)—Fiction. 3. Artists—Fiction. 4. Summer—
Fiction. 5. Life change events—Fiction. I. Title.
PS3561.E38578S86 2006
813'.54—dc22   2006000210

Set in Simoncini Garamond • Designed by Elke Sigal
Printed in the United States of America

For Amelia and Libby, who brightened my life
as I completed this story.
May they grow up knowing themselves
and never forget who they are.

Acknowledgments

All my gratitude to my many friends who read this book and gave me sage comment. Sue Dyke, Moey Rutledge, Blythe Thomas, Leta Worthington and others. For the support and encouragement of my agent, Helen Breitwieser, and my editor at New American Library, Ellen Edwards, both of whom struggled with me for a title for this book.

A Summer All Her Own

One

In the early morning of the fourth day, Anna Sandoval knew that she had been wise to make this journey to Crete. It was the luminous light. Here on this stark island where Western civilization had begun, the light appeared to emanate not only from the sky but from the earth itself: from the craggy hillsides and sepia-colored fields, from olive trees—leaves green on one side, dull silver on the other—from the scattered confetti of wildflowers with poppies waving in the breeze like small red flags. The light illuminated the folds of distant hills and gathered in the waters of the gulf.

But what drew Anna's attention was the color of the water. Far below the high bluff where she stood on the terrace of her tiny villa, this little corner of the Aegean glinted sun strikes of silver across the inky cobalt blue in the distance. The water faded to crystal azure in the rock-ribbed coves, turning lavender as it washed a shoreline as mysterious and enigmatic as a myth. Anna sank onto the chaise longue on her terrace with the sun full on her face, closed her eyes, and took slow, deep breaths, willing the light to fill her, to chase away the shadows of sorrow. *What am I going to do now?* The question reeled through her thoughts like a mantra. She had come to Crete to find answers. But not today. There was plenty of time.

Then she smiled, remembering her arrival three days earlier in a taxi that smelled of gasoline and had a worrisome clatter under the hood. As the vehicle roared at breakneck speed, horn blaring, along the winding road from the airport in Iráklion, Anna had barely noticed the landscape—more concerned that her life was in peril. In her jet-lagged state she had only a fleeting impression of a starkness as somber as the faces of the black-clad people she saw in a blur along the roadside as she sped by, some with donkeys laden with hay or sticks of wood or water jugs.

At last, in a cloud of dust and screech of brakes, the taxi pulled up in front of Anna's hotel. The Villas sat perched on the top of a hill overlooking the town of Ayios Nikolaos across the sparkling crescent of the Gulf of Mirabello. Built in the style of a white limewashed Greek village, rows of small villas descended like stair steps down the steep slope toward the water below.

Anna checked into the hotel, then followed a porter, who couldn't have been more than thirteen, along the warrenlike passageways. They had turned several corners and gone down two flights of stairs when she heard a shout. "Hey there," a voice called from some distance behind her. "You've dropped something."

Anna looked back to see a tall white-haired man running toward her with her purse dangling on the end of one finger—the bag that contained, among other things, her passport and all her money. Then she noticed what was clutched in his other hand. Obviously the bag had fallen and dumped out her makeup, her book, a bouquet of tissues, all used, and, of all things, the extra set of underwear she'd thrown in at the last minute in case she had an unexpected layover somewhere. In the confusion of the moment, she didn't even look the man in the face, only stuttered something incoherent. "God, I'm so . . . I don't know, please excuse . . . I'm so tired." The only thing she remembered later was that he had an open book draped over his arm.

He stuffed her belongings back into the bag and handed it to her. "Nothing lost. Go get some rest. You'll feel like a new person tomorrow."

"Thank you," Anna said, grabbing the bag and turning to catch up with the porter before she lost him in the labyrinth of walkways. What a way to begin her pilgrimage into the future . . . dropping her underwear first thing.

Rushing after her guide while trying to preserve some degree of dignity, she heard the man shout from behind, "Welcome to Crete, by the way. Have-a-good-day." Only the next morning had it sunk in that her savior had been an American. No one else would have said, "Have-a-good-day" as one word like that.

Trailing after the boy, Anna climbed the two steps under the archway into her tiny private courtyard and walked through the heavy blue door of her own little "villa." She tipped the boy, barely taking in the woven wall hangings scattered throughout the rooms, the black wrought-iron chandelier, the fringed lamps in the bedroom. Dropping her clothes on the floor, she showered and stumbled into bed.

During the next three days, Anna moved trancelike from her rooms down the serpentine path to the beach and back, the sun and solitude a solace, the sense of being away, far away, comforting. She still felt carved out, a shell of a person like one of those bland-faced porcelain dolls with a hole under its feet from which everything that had made it solid had been emptied. But the past seemed distant here, as if she were looking at it through the wrong end of a telescope. For these three days her grief had moved to a quieter place. Here on Crete, there was nothing to stir old memories. Anna shifted in her chair late one afternoon, feeling the Aegean sun warm her clear to the bone. Greek sun. Healing sun.

She was awakened by her rumbling stomach. In the kitchenette cabinets she had found a cache of cereal, crackers, and cookies when she arrived. The small refrigerator in her kitchen nook had been stocked with several bottles of wine, mineral water, and an assortment of cheeses. And, along with flowers, each day a fresh bowl of fruit appeared on her table. But Anna had been more tired than hungry until now. She looked at her watch. It was seven o'clock, a good time to venture out to the Taverna, the hotel dining room, for dinner.

When she was shown to her table, she wondered why she was the only person there. Later she found that Greeks would never think of eating dinner before nine or ten. But the waitstaff, being used to Americans, no doubt, were accommodating. Anna enjoyed the subdued light and soft music. Out the window she could see the water changing color, reflecting the sunset. By the time she had finished her dinner of moussaka and ordered coffee, the lights of Ayios Nikolaos in the distance had begun to flicker on.

She was almost ready to leave when the man who had rescued her purse came in. She smiled, hoping to attract his attention so she could thank him properly, but he didn't look her way as he proceeded to a table on the other side of the room, appearing to be absorbed in his own thoughts. He didn't glance around, just sat with his back to Anna and pulled out a book. It was just as well. As soon as she put down her spoon, a wave of lingering jet lag came over her and she stumbled sleepily back to her little villa, full and satisfied.

Before she went to bed, she stepped out onto the terrace and sat in her chaise longue, her thoughts riding on the rose-scented breeze, cool from the sea, smoothing away the heat of the sun. She was glad she had decided to come here.

In the spring, her friends in Washington had tried to talk her out of going to Crete. "It's so strange, so isolated. Too near the Middle East and all that unrest. Why don't you go to Hawaii or the South Pacific if you want beaches?" they pleaded.

Anna didn't tell them that she couldn't bear it. She had been to the Pacific islands so many times with Paul.

Peter, her son, a graduate student at Princeton studying anthropology, had been more enthusiastic. He had been to Crete on a student trip. "What a great idea. Be sure and go to Knossos! That's where our culture began. And don't miss Lato. It's magical." Then he added, "If I didn't have all these papers to write, I'd come along as your porter and guide."

Her daughter, Christine, so caught up in living happily ever after for the past year and a half of wedded bliss, only said, "Whatever makes you happy, Mom. Go for it." When Anna told her that her friends thought Crete was risky because of terrorism, Christine said, "Don't worry. Terrorists would be terrified of you anyway." She grinned. "Just kidding, Mom. But if you see one, tell him to *go to your room* with that 'look' and you'll have no trouble."

Both of the children had lots of practical advice as well, in their new roles as adults taking care of their widowed mother. Mostly they were glad to see Anna stepping out, going on an adventure. "You can't keep rattling around this old house, Mom. It's been a year since—"

Yes, it had been a year since her forty-six-year-old husband gave her a peck on the cheek and went out for a run . . . never to return. Dead of a heart attack. A year since the policeman came to the door that late April day and asked, "Are you Mrs. Paul Sandoval?" A year since the *Washington Post* published headlines about Paul's untimely death on the front page, listing all of his broadcasting awards, including an Emmy for hosting *Fourth Dimension*—the comprehensive, in-depth television talk show Paul had anchored, which Anna could no longer bear to watch. A year since the last showing of Paul's unfinished documentary series—the award-winning, nine-year-running *Religions and Cultures of the World*, which had taken Paul and Anna all over the world as he did research and interviews and filmed festivals, rituals, and so many fascinating people. It had been a terrible year.

Anna's friends were concerned that she was doing something irrational and perhaps dangerous. Her children were concerned that she was going to wither away living alone. Anna had just known it was time. Time to move on.

Then the phone rang one day. "Don't do it!" yelled the voice on the other end of the line, without salutation. It could only be Maggie, calling long-distance from Dallas. "I just got your letter about this crazy idea you have of going to Crete, and I'm coming to Washington to head you off at the pass. I'll be there this afternoon." She gave the time and flight number. "I'll talk to you then."

Anna smiled as she hung up. Maggie Bradford, her oldest and best friend. She'd be glad to endure Maggie's admonitions just to get a chance to have a good visit with her. They had known each other since they'd entered St. Mary's High together. Later, in detention hall for being part of a group that set off firecrackers behind the toilets in the restroom, they became comrades. For five days, they passed illicit notes under Sister Mary Margaret's nose, a correspondence that had bonded their friendship forever.

The evening after Maggie arrived, she and Anna lounged in front of a crackling fire, sipping cocoa, their feet stretched out on the coffee table in what had once been Paul's study. Paul had called this room "the hole," and for Anna it had become a sanctuary. She felt closer to him here than in any other place in the house. He had certainly left his mark. The desk, uncluttered now, held only a picture of the family taken when Christine and Peter were in their early teens, a carved wooden statue of a Masai shepherd, and a brass lamp with a green glass shade. Books, carvings, sculptures, and pottery that Paul had brought back from all over the world filled the shelves. As they talked Anna noticed one of Paul's sweaters was still hanging on the bentwood rack. Had she simply not seen it before? Or had she left it there on purpose? "I have to get away for a while. I've got to get out from under the weight of Paul's shadow."

"That's a strange thing to say."

"I know, because he's been . . . he's been dead for a year now. But people still think of me as Paul Sandoval's wife. I'm still clothed in his image." She cleared her throat, determined not to cry. Again. "It's strange," she went on. "I've learned something these past few months that I simply didn't know, or was in denial about. My whole identity all these years has been bound up in other people's needs—not only the family . . . everything, all that volunteering and stuff. I allowed myself to become merely one of life's supporting players. I guess I just didn't notice when Paul was still—"

"Are you talking about all that wife and mother and sterling-member-of-the-community stuff? Or are you talking about the demands made on the wife of a celebrity?"

"All of the above. I did what I was supposed to do. What I was schooled to do from the day I was born. 'Stand by your man. Follow his lead.' Isn't that what all good little Catholic girls are taught?"

"All good little girls, yes. It didn't take on some of us," Maggie mused.

"Well, while I was doing it, I loved it . . . for the most part," Anna went on as if she hadn't heard. "Do you remember how excited I was when I got the job in graphic art with *Travel Magazine?*"

"The way I remember it, they came after you and begged you to apply!"

"And then, after nine very enjoyable months, I met Paul."

"In the elevator."

"Well, he worked in the same building." Anna didn't speak for a long time. "I chose to marry him knowing that in doing so, I couldn't keep my job because he was making those documentaries and was always traveling, living in one place after another." She took a sip of cocoa. "I know there was a lot of talk a while back against women having to 'give up' their careers in favor of their husbands'. But I didn't give up anything. I could have had a career. A very gratifying career. I chose to marry Paul instead. Besides, I was pregnant in the first minute." She laughed. "In only two years I was the mother of as many children. My new career as supporting player was launched."

"You did it well. Your terrific children have certainly glowed in the limelight and proven their mettle. Christine was a child bride, but she married a super guy, and Peter, who did his undergraduate work in three years, was accepted to Princeton for this spring semester and is plowing on through the summer so he can finish his master's in record time. Since they flew from the nest, you've distinguished yourself as Washington's volunteer of the century."

"But I'm trying to discover what people in supporting roles are supposed to do when the stars, the lead players . . . are gone."

Maggie didn't say anything, so Anna went on. "I need to figure out who I am now, without following a script written by someone else."

"But why Crete?" Maggie asked.

"Because it's unusual and piques my interest. Because in pictures it looks bare and rocky and sun soaked. They say the air is different there, that it has more clarity. I need that. Someplace simple and spare. Maybe a land like that can scour away this"— she had to clear her throat—"oppressive sense of emptiness."

"Oh, Anna," was Maggie's only response.

Anna held up her hand to ward off any sympathy. "Mainly, I'm going to Crete because it is one place we never went, the one place where I won't expect to see Paul at every turn." It was time to change the subject. "Have you redecorated your house lately?"

"You mean since I changed it from Scandinavian to Japanese?" It had been a standing joke for years, Maggie's drastic renovations of her various houses.

"Are you still sleeping on a futon on the floor and eating raw fish?"

Maggie nodded. "It's healthy. I had my yard transformed into a tea garden since you were there last. It's a beautiful and peaceful place. I've even been studying with a Zen master."

"Buddhism?"

"More like mysticism. I just keep thinking there's something I'm missing. Maybe this will . . . anyway, it's healthy."

"I've heard that a glass of blackberry brandy every night after dinner is healthy too—good for the constitution. Would you like some?" Anna poured two glasses without waiting for an answer and they sat quietly in the way of old friends who can share an easy silence. Then Maggie asked, "How are you doing, Anna? How are you feeling now?"

"I'm doing all right."

"Anna, this is Maggie, your old friend. You don't have to be brave for me." She kicked Anna's foot lightly. "Tell me. How are you?"

"Do you really want to know?"

"I wouldn't have asked if I—"

"I'm angry," Anna interrupted abruptly. "These days I'm angry!"

"How so?"

Anna felt reluctant to answer. In truth she was *very* angry.

Angry at her friends in Washington who handled her with kid gloves, never mentioning Paul's name for fear she'd burst out weeping. So, to show how plucky she was, she had become a closet mourner. She had smiled so much these past months her face hurt. But that was not the worst of it. "I'm angry at God," she told Maggie. "It's all so unfair. Why Paul? Why not a murderer instead? A child molester? Someone dying of a dread disease? A man whose wife hated him?"

"It never works that way, Anna. Expecting life to be fair because you are a good person is like expecting a bull not to charge you because you're a vegetarian."

"But that is only part of it. I'm angry at . . ." Anna remembered now how hard it had been to confess this. "I'm furious . . . with Paul."

"With Paul." It was a quiet statement, not a question.

"How could he leave me? What did I do to deserve that? I did everything I was supposed to do, was there through thick and thin, as they say, for better and for worse. He was my life . . . and my future." She reached for the rings, the wedding rings, hers and Paul's, that she wore on a chain around her neck. "My future." She looked away and said, "God, how I miss him. I feel bankrupt, abandoned. And then. . . . and then I feel guilty."

Maggie didn't speak for such a long time that Anna wondered if she had shocked her, disappointed her. "I'm sorry. I shouldn't have said all that. The awful part of grief, Mags, is how sorry you feel for yourself."

"There's nothing wrong with honest anger, Anna. You should be able to say anything you feel like saying. Saying something out loud often takes away some of its power." Maggie had shifted so she could look straight at Anna. "I don't know if this is the time to say this, but I've always envied your marriage. Well, actually, I envied you from the day I met you . . . tall, slim, with that aquiline nose and fantastic hair. Then your fairy-tale romance with Paul. You and Paul had such a magnificent marriage, something I never got right. Either time. On all my visits here, I couldn't help noticing the constant current that flowed between the two of you. No wonder you feel sorry for yourself. You must be very lonely."

"Yes," Anna answered. A log fell and the fire sputtered. She got up and put on another log. Then she asked, "Maggie, you've lived alone for a long time. Do you ever miss . . . do you ever feel desperate, a sort of desperation that . . . ?"

"Are you talking about sex?" Maggie laughed.

Anna shook her head. "That's not exactly what I meant, but it will do for starters."

"How about you, Anna? It must be terrible for you."

"But it's not only that. It's . . . I don't know. . . . It's something more, something that tears at me, makes me feel anxious in a way I don't understand."

Maggie took a sip of brandy, nodding. "I know, Anna. Just having someone there. I don't know how many evenings I find myself sitting, alert with expectation, waiting for the sound of a car door slamming, a familiar footfall on the step."

"That's it. Just someone to be there." She stared into the fire. "I would pay anything for a good laugh, a good fight. I . . ."

Maggie smiled. "Then as long as we're on the subject, there is the matter of pure, unadulterated sex."

Anna snorted. "Yes, there is that. I'm not prepared to deal with that. I just try to put it out of mind . . . and body."

"Hell," Maggie said. "That's ridiculous."

"Do you have a better suggestion?"

"Find somebody who . . ."

Anna stiffened. "You're not going to suggest I get married again? How many times have I heard—"

"I'm not talking about getting married."

"Good. Because I could never—" She stared into the fire.

"You may change your mind about that." Maggie raised her hand to still Anna's protest. "But I'm not talking about anything so drastic. I'm talking about just having fun. Somebody to talk with, to have a drink with, and . . . to you-know-what with."

"An affair?" Anna was looking at her wide-eyed. "Have you—?"

"Come on, Anna. We're no longer in the Dark Ages. This is the twenty-first century!"

"But wouldn't you . . . feel, uh, embarrassed? Guilty. You know, we good Catholic girls were taught how to deport ourselves." She grinned over at Maggie.

"Guilty? Ah, guilt." Maggie laughed. "I savor the guilt. That's part of the fun." She stopped laughing and stared into her hands, then up at Anna. "Anna, you're talking like an innocent, blushing nineteen-year-old virgin, if there is such a thing anymore. But your innocence is the product of experience, not inexperience. A marriage like yours could never be repeated. I know that. But, hey, a little fling never hurt anyone."

"Innocent? I was married for twenty-three years! I had two children by age twenty-four!" But there was some truth in what Maggie said. Anna had slept with only one man in her life. "The thought of . . . of . . . I never thought of sex as something you *do*. I just never considered it a thing in and of itself. Making love was always a part of something more—the culmination of everything, of the day's joys and sorrows, even fights . . . a part of everything." She stared into the fire. "It was a sort of sacrament," she said in a low voice.

"Anna, I don't know how to tell you this, but I would guess that the love you had is so rare as to be almost nonexistent. The Hope diamond, world peace, unicorns, and thin hips after forty are more common. Can't you see how fortunate you are?"

Anna was appalled. "How fortunate I *was*, you mean."

Maggie's eyes filled with sorrow.

"Okay, yes, I know," Anna finally said. She got up and spread the fire to make it go out. "So, now how do I live out my days being . . . not so fortunate?"

"With your luck, Anna, something wonderful will happen. Believe in it. You do have a lot of choices, you know."

"That's too true to be good, Mags. A lot of choices? Yes. I do have a lot of choices." Anna got up and closed the doors to the fireplace and turned off the lamp at one end of the couch. "I am free to do anything . . . go anywhere . . . for a while. The house is paid for. We had become reasonably well-off financially, and Paul was not only a good investor, but I found out in dealing with the estate settlement this past year that he bought a life insurance policy before every trip he took. I'm not wealthy, but I don't have to worry about money. But what am I going to do with . . . with my life? Too many choices can feel like . . . like a free fall through outer space. Nothing to cling to."

Maggie stayed for three days, wonderful days. The Monday after she left, Anna began packing to go to Crete. She took Paul's picture down from the mantel in their bedroom and looked into his face. Many studio portraits had been made of him over the years, but this snapshot was Anna's favorite. Paul, so strong and vital, stood at the helm of the sailboat they had rented in Barbados five years before, the wind lifting his blond hair. The trip had been a gift to celebrate Anna's fortieth birthday.

She carried the picture to her chair and studied the familiar smile. He was in his element, tan and lean with the well-defined muscles of a runner. Tears blurred the face Anna would never see again. How could someone so healthy have a fatal heart attack? There had been no warning. He was never even sick. Anna sighed. At least he got to see their daughter married and their son accepted to graduate school. She walked over to put the picture in the suitcase, but something stopped her. She turned and put it gently back on the mantel and snapped the suitcase shut. Anna left Washington on a cool, rainy day in late May, her mind in a fog as gray as the clouds that rushed by the window as the plane took off.

Waking early to a bright Aegean morning, Anna still couldn't quite shake her jet lag. She read and dozed on the brightly cushioned ledge that served as a couch in her sitting room. Except for a basket chair across from the couch and the rough-hewn coffee table, all the furniture was built into the walls, even her bed and the shelves of her tiny bedroom. She ate an orange, then pulled on her one-piece Jantzen, slipped her feet into thongs, and made her way down the hill for her late-morning swim.

Since the Hotel Villas was high on a hill, the beach was sev-

Daven

eral hundred yards down a steep, rocky path. Each day, Anna had gone for a swim at the beach. Her legs were sore from the climb down and back.

"Beach," to the Greeks, she discovered, means where land and water meet—not always including sand. The Villas beach aptly fitted this definition. Except for one small crescent of gravel, the shoreline was solid rock, rising straight from water so clear that the bottom, ten or twelve feet below, was almost undistorted. The rocks were naturally terraced, forming flat tiers where one could spread a mat to soak up the sun.

So far, there had been few other people on the beach when Anna went there in late morning, since she had arrived during the week. She had a favorite place around a curve in the rocks that was secluded and partially shaded by a rock outcropping. Occasionally, a young man about the age of her son appeared on the beach with a spear and goggles and left with an assortment of octopuses and fish, which were later, she suspected, the very ones on the menu. Peter would love it here, she thought, watching the young man dive with such abandon.

To get into the water, one could dive straight off the rocks or wade down the more gradual descent of the gravelly crescent. Anna was glad she'd brought along a pair of thongs to wear down the path and to protect her feet from the rough beach itself. A swimmer from early childhood, Anna glided with long strokes through the liquid-crystal water, straight out from shore, then let herself be carried back on the swells, salt tasting bitter on her lips. When she tired of this, she spread her mat on the smooth rock and sunned herself under the cloudless Cretan sky.

Back up at her place, she passed by the nook that was her "dining room" set into the wall in front of a window framing bougainvillea, sea, and distant mountains, and headed for the shower. The bathroom was laughable, one large tile cubicle with no division between the shower stall and the rest of the room. The toilet actually sat next to the showerhead. At any rate, water sprayed so wildly that Anna had to put her shower cap over the toilet paper and learn to live with wet hair.

Today, for the first time, she had climbed back up the trail without feeling breathless. That was a good sign. She sat out on her walled terrace drying her long dark hair, brushing it out in slow, easy strokes to catch the sun. It was grayer lately, especially at the temples, but she liked it. *I deserve every one of these silver threads. I earned them.* She had always taken pride in her hair. It was one of the things about her that Paul had liked best.

Through the archway, the Gulf of Mirabello and the distant tumble of white cubes and rectangles of the village of Ayios Nikolaos made a postcard picture. The water of the gulf, its surface whipped to scudding whitecaps, was streaked with fingers in different hues of blue. Anna ran the brush through her warm hair one last time. No matter what she did, it curled in wiry ringlets at her temples and forehead. It would never lie flat and sleek. There had been years in Anna's early teens when almost all her creative efforts went into trying to straighten her hair. Now she rather liked the curl. Tying it back with a red silk scarf, she stretched her sore muscles, raising her arms above her head, then bending to touch her toes. Something clanked against her teeth. The rings— the wedding rings. Clutching them in her fist, she stared across the water. Then she raised her head and squared her shoulders and strode into the coolness of her rooms in search of something to eat. Seeing her almost-empty larder, she decided that this would be a good day to go to the buffet lunch at the pool. She changed into a skirt and sleeveless blouse and grabbed up a paperback. She had never been to the pool. Because her apartment was at the far end of the "village," she had seen only the tops of colorful umbrellas from a distance.

Anna entered the sunken pool area surrounded by a deck scattered with chaise longues, tables, and chairs overlooking the sea far below, then stopped in her tracks, trying not to stare. It was like entering a museum—a gallery of living sculpture. A variety of young men in very scant bikinis stretched their hard, sunvarnished bodies out on towels or deck boards. They were beautiful to look at. But it was the women who caught Anna's attention. With few exceptions, none of the women at the pool were wearing the tops to their bathing suits. All ages and sizes of bare-breasted women sat, perfectly at ease, drinking, reading, smoking, talking. Some were strikingly lovely. Others—not so.

In none of the life-drawing classes she had taken years ago had there ever been such a wealth of subjects. As the waiter led her to the table, she was tempted to reach out and touch. She wanted to run her hand over the wet brown muscles of the nearest young man, who had just lifted himself effortlessly out of the pool. She even had the urge to touch the shapely curves of the young woman leaning back in her chair at a nearby table with a group of men, speaking in German. Her startling white teeth flashed in her tan face as she laughed, taut, thin skin moving smoothly over her lower ribs below her firm, full breasts. Michelangelo would have had a field day at this pool. Anna felt overdressed.

Later, back in her bedroom, she stripped down and took a good look in the mirror at her own tall naked body, light tan now with the pasty white outline of her one-piece suit. What she saw was certainly not the creamy swell of bosom one read about in novels, but it wasn't bad for a slightly over-the-hill woman, Anna thought. She touched the blue-veined paleness of her breasts. The skin was cool.

She went over and searched through a drawer for the bikini given to her as a joke at a going-away party before she'd left Washington. Being too prudish, as her daughter would say, she had not worn it before. She slipped on the bottom half, trying not to notice the faint map of stretch marks near her navel. Checking to make sure no one else was around, she ventured out onto her courtyard. Pulling the chaise around so she faced the sun, she lay back in the chaise longue, frequently rubbing lotion into the soft skin of her iridescent white bosom and abdomen.

Drifting on the edge of sleep, she heard footsteps and voices on the path in front of her villa. A jolt of panic tore through her. Could these people see her as they passed by? Should she run back into the house? No, too late. She lay perfectly still with her eyes tightly shut. When she could hear the voices receding down the hill, she raised her fists in triumph, feeling a sort of gleeful wickedness. This was some sort of milestone.

The day after her lunch at the pool, Anna realized she had finally recovered from the bone-leaden tiredness of the drastic time change. Invigorated by her morning swim off the rocks below, she was ready to venture out. It was a good day to go exploring. Besides, she needed to shop for food. After she dressed, she emptied her big straw beach bag and took the hotel shuttle to Ayios Nikolaos. The road skirting the Gulf of Mirabello was lined on the landward side with hotels and bungalows piled up the hillside, the rocky beaches below littered with the well-oiled, almost-naked bodies of sunbathers. Surf sailors skimmed the water.

The little town was far different than Anna had expected. A stack of whitewashed blocks from her archway, it was quaint and colorful up close, nestled around a miniature harbor where boats of all kinds bobbed on water reflecting the buildings hovering at its edge. Docked among a few white sailboats and sleek yachts were Greek fishing caïques of various sizes, always painted in at least three bright colors—yellow, apple green, turquoise, orange, royal blue.

Crossing the cobblestone street around the harbor, however, was hazardous. Motorbikes and bicycles along with buses, cars, and trucks screeched around the corners, blaring a cacophony of horns. Anna breathed a sigh of relief when she finally made it across, then wandered from shop to shop enjoying watching the people as much as admiring the merchandise. Most of the stores near the harbor catered to tourists, selling souvenirs or printed T-shirts, and cheap imitations of ancient Greek art objects. Anna made her way along the narrow sidewalk through hordes of mostly Germans and Australians and a few Americans.

Rounding a corner, she discovered a small, chic gift shop. The sign in Greek with English underneath read THE BLUE DOLPHIN. When she opened the door a little bell chimed and she stepped into a room decorated like an aristocratic parlor. Blown-glass lampshades, paintings, ceramic figures, and excellent reproductions of the best of ancient Greek art were displayed as if each belonged to the spot where it had been placed. Flute music wafted on the fragrant air from some unidentified source. The proprietor, a woman of perhaps thirty-five, her reddish blond curls pulled up on top of her head in a well-crafted manner of careless abandon, smiled when Anna complimented her line of goods. In perfect English, with a lilting Greek accent, she offered Anna a cup of tea, then left her to wander about the shop, sipping the hot, sweet drink. A string of green glass beads caught her eye, simple and heavy, draped over a piece of driftwood. She liked them. They felt cool to the touch as she lifted them and laid them on the counter and fished out a few euros.

It was when she sat in the wicker chair offered to her that she spotted the painting, a watercolor of two fishermen, a common subject for paintings in Greece. But this one was different. The mirthful expressions on the two men's faces—one with his head thrown back in laughter, the other with a smile that crinkled the corners of his eyes—made Anna wish she had heard the joke. The detail was so distinct that she could almost hear the lapping of the water on the shore at their feet and yet . . . she looked more closely. . . . No, it wasn't all that distinct. The water, with only a hint of motion, was a series of smears. The minute detail was in the faces. No matter where in the painting she looked, Anna's eyes were drawn back to the faces. The signature read, "Demetri."

"Do you know this artist?" Anna asked, pointing at the name.

"I know who he is. Demetri Anistopolis. He is Greek-American. He spends a great deal of time in Greece. He is very good, don't you think?" She handed Anna her change along with the beads wrapped in a tissue package. Anna took one more long look at the painting as she left the store.

Back on the street, Anna was delighted with the contrasts. Scantily clad, mostly young tourists shopped at stores run by local women wearing black dresses and black head scarves. Shiny modern cars and motorcycles of every make shared the street with carts drawn by donkeys. Sailboats with blinding white sails bobbed next to medieval-looking fishing boats and ancient stone jetties. She was sorry she hadn't brought a sketch pad to Crete.

This thought made her stop and lean against the rough stone balustrade. She hadn't touched a pencil in years—except to make lists and write things on her calendar. Suddenly it was as if everything came into focus. Not only did Anna see the scene around her, but she noticed perspective in the angles of the jetty, the light reflecting on the faces of people passing by, the contrast between the sleek lines of the yachts and the rough, quaint roundness of the caïques. *I remember when I couldn't wait to—what did I used to say?—to pour myself out on paper.*

During high school and the years at Denison, where she got her degree in studio art, Anna had felt withdrawal symptoms when she couldn't find a pencil. She could hardly think of anything else. She had done illustrations for flyers and posters, the annuals and newspaper. Somewhere, buried in the attic, there was a box of ribbons and certificates for all the awards she had won.

Thoughts swirled around in her head. *Wonder when I stopped drawing. Wonder when I packed away the most important thing in my life, considered it less important than . . . than what?* Anna turned and leaned back against the rough stone, watching the people, noting their expressions—excited, bored, smiling, talking with arms akimbo, hunched frantically over maps. *I just didn't have the time. Well, didn't take the time. I wonder if I could even do it now. You have to be in a certain—*she thought for a moment—*a certain poetical frame of mind. You have to be in . . . you have to be in a state of grace.*

How long had it been since she had felt that state of grace? She had been too busy, never having a stretch of time to herself. Marriage. Children. Then after Christine and Peter went off to school, Paul had wanted her with him on his trips, and she gladly went along, arranging her schedule around his. As she told Maggie, she had embraced her life with him willingly, never feeling that she had sacrificed her own calling so much as that she had simply chosen another.

Standing on the busy thoroughfare in this small village, she knew then that she wanted to try again. With a growing sense of anticipation, she wondered if there was a place she might buy some pencils, maybe charcoal, a board, and paper. She'd ask the woman at the Blue Dolphin later.

Before that, though, she had to buy some food. Anna knew that this part of Ayios Nikolaos did not represent the "real" Crete. It had evolved to meet the needs of tourists who flocked here year-round. The only Cretans near the water were shop owners and a few old men who sat in the sun by the dock, refusing to yield their privileged place to the sunburned, half-dressed visitors. In their black suits and billed hats they reminded her of the Demetri watercolor.

Only when she was streets away from the water did she begin to see other local people. She was directed toward a cheese and fish market on a small square several blocks inland and actually found it, eventually, by following her nose. There she joined a few women dressed in traditional black, carrying bulging string bags stuffed with their day's shopping items. Using her small English-Greek dictionary and lots of pointing, Anna bought several kinds of cheese and some fillets of grouper.

Noting the fresh vegetables in other women's bags and asking in gestures where they had gotten them, they directed her, in Greek, with much gesticulating, to a fruit and vegetable stand down the way. There she picked out salad makings.

Last on her list were wine and bread. An old man with cheeks so pink that they matched the flowers he was selling pointed to a bakery, a stone edifice that appeared to have been in the same location for centuries. Anna bought a bouquet of flowers from him and walked across the square.

The ovens were large stone domes that radiated heat out onto the street. The baker, a dowager, again in black, with the reddest face Anna had ever seen, retrieved loaves with a wooden paddle from the depths of the glowing cave. They all looked delicious.

The woman handed her the bread without wrapping it. Anna topped off her bag with the still-hot, hard-crusted bread, sticking the flowers in the end away from the heat.

She picked up a bottle of wine on the way back to the Blue Dolphin, lugging her heavy bag with both hands. A small bell tinkled when she walked into the shop. "Do you know of a store that sells art supplies?" she asked the young woman.

"What is it that you need?"

"A sketch pad and pen—"

The woman waved Anna toward the wicker chair and disappeared through a doorway hung with clicking strings of colored beads. Relaxed, listening to the music, admiring the Demetri painting, Anna wondered how he could capture every detail and emotion on a canvas only two by two and a half feet.

Returning with a stack of pads, pencils, charcoal, kneaded eraser, the proprietor said, "I have a few things on hand because, from time to time, a person like you comes along." She laughed. "If you have it in your blood, I think, it starts to boil in Crete." She put everything on the counter.

But Anna was barely listening. "I would like to buy that painting," she said in even tones.

After a sharp intake of breath the woman smiled. "I am sure you will not regret owning such a work of art." She took it down and laid it on the counter.

Watching the young woman's careful hands as she lovingly wrapped the painting, and seeing regret in her face, Anna felt drawn to her. Who was she? What was her life like? "This is a wonderful shop." She looked around and then back. "I'm Anna. Anna Sandoval."

"And I am Sophia Papathanasiou." She handed Anna her business card. "This shop is my life."

Getting out of the taxi back at the hotel, Anna struggled with her bulging bag and unwieldy package. Ahead of her down the passageway, that same tall man, in bathing trunks with a towel and book under his arm, was striding down the first set of steps. Now she really knew he was American. No European man would be caught dead in those trunks. Anna started to call out to him to see if he would help her carry her things. But when he got to the bottom of the steps, he turned a corner. She looked at her pile of shopping bounty and sighed. *I guess I'll have to make two trips.*

Just then, the young man Anna had seen down at the beach emerged from the office smiling and, without being asked, picked up the bag. Anna carried the Demetri painting.

The first thing she did when she got to her rooms was to take down the woven wall hanging and replace it with the picture. Next, she unpacked the drawing materials and spread them out on the table. She almost let the vegetables wilt before she remembered to put them in the refrigerator.

Pleased with herself, she cut slices of bread, made a cheese sandwich, and ate it sitting in the chair, gazing at the painting, a kind of gaiety she hadn't felt in a long time spreading through her chest. She wanted to celebrate, to invite people in to see her work of art.

But she knew no one to invite.

After lunch, Anna still felt restless. She paced around her rooms, and then went into the bedroom, trying to decide whether or not to go back down to the beach. Automatically, she reached for the Jantzen. Then she hesitated. Did she dare try her new look at the pool?

Holding the one-piece suit in her hand as she eyed the bikini, Anna shrugged. What the heck. If she was going to do it at all, it might as well be now. She put the Jantzen back and took out the bikini. As she pulled on the scanty bottom half, it seemed even more brief than the day before. Anna flipped the top of the suit into her bag, in case her nerve failed. Pulling on a T-shirt over her unharnessed breasts, she walked to the pool.

Several people were there along with a couple of naked children. Casually, Anna spread her towel on a lounger, then just as casually skinned off the shirt and leaned back, bare-chested. *Ta-dum!* Feigning sleep behind her dark glasses, she watched through slits of her eyes for any reactions.

There were none. The absent gazes of the young men, if they looked at her at all, flicked away as if she weren't even there. She might as well have been dressed in a nun's habit. The older European men, distinguished by their nylon bikinis no matter how large their stomachs, stared frankly around the pool as they arrived, with no apparent ogling either, then ordered tall glasses of beer and settled into gruff conversations.

Everyone was perfectly at ease. The topless young women sitting poolside barely gave Anna or anyone else a glance. They leaped around with total abandon, springing on the diving board, splashing their escorts. The older European matrons came down to the pool in one-piece suits, usually black. After they had laid out their books and towels and ordered drinks, they rolled the suits down to their waists. Even the heftier women seemed to feel no compunction about this, their heavy breasts falling loose like ripe melons, flattening and sagging back to their armpits as they lay back on the chairs.

Paul would have been mesmerized by this panorama of bare breasts. She almost laughed, thinking what his reaction would have been to find hers among them. He would have loved it, she decided, feeling deliciously wicked.

She settled back and tried to read, but she couldn't concentrate. She did begin, however slowly, to feel more natural. She looked around at all the makes and models of figures. Why did Adam and Eve feel so ashamed of their newly discovered nakedness that they wanted to hide? Why did we? God, we made life so complex! She stretched, feeling the sun warm the length of her body. *This is how it was meant to be.*

It was only later that she realized she had thought of Paul for the first time without a rush of sorrow.

Two

The next day, Anna decided to forgo sun and water. She had forgotten the day before that parts of her body had a head start on other parts in getting a tan. She had a painful, isolated sunburn across her breasts.

As she ate breakfast in front of her "Demetri," Anna knew she had never bought anything that pleased her more. How was this artist able to capture a moment so delightfully? Not only did she enjoy looking at it; she found herself scrutinizing every brushstroke. How did he get that effect of movement? Those subtle shadows? It called forth the old inner passion and she remembered happily the brand-new pencils she'd bought from Sophia.

Anna stretched, energy coiled like springs in her muscles, begging to be released. She hadn't felt this invigorated in months. Emboldened by her brazenness at the pool, she brushed her hair and twisted it into a haphazard bun and slipped out of her robe. Shunning a bra because of her sunburn, she slipped into a cool sundress, and gathered some fruit and cheese, half a loaf of bread, and a Crete guidebook into her straw bag. Then she rushed back into her bedroom and grabbed the smallest pad of drawing paper with the box of pencils, and dropped them into the bag along with her lunch.

On the shuttle into Ayios Nikolaos, she decided to try to get a taxi to take her up to the ancient ruins at Lato, in the mountains above the harbor. When she arrived at the village, however, she was at a loss. She wasn't sure how to negotiate the price in the nonmetered taxis, and she had no idea how to choose a reliable driver. Paul had always arranged these things when they traveled. She knew she didn't want to go on the guided bus tour. She wasn't sure what to do.

She leaned on her elbows on the stone wall surrounding the boat harbor, enjoying the colorful sight of boats and gulls and milling people. Fewer tourists were out than she had seen on her last visit. The sun fell across her shoulders like a benediction, and she turned to face it, to receive its blessing. At that moment she saw Sophia coming out of her store. *She can advise me about the taxi,* Anna thought. Crossing the street after letting two mopeds and a donkey cart go by, she caught up with the woman. "Good morning," she said, falling into step with her.

"Oh, hello. Lovely day, isn't it?" Sophia's English, colored with a rolling Greek accent, was a delight to hear. Her reddish hair was piled on top of her head as before, a few curls falling loose. She jangled with many bracelets, mostly gold. "Are you going to church too?"

Was it Sunday? Anna hadn't even been wearing a watch, much less been keeping track of the days. "Actually, I was going to try and get a taxi to Lato, and I was wondering if I could ask your advice."

"My advice is—don't."

"Don't?"

Sophia laughed. "At least don't get one of these you see driving around here in Ayios Nikolaos. I have a cousin who will drive you."

Anna started to protest. "I wouldn't want to impose. . . ."

"No, it is his business, in a way. He is a—what do you say?—a courier."

"But it's Sunday."

"No, that is all right. His wife is expecting a baby, and he will be glad for the money. That is"—she smiled—"if you want to chance getting up that road in his asthmatic old Mercedes. The only thing is, he doesn't speak English very well." She looked at Anna hesitantly. "But I'll tell him where to take you. You must see Lato. Come, I'll telephone him." She turned and hurried back to her store, unlocked the door, motioned Anna in as she picked up the phone.

"I . . . I can wait until later to go," Anna said. "I have no schedule. Perhaps you would like to . . ." She wanted to invite Sophia to have coffee somewhere or at least see if she would like to come to Lato too. She would even have gone to church with her if she had been asked, but Sophia was already talking on the phone.

She hung up. "He will be here in five minutes. And I can *just* make it to church"—she looked at her watch—"without being too late, if I hurry." She locked the store, waved, and walked quickly away. "By the way, he is called Stiros," she shouted back.

As she watched Sophia move up the street, heels clicking a staccato pattern on the pavement, Anna had a sinking feeling. It would have been nice to have her along. For company.

True to Sophia's word, a dented blue Mercedes turned the corner five minutes later. Stiros was much younger than she had expected, a thin, tightly wound young man with a solemn face and a shy smile that matched his equally shy, dark eyes. Stepping out of the car, he carefully put out his cigarette before opening the back door for Anna.

Turning the corner with grinding gears, he ran up on a curb to pass a truck on a curve going up a hill and leaned on his horn as a boy on a bicycle came careening down the other side. Anna found herself saying Hail Marys for the first time in years.

Stiros started up the winding road at breakneck speed, but Anna put her hand on his shoulder and said, "Please, not so fast. I want to see your beautiful country."

"Sorry. I too much hurry," he said, and slowed down to a reasonable speed.

"Thank you," she said in relief.

They drove by groves of olive trees, some so old their gnarled trunks were hollow, their cores long since gone back into the earth. Anna had heard that shepherds sometimes took small flocks of sheep into these hollow old trees, seeking refuge from the rain. They had been planted long ago in rows that flowed over the rocky hills and down into the valleys, their leaves blowing pewter, then green, lifting in patterns as a light breeze played through the branches. Around another corner, Stiros had to pull around a man riding a donkey, his saddle made of wood. On a hillside, Anna saw a flock of sheep herded by an old woman, her shawl tied around her waist.

Once, Anna caught sight of a man on horseback, wearing the shiny black boots that are part of the Cretan traditional dress. He rode between rows of olive trees, his dark hair lifted on a gust of wind, his white shirt resplendent in the morning sun. His roan mare stepped high in a steady canter. Anna closed her eyes and took a deep breath, remembering the power and freedom she had felt as a child on the back of a horse. She hadn't ridden in years.

The narrow blacktop road with crumbling edges wound higher into the hills. Going around one curve, Anna looked back and caught the distant glint of the sea just before they got to the village of Kritsa. No people were about. Probably because it was Sunday.

Stone, red-roofed buildings covered with peeling plaster were stacked at random against the hillside. Goats and sheep grazed in yards Anna could see through sagging gates. The village looked as if it had been there in that high valley for hundreds of years. It probably had. What must it be like to live in a house that had been in your family, not only for generations, but for centuries?

At the edge of the village, Stiros made a sharp left turn and drove down a street that was paved for only about a hundred yards. Then they lurched along a dusty trail with olive branches slapping the sides of the car. Occasionally, a break in the trees gave Anna a glimpse of stone houses or barns surrounded by stone fences. Farther along, a man was sitting on a pile of rock by a wooden gate. He was smoking a large black pipe.

"Stop!" she cried. Stiros slammed on the brakes, enveloping the car in a cloud of dust.

He leaped from the car with alarm on his face to open the door, but Anna was already getting out with her bag hanging from her shoulder. She walked over to the old man. He was at least eighty and had the most wonderful mustache Anna had ever seen, thick and wiry, white like his hair. He was hatless, dressed in black, his pants tucked into high boots. He watched Anna's approach grimly, his scowl stern and forbidding. She swallowed. "Is this the road to Lato?" she called. It was a stupid question—the first thing that entered her mind—but she had to get a closer look at this marvelous man. Slowly he stood, and after a slight bow in her direction, he smiled. Light filled his faded eyes, and his face, like a medieval painting, cracked into a thousand tiny lines radiating up into his hairline.

"Lato?" Stiros asked. What he said after that, Anna couldn't understand. With a puzzled expression Stiros caught up with Anna and walked beside her as she approached the old man. His suit looked like wool and smelled a little of sheep. His hands were as thick and gnarled as the branches of the olive trees.

Concentrate, Anna told herself. *Memorize this scene—the way his cheeks have turned pink, the gap in his yellow teeth, his full lower lip, smooth as a baby's, his hoary eyebrows, the way he cradles the pipe, his jagged fingernails.*

"*Kyria,*" Stiros said to Anna. "You asked to Lato? Why you stop? I know way."

Anna smiled. "I know, Stiros. I just wanted to meet this man. Do you know him?"

"Meet man? I not understand."

"I'm an artist." Anna made drawing motions in the palm of her hand. At his confused look, she dug through her bag and found the pad of paper. Quickly she sketched a rough outline of Stiros' face, bracing her purse against her waist as a drawing board. She handed it to him. Then she smiled at the older man. "I'd like to draw your picture," she said, pointing at the drawing of Stiros.

"Ah," he said, smiling. Then he shrugged and shook his head side to side. "*Ne. Malista.*"

Anna's heart sank. She had probably offended him. Then suddenly he put his foot on a pile of stones and puffed out his chest, cupping his pipe in the hand resting on his knee, and assumed a dignified expression.

It took Anna a moment to realize he was posing.

Confused, she turned to Stiros. He was smiling.

"*Ne.*" He shook his head. "He say, '*Ne*'—yes."

"*Ne*" meant "yes" when one shook his head no? She'd have to remember that. She looked back at the man. "Ask his name."

Stiros frowned; then his face brightened. "Name?" He turned to the old man. "*Kyrie . . .*" He asked the question in Greek.

The man answered in a rumbling voice.

"Simone, *Kyria*. Name, Simone Syriotis," Stiros said.

"Thank you, Mr. Syriotis," Anna said. She sat in the grass and did several quick sketches, using the soft pencils to get the texture of his clothes. She traced the pattern of his wrinkles, the rough pockmarked nose, the grand mustache. Then she asked him by gesture to smile and did several more sketches. Finally, turning to a new page, she did a last drawing, quickly, sensing her subject was tiring, and using her finger to burnish a shine onto the boots, she tore it out and handed it to him. It was just a rough sketch, but she wanted to give him something.

He stared at it, his eyes stern. She could see them move over the page from top to bottom as though he were reading it. Then he shook his head and said, "*Ne, ne.*"

"He like," said Stiros.

Anna's hands were tingling. She felt a lump in her throat and a soaring sensation under her breast. Tears burned her eyes. This was the "state of grace." It flooded through her like light. Turning to Stiros, she asked, "How do you say 'thank you' in Greek?"

"*Efkaristo, Kyria.*"

"*Efkaristo, Kyria?*"

He smiled, pointing to Mr. Syriotis. "You must say to he, '*Efkaristo, Kyrie.*'" He pointed to Anna. "*Kyrie* is for man. *Kyria* is for woman."

Anna held out her hand and said, "*Efkaristo, Kyrie* Syriotis."

His hand felt like a piece of wood. Anna was glad she had gotten to touch him.

He held up the drawing in the other hand. "*Efkaristo, Kyria,*" he rumbled.

"Anna," she said, pointing to herself. "My name is Anna."

"Ahn-nah," he repeated.

Back in the car she was sorry she hadn't tried to find out where he lived. Was he from the house out there or had he just taken a walk from town? Did he have a wife? Children? Anna regretted that she hadn't gotten Stiros to ask him.

Stiros was looking anxiously at his watch, and Anna was surprised to discover that it was after two. Had they been there more than two hours? "Stiros," she said, "let's go back to Ayios Nikolaos. We can see Lato another day."

"Go back?" he asked, looking relieved.

"Yes. Please turn around. It's too late to go to Lato."

Anna didn't watch the scenery on the way back. She thought of Simone Syriotis, so comfortable in his surroundings that he was almost a part of that olive grove. Her palm still held the memory of the hard roughness of his hand. Could she finish that in pencil, or would it take ink?

Back at the hotel, Anna paid Stiros and then was again frustrated, trying to thank him for making the day special for her—for being so patient while she was drawing old Simone. She'd have liked to buy him a beer, to talk with him about his family. But it was no use.

"*Efkaristo*, Stiros," she said, dismissing him with a smile. As she watched him drive away, she felt bereft, as if she had said good-bye to her only friend.

Anna took a deep breath and sighed. Such an enchanting afternoon. She trudged slowly back to her apartment. Crete was the most foreign place she had ever been—even more foreign than primitive cultures in the hills of the Philippines or the wilds of the Amazon, where the people, even when they were almost naked, smiled and welcomed strangers. There was mystery here, something hidden in the scowls. It was strange. This was where Western thought had been conceived, and yet, the descendants of those ancient cultures had avoided the sweep of the main current.

Perhaps the rough, forbidding terrain bred into Crete's inhabitants a natural resistance to materialism, bright, flashy advertising, and lavish lifestyles, she thought. Here people lived with a simplicity that was like clean, raked gravel, with a harsh beauty all its own.

Simone Syriotis, she imagined, had lived through revolutions and wars and, being so old, had surely suffered the deaths of many loved ones. Hardship and sorrow were written in the lines of his face. Yet he stood so proud and confident and content. He was deeply rooted in that rocky ground. Anna could see that in the way he stood, his boots planted in the earth.

It was five o'clock, hours before the Greek dinnertime, when Anna got to her villa and spread out the drawings. They were pretty rough, she thought, the exhilaration of her encounter with eternity still racing through her veins. Those two hours with *Kyrie* Syriotis had simply vanished in the clear Cretan afternoon. Time out of time. Looking at the sketches, Anna could still feel the old man's grasp. She could smell the sun on his wool jacket, see the light in his wise eyes when he finally smiled.

From experience, she knew she dared not try to work with those drawings just yet. She needed to get away from them for a while, to let the images solidify. With a cup of tea she wandered out onto the terrace and settled into the chaise longue. *Timeless moments feed our souls,* Anna thought, remembering the two hours this afternoon that had vanished as she tried to capture the spirit of Mr. Syriotis. The tea was hot and lemony, the Gulf of Mirabello smeared with cool hues of blue, cool, inviting water, winking in the late-afternoon sun. A swim, she thought. That would be the perfect ending to this glorious afternoon.

Slipping out of her dress, she stepped into the bikini bottom and put on an oversized shirt, tying the tails around her waist. Stuffing the suit top, her book, a towel, and a straw mat into her bag, she started down the trail. As an afterthought, she went back for her sketch pad.

The stone beach was crowded, more crowded than she had ever seen it. Anna could hear a half-dozen languages as she made her way between reclining people, most of the women bare breasted, most of the men in bikinis. She found a smooth empty shelf of rock on the water's edge and spread her things. A flock of pelicans skimmed the water, but by the time Anna pulled out her pad and pencil, they were gone. Her gaze fell on a child playing at the water's edge on the gravel crescent. After trying to do some quick studies, she realized she was just doodling.

The heat had gone out of the sun's strike but still radiated up from the rock in perfect complement to the cool breeze that wafted off the water. It was too late in the day to fear more sunburn.

Holding her breath, she took off her shirt. . . . It still took a moment of courage to get over that hurdle. Then, when she started breathing again, she relaxed. She pulled off the scarf that held her hair back, letting it loose on her shoulders. Then kicking off her thongs, she dived off the rock and slipped through gentle swells, the cool, salty waves stroking her body like silk. Her hair floated out from her head like seaweed, undulating with the movement of the waves. She was weightless, levitating between earth and sky, letting the current carry her away.

When the voices of other swimmers, bobbing in groups of two or three, grew faint, Anna realized the current had taken her far down the beach. She turned over, swimming in long, lazy strokes back to the gravel crescent, and made her way on tender feet back to her things. She toweled off before settling with her back against the warm stone to read, but she was distracted by several pelicans skimming the water, their silhouettes against the powdery sky like a flock of pterodactyls lost from prehistory. They soared and dipped as if the currents of the wind were hills and valleys they were following together. A flock of quarrelsome gulls down the beach cried their plaintive wails, keeping watch out to sea for passing fishing boats that might throw scraps overboard.

The breeze, almost imperceptible in the late afternoon, dried stray wisps of Anna's hair and fluttered the pages of the book she couldn't get interested in. The soft hiss of the swells breaking against rock was soothing. She felt contentment in every part of her body, the perfect temperature, the whisper of the swells, the voices getting fainter and fainter.

A man's voice jolted her out of the soft, misty drowsiness. "Excuse me, but . . ."

"I beg your pardon?" Anna opened her eyes and blinked, shaking the sleep out of her head. The sun, low on the horizon, blinded her. All she could see was the silhouette of a tall man against the western sky. She squeezed her eyes shut.

"This must be yours."

Anna struggled to sit up, squinting against the light. At the end of her mat she saw a pair of muscular brown legs grizzled with silvered hair, then well-fitted, blue cotton swim trunks on slim hips, a broad chest covered with the same silvered mat, and a head of almost-white, wind-mussed hair. His face would have rivaled that of Walter Matthau or Joe E. Brown for compelling homeliness—grained, carved by a rough hand. The nose was beaked, hawklike. Brown basset hound eyes looked down at her, and the corners of his mouth twitched with a held-back smile. Her bikini top dangled from the same finger he had dangled her gaping purse on the day she'd arrived.

"I found this on the trail," he said, his expression deadpan, "and, uh, it seems to match." He pointed to Anna's bottom half.

My God, she thought. She willed herself not to grab the book up to her chest. She felt as if something were crawling over her skin. "Yes, th-thank you, I . . . I must have lost it." As she said this, she was sure he was picturing her walking down the trail, her suit top—which she remembered putting in her bag—falling from her body unbeknownst to her. God! "I mean, I must have dropped it. Thank you." She held out her hand, looking away.

"Hey, you are American," he said. "I thought so the day you arrived . . . scattering things all down the path. You must be the only other person from the States here." He was smiling down at her.

Anna smiled, nodding slightly, looking out to sea. It wasn't only her bosom that felt exposed. She felt naked.

"Do you mind if I join you?" He gestured around. "There seems to be no place left."

Anna looked around. The Sunday crowd of people occupied every available flat space. How could she refuse? And how could she stay here?

"Actually I was just leaving," she said. Looking back up at him to gesture toward the spot next to her as she started to gather her things, she found him staring openly at her breasts, as appreciative as the older Europeans, not in the least self-conscious or embarrassed.

"Lovely," he said softly. She barely heard him. Then he rolled out his towel, sat down, and picked up a book. "Lovely day," he said, perching a pair of half-glasses on the knobby arch of his nose.

Anna thought she could feel his eyes on her as she walked away, her belongings clutched helter-skelter in her arms hugged to her chest, but when she rounded the corner and sneaked a quick peek back, he was reading.

That evening, after finishing her solitary meal in the Taverna, Anna looked around the dining room. A boisterous group of Germans sat talking like old friends. Near them, at two tables pushed together, the group of British women were conversing in lofty, piping voices. Anna wondered what they were laughing about. At another table, four Middle Eastern men in Western suits bent their heads in earnest conversation. Then her gaze fell on a table near the window. A man and a woman leaned toward each other, the man listening raptly to the woman, who gestured like a ballet dancer as she talked. He smiled and reached for her hand, from which a wedding ring gleamed. Anna couldn't hear their conversation from that distance, but she could read his lips as he said something she herself hadn't heard in a long time. "I love you." She clasped the rings on the chain around her neck and, before her coffee came, headed back to her rooms.

Before she went to bed, Anna poured a small glass of wine and stepped out onto her little terrace. The star-flung sky that hung down to the sea was vast and lonely. She lit the squat candle she had put in a seashell on the table, and was warmed by the comfort of its flickering light. The dry wine tasted tangy and cool.

This had been a wonderful day. A gift. When had she lost that knack for timeless hours? Hours when she was living totally outside herself, unaware of any ache or itch or sadness or even hopes for the future, just a total focus on "now," every breath seeming to pull in energy as she watched a drawing take shape under her hand. She remembered telling Maggie on that visit to D.C. just before coming here that she needed to find herself. *When did I lose myself? When did I stop allowing time for myself?*

Anna took another sip of wine. Maybe that capacity for timelessness withered and fell from the vine like a dried blossom if it wasn't nurtured. Could it be brought back to life? she wondered. The lights of Ayios Nikolaos looked like reflections of the star clusters overhead and out on the dark expanse of the Mirabello Gulf, the single pinpricks from fishing boats formed constellations of their own. If only—

If only what? Anna sat up in her chair. She was in Crete trying to rid herself of these empty, fruitless questions and longings. But over and over the effort seemed hopeless. Even here on Crete, especially at night, she kept waiting for "a familiar footfall on the step." Someone to talk to, someone who would listen with interest as she told about her trip that day, who would discuss this zany notion of timelessness and loneliness.

She missed Paul.

The unaccountable anger flashed through her again, followed by the inevitable guilt. Why did she continue to be so angry with him? Anna's hand went automatically to the rings at her neck; then she held her left hand out, fingers spread, and looked at it in the light of the candle. The white indentation on the fourth finger was gone now. It had glared like a scar the day she took off her ring and laid it beside Paul's—the mark of a widow.

Widow. The word echoed through her mind. It sounded hollow, empty, a death word calling to mind spiders and weeds and black. She had mouthed its shape that long-ago day, not daring to speak it aloud. But the current of horror that ripped through her body was just as violent as if she had shouted it.

Like a movie replaying in her mind, she remembered her dev-

astation those first months after Paul's heart attack. Her friends
had been wonderful, if wary, treating her as though she was very
frail and fragile. They had invited her to so many meals she had to
have a calendar just for eating. She never knew for certain if they
got together to plan her time so she would never be alone, but it
seemed that way to her.

She always went, desperately afraid of being alone. Once
there, however, she felt even lonelier in their presence.

It was their offhand, everyday affection with each other that
got to her. Anna had never realized how much casual touching
went on between husband and wife. Little pats. Pecks of kisses.
Straightening a tie, pushing back a lock of hair. Intimate looks
that promised more later.

In those first months after Paul died, there were so many details to attend to, so many decisions to make. Anna did what she
had to do so methodically that she became an automaton. She
could live for days at a time without having a single feeling.

But when she started being invited to parties where she was
carefully introduced to "eligible" men, she realized that the time of
mourning was over for these friends. They were ready to move on.

After that, she mourned alone.

Mourning. It was like a fever that wouldn't go away. No matter how much she smiled, no matter how much she tried to get a
grip on her life, she ached with loss.

Anna swallowed. Images of evenings like this crept into her
mind, when she and Paul sat under these same stars and listened,
together, to night sounds like these, just enjoying being together
before they went to bed.

Bed. Oh, God, Anna thought.

The wine tasted bitter. She poured the rest of it over the balcony and reluctantly went to her lonely bed. Her body crawled
with unfulfilled yearnings, and she moaned, her hand between her
legs as if covering a wound.

Three

The next morning after breakfast, Anna went into the hotel office to see if they had brochures. She found the manager's wife, sitting behind the counter, reading a romance novel by an American author. "A good way to learn English, yes?" the dark-eyed woman commented, raising her eyebrows with a grin. "Take any of these that interest you," she said, pointing to a colorful display.

Nodding, Anna gathered up a few of the flyers. One of the brochures showed pictures of windmills near the village of Elounda, four kilometers to the north. She wanted to find them and do some sketches. Looking around, she noticed a schedule on the bulletin board in the lobby showing that a local bus passed the hotel every hour. The bus to Elounda was leaving in thirty minutes. "Thank you," she said, hurrying back to her rooms to gather up her pad and pencils. She then went out to wait for the bus by the road.

The stones of the wall where she sat were already warm. She leaned back on her hand, looking around. There was nothing flat in this part of Crete. The mountains she could see in every direction, rather than towering above like the Alps or Himalayas, rolled back from the sea as if stepping back to look at it, the jagged-edged ridges and peaks marking the division between heaven and earth. She noticed again the special clarity of the air and light. Sitting there by the roadside, Anna felt she could breathe the very blueness of the sky. Down the winding road that hugged the hillside, its seaward shoulder sloping steeply to the water far below, she could hear the drone of traffic toiling its way up the hill or zooming down toward Ayios Nikolaos.

The bus, when it came, fifteen minutes late, was an adventure in itself. The belching, vintage Mercedes shuddered, gears of metal teeth gnashing, as the driver forced it, apparently against its will, over the hills and around the curves skirting the gulf.

The passengers were a rare mix. Several mustached young men with dark good looks, who must have been commuting to work, laughed and smoked. A group of high-spirited Aussies juggled beach gear. A teenage girl with a peeling nose and greasy blond hair scowled sullenly. A young mother had her hands full with three children under the age of three, one in her arms, the other two bright-eyed and agile as they climbed over and under the seats. An old Cretan man in black clothes and the inevitable knee-high boots sat holding a box of baby chicks, a dog at his feet. A strange smell that Anna couldn't . . . didn't want to identify wafted through the diesel fumes.

The bus stopped many times, taking on more new passengers, making the ride of only four kilometers last almost half an hour. Anna enjoyed it despite the smells. She was almost sorry when it was time to get off.

Elounda, too, was nestled around a small harbor. A row of seaside restaurants along the water faced onto a park with benches shaded by trees and shrubs. The grass here was thin and dusty from the constant activity of playing children, judging by the look of the soccer game going on.

On a small, rocky island across the harbor, Anna could see the impressive medieval Venetian fortress of Spinalonga, mysterious even in the light of the morning sun.

She walked up one of the streets heading away from the water to look for the windmills she'd read about. The buildings were much like those in Ayios Nikolaos, though shabbier. In spite of being run-down, they appeared to be fairly modern. Anna had expected a quaint, old city. In the next block, she came to a small coffeehouse. She could see through the flyspecked glass that it was crowded with people sitting around plain wooden tables littered with the demitasse cups that meant Greek coffee. Coffee would taste good. Thinking it would be more interesting to go where local people congregated than to the outdoor tables near the water that obviously catered to tourists, she entered the open door and asked, with a friendly smile, "Excuse me, but could anyone tell me where I would find the windmills?"

Everyone just stared. Actually, they glared. Acrid smoke filled the air, not quite covering the smell of stale beer. That was when she noticed that all the people in the room were men. Maybe they didn't speak English.

"Windmills," she repeated, making a windmill motion with her hands.

This instigated a short discussion. Some of the men just shrugged and shook their heads, looking away. But one pointed to his left. "Up there. Up, up, two, three kilometers. Very . . . uh . . . difficult to walk. Very—" He indicated steepness with his hand. Then they all turned away and resumed talking with one another. The man behind the counter did nothing to encourage her to stay.

Well, so much for windmills and getting to know the locals, Anna thought. Back by the quay, she passed several outdoor cafés with colorful umbrellas over white chairs and tables and finally chose one on the edge of the green where she had a view of boats and the children playing ball. She ordered Greek coffee and watched.

The game was a variation of soccer that seemed to have few rules. Anna got out her pad and quickly did some sketches of the children. The pencil felt awkward, as if, right-handed, she were trying to draw with her left hand. She couldn't get a fix on them before they moved, and she seemed to have forgotten everything she had once learned about anatomy.

Giving up on the moving children, she decided to try the more geometric lines of the boats. She had done a few practice sketches when she noticed a man on a bright blue caïque near her. He was bent over, working on the motor. This was more the kind of thing she wanted. She tried to focus on the strength of his blackened hands, but after a few moments, she realized the hands in her drawing were out of proportion. She was distracted by the shouting children, the people walking by, the boats slicing across the harbor.

She looked at the fortress across the water, its castlelike, crenellated stone walls and turreted balustrades looking formidable and forbidding. Shaded by a mountain, its lines were shadowy. Just looking at it was like entering a time warp. Anna could imagine medieval ships with colorful, square sails skimming across the harbor. The hills on the islands to each side were lined with peculiar stone fences. They made a nice geometric pattern in contrast with the choppy water and the craggy hilltops.

It was no use. She tore out page after page. She couldn't concentrate. She failed to get the perspective right in any of the sketches.

Anna leaned back in her chair and ordered another cup of coffee, cradling the demitasse cup in her hands. The thick, bitter coffee, sweetened with coarse sugar, was delicious, though she had learned by experience to be careful not to drink the mudlike dregs at the bottom.

More people were milling about the square now, filling the tables of the cafés, walking out on the docks. Some were in groups, getting ready to take the water taxi across to Spinalonga. Others milled in and out of the shops on the far side of the green.

The children's shouts caught Anna's attention. Their ball had gotten away and was floating in the water. A small boy in a green sweater and short pants, his mass of black curls bouncing in the sun, jumped onto a boat and, grabbing an oar, leaned far out over the side, using it to try to reach the ball. It was just beyond the tip of the oar. From his friends on the bank came all sorts of shouted advice, their young voices lyrical with the beauty of their language. The boy was in no real danger. Even if he couldn't swim, he was very near the man working on the motor, who had looked up and was watching.

Anna sketched furiously, trying to translate the boy's effort onto paper as the breeze slowly moved the ball back in his direction. Long after the boy had retrieved the ball and the game had resumed, she worked on the drawing—shading, erasing, trying to show his teetering balance.

Damn. It just wouldn't come. It was wooden and smudged.

She was about to rip out still another page when a voice behind her said, "Don't touch the water. It is perfect. Look, there you captured the sense of movement, the effort of the small arm holding the heavy oar. But you overworked it. If only you had left it to speak on its own."

Startled, Anna whirled around toward the deep voice to find herself looking into the gaze of an intense elderly man, the dark eyes under grizzly eyebrows penetrating to her very soul. He was sitting in a chair at the table just behind her.

The stern face broke into an embarrassed smile. "Pardon me for my intrusion," he said with a small bow. "But I sense you are a little discouraged and you needn't be."

Anna looked down. "Not a little . . . a lot discouraged." She could hear the bitterness in her own voice.

"You have been an artist for a long time, I can see that," he said.

She smiled, shaking her head. "I started long ago, but I retired early. Too busy with, well, other things." Gesturing toward her drawing, she added, "I had thought to come out of 'retirement,' but I don't know. I think I've lost the knack."

"No, you must not think that. You are just out of practice." He was silent for a moment, then cleared his throat. "Please forgive me. I have interrupted you. I had no right." He reached for the handle of the wooden box at his feet and stood up to leave.

Feeling an unaccountable panic, Anna gestured toward a chair at her table. "No, please." Her unspoken request hung in the air. She was surprised at the urgency she felt. She didn't want him to leave. She almost reached out. "Won't you join me for a cup of coffee?" she asked. "I mean, if you have time." A nervous laugh bubbled up. "I'm . . . I—" *Please stay,* she begged in her thoughts. She wasn't sure why.

He turned his broad-brimmed straw hat in his hands, hands that were strong and brown and, Anna noticed, stained with color. "Are you a painter?" she asked.

He smiled and nodded. "Allow me to introduce myself. I am Demetri Anistopolis."

Anna just stared. This man, with his white hair in wisps over the tops of his ears, his carefully trimmed mustache, the deep laugh lines at the corners of his eyes, smiled. A scarf of brown silk, the color of his eyes, was knotted above a faded blue shirt and a shapeless sport jacket with sagging pockets. He bowed as if dressed in evening clothes.

Anna had met many famous and accomplished people, but there was something about this man that made her want to stand. She didn't, however, knowing that that would have embarrassed him. His countenance reflected a spirit that had long ago said, "Ah, yes" to life. He had the look of someone who had come to terms with the world and liked what he found.

Anna didn't realize how she knew so much about this person after only a few moments. It was as if she recognized him, as if he were someone she had known long ago. She knew only that if she had attempted to draw a picture of the artist who had created her "Demetri" painting before now, she would have drawn this man.

"Mr. Anistopolis," she said. "It is a pleasure to meet you, although I feel that I already know you."

He looked at her, puzzled. "Have we met before?"

"I met you when I bought your painting *Fishermen of Mykonos*." She smiled. "It has given me great pleasure to own it."

"That pleases me," he said, with a broad smile that lit his eyes. "One always hopes that whoever buys one's work will enjoy it." He spoke with only the slightest accent.

"Please," Anna said, indicating a chair. "Do join me."

He sat down at the table but refused the coffee. "What brings you to Crete, Miss . . . ?"

"Anna Sandoval. I'm here on vacation, staying at the Hotel Villas near Ayios Nikolaos." Anna cast about among her thoughts for a more original reason. "Just here to see a part of Greece I had not visited before and to soak up some sun," was the best she could do.

"Not to draw pictures?"

Anna pressed her lips together in a tight grin and nodded. "That too. Actually I didn't think of it until I had already arrived—after I bought your painting."

"I am flattered. You are quite good, you know. I encourage you to keep it up. The technique will come back as you practice, as you let yourself enter into the current." He pulled a watch from his pocket. "Oh my, I must be going. It is past my lunchtime. My wife will be wondering what has become of me." He stood up and put on his hat. "It was very nice to talk with you, Miss Sandoval. I hope you . . ."

He paused in thought and Anna said, "It was an honor to meet the artist who painted my picture, Mr. Anistopolis. I look forward to seeing more of your work."

"And I look forward to seeing yours," he said with a little bow and wry smile. Then he looked at her and raised his eyebrows. "If you are free, that is, if you were going to lunch alone, why don't you come to my home and meet my wife, Maria? We live in the village above Elounda. That is, if you would care to."

Anna resisted the temptation to shout, "Yes, please" before he had second thoughts. Instead, she asked, working to keep her voice calm, "She would welcome a visitor for lunch with no notice at all?"

"She always welcomes company."

"In that case, I'd be delighted to come."

Demetri directed Anna to his battered Fiat, a model from the early sixties, and drove slowly through the backstreets of Elounda and up the hill on a very narrow road lined with stone fences. Chickens scratched at the dusty yards of houses along the way and once Demetri slowed to let a small girl tugging at a reluctant goat pass down the hill. She smiled and waved at him.

The car wheezed and clattered, and Demetri applied his whole attention to coaxing it up the hill. At that speed, it was easy for Anna to relax and look around—unlike on the hair-raising ride from the airport or the white-knuckle jaunt on the road to Lato yesterday.

At a turn of the road, Anna looked down on the red tile roofs below, the original town set back from the harbor. This was the old village of Elounda Anna had expected. She just hadn't ventured far enough. It was a scene from a forgotten era painted in old-master colors, the tiny houses stacked along crooked, cobbled streets just wide enough for a laden donkey. The church gleamed white in the early-afternoon sun, its dome bearing the Greek cross.

The people along the road waved as Demetri drove by. He nodded, keeping both hands on the steering wheel. At a break in the trees, Anna's breath caught. Standing on a distant ridge was a windmill, its white triangular sails turning slowly. "How beautiful," she said.

Demetri glanced over to see where she was looking. "Yes, they are beautiful. And powerful. Have you not seen one before?"

"Not on Crete."

"There is one near our home. We can walk there after lunch if you like."

For some reason, tears came to Anna's eyes. How lovely to feel so welcomed. She turned to look out the window. "Yes," she said, keeping her voice steady. "I'd like that very much."

Four

When Anna first looked into the eyes of Maria Anistopolis, as with Demetri, it was as though she already knew her though they had never met. Maria was a tall, delicate-boned woman with a profile that could have been stamped on an ancient Hellenic coin. Her straight, high-bridged nose, smooth, wide forehead, well-defined lips, and strong chin softened by age were framed by softly feathered, white hair—classic in Greek art. Her eyes, large and sorrowful, reflected wisdom and humor and, more than that, concern and interest in everything around her. The child in Anna wanted to pull Maria down beside her on the couch and tell her how frightened and alone she was. Blinking fast, she turned away on the pretense of straightening her hair. When she looked back, Maria was leading the way into the house. She was beautiful. And like most women of distinctive beauty, she was aware of it. This knowledge was evident in her regal bearing and slow, stately movements. One would expect her to be wearing the draped robes of the ancient Greeks, but she had on instead slacks and a silk blouse of delphinium blue.

"Come in out of that sun. It's so bright today that it could strike you dead." Laying a hand on Anna's arm, she said, "I'm so pleased you would take time to join us for lunch." Her fingers were twisted by arthritis.

"It is such short—or rather no—notice. I hope it isn't an inconvenience."

"Never," Maria said, leading them through the door. "We always have a cold lunch that can be eaten at any time by any number of people, because this wandering artist here with his head in the clouds is almost always late," she said, smiling at Demetri, "and often brings home the person with whom he last speaks."

"I used to know someone like that," Anna said, smiling at Demetri. "But I do appreciate your invitation," she added.

"Let's rest here in the sitting room for a moment and relax while Mina gets lunch ready."

"The ride up that hill always puts one in the mood for a glass of wine, wouldn't you agree?" Demetri asked. "To calm one's nerves, of course." He chuckled.

"You don't have any nerves," Maria said, shaking her head at him. "And most things put you in the mood for a glass of wine. I'll be right back." She stepped over to a small table to get the wine. The tray was waiting, with a tall, blown-glass decanter and two glasses. She added another glass and put the tray on the coffee table.

Every movement Maria made was a ritual, Anna noticed. Her hands, though misshapen, were two graceful birds flitting about the table, lighting the candle standing in a tall, silver candlestick on the table by the tray, slowly pouring the wine, gesturing with each word she spoke. The heavy, rose-colored draperies pulled against the noonday sun gave the room a dawnlike glow, peaceful after the harsh glare of midday outdoors. Anna smiled. She had thought she was the only person in the world who lit candles at midday. She and Paul had had candles at every meal, even breakfast. She felt a warm rush of kinship with this woman she had just met.

Demetri raised his glass. "To new friends," he said, bowing his head a little toward Anna.

Anna nodded, lifting her glass. "To new friends."

From the moment she entered the house, Anna felt as if she were in a holy place. The drinking of wine in the quiet atmosphere of the sitting room was like the first part of a solemn liturgy. They talked of ordinary things, but the atmosphere was different, a spiritual element that Anna couldn't put into words, but it was as real as the air she breathed.

When they finished their wine and Anna was ushered into the dining room, a room as stark and simple as a monastic refectory, the sanctified feeling was intensified. She was infused with reverence—not a sense of worship so much as of gratitude. Floor-to-ceiling drapes of forest green held back the light here. A single painting in muted tones was the only decoration on the roughly plastered white walls. More candles burned on the table beside a low flower arrangement.

The dark wood of the table, sideboard, and chairs was polished to a high gleam, and the table was scattered with small mats and napkins of white and deep red. It looked like a still life, each article placed to catch the bath of candlelight that revealed its color or texture.

The food was simple—slices of cold lamb and a light white cheese with dark bread in thick chunks. Wedges of cucumber and lettuce with florets of radish and cauliflower filled a plate beside a bowl of peaches, grapes, and dark purple plums.

Maria served each plate, adding condiments as if she were arranging flowers, each plate a work of art. She chatted with Demetri about her morning, his morning. She asked Anna how long she had been in Crete and about her home and family. Anna found herself telling about her daughter Christine's wedding, and Peter's successes at Princeton, talking on and on as though she were with old friends. She even described her house in Washington. She told them about her aborted trip to Lato, and the old man, Simone, she had drawn.

For dessert, a woman dressed in black served them a small mound of caramel cream custard that was so delicious that Anna actually moaned. Maria poured Greek coffee into demitasse cups. She was a priestess, her every move a sacrament.

After lunch, Demetri excused himself to put away his paints, leaving Maria and Anna to finish their coffee.

"And your husband?" Maria asked.

Anna hesitated before saying, almost in a whisper, "He died. A little over a year ago."

"Ah, I thought so. Was it sudden?"

Anna looked up in surprise at the abrupt question and then nodded. "Very. He hadn't even felt ill."

"Did you have a good marriage?" Her voice was musical, pronouncing perfectly grammatical English in Greek tones.

Again Anna startled at this direct question concerning Paul. "Yes." Anna was looking into her hands. "Yes. We did"—she swallowed—"have a good marriage."

At a small gesture of Maria's hand, they moved back into the sitting room. Anna's chair was deep and comfortable. The flickering candlelight played across the faded flowers of the chintz cover and the dark wood of the other furniture, giving the rose-colored air an added glow. The wine and delicious food had put Anna in a mellow mood, removed from past or present, until she was shaken back to reality by Maria's questions. She could feel the plastic smile she had practiced back in Washington start to slide into place and words forming that would change the subject—to the weather or things to see and do in Crete—when Maria said quietly, "Then you are fortunate."

"Fortunate?" That was what Maggie had said.

"Yes. That you had a good marriage. Many people cannot say that."

"But that's what makes it so"—Anna heard her voice crack and willed herself to get control—"so hard to bear." She blinked back the tears that burned her eyes. *I can't cry,* she thought.

"To bear death? Death is almost the only certainty we have in life."

"But he was so young. It was so unexpec—"

"Death is no respecter of age, Anna." Her gaze made Anna look away. "Had he done what he wanted to do in life? Was he happy?"

Anna hadn't thought about that. "Yes. In many ways he had reached the top in his field." Why was this woman doing this?

"What a fortunate young man." There was that word again. "To have a lovely wife, two accomplished children, the satisfaction of reaching one's goals—and to die suddenly, with no long illness or violent accident to mar his dignity."

The pent-up anger exploded through Anna's body. She sat
forward in her chair, almost upsetting the coffee on the table beside her. "Yes, that does seem 'fortunate' when put like that. But
he wasn't ready to die, and I wasn't—"

"You were not prepared." It was a statement.

"I certainly was *not* prepared," Anna said, her voice tight
with control. How could this woman who didn't even know her
sit here and tell her that Paul's death was fortunate, then make
light of the whole thing by simply saying that she, Anna, was "unprepared"? She looked at the door, visualizing herself flying
through it and stomping down that hill back to Elounda—away
from this place.

"I know how you feel, Anna," Maria said, handing Anna a
soft embroidered handkerchief. "I too was a widow. My young
husband was killed in a border skirmish. He was in the army."
Her eyes turned inward as if filled with the memory. "One morning he was there, holding me, loving me, talking about our future
after he had done his duty in the service. Then, only hours later,
they brought him back home to me, wrapped in a blanket."

The look in Maria's eyes was like a fist to Anna's stomach. "I
didn't even get to tell him good-bye."

"Oh, God."

"One does survive, Anna."

"How?" The word echoed through her brain. She could feel
the "Why?" that she had been asking with each beat of her heart
for this past year dissolving—the question that had tormented her
sleep and roused her anger so that she woke with deep fingernail
marks in her palms. Why? Why? Why? There was no answer.
Now it was replaced, for a time anyway, with a new question,
"How? How do I survive this?"

Maria reached over and laid a cool hand on Anna's arm. "You
forgive. Then you go on. Go on!"

"Forgive? Forgive whom?"

"First yourself."

"But . . . for what?"

"For living. For being healthy and very much alive when he is very much dead. Survivors of accidents in which other people are killed often have feelings of guilt. In fact, I think it is called survivor guilt. They ask, 'Why was I spared?' And they are afraid of the answer—afraid something is now expected of them that they can't fulfill.

"There were two of you in your good marriage and he was struck down. You must be wondering if you are somehow responsible in some way. You must have wondered, 'Why him, not me?' " She patted Anna's arm. "You must forgive yourself for continuing to live."

"And if one can accomplish that?"

"You must forgive your husband for dying, even as you must know he would never have chosen to do so. What was his name?"

"Paul." When Anna said his name, something broke inside her. She wanted to scream it, as if by calling out she could summon him. "Paul," she said again, but instead of a scream it was almost a whisper. No one had asked her to say his name except Maggie. No one, not even her friends in Washington, had even said it to her in a long time, much less asked questions about him.

"Are you still angry? With him?"

"What?" Anna looked sharply at Maria. "How could you know?" Maria didn't answer. Then Anna whispered, "Yes," her throat hurting. "I don't know why. I know it's unreasonable but—"

"Did you see him? After he died?"

Anna nodded, wondering why she had asked. "They took me to the hospital. For identification."

"Did you touch him?"

Anna looked into Maria's eyes. "I couldn't. I didn't want to . . . know. I didn't want to believe it."

"That's too bad. You should have been allowed to hold him in your arms, be alone with him. And then, to look up and say good-bye."

"Look up?"

Maria smiled. "People who have actually been medically dead, then are revived, tell of floating, in spirit, above the place

where their body lies, watching from above as people minister to
them."

"But—"

"I like to think that's what will happen to me. And that my
loved ones will be holding my body long enough to realize I am
no longer in it and then look up, and smile."

Anna blinked and shook her head as if to clear it. She had
never once considered Paul's spirit. For her, he was just gone.
"That's beautiful. But for me it's a little late."

"When Dominic was killed, I'd never heard of that either. I
did hold him in my arms—Greek peasants have a lot more freedom to weep and wail than Americans do. But for a long time I
was angry"—she looked at Anna—"like you, because I felt it was
so unfair. Because there was no good-bye. I was angry with Dominic. Angry at God. Many years later I realized that perhaps my
young husband had been there all along, just above me, waiting
for me to look up at him and give him his leave."

"Give him his leave?"

"Permission, of a sort. That's what a good-bye really is. Permission to take one's leave. When I finally did that, I was able to
forgive him—and God, and life, and myself."

"How . . . how did you do it?" Anna asked, her throat aching.

"Each person has to find the way best for herself." She gave
Anna a long look, compassion softening her gaze. "And time will
help, Anna. Time is your friend."

"Maria." Demetri's voice fell across the sweet gloom as he entered the room. Anna noticed the look in Maria's eyes—patient
and loving—as she smiled up at him. "Would you like to walk
with Anna and me up to see that old windmill?"

Barely hearing this, Anna was seeing only Paul's face in her
mind's eye. First it was the face in the picture on her mantel; then
it was the waxen mask she had cringed away from at the hospital.
At the sound of her name she was startled her out of her reverie
and she found herself clutching the gold rings on the chain
around her neck, staring into the flame of the candle.

"We too used to have candlelight at every meal," she said.

"I think Anna could use a good walk," Maria said. "You'll love that old windmill," she added.

"You aren't coming?" Anna asked.

Maria just smiled. "No, you two run along. My old bones have trouble on that hill these days." To Demetri she said, "I'll call Zino." She added something in Greek, a sad look on her face.

Demetri nodded.

Anna was barely aware of the tree-lined lane that led between two neatly stacked stone fences up the hill behind the Anistopolis house. Demetri pointed out the circle of stones about thirty feet in diameter, saying, "That is a threshing floor." She only nodded. As if from a great distance she heard him explain, "The donkey pulls the—" but she couldn't listen. Maria's words repeated themselves over and over in her mind. *Forgive. Time.* She felt as if this woman had laid open her heart with the skill of a surgeon and, with words of equal power, begun to stitch it back together.

They topped the hill to find the windmill, its reefed sails spinning slowly in the gentle breeze. Anna viewed it distractedly, noting its beauty, but in her mind she played scenes from the year before—again, at the hospital, Paul lying on the metal table as though made of wax. She had been so horrified that she hadn't even wanted to look. *It isn't him,* she kept telling herself. It couldn't be. She couldn't make herself touch him. Couldn't rid herself of the icy disbelief that this could have happened.

Demetri sat on a stone wall and lit an acrid cigarette. "I never smoke in the house," he said apologetically.

Anna leaned against the wall a little apart from him, still immersed in the past.

"I can see that Maria has perhaps upset you a little." He laughed gently. "She has X-ray vision which permits her to see straight into people, and"—he shook his head, smiling—"she asks a lot of questions."

"Questions I need to answer, I think."

"Out of sorrow has come some of our greatest works of art,"

Demetri said, gazing off across the hillside. Anna turned to look at him. "Maria told me you are a recent widow. I am sorry." He sat and smoked for a while. "I am glad you've decided to 'come out of retirement from art,' as you said."

"It seemed a good time now, in this interesting place, when I have little else to do. But I was so disappointed with my efforts today. The pencil feels awkward in my hand. When I sketched Mr. Syriotis in Kritsa yesterday, I thought I had the magic back. For a couple of hours I was lost in it. But today it eluded me. I don't 'see' as well as I used to—angles, lines, positive and negative space, perspective." Anna looked at the ground, then at Demetri. "As for sorrow, I find it a distraction."

"Sorrow opens avenues into our deeper selves, Anna. It is the touchstone to deeper understanding of life—because it is part of life. Technique takes only time to master, or to remaster, if you have the talent. You need to relax, not try for perfection. Enjoy it. Let it come back slowly, in its own time."

"I need a teacher," Anna said. She had spoken without thinking, but as soon as the words were out of her mouth she knew they were true. "Maybe you know of someone."

"Would you let me help you?"

"Oh, you must be much too busy to take on students. I couldn't take your time."

"I never take on students." He spoke sternly, looking at her with his bushy eyebrows knit in a frown. He took a long draw on his cigarette. "Occasionally, however, I do come across a person who has that magic, as you say, that strength of delivery, that vision that holds great promise." His voice lost its edge. "Usually, all it takes is a suggestion or two to encourage them to let it free." He looked at Anna. "I see that in you."

Anna stared back, her heart beating in her throat. "I would be honored and privileged. The cost is not a problem. I would pay anyth—"

"The cost will be greater than you think. Not in money. I would never accept money. It is my obligation to help others as I myself have been helped. The cost will be change. If you are unwilling to yield to the demands of your art, nothing I can do will help. If you are open to change, you will find that as you explore all the possibilities, you will be transformed—not into a different person but into all that you were meant to be." His eyes as he looked at Anna were filled with compassion. "This can be painful."

Had the temperature changed? A chill flitted over Anna's bare arms. She had the urge to run. Away from this man who spoke words that echoed from a great distance, calling her to let go of . . . what? All she wanted to do was enjoy drawing again. A few lessons. A little critique. Why would he ask her to change?

"Sometimes we get so comfortable even with our inadequacies, our irritations, our deprivations, that we don't truly want to change. It gives us security to say, 'I can't.' An excuse for—"

"When can I come for my first lesson?"

Demetri let out a long breath. "I must go to Athens until Thursday. Would Friday be a good day for you?"

"Excellent."

When they got back to the house, Maria told them that a young man, Zino, from up the hill, would be glad to take Anna back to her hotel in his truck. He was going into Ayios Nikolaos for a load of concrete blocks.

Anna shook Demetri's hand and said, "Friday."

When she tried to shake Maria's hand, Maria drew her close in a hug. Anna thanked them both, her eyes stinging with gratitude that couldn't be put into words.

"I look forward to Friday, when you will come back to us," Maria said as Anna climbed aboard the cab of the wheezing flatbed truck.

On the way along the winding road back to Elounda, she exchanged a few pleasantries with the dark, muscular young man, whose black curly hair and great mustache gave him an air of bravado not borne out by his soft voice. His English was very limited, so the trip into Ayios Nikolaos was mostly silent. Anna took the time to reflect on what Maria had said. Could it be that Paul had been there with her all this past year?

Out on her veranda that evening, Anna lay back on the chaise under the quiet of starlight. Was he out there, waiting? She couldn't picture Paul as a spirit.

Time, Maria had said. *Time is your friend. Forgive.*

Anna sighed and went in to bed.

Five

The next morning, Anna was crossing the street in Ayios Niko-laos when she saw Sophia unlocking her door. She sat down on a bench to wait until the store was fully open, watching as Sophia polished the etching on the beveled-glass pane with a cloth and then stepped out into the sunshine. The old woman in the shop next to the Blue Dolphin nodded, her face in the grim set of most Greek women over the age of sixty.

"Good morning, Isidorou," Sophia said.

The woman, dressed in black, smiled briefly before letting a scowl settle back onto her features. It was the Greek matron look, Anna thought, a way of closing out the world perhaps, especially the past in which so many women saw their husbands, sweet-hearts, and sons die in the horror of one conflict after another. Isidorou trudged back inside to get more needlework to put on low display tables outside her door.

Sophia turned the crank to let down the blue scalloped awning, adding to the picture the quaint little shop with a propri-etor in a flouncy skirt, silky peach-colored top complementing her reddish-blond hair. *She always looks as though she has just walked out of the pages of a fashion magazine.* Anna watched as she turned on the lamplights, then entered the door to the chime of the bells. "Good morning." Anna's voice from the doorway startled Sophia. "Are you open? The door was unlocked."

Sophia smiled. "What a nice surprise to see you again," she said. "Please, come in . . . Miss Sandoval, is it?" She frowned. "Stiros told me you didn't get to Lato on Sunday." Before Anna could explain, Sophia added, "He said you are a very good artist. Your drawings of old Syriotis impressed him."

"It was my fault that we had no time for Lato. Those drawings took time and—" She dismissed their importance with a wave of her hand. "Stiros was very patient."

"You must plan to go to Lato sometime, though. It is worth seeing. May I help you with something?" She pushed a switch behind her and Pachelbel's Canon filled the room.

"What I really came for was more paper, but let me just wander around in here for a while. You have such wonderful things. Where do you find them all?"

"Auctions, estate sales, trips to small country fairs. I try to discover unknown artists when I can. And, of course, I look for antiques everywhere I go and good-quality replicas of antiquities."

"When do you have time?"

"Ah, that is difficult. I sometimes wish I had a twin." Sophia poured Anna a cup of tea.

Anna slowly examined each shelf. "It must be hard letting some of these pieces go after you have gone to so much trouble finding them."

"Yes, that is true. If they are here a while, I get used to them. Sometimes I even take a painting or a sculpture to my rooms upstairs. I feel that being treasured, even for a little while, enriches objects of art. They seem more beautiful when I bring them back down to the shop." She grinned sheepishly. "I had the Demetri painting on my bedroom wall for a week."

"I think that was part of why I loved it. It seemed cherished," Anna said. "How long have you had this shop?"

"Ten years. My father died, leaving me the proceeds from the sale of his farm." She looked over at Anna. "As I told you that first time you came in, this store is my life."

"Well, you have certainly filled that life with beautiful things."

"I decided that I would never yield to the impulse to stock the usual cheap tourist trinkets—though they do sell well."

"You must love the look of delight . . . and relief on the faces of your customers when they walk in the door after seeing all those shops over by the harbor."

"Yes, that. But most important, I found something to do so I didn't have to leave my beloved Crete as most of my friends have done."

Anna picked up a brown ceramic bird about the size of a small orange, fat and content looking. She made a nest of her hand, cupping it in her palm. "Just fits," she said. "I always think it is nice to have small sculptures about, to hold on to in times of . . . of contemplation." She laughed, looking at the bird. "I keep expecting this to chirp. It's delightful"—she looked up at Sophia—"and I think it's chosen me." She laid it on the counter.

"Will you be staying in Ayios Nikolaos long?" Sophia asked. "Most Americans are here only a day or two."

Anna was looking at a set of four matching long-stem wine-glasses. "That's a question I've asked myself," she answered with a laugh. "I leased my little place at the Villas for a month with the option to stay longer. It seemed simpler that way." *Has it been a week?* "So, I haven't decided yet. It's so beautiful here and—" She held a wineglass to the light. It was obviously hand-blown but not by an expert. It had a few bubbles in the stem Anna thought added character. "I have no place to go—no place I'd rather go," she amended. "And the Villas is beginning to feel a little like home to me as I venture about more." She sat the wineglass beside the little ceramic bird on the counter. "It's a nice place to go back to, and I'm reluctant to . . . well, I just don't know." She laughed a little, nodding her head, eyes closed. When she opened them, she said, "How's that for a direct answer?"

She picked up another glass. "I've been drinking wine out of a juice glass," she said. "If I'm going to call this home for now, I guess I should think about setting up housekeeping. I'd like to have this set."

Sophia smiled. "There is an old saying that if the first customer of the day buys something, the rest of the day will be prosperous." Sophia took the other glasses down and placed them on the counter. "How about dishes? I have the feeling those provided at the hotel are not very elegant." She walked over to a place setting of hand-thrown pottery, a platter, plate, bowl, and mug tied up in a ribbon. It was off-white with a dark blue border. "These were made by a local potter here on Crete. They are not expensive, but I think he does very nice work."

"They're lovely." Anna untied the bow and picked up the mug and found that the handle just fitted her hand. "And you're right. I have been eating from the cast-off dishes from some army base, I think. I'll take one place setting. No, I'll take two now."

"If you want more later, I can get you as many as you want."

"Great. I'll take the glasses and dishes today." She smiled at Sophia. "That is, if you'll accept my invitation to dinner sometime this week . . . to break them in." She handed Sophia her credit card.

Sophia looked up in surprise, considered for a moment, and said, "That's very nice of you."

"Would Saturday be a good day? Seven? No, I forgot. Greeks never eat until almost midnight. How about nine o'clock?"

"Unfortunately I am scheduled to go to Athens on Friday and won't be returning until"—she looked at her calendar—"the following Thursday."

Anna tried to hide her disappointment.

"I'll call your hotel when I return"—Sophia glanced at the name on the plastic card to be sure—"Miss Sandoval."

Anna nodded. "Good. I'll look forward to your call. Now, please tell me your last name again—slowly."

"Papathanasiou. Sophia Papathanasiou."

"Would you mind if I called you Sophia? My tongue balks at that many syllables."

Sophia blinked and then shook her head. "*Ne,* please do."

After Sophia had boxed and wrapped Anna's purchases, remembering to add the pad of drawing paper, she put them in a bag. "*Efkaristo,* Miss Sandoval."

Anna nodded. "Thank *you* for saying you'll come. And

please, call me Anna." At the door she paused and turned to say, "By the way, did I tell you I met Demetri Anistopolis?"

"No. How wonderful for you."

"He's as unique and as wise as his painting reveals," Anna said. "I'll always be thankful that you introduced him to me."

Six

Anna arrived back at the Villas at four in the afternoon, the taxi piled high with groceries, packages from the Blue Dolphin, and a few things she had bought at a weaving factory she discovered. She had gone there specifically to get a small red rug with the black design so typical of Crete, which she had seen hanging in the window, but she couldn't resist a blue tablecloth and napkins of soft wool, fringed around the border in a pattern of darker blue and green. They looked handwoven, but the price belied that. Another package contained a string bikini she had bought at a store that specialized in T-shirts, snorkels, beach mats, and rubber thongs.

It must be a nesting thing, Anna thought, surveying all her purchases. She had never been tempted to impulse spend. Certainly she and Paul had been comfortable and had risen to a certain degree of affluence in later years, but she didn't really need anything. That didn't matter. She suddenly wanted to make a little home here, a small hermitage to settle into.

The taxi driver set all her bags and boxes on the low wall beside the walk and drove away, leaving her in a cloud of dust. She was contemplating how many trips it would take to get all this to her rooms when she heard a car drive up.

"Looks like you need one of those donkeys you see along the road." She turned to see the American man from the beach unfolding his tall frame out of a tiny rental car.

"Oh, I can probably make it. Walking back and forth will do me good." She picked up the basket with groceries in one hand

and, with her huge purse slung over her shoulder, grabbed up the paper-covered rolled-up rug in the other.

"Your apartment is at the end of the line, and there are about a hundred steps up and down between here and there. Now, I would be one of those donkeys—a real ass, as a matter of fact—if I didn't help you pack some of that over there." He picked up the boxes with the dishes by their strings and weighed them like a balance scale. "You buy rocks or something?"

"Be careful with those," Anna said. "They're glass."

As they walked along, she asked, "Do you know where everyone lives in this hotel?"

"Only those who catch my attention," he said, giving her a sidelong glance. "I have the apartment at the top of the hill, with a view not only of the gulf—is it Mirabella? I've seen you down there."

Warmth flooded Anna's cheeks. Could he see her terrace?

"Let's see, you've been here about a week now, haven't you?" he asked, shifting the dishes from one hand to the other and taking the rug from her. "Must like it to have stayed on."

"I do like it. It's just what I needed." Anna regretted saying that, but he didn't respond. "How long have you been here?"

"I came the day before you scattered your underwear along the path here."

"I was laying a trail in case I lost my young guide through this warren and had to make my way back," Anna said with a straight face.

"Likely story. I believe this is your place—the one with the big pot of geraniums by the door."

My God! He could see it.

"Don't worry," he said as if he could read her mind. "I can't see it from my balcony. Just noticed the geraniums through the archway once when I was out for a walk. I've tried to grow them like that myself on Long Island, but I've never gotten them to grow like trees the way they do here." He turned through the small archway and up the two steps, then stood back so that Anna could unlock the door.

"Where do you want these?" he asked as he walked into the sitting room, looking around for a place to set the package.

"Just put them on the table over there," Anna said, indicating the nook in front of the window. "I'll deal with them later." She walked around the bar into the kitchen and put the basket on the counter.

"This is real nice," he said, smiling as he looked around. "Mine's a lot more compact. Of course, I had to take what I could get, coming out here unannounced like that."

"You came to Crete unexpectedly?"

"Yes and no. I came on a whim. I planned to stay at the Minos Hotel, where we—my wife and I—stayed on our . . . when we came here once before. Only I found it had burned to the ground many years ago. Anyway, the good people at the tourist agency down there in town sent me here."

"Is your wife here with you?" Anna liked this no-nonsense, no-pretense man. If his wife were half as nice, she would enjoy meeting her. It would be pleasant to have some people she knew nearby, she thought with a smile, so she would have someone to share her new wineglasses with.

"No. She's—" His craggy face sagged, making his nose appear more hawklike. The lines on his forehead deepened. "My wife died two years ago."

"Oh, I'm so sorry."

"It's all right. This trip is sort of a nostalgic bit of nonsense I decided on. I was in Athens on business and just decided to come over here and . . . you see, we spent our honeymoon here at the Minos. And I thought . . ."

He shrugged a little and let his gaze wander around the room as if he was trying to think of a way to change the subject. When he noticed the Demetri painting, his face brightened. "That's a wonderful picture. The one I've got is just a wall hanging. But this—"

"It's mine."

He looked at her, bushy eyebrows raised.

"I bought it."

"Oh." He turned and looked at it appreciatively.

"Well," he said, "you sure know how to pick 'em. It's strange. When I see something like this in other people's houses, I wish I had it. But when I go into a store, I never seem to be able to find anything. My wife . . . she always used to decorate the house. We do, uh, did have some beautiful things. Well, I still have them." He walked over to the other side of the room to get a different perspective. "She would have loved this."

"It is a wonderful painting," Anna said. "And I've met the artist, Demetri Anistopolis. He lives in a town not far from here."

"Is that right?" He smiled at her. "You really get around, don't you?"

"And I'm forgetting my manners, Mr.—"

"Sam. Sam McDonald, Miss—" He was looking at her left hand.

"Anna Sandoval." He regarded her with his brow wrinkled as if trying to remember something. Anna held her breath, waiting for him to ask if she was Paul Sandoval's wife, but he didn't make the association. After all, Sandoval was a fairly common name.

"Can I offer you a cup of tea, Sam?" She started searching through her cache of food on the counter. "And I have here"— she picked up one of the unwrapped loaves—"some of the most delicious-looking bread."

"I have a better idea, Anna Sandoval. I have two ice-cold bottles of Amstel beer in my icebox and a slab of the best cheese I've tasted in years. I was planning to go down to those stone shelves they call a beach. How'd you like to join me? And bring your bread."

"That sounds wonderful. I was going to go myself after I put all this—"

"I'll meet you in ten minutes at the top of the trail."

After Sam left, Anna put away the groceries quickly. It was only when she went into the bedroom to put on her suit that she had a memory flash of the scene with Sam standing there with her suit top hanging from one finger. *Oh, God,* she thought, her face in her hands. *Now what am I going to do? What can I wear that will be an encore to that?*

She got out the one-piece Jantzen. Holding it up, she looked

in the mirror. To her Greek-beach-acclimated eyes, it looked like
something Whistler's mother would have worn. Reaching into the
paper bag she had just brought in, she lifted her latest beach attire—the suit she had bought today that was only strings and tri-
angles. No good. She hadn't the courage.

Finally she compromised. Tossing that one aside, she put on
the bikini that had seemed so daring when she'd first worn it,
and resolutely hooked on the strapless top. Throwing on her
beach robe, she emptied the straw bag and put in all her beach
paraphernalia, adding the loaf of fresh bread, a knife, and a couple of peaches.

Sam was waiting at the top of the first flight of stairs leading
to the path, looking like a tall, angular athlete. His swimming
trunks announced his nationality as much as if he were waving a
flag. They resembled track shorts, fitting snug around his hips. He
wore no gold chains to tangle in the grizzled hair of his chest, and
he stood, feet apart, his hound-dog eyes crinkling at the corners,
as if to say, "Here I am—just me." He was definitely not a poser.
He had the beer wrapped in a hotel towel.

There were only a few people on the beach. Sam and Anna
spread their things out on her favorite spot, the shelf by the water
where a rock outcropping gave them something to lean back
against. Anna dropped her robe and took off her sunglasses. "I'm
going to take a swim first," she announced. She was already standing up, looking out at the water.

She was reaching up to loosen her hair when Sam spoke from
behind her. "I hope you won't think me presumptuous," he said,
"but I've seen you down here before, and although I usually don't
do this on a first date, I want one thing understood from the beginning. You can do as you please around me. None of this false-
modesty stuff." Before Anna realized what he was doing, he had
unhooked the back of her swimsuit top. She gasped, barely keeping herself from shrieking. "Don't worry, I've already seen them
and you've got nothing to hide." He slid the top off from behind.
"Now, Mrs. Sandoval, go for your swim."

Anna dived in before she could think and swam underwater

as far as she could. When she surfaced, she swam in long, fast strokes straight out to sea, almost choking with laughter. *I can't believe I just stood there and let him—*

The water slid like quicksilver over her almost-bare body. She swam as if something were after her. Finally, spent and out of breath, she rolled over on her back and stared up at the sky, suspended in blueness. She was beginning to love it here in this corner of Crete.

"You in training for the Olympics or something?" Sam sputtered, breathing heavily as he treaded water beside her.

Anna still felt the urge to turn her back to him, so she willed herself to face him. "I race the dolphins when I'm out here alone."

"I bet you win, too. I sure as hell wouldn't want to race you. I'd drown of a heart attack."

At the words "heart attack," Anna felt her veins fill with lead. She swam a few strokes away and back to shake off the feeling. "Nah, I'd save you," she said. "I've got a genuine Red Cross certificate in lifesaving."

"For that, I'd gladly drown."

Anna gave him a sidelong glance and started a slow swim back to shore. Sam was a strong swimmer. Even when she sped up, he stayed alongside her.

"Those Dutch sure know how to brew beer," Sam said, leaning back after spreading his towel as a cushion against the rocks, his legs stretched before him.

"And the Greeks know how to make cheese." It was a wonderful picnic. Anna hadn't felt so relaxed and natural in months—years. She had, however, pulled on a T-shirt.

"How long do you plan to stay here on Crete?" he asked.

"I don't know. I'm at loose ends right now, sort of, and I guess you could say that I have no definite plans." No plan at all, she thought.

"I've noticed you drawing things when I've seen you here before. You an artist?"

"If an artist is a person who carries around pads and pencils, yes, I guess I am."

"I wish I were." His voice was sincere.

"What do you do, Sam?"

"I'm a pilot. I've flown for American Airlines since I got out of the air force."

"That must be exciting."

"Well, in the movies it's always exciting. In real life it's pretty routine about ninety-nine percent of the time."

"I would guess that the one percent that's not routine is—"

"More exciting than anyone would wish for," he said.

"You must have been to many interesting places."

"Oh, yes, like St. Louis, Dallas, Salt Lake City?" He grinned.

"You only fly domestic routes?"

"Recently. When I was copilot, I flew international. But when you get promoted, they clip your wings a little. I'll have to be more experienced on the domestic circuit before they let me captain an international flight."

"I've always admired the flight personnel I've met here and there. They look so snappy in those crisp uniforms." She turned to him. "Everyone always seems so debonair, moving with such ease and aplomb about the world's great cities."

"Now, I don't want to ruin your image. I'd like you to think of me as this suave stud who flies all over the world with dash and glitter. But appearances aside, it's just a job. And most of those debonair people are just family men and women who would really, if the truth were known, like to be at home." He shook his head. "We stay such a short time in each city that, what with dealing with jet lag and trying to get enough sleep to go back, we have precious little left to spend glitzing about." He turned on his side, leaning on an elbow. "Or as the movies would have it, jumping in and out of bed with each other."

Anna looked away, somehow unable to picture Sam leaping from bed to bed. "You said you wished you were an artist," she said quickly. "I've seen those panels of switches, knobs, gears, and lights in an airplane. I should think it would take an artistic touch to make a plane fly—a phenomenon I've never really understood. It has to take real mastery to get it off the ground and back down again."

"Mechanics. The pilot might add finesse, but there isn't much room for improvisation or originality. It's one of those things where there is a right and a wrong way to do it." He chuckled. "Unless you go in for stunt flying."

"I take it you don't."

"Not since college. As an undergraduate, I impressed all my girlfriends with my loops and spins in the flying-club biplane. By graduate school I was above such maneuvers."

"Oh?"

"I met my wife. She didn't like to fly." He stretched and got to his feet. "I have an idea. If you don't have other plans for this evening, how would you like to join me for dinner?"

Anna felt a little twist in her heart. She began gathering her things in the basket. Inside her head it was as if she had become two people. How nice, one part of her said. It would be so good to have someone to eat with, to talk with. The other shrank back with wide eyes, as if against a wall. *I can't do this,* that part of her said. *He's only asking you to eat with him,* the first side coaxed. *I'm not ready,* said the other. *He's a nice person. And lonely. But I need time.*

Anna straightened, picking up the basket, and looked at Sam. He stood, feet apart, his head a little to one side, his face passive, his doleful eyes pleading. "I . . . I'd like that," Anna said.

Sam came to Anna's door at nine sharp, and they walked up to the Taverna and had a drink at one of the tables by the pool. When Anna had realized that tonight it was a little cooler than usual, she had searched around for a light wrap, and ended up wearing her new blue tablecloth as a shawl. It was a perfect weight for the soft breeze that blew off the water far below.

They decided on a traditional Greek dinner beginning with hors d'oeuvres of pickled olives, squid, prawns, and vine leaves stuffed with rice. Sam washed this down with ouzo, a thick, sweet aperitif with the flavor of anise. Anna had tried ouzo before, and it had no appeal for her. She asked for mineral water. Then they had souvlaki, a kebab of lamb's meat, and moussaka, the Greek version of eggplant lasagna.

"May I suggest a wine?" Anna asked. "This one," she said, pointing to the wine list, "Naoussa Boutari, is delicious. A Macedonian wine. It's really a pretty inexpensive wine, but I've never tasted better."

"By all means."

When it came, Anna took a sip, savoring the full flavor of the smooth, fruity wine.

"Where did you discover this?" asked Sam, swirling the wine in his glass, then holding it under his wonderful nose to inhale the bouquet.

"In a taverna in Athens. It is good, isn't it?" They ate in silence for a while, enjoying the wine and the food. Anna and Paul had discovered this wine at dinner one night a few years before when they were wandering around the Plaka below the Acropolis.

"You didn't draw any pictures this afternoon," Sam said.

"I know. Too busy talking."

"I'd like to see some of your drawings sometime, though I know I'd be envious. Like I told you, I've always wanted to be an artist."

"You said this afternoon that you like to garden. That's art."

"I used to putter around in the garden. But it was Grace who was the artist with it. Pilots are gone a lot and a beautiful yard needs constant attention. She was the gardener. I was just the yard man—you know, cut the grass, trim the hedges, fertilize, irrigate—all that."

"But you were interested in more than just yard work. You said you tried to grow geraniums—"

"Because she loved them. She placed them. She trimmed them and, of all things, talked to them. I read up to find the best plant foods and all that to make them what she wanted."

"How thoughtful."

"It was the least I could do. She had to go it alone so much. I'd be gone for four, five days at a time, and then I'd be there in her hair for several days between trips. Sometimes more, when I'd get the Europe beat. You know, a hotel in Paris, then we'd fly out of there to all the major European and Middle Eastern cities for a while."

"She didn't come with you?"

"The kids—we have twin girls; they're twenty-six now—were in school. And no, she seldom came with me. She didn't enjoy flying and . . . was kind of a homebody." He pulled his ear and took a swallow of wine. "Oh, on vacations they'd all come. We could go anywhere, space available. She'd come for the girls' sake. Then after the kids grew up, she'd come on short trips sometimes. But there was the garden club and women's groups. You know." He shrugged.

Anna remembered all those things women do to keep busy while their husbands are off on business trips—and how those things can take over and become a way of life as rigid as the husband's demanding schedule. "Tell me about her, Sam. What was she like?"

A look of pain crossed his face before it settled into lines of deep contentment. "She was an old-fashioned girl, built for comfort, not for speed. She was a cute little thing when I met her, fresh and pretty. After the children, she got, well, a little rounder—but still pretty. In fact, she was beautiful."

He picked up his spoon and drew patterns on the tablecloth with the handle. "It was good to go home to that house, with Grace—you know the saying—keeping a light burning in the window?" He took a deep breath through his nose and let it out slowly through pursed lips. "Well, that was Grace—always waiting with open arms."

"Did you love her?" It was obvious that he did.

"Very much."

"I'm glad." Anna was doing this on purpose. She knew how painful it was for him to remember, but she also knew what a relief it was to find someone who would ask about it. "Do you still live in that house?"

"No, like a crazed idiot, I sold it. The twins had both moved from Long Island, one to California, one to Arizona. And the house was so big and, well, it was too full of memories. I just couldn't face going back there after my trips and finding—"

"No light in the window?" Anna couldn't bear to add, *No open arms?*

"No light in the window," he said softly. He leaned forward and broke off a piece of bread. "But enough of that. Let's have dessert outside, okay?"

Anna chose fruit after that heavy meal. Sam had baklava, layers of thin, crusty pastry oozing with honey and nuts.

"I want you to know," Sam said after they ordered, "that I was very sorry to hear of your husband's untimely death."

Anna looked up at him in surprise, a slice of peach halfway to her mouth.

He pulled his ear. "I, of course, didn't know him, but I knew who you both were. I've flown into Washington many times these past few years." He smiled. "It took a while for me to remember where I had seen you before. Your picture was in the Washington papers after your husband received the Drummond Award." He pressed his lips together and looked at her with concern. "It must be real hard for you. He seemed like a fine person. I'm sorry."

Anna nodded. Something in her tensed, then relaxed. She had expected this to come up eventually, and even as she longed for the opportunity to talk about it, she had dreaded the moment she would have to shape those first words of explanation. But with Sam it was easy. "He would have enjoyed this evening," she said. What a relief to just be natural. "He loved Greek food." Loved. Always past tense.

There was an awkward silence that Anna couldn't find a way to break as she sat staring at the slice of peach. Finally, she looked up and smiled. "Thank you, Sam. Thank you for remembering."

After she finished her dessert, she reached into her bag and pulled out a small pad and a pencil. "Now for some art. When I was younger, I drew a picture for every important event of my life." She told him about her files of drawings and that led to anecdotes about the events she had chronicled in those illustrations. Then she told him about her childhood, summers on her grandfather's Texas ranch. Sam recounted trips he'd made to Texas when he was in the air force. Anna described trips she had taken with Paul and the picture she *didn't* draw the time Peter was suspended from prep school for mooning from the track-team bus. As they talked, she sketched the pool area, their table in disarray with empty cups, crumpled napkins, and half-filled glasses of Greek cognac. Surreptitiously she sketched Sam.

Sam countered Anna's tales by telling her how he'd met his wife. "She used to sit and look at me with those wide blue eyes and listen while I talked on and on for hours. I thought she was the best conversationalist I'd ever met."

It was well after midnight when they finished the meal with coffee and the waiter brought the tab for Sam to sign. Anna then handed Sam a portrait of himself.

Almost a caricature, it exaggerated his nose and mournful eyes and caught him pulling his ear, a characteristic gesture. "To remember this evening," she said. "And now, I can find my own way back to my place."

Sam stood and started to protest.

"I enjoy a solitary walk before I turn in." She picked up her bag and pulled her "shawl" closer. "Thank you, Sam, for a very nice evening."

"Will I see you tomorrow?"

Anna had no plans at all. After a moment, she said, "Come for breakfast. Ten o'clock." She smiled and turned away. When she got to the steps that led up to the path Sam called out, "Anna! Thanks for the drawing but I didn't need it—"

She stopped and looked back at him.

"—to remember this evening."

Anna smiled and waved. *I didn't either,* she thought as she climbed the steps.

Seven

Anna served breakfast on her terrace. Dressed in shorts and an orange tank top covered by an oversized shirt with its tails tied around her waist, she stretched in the sun feeling as if she owned the whole scene around her—water, mountains, and small, distant town.

With the flourish of a bullfighter, she covered the stone table with her "shawl" of the night before and filled the wineglasses with freshly squeezed orange juice. She stood back to see if she had forgotten anything. Flowers. Going in to get one of the little vases that the maid filled with fresh flowers each day, Anna threw out the droopy bouquet from the day before and put the rose in the center of the table. Before turning to pick a sprig of bougainvillea from her bush, she looked everything over again. She was pleased with the effect. The dark blue shawl/tablecloth looked nice with the new dishes.

How many times had she done this before for the meals she and Paul hosted in Washington? Even those last years when they'd had a cook, Anna had always set the tables. It was something she had enjoyed immensely.

"Good morning," Sam shouted from the arched gateway at the foot of the steps. "It's a pleasure to find someone so full of life so early in the day."

Anna didn't know how long he had stood there watching her. But what did it matter? She smiled and said with a dignified bow, "The house bids you welcome."

Sam brought his hand out from behind his back, offering

Anna a handful of white and pink bougainvillea blossoms. "I've discovered the most delightful florist," he said.

"Why, thank you, Sam. How thoughtful. I was just about to go to that same florist myself." Anna put the bouquet in the vase.

When they were seated, Sam looked the table over appreciatively. "Up at my place, the dishes are plastic," he said, examining a plate. "You must really rate around here."

"You carried these in yesterday. Another item I just couldn't resist down at the Blue Dolphin."

His eyebrows rose.

"That's a gift shop in Ayios Nikolaos." She served up omelets stuffed with lightly stir-fried vegetables and a grating of cheese, and filled both cups with steaming coffee, setting the pot beside the vase that now overflowed with Sam's flowers. On impulse, she picked out a stem covered with blossoms and tucked it into her hair, laughing.

"Wherever you got all this, it has a powerful effect." He took a bite of omelet. "Elegant and delicious." The morning light only emphasized Sam's craggy face and wide, disarming smile. His eyes were just as sad as the night before. No, not sad, Anna thought. Woebegone. The hammered leather of his face crinkled at the corners of his eyes as if he had spent a lot of time squinting into the sun.

They ate in silence, gazing out at Anna's postcard view. There was no need to talk. Sam was already like an old friend. Feeling perfectly at ease, Anna plopped her bare feet onto an empty chair and leaned back, sipping her coffee.

"It is certainly beautiful here," Sam said finally. Turning to Anna, he asked, "You plan on taking up residence?"

She smiled at him. "I just don't know what I'm going to do. It's been good for me to come here. Made things easier, in a way. At least I don't expect Paul to come walking through the door here like I did back in Washington."

"I know how that is." He pulled at his ear. "But you can't run away forever."

Anna was startled. "I've always thought of this trip as 'getting' away, not 'running.'"

"Well, you picked a nice getaway," Sam conceded.

Anna was silent for a while, wondering if he was right. Was she running away? Hiding out? "How about you, Sam? How long will you be in Crete?"

"When I came over here, I intended to spend four days—just enough time to revisit some of the places—" He shifted in his chair. "But I like it here. I have to go back to Athens for another meeting as soon as they set it up. They are making renovations at the airport to accommodate the new security regulations and they have this architect there who is real busy, so since I am apparently not, I got chosen. This was supposed to be my vacation, but since they knew I was coming to Athens, they asked me to spend a day or two at these meetings."

"How long were you in Athens before coming to Crete?"

Sam shifted in his chair once again, looked directly at Anna, and said in a flat voice, "I came to Athens to get"—he cleared his throat, then pressed his lips together and looked away—"to get a new perspective on my life." He turned back with a sheepish grin. "You know, men who have just turned fifty are at a dangerous age." He pursed his lips and looked solemn. "We're plagued with questions. 'Have I measured up? Was I a good husband? Have I done my job well? Is this what I wanted out of life?' "

He rubbed his nose. "Well, I've been at this fifties business for three years now, and of course, losing Grace hasn't made it any easier." He stared across the table a moment. "But I want to get all I can out of the years I have left on this earth." He looked across the table at Anna. "I would guess that we're both here for the same reason. To decide what to do from here on out."

Anna just nodded.

"So, as long as we're both looking for the tag ends of our lives, I suggest we start by taking a short trip today. You ever heard of Lato?"

"Yes. I've been wanting to go there." She told him about her aborted attempt with Stiros.

"Well, let's go. I have this little bitty car rented, and in the hopes that you would accept, and knowing I'd never be able to compete with a meal you had prepared, I asked the Taverna people to pack us a lunch. What do you say?"

"What are we waiting for? Just let me change. In the back-country, all the women are swathed in black dresses with long sleeves and scarves. I'd feel more comfortable in a skirt."

Anna looked in vain for Mr. Syriotis as the Opel bumped its way between the olive groves up the rocky road to Lato. From a brochure, she read out loud, "Lato, a fortified Doric town built on terraces, founded in the seventh century B.C., named after the vegetation goddess Lato."

She flipped through her guidebook. "Crete is an interesting place. Some say it's the birthplace of Western thought, the culture that was the forerunner of the golden age of the great Greek philosophers who shaped Western civilization. I'm looking forward to seeing the ruin at Knossos sometime, the heart of the Minoan civilization. It's near Iráklion."

"Where the airport is?"

"Mmmm." Anna looked out the window and watched as a single hawk glided on air currents, engraving slow circles against the cloudless sky. In the loneliness and strangeness of Crete, her senses had sharpened. Time had slowed. She had time to really see what was around her. She watched the bird, craning her neck to keep it in sight. She knew she would remember this moment—the smell of dust rising from the road, the hum of the motor as Sam changed gears over the hills, the heat of the sun pouring first through the windshield across her knees, and then, as the road curved, warming her arm where it rested on the window ledge. Finally, the hawk disappeared behind a hill.

"Crete is the most foreign place I have ever visited. I can't seem to put my finger on exactly why. Most of the trees and plants are familiar. There are places in the States that have this wilderness atmosphere. But have you noticed how it still seems strange?"

"Maybe it's something in the air."

They passed a couple of black-clad women prodding a donkey piled high with loose hay. As the car went by they scowled, ignoring Anna's wave. "Or in the history," she said. "The people are different. The look in their eyes, their faces in repose are so . . . closed. I'm not sure if they dislike and distrust foreigners, or if they are grim with each other, grim about life in general."

"They haven't had an easy life, as I understand it. They've been in almost constant war, certainly in this century."

The road broke out of the olive trees and snaked along an arid ridge with a view of country as wild and mysterious as Anna had ever seen. Craggy mountains sawed through the sky in every direction, tier upon tier. Far across the valleys, small clusters of red-roofed houses huddled together as if for protection.

At one turn, the road came to an abrupt end where the stones had been scraped into a turnaround, leaving mounds of dry, rocky earth. Sam stopped and parked. The road was only a trail after that.

"According to the map," Anna said, "this is it." She peered through the dust billowing around the car. There were no other cars there. "It surely is a lonely place." They got out of the car and climbed over the rough ridge of earth bladed to one side.

Before them was a rambling ruin spread over the hillside, overgrown with bushes and trees of this century. A grand staircase that could have served as an amphitheater was built into the slope of the hill. Opposite that, a huge, ancient olive tree had broken through a wall indented with niches reserved for the statues of gods, long since removed by looters or placed in museums. In the semicircle of stones was, according to the guidebook, a solemn place of worship.

The silence was expectant, as though the place itself were holding its breath. The repetitious crick of cicadas drilling into the hush, even the crunch and scrape of their feet on loose stones, emphasized the quiet. "Sacred places always retain that sense of sanctuary, don't they, even centuries after they are no longer used?" Anna said.

Sam smiled at her but didn't answer. They climbed to the upper part of the ruin, high in a saddle, on a stone pathway up the

northern slope to the agora, or marketplace. As they followed the
bends and curves, they saw a perfectly round circle of paving
stones, smooth and even, encircled by a wall about knee-high,
continuous except for one small opening.

"I know what this is," Anna said.

"What? Another temple of some kind?"

"No. It's a threshing floor. There is one near Demetri's house
that looks just like this. It is still in use." They moved on. Passing
between crumbling town walls with towers, up narrow streets of
huddled, mostly roofless, but amazingly well-preserved stone-
walled houses, Anna and Sam stopped and looked in the door of
a small windowless room. The stone doorjamb was intact. Even
the supporting stone beam above the door was still firmly in place.
They both had to duck to enter the dark interior.

A shaft of sunlight pierced through a hole in the roof that
someone had fashioned out of scrap boards gray with age, and
light poured onto the floor of the twelve-by-fifteen-foot room. It
had the dank smell of moist earth. Anna shivered, though it was
quite warm.

A bee buzzed drunkenly through the shaft of light and out
the door. Anna reached out her hands into the mote-dusted beam,
and the light filled them as if poured. She felt as if she were being
given something of great value.

"Well, if this was a house, the inhabitants must have been
small people," Sam mused. "At least housework would have been
a cinch. You could clean this whole place standing in one spot."

Anna bent down to where the light pooled on the floor and
scraped at a piece of stone with her finger. She finally pulled loose
a natural-colored half-moon of pottery. "The top of a jar," she
said, turning the shard in her hand. Clasping the piece of pottery
to her breast, she said, "Can you feel the ghosts?"

"Ghosts?"

"The spirits of people who lived here, those who used this jar,
who played here as children and grew up and fell in love and gave
birth and went off to war and returned as heroes . . . or didn't return." As the words were said, she looked away.

Sam put his hand gently on her shoulder. "Life never changes, generation after generation. It's the same for everyone. We are born, we grow, we love, we hate, we die. Everyone dies."

Anna nodded. Turning to duck back out the door, she took a deep breath. "Life is hard for people of every age, I guess. But all people have such great hopes, don't they? They search for meaning. Then they concoct religions to reach beyond the cycle of birth, life, death, birth, life, death."

"You think religions are concocted? Made-up?" Sam asked.

"I've lost faith in mine. God doesn't seem involved in my life these days. So much of what I was taught as a child just isn't true. And the rest doesn't make sense."

"Hmm, I've always thought religions took a very simple fact and made it complicated," Sam said. "But I know that we are part of something bigger than ourselves. I believe that our short life span here is only a thin slice of what we can expect. Otherwise, it's all a sham. So we search for what it is that we are a part of. People do that in different ways."

"How do you do it?"

"I just live."

"Aren't you angry with God for ta—for taking Grace from you?"

"God didn't take her. She died of cancer. Like the sharp teeth of wild animals and fast-moving motorized metal carriages of high horsepower, cancer is just another of the dangers of living." He looked over at Anna with his serious, sad eyes. "So's a heart attack. It happens. None of us is exempt."

Anna nodded. She was looking down, watching her step.

"The way I look at it," Sam went on, "it's the way we conduct our search that counts—the way we live. The way we die . . . well"—he shrugged, palms upward—"that's incidental." His eyes shifted to something beyond Anna. "Will you look at that!"

When Anna looked up, her breath went out in a rush. Before them, the land sloped sharply away, all the way to the Gulf of Mirabello. The distant sea winked in the sun and Ayios Nikolaos was nestled around its tiny harbor. The undulating hillside fell into deep folds of land, rills, and draws that flattened into a broad sweep of textured velvet to the water.

As she tried to take it all in, Anna felt Sam's hands on her shoulders. He turned her around to look at a scene behind them that was equally breathtaking. One mountain range after another, each a lighter color of gray blue, rose tier on tier into the haze, the jagged rock formations on the peaks piercing the washed blue dome of sky.

"It's so beautiful that it's frightening," Anna whispered.

"No one could make a surprise attack on this place. That's for sure."

"How did they know to build here?" Anna asked. "Did they wander all over this wild country and just find this?"

"I don't know," Sam said. "But since they don't seem to have a restaurant here, I suggest we go down and get our lunch basket. Where do you want to eat?"

"I'm feeling majestic today. Let's eat on the grand staircase."

When they got back to the lower level, several other people were milling about, a group of Frenchwomen and two or three couples speaking German. Sam got the basket from the car, and he and Anna settled on the far end of the broad stairs. The basket from the Taverna contained white, restaurant-china dishes and two wineglasses. The wine, chilled in a small zippered container with a corkscrew in a pocket on the side, was dry with a fruity bouquet, the food more delicious for being eaten outdoors.

The afternoon hummed away with the background rhythm of cicadas. They talked of trips they had taken and people who had influenced them during their school days; summers at camps; horseback riding.

"I used to have a horse," Sam said. "I guess I was about seven when I got it. I had full responsibility for it. Some of my best childhood memories center around that horse. Her name was Arabella. Bell and I had an intimate relationship. She was my best friend. I used to go out to the stall in the middle of the night during a thunderstorm to brush and soothe her.

"You know, as we get older, we get into the 'thing mode.'

We're never satisfied, just want more and more, bigger and better. But when I was out there with my horse and lightning crashing all around, I had everything I needed or wanted. I was perfectly satisfied."

Anna smiled. "There is something very satisfying about being alone with a horse," she agreed. "All those summers I spent at the ranch I practically lived on a horse. I had so many happy memories there. Horse memories. People memories. I inherited it after my father died a few years ago. But there was no way I could keep it. Regretfully, I had to sell."

"That must have been painful."

"Yes, but it just wasn't the same. The nearby town had sprawled almost up to the gate and . . . I don't know. Paul, he was a city boy who begot city children. Both the kids loved it while my father was living. But we were all so busy we could never go there. I had to let it go."

"Well, you'll always have the memories."

Anna nodded. *Of so many things,* she thought. Then she smiled and told Sam about Maggie. "She's probably one of the best lawyers in Dallas, but she still looks like a teenager," Anna said. She told him about the time in ninth grade when she and Maggie had smoked a cigar "all the way down to the butt."

"Sounds pretty tame considering what kids do today. Make you sick?"

"She nearly died, but I kind of developed a taste for them. Since then, I've always enjoyed the smell of cigar smoke."

Sam smiled. "I envy women their close ties like that. Grace had a few gals who were like sisters to her."

"I don't think we're allowed many friendships like this one," Anna said. "You'd like old Mags."

The shadows were long when they drove back down the rough road, then on through Ayios Nikolaos and back to the hotel.

In the lobby, Anna picked up her mail while Sam read the advertisements and flyers on the bulletin board. "Would you care to get down and boogie in Ayios Nikolaos tonight?" he asked. "Or would you like to go back to the Taverna and see some authentic Cretan folk dancing? Tonight's the night the troupe from Iráklion will be here."

They stayed at the hotel Taverna and even learned a couple of folk dances—Sam with a great show of reluctance—when the dance troupe invited the audience onto the floor.

The next day, they breakfasted again on Anna's terrace. This time, Sam brought his tape recorder. "I'm a little old to be calling it a 'blaster,' but that's what it is." He put on a tape of *Ancient Airs and Dances* by Respighi. "Seems like good morning music." After that, the blaster and Sam's shoe-box repertoire of CDs were always with him.

In the afternoon, after a trip into Ayios Nikolaos to buy beach chairs and beer, they went down on the rocks by the water, Sam reading a thick book called *The Dancing Wu Li Masters*, Anna sketching the people around them.

Eight

On Friday, Anna arrived at the Anistopolis house breathless. She had walked up the hill from Elounda, a good three-kilometer hike. She had her drawing board and supplies in a brightly woven packsack she had bought in Ayios Nikolaos. The wool itched through the back of her cotton shirt. She should have worn shorts today instead of jeans.

Maria opened the door as Anna walked up the drive. "Why didn't you take a taxi?" she asked, shaking her head. "We didn't know you were taking an early bus. Demetri planned to come and meet you later."

"I enjoyed the exercise," Anna puffed in short gasps. "But I'm glad I'm finally here." She took off her pack and set it in the hand-carved chair of dark wood in the foyer. "Could I have a glass of water?"

"Come, I'm having breakfast. Please join me."

Anna settled into a wicker chair in the solarium as Mina set a place for her and poured water from a tall glass carafe.

Maria was silent, letting Anna catch her breath and cool off a bit. "Demetri doesn't make a showing until after eleven," she said. "He's such a night owl. He loves to putter about in his studio until three or four in the morning."

Anna's coffee had been poured and she buttered a hard roll.

"How have you been, Anna? I worry about you, you know, being all alone up at that hotel. Are you sure that is best?"

"You worry for nothing. I've made some friends—the young woman who owns the Blue Dolphin in Ayios Nikolaos. And a very

nice man who is also staying at the hotel. His name is Sam Mc-
Donald."

Maria's eyebrows rose.

"He's in Ayios Nikolaos because he spent his honeymoon
there. He and his wife had always planned to come back here together. But . . . he's a widower."

"How sad." Maria looked Anna over. "You are browner. You
must be spending a lot of time in the sun. You look more
relaxed."

"The sun has healing powers. New friends and sun." Anna
smiled at Maria.

"And time," Maria added.

"It used to make me angry when people told me time would
take care of everything. I felt like a violinist who had lost the fingers of her left hand. How could time take care of that?" She
lifted her hands, palms up. "But maybe everyone was right. Distance does take the edges off." She stared out over the garden
without seeing it. "I wonder, though, if the violinist ever stops
missing the music." As soon as she said this, she was sorry. Her
question, half-whispered to herself, was all it took for the sorrow
to rush back like a tide, washing over the peace of these last few
days as if it had been a sand castle. She didn't want to burden
Maria with her pity party. "Ah, well," she said. "Maybe time does
take care of things."

Maria didn't go for it. "Each person, Anna, must find her
own music. It can't depend on another person or a set of circumstances. Great loss changes the tempo, certainly, and the mood,
but the music is still there, if you care to listen for it."

Anna said nothing. She hardly knew this woman, yet
strangely, Maria seemed to know her. Intimately.

"Let me ask you this," Maria said. "If you had been asked,
let's say ten years ago, to describe yourself in one word, what
would that word have been?"

"May I have two?"

"Sure. I'll be generous." Maria smiled. "Two."

"That's easy. Wife. Mother."

"How about twenty . . . say twenty-two years ago?"

"Subtract 'mother.' One word. Wife."

"And the years before that?"

"Well, for the first eighteen years—daughter. Then from college until I met Paul—"

"What then? How would you describe yourself in those years?"

"Student, then career woman, for a short while."

"Do you realize you have described every age of your life with a role? Do you really see yourself in those stereotypes?"

"Oh, you want description? Okay. Start with dreamer—the first eighteen years. Then, let's see, in college—passionate artist. Then I got a job in New York I thought I had no chance for at all."

"And how would you describe yourself then?"

"Fearless. No, adventuresome. I was full of myself. Totally confident."

"Then?"

"During the next twenty years? Capable. Devoted. I need more words."

"And now, Anna? How would you describe yourself in one word now?"

Anna thought about that. These past days had been so relaxing, so without care, that she had forgotten. Now, thinking of the past, she felt desperate. Finally she said, "Scared."

Maria looked surprised. "But after all these years of being daring and capable, why would you be scared now?"

"My grandfather used to have an interesting theory," Anna said. "He spoke of dying to things, letting them go, giving them up, so that you could be reborn. He was no fundamentalist, that's for sure," Anna explained. "I never heard him refer to this being reborn as a 'born-again' conversion experience. But he said that throughout our lives we have to *die* to conditions, positions, roles that are over, in order to be *born* into new experience."

Anna pushed back a strand of hair that had escaped the scarf holding it back. "The trouble is, to go on with this analogy, death and birth are mysteries. We don't know what's on the other side—either way." She looked hard at Maria. "I'm not explaining this very well. I know he wasn't talking about physical death and birth. He was talking about realizing something is over and *letting go of it* so the next thing can happen."

"And some people spend their whole lives being afraid to do that," Maria said, "afraid to admit something has ended and let it go so that they can be open to new opportunities. Is that what you're saying?"

"Exactly." Anna examined the dregs of her coffee. "But what if one does face up, and die to . . . let go of whatever it is . . . forgive, as you told me before? And suppose then, they wait to be *born again*, only to find that they are"—she cleared her throat—"that they are stillborn? What if there is no life after death?"

"You didn't die with him, Anna."

Anna looked over at Maria, her hands gripping the wicker arms of the chair.

"I'm sor—" Maria started to say.

But Anna had already begun to speak, her voice steady now. "Don't be sorry. You have helped me more than you know. Maybe one day I'll stop beating my hard head against this particular wall and—"

"And how will you describe yourself then, Anna? In one word? What do you want to be?"

Anna had reached up with one hand and was gripping the rings on the chain.

"When you find the word, what will it take to make it happen, to make it true?" She put her hand on Anna's arm. "You are only limited, Anna, by physical impossibilities and decisions you have already made."

Anna flinched.

"You didn't choose to be a widow. But you did choose many things. And I think you did them well."

"I've had a good life. But I spent these last few years entirely in Paul's shadow. And I got lost in it. That's why I'm so afraid. And angry. Everything I was came to an end with his death. With the children grown, I had already ceased being a mother in the real sense. My role was 'Paul Sandoval's wife.' I once even discovered that I was introducing myself as just that—Paul Sandoval's wife. For years I haven't done anything, really, on my own. I wonder if I can." She smiled sheepishly. "Cowering is new for me."

"Think about the word, Anna. Words have great power. What do you want to be, now that you no longer can be defined as wife and mother?"

"Only one word?"

"How would you like to be described?"

Anna thought about it for a while, casting about for a powerful word. Finally she said, "Invincible. I want to have that feeling of soaring that I felt when I began my short-lived career as a graphic designer during that year before I met Paul. I felt I could do anything then."

"Then be!" Maria said, passion trembling in her voice. "Be yourself, Anna Sandoval, and you will find that you are just that. Invincible."

Demetri came in just then, looking well scrubbed, his cheeks pink, his mustache like spun silver. "Well, Anna, I expected you later. What a nice surprise. May I join you ladies for coffee?"

Anna shook her head, blinking like someone suddenly awakened, then smiled with genuine affection. "By all means, join us. Maria has been lecturing me, and you've saved me, I think, from having to take a final exam."

He had on a crisp blue shirt and a string tie. His worn cords were neatly pressed. "This is a treat," he said, slathering butter and jam onto his roll, then spooning sugar into his coffee. Smiling at Anna, he said, "I thought we'd go back down to the wharf now that you have toiled your way up here. You did say you wanted to concentrate on people, didn't you?"

"I did."

"We can stop if we see any willing subjects on the way."

As they were leaving, Anna gave Maria a hug. She clung to the older woman for a moment, hoping she could somehow draw into her own being Maria's peace and tranquillity, and that at the same time she could pour into Maria her love for her. As before, just being with her for a short time made Anna feel as if she was trembling on the brink of something wonderful.

"Invincible," Maria whispered into Anna's ear.

"Thank you. Thank you for everything you are doing for me."

Demetri and Anna chose a table at a café on the park by the water. Since it was a weekday and early afternoon, there were fewer tourists. Only some local people had ventured out. Demetri set up his easel for Anna and then ordered coffee for both of them.

She got out her pencil box and opened it, waiting for Demetri to tell her which one she would need. She picked up the thick pad of paper.

Leaning back in his chair, Demetri sipped his coffee like an idle old man enjoying a morning with nothing to do. His eyes were half-closed, as if he was daydreaming.

Anna put down her pad and pencil. She wondered if she was to get a lesson after all.

"Look around you," he said. "See that old woman with the child? What is she thinking? What is she feeling?"

"She looks tired," Anna said. "I don't think she likes the child."

"And the child?"

"He hates the woman."

"Hatred. That would be the soul of a drawing of those two." He sat for a long time, still leaning back, his hands folded across his chest, his legs stretched out. Anna thought he might be dozing, but he said, "The artist must 'put on' his subject." Anna noticed that his eyes were not closed but that he was squinting at the scene in front of him. "He must become the person he draws—have his memory, feel his pain. To do this the artist must know himself. He must be in touch with his own center."

Anna thought about that. Centered. It was a potter's term. She hadn't felt centered in a very long time.

"See those two people over there?"

Anna looked. A couple, not so young, sat on a bench. The man held the woman's hand to his chest as he spoke earnestly to her.

"They are lovers, obviously. What tells you of their love?"

"The hands. The way they look into each other's eyes. And the way she keeps checking her hair as though she wants it perfect for him."

"Ah, it will be a pleasure to work with you, Anna. To find the soul of your picture, you must find the focal point. Then it comes alive. It is the same with still life. It is the same with sea and landscapes."

Anna moved her board to a comfortable position and lifted her pencil to start with the lovers, but Demetri put a restraining hand on her arm. "Not yet."

"Not yet?"

"First we must talk about you. Have you ever worked at a potter's wheel?"

"A long time ago, in college. I found it very satisfying, though I never really mastered it."

"It is satisfying because it is a centering experience. That and the fact that clay has restorative properties. There is nothing like working with one of the basic elements—earth, fire, air, water. Clay embodies them all. But the important thing about making a vessel on the wheel, as you know, is that not only does the clay have to be centered or it slings itself off, but the artist must also be centered, concentrating his energy, his creativity, in the ball of earth spinning in his hands. And when he starts to pull up the walls of the pot, the control must come from his own center or he will pull it out of balance and it will wobble off the wheel." Anna nodded.

"It is true with all art, with all artists," Demetri said. "Before we make the first mark, the first brushstroke, the first strike of the chisel, we must first center ourselves." He closed his eyes and breathed slowly, a satisfied smile touching his face.

Suddenly he clapped his hands in front of his face, startling Anna so that she dropped the pencil. He grinned at her. "It's a

Zen thing. Gets rid of the mind chatter that always tries to in-
trude." He leaned back again, relaxed.

"You were speaking about centering. . . ."

He nodded. "Yes, our center point. That incorruptible core
deep inside us. It is the nucleus of the soul, from which radiates
all creativity, all love, all passion for life."

"That sounds like meditation."

"All art is meditation, Anna. It is a mortal's way to be cocre-
ator with God. Theologians write tomes and treatises trying to explain the mystery of God and his creation, but it is the artist who
communicates the essence of the cosmic creation. Words, unless
they are very metaphorical or poetic, are too confining to express
something as grand as love or sorrow or beauty. The person who
said 'A picture is worth a thousand words' was right."

His voice was as soothing as his words. Anna closed her eyes
and breathed deeply, aware of her breath, aware of this wise man
that was her teacher.

"Now, choose a scene and draw only the essence." The lovers
had gone, hand in hand, into a small hotel near the water, and the
reluctant babysitter with the unruly child had moved on. But a
small old man sat primly on the end of a bench smoking a huge
pipe, his face turned to the sun.

Anna drew his hand on the pipe and a detailed sketch of his
face, highlighted in white. When she started filling in his body,
Demetri said, "You finished minutes ago. Leave it. That part is
not important."

Two men sat astride a backless bench playing chess. One of
them could hardly see the board over his paunch. The other was
a wizened scarecrow whose wispy white hair lifted on the breeze,
silvered in the sunlight. The large man was stoic and slow, the
other birdlike, with quick, impatient movements.

Anna watched them for a long time, trying to see what
Demetri would see in the scene. Finally she made a quick drawing, using a soft pencil, of heavy lines that showed the sagging
weight of one man. The chess set was a scramble of lines that only

hinted at the pieces. Then she drew the smaller man with a harder
pencil, in thin, light, broken lines.

"Beautiful," Demetri said.

"I don't know how to do his hair—it's so fine and light."

"Do it with the background."

Anna looked. The background was a confusion of buildings,
trees, cars. It would ruin the drawing to put that in. She looked at
Demetri with a frown.

"Look at that cloud over there." He pointed behind Anna.
"The dark one with no texture." He laughed. "Put that in your
picture behind the men and let the whiteness of the paper be his
hair." He pointed away from the men. "And at their feet, put in
that wadded newspaper blowing down the dock there. That will
show that they are in a dusty, ill-kept park."

Anna shaded in the background and drew a sculptural replica
of the newspaper.

"Stop!" Anna jumped and almost dropped her pencil.

"Perfect. That is one you will want to keep, Anna. Don't do
another thing to it or you will ruin the effect. We are tempted to
draw pictures as we wish to 'draw' our lives—every detail perfect." He took another sip from his small white cup. "We want to
keep adding, touching up, making it more perfect. Until . . . we
ruin the piece. What we need to do is trust."

"Trust what?"

"Trust the medium. Trust that a series of lines will communicate better than something worked to death with detail. We need
to trust our own instincts in this. And we need to trust that those
who view our work will get its message more forcefully if we leave
a little to their imaginations.

"You want your eye to be drawn to telling details only, the soul
of the painting that pours forth from the work through the eyes of
the viewer, straight into the heart. Just enough. Give the viewer the
pleasure of filling in the rest from his own center of creativity." He
sighed. "Finally, we have to trust when it's finished and let it be.

"It is like finding the Truth, Anna. Art is a holy quest for
truth. At the same time, it is a quest for one's true self. The artist

seeks wholeness, completeness, essence." He smiled. "To find wholeness is to find holiness. To be whole is to be holy."

He picked up Anna's pad, carefully holding it by the edges. "God created these two men and this day. You, the artist, have immortalized them on this paper." He smiled at Anna. "You are a very talented artist because you can *see*."

Time rushed by. Demetri's voice was like a force guiding Anna's hand, and though she wasn't always pleased with the effect, he always pointed out the good in each attempt. He didn't really let her finish anything. "This is a day for beginnings. Finishing is done in the silence of night," he said.

She knew she was getting much more than a lesson in the art of pencil drawing. It was difficult to distinguish when he was talking about her art and when about her life, although he never referred directly to her life. She didn't really try to distinguish between the two. It all seemed woven together. He didn't ask questions. He didn't relate anecdotes from his own life. It was as if he, like Maria, could see through her with X-ray vision.

Exhausted, she climbed aboard the last bus back to Ayios Nikolaos. Turning to Demetri, she said, " 'Thank you' is too small a thing to say for today."

"Then don't say it. Just come back to us. Soon."

"I will. I'll call you."

"You'll have to send a message. We have no phone."

The bus complained all the way back to the Villas, but Anna's thoughts followed the birds that rose in reeling flocks, dipping and gliding from stony field to stony hillside. Looking across at the grape blue outline of distant mountains on the other side of the gulf, she felt purified. Hands had been laid on her soul, healing hands.

Nine

Early the next morning, Anna sat on her terrace in her robe, savoring a cup of coffee. The sun had come up over hills that looked like cutouts of gray cardboard. As she watched, the water changed from the color of ink into a kaleidoscope of different blues. The sky brightened from smears of dark salmon pink to mother-of-pearl, inhaling the blue from the water as it got lighter.

At the sound of footsteps on the path, Anna looked up to see Sam walk by. He glanced absently through her archway as he passed; then she heard him say, "Today is my lucky day." He peeked back around the wall. "You're certainly up early."

He was obviously fresh from a shower. His damp hair still showed comb marks, and his cheeks had that fresh-shaved glow. How had she ever thought of him as homely? When she saw how his eyes lit up with a pleasure he wasn't afraid to show, she had the answer to that question. At first meeting, one might notice only the rough-cut lines of his face. But all it took was a smile to assure anyone that here was a man with no guile. He was truly himself, all the time. "I could say the same for you. Want some coffee?"

"I'd love some."

Anna took a turn through the bedroom, pulling on shorts and shirt before taking the steaming cup of coffee out to Sam. They shared the new morning in silence for a while. Then Sam said, "I missed you yesterday."

"It's nice to hear that you're missed."

"Well, I called the girls. I call them every week. I tell them I'm checking up on them—but really, I'm just checking in so they won't worry about poor old Dad."

"Isn't it strange to find that you have been moved from the role of caregiver to children to the recipient of their care and concern?"

"And nosiness sometimes. Ah, well, along with the relief, it is comforting." Sam smiled. "They're good kids." He picked up his coffee cup. "Where did you run off to yesterday?"

Anna told him about Demetri and Maria and what a pleasure it was to spend time with them. He listened with interest as she described her lesson.

"I'd like to meet them sometime," Sam said. "Hey, listen, I've heard they have beaches with real sand on the south shore. How would you like to go exploring with me today?" He turned and added, "Unless you have other plans."

"It sounds wonderful."

They drove to the town of Ierapetra on the south shore of Crete, where there actually were stretches of real sandy beach, and found a place to spread their things before taking a long walk in the edges of the Mediterranean surf that rolled up on the sand.

They lay in the sun for long hours. Anna now felt perfectly at ease in her next-to-nothing Cretan swimming attire. Sam seemed at ease with it too. He, however, had not given in to the bikini fashion of the European men, sticking with his cotton trunks. He unfolded the new beach chairs, and while Anna sketched—the birds, the children at the water's edge, the people around them on the beach—Sam read.

He always had several thick books in his gear, Anna noticed. "Your luggage must weigh a ton," she teased.

"It starts out that way. I send them home as I finish them, so, unlike some people I know"—he peered at Anna over what he called his "half-assed" reading glasses—"who acquire more and more junk as they go along, my baggage gets lighter and lighter."

"It is nice, though," Anna defended herself, "to eat off real dishes instead of plastic, don't you think?"

"And to have real art on the walls and authentic carpets

under your feet. And pottery from this island and . . ." He sighed
in mock boredom. "You're right, though. It is nice . . . just as long
as I don't have to carry out all that stuff I've packed in for your
place. Your humble abode has turned into the most fashionable
house on the block"—he pushed his glasses up—"if not into a
museum."

Later, after sandwiches washed down with Amstel beer, Sam
fell asleep, his book slipping onto the sand beside him. Putting
down the sketch she was doing of a large pelican standing sedately
at the water's edge, Anna picked up the book to dust it off, and
leafed idly through the pages. It was about new concepts in
physics.

When Sam woke from his doze, she asked, "Do you really understand all this? I can't even comprehend the description on the
dust jacket."

He stretched and yawned. "Let's put it this way. Science has
changed since I was in school. So many new discoveries have been
made. With computers, the processes that took years to work out
before when somebody came up with a new theory, now take only
minutes. So everything is being turned upside down, practically at
the speed of sound. When I'm reading this new stuff, it makes the
best of sense. And a lot of the random information in here"—he
pointed to his temple—"clicks into place." He scratched his head.
"The breakdown comes when I try and explain it to someone else.
I'll just say I find it very interesting. We live in exciting times."

"Quantum physics? Ontology? Cosmology?" Anna was reading the table of contents.

"We are a part of something so vast and grand that we can't
even see it or touch it or taste it or smell it. We can only feel it and
know it is true. But we want to know what it is. And we want to
know how important our part in it is."

They sat in silence for a while, the sound of surf washing
through Anna's thoughts. "Don't you ever feel angry, Sam?"

"Angry? About what?"

"About Grace dying. About being in . . . in the prime of your
life, alone."

He pursed his lips and looked out across the water. "I was angry, for a while. I was never honest enough to admit it at the time, but I was."

"Did you ever talk with your friends about the way you were feeling?" Anna asked, remembering how it had been with her friends in Washington, and the relief when she could talk with Maggie and, later, Maria.

"Men don't talk about feelings. They talk about football." He drew overlapping circles in the sand with his finger. "I finally had to let it go—the anger. It was doing me no good to let it eat at me." He looked up at Anna and said, "I finally just said goodbye." Tugging at his ear, he let out a long sigh. "RIP. Rest in peace. Isn't that what it means? I decided to do that. Let Grace rest in peace. And I try to do the same."

Anna looked out over the water. *God, I wish I could do that.* She remembered the handful of dirt she had been unable to let go of at Paul's graveside as everyone else tossed theirs on the casket with thuds. Anna had held hers all the way back to the car and dropped it there, anxious to get somewhere to wash her hand.

"How about a little snack?" Sam said. "I think there are some little cakes in there."

"Cakes? Lord, Sam, where do you put it all?" Anna watched him eat the cake, savoring each bite. "I'll say this for you," she said. "You are a man who enjoys." She laughed. "Enjoys the good things in life."

"Now that I've gotten old enough to appreciate them," he said. He looked over at Anna. "How about you, Anna? How do you feel about growing, uh, growing . . . older? Oh, you probably haven't thought about it. What are you, thirty-eight? Forty? But for me . . . for most people, according to the press I've read, some-how turning the corner at the big five-O makes you wonder about things. Makes you wonder if you are growing wiser or just more doddering. I know I'm more appreciative. Used to take things, important things, for granted. But how about you?"

"Well, I certainly wouldn't want to be young again. I'm be-yond all that birthing and trying to do everything right, the car pools and the PTA and the knock-knock jokes." She tucked a lock of stray hair back. "I just don't want to get any older. For a while. I need some time to get used to being where I am now."

"And where is that?"

"That's a good question. I never thought about it until this past year. No, it began even before that. When the children left I started thinking about it. I had done the expected all my life— school, marriage, children, community service. But suddenly I realized that I had nothing to show for it. I, along with almost every other woman over the age of forty, had been following a set of cultural rules that are so deeply ingrained that they are almost genetic." She gave him a long look. "It's hard to break out of that."

Sam was quiet for a while. Then he said, "It's hard for men too. We're told, 'Be tough. Don't cry. Be successful. Don't be a sissy,' which covers the whole area of feelings and what is acceptable to show. And every little boy grows up in the sure knowledge that he will probably someday be asked to be a killer."

"What?"

"Join the military service. Even though they no longer have a draft, every young man is asked to consider that option. I chose it because I wanted to learn to fly and because I somehow felt obligated. I didn't think so much about *being* killed. I don't think any of us believes it can happen to him. But I did think about killing." He sighed. "I was lucky. After flight training I was never sent into danger. But we were taught to be killing machines. I never had to use my guns except to practice. But I knew I had them. And I wondered if I really could make myself use them if I had to. It scared me."

Anna hadn't thought about that. She had always thought that men had it made. They could do what they wanted, choose their own course. Have a wife to follow them around and make it possible for them to achieve their ambitions. Paul had been so confident, so self-possessed. She wondered, after what Sam had just said, if he too had had self-doubt, hidden fears he wasn't allowed to share, dread of what a man is supposed to do . . . to be.

"Will you sit for me sometime? For a drawing?" Anna asked.

She wondered if she would be able to capture the essence of this man. But she wanted to try.

Sam looked at her in surprise. Then he said, "Sure." He struck a bodybuilder pose.

"No, I mean . . ." Anna laughed, gathering up their gear. "Come on, let's get back to the hotel. I know just where I want to do it. On my terrace."

The next day was Sunday. Sam met Anna at the hotel Taverna for breakfast. But instead of offering that easy smile and the constant flow of half-serious banter, he was distracted and noncommunicative, speaking in monosyllables while staring out across the gulf. Anna didn't mind. She had no need to talk, though she was a little concerned.

Finally, Sam took a deep breath and said, "I'm going to the Lassithi Plateau today and . . . I'd like you to come along. That is, if you're not busy."

"I've heard of that," Anna said. "And I'd enjoy coming." She looked at him closely. "If you really want me to."

"Well, at first I didn't." Anna couldn't help feeling a little taken aback. "But I've changed my mind. I—" He apparently changed his mind again, about what he was going to say. "Let's go," he said gruffly.

Mystified, Anna got in the car. She had never seen Sam like this. They drove toward Iráklion first, then, at Neapoli, started up the treacherous switchbacks of the Dikti mountain range to Lassithi Plateau, a sweeping expanse of flat farmland tucked into a high valley almost three thousand feet above sea level, according to Anna's guidebook. After being silent all the way, Sam said, "It was Grace's favorite place."

"Oh."

When they reached the top of the pass, Sam pulled over, and they got out of the car to look at the view. There, spread before them, was a wide, flat plateau as varied in colors and patterns as a quilt, embraced by high, forbidding mountains on all sides. The floor of the plateau was an irregular grid of farmland, divided by

paths and roads to allow the farmers to get to their fields. The
edges were studded by small communities huddling against the
mountains. But what lifted Anna's heart were the windmills. Hundreds of white-sailed windmills, looking tiny in the distance, their
resplendent triangular sails whirling in the late-morning sun like
small pinwheels.

Sam stood a little apart, his arms hanging at his sides, as he
stared out across the plain. Slowly, he propped his foot on a large
boulder, elbow on knee, chin in hand. Anna was sure, for that moment, he was living in the past. "I can see why she liked this
place," she said softly. "There's a magic to it, with those spinning
windmills. It frees one's spirit."

"It seemed only fitting to come up here today. It's our, uh, *was*
our anniversary." He took a long breath and let it out through
pursed lips. "Grace was a farm girl. She grew up in the Midwest.
The thing she liked about this place was the water. She was fascinated by the fact that with those windmills they could get enough
water up to this altitude to irrigate the farms." He picked a blade
of grass and chewed it thoughtfully. "She wasn't much for ancient
history, and she was a little fearful—intimidated is a better word, I
guess—of the people here. But farms she understood. We drove
down there so she could see some of the local farming techniques."

"That was practical for an avid gardener."

"Uh-huh." He looked over at Anna, his lips still pursed in reflection. Then he smiled. A sad smile. "I can see that you're just
itching to get at your pencils and draw those windmills, and I
think I'd like to take a walk. How about if I make off down this
road and you stay here and do your thing. Then you meet me at
the little town of—" He pulled a folded map from the glove com-
partment of the car and spread it on the hood, tracing their road
with his finger. "Look here, I can't pronounce the name." He
pointed at Tzermiado. "There's bound to be a public square of
some kind there. I don't remember exactly how it's laid out, but
I'll look for you in, say, an hour and a half. Will that be enough
time?"

"That sounds fine."

"I'll be waiting for you."

Anna watched him walk away down a dip in the road. She knew, with an ache in her throat, that he was torn between past and present. She also knew that this hidden valley had been a place of refuge for Cretans in troubled times over the years. *May it be so for this troubled man,* she thought, watching as Sam turned to wave before he disappeared around a curve.

Her drawing was not of the plateau or the windmills. It was a character study, from memory, of Sam as he had stood, before he put his foot up on the rock, looking out at the Lassithi Plateau through the beloved eyes of someone long dead. What had he said? Grace was interested in the irrigation systems? She must have been even more down-to-earth and practical than Sam.

Anna drew him from the back, at a quarter angle, with only lines to give the impression of his military bearing, his broad shoulders squared as if facing some unseen foe. From this angle, she got the ax cut of his jaw and his breeze-tossed hair, silvered in the light. His eyes were lifted, looking through time, his nose like that of an Indian warrior. She had chosen this angle because she hadn't wanted to try to capture the look in his eyes—lost, confused, pained. Without blending the pencil strokes, she let the rough paper show the texture of his face. She left it white for his hair and the highlights on the planes of his face, adding only a few lines to point up the shadows. Then she glanced at her watch.

"Good grief," she said out loud. It had been over two hours since he'd left. Throwing her things in the backseat of the car, she took off in search of the subject of her drawing. Her heart warmed at the thought. Having had this time away from him somehow made her feel she knew him better.

As she drove carefully down the winding road, Anna became aware of an insistent sensation, not new, but one she hadn't experienced for a long time. No rush of emotion, just quiet gladness. *Not too far away, someone was waiting for her.* After she passed the sign announcing the city limits of Tzermiado, she watched carefully for Sam.

She couldn't have missed him. He was sitting in an outdoor

café, at the table nearest the road, pretending to read a Greek newspaper, looking comical with his half-glasses perched halfway down his nose. Anna parked, and walked up to the table. "Excuse me, sir, is this seat taken?"

"You aren't the lady they usually send," Sam answered, without looking up.

"So unappreciative," Anna answered.

They ate a lunch of bean soup called *fasolada*, and downed it with Greek beer. Sam was his old self again, more relaxed, though his talk still centered on Grace. Anna was glad to listen. He told about how his wife had gotten up the courage to ask people here and there if they would snap their picture together, in front of this statue, that windmill. She had loved showing the album when they'd returned home. He described her interest in the way the women here wove their colorful cloth. How she had been reluctant to spend any money on souvenirs.

As they got up to leave he said, "Let's drive around some before we head back, okay?" As they drove Sam said, "I called the girls again last night, both of them."

"How are they?"

"They were a little sad. They knew this was our anniversary and in the past they have always come to see me."

"They are very thoughtful young women."

"That they are. They have been a pleasure from the day they were born . . . aside from a few years when they were teenagers. But they made it through."

"I'm glad you got to talk with them."

"So am I."

They drove along the edges of the farmland as Sam continued to reminisce, and made their way back up to the ridge, but as they started down the mountains, he fell silent. The look on his face was one of contentment.

Later, Anna dozed, lulled to sleep by the motion of the car. When she awakened, Sam was pulling in at the hotel. Stretching and yawning, not feeling the least bit guilty that she had been such poor company all the way home, she looked over at Sam and said,

"I loved this day. Lassithi was beautiful, the food was good and the company, well . . . amiable."

"Thank you, Anna." His voice was gruff again.

"For what? It's your car. It was your idea."

"For just being you, and for going with me to remember . . . so I can forget." They were at Sam's door. "I had intended to take that trip alone. I'm glad you were along."

Anna nodded. Maybe Sam had the answer. Take along a friend. She hadn't thought of that before. He gave her shoulder a squeeze and she smiled up at him. But it would only work with a new friend. Her heart warmed again at the sight of this kind, honest man who had become her newest friend.

"I'm glad I was along too," she said.

The next week, it seemed perfectly natural to find herself eating almost every meal with Sam. Afternoons, they met to walk down to the beach, or the pool when they weren't out exploring the countryside.

One day, just before noon, Anna heard a strange squeaking, rattling noise. She looked out and couldn't believe her eyes. It was Sam, riding down the walkway on an old-fashioned woman's bicycle two sizes too small for him, its wicker basket piled full, topped with a thich spray of pink bougainvillea that left a trail of blossoms sprinkled behind.

"Wha-what are you doing?" Anna gasped, laughing.

He dragged his feet to stop. "I'm looking for a place to have my picnic."

"How did you get that bike down all those stairs?" She shook her head. "And why?"

I was trying to carry this stuff when the manager's wife pulled up on this here two-wheeled basket. So I asked if I could borrow it—the basket. The bike came with it."

"But those stairs!"

"She told me about a secret way around back where they pull the cleaning carts."

"Ah. I see. And are you planning to ride down those switch-backs to the beach?"

"I was hoping you'd offer your courtyard." Hand to heart, he added, "I brought you flowers.

"That you stole!"

"It's the thought that matters." He gave her a woebegone look.

"Come on in," Anna laughed as she helped Sam unload his basket. "Park your two-wheeled basket over there by the wall."

The next day, they drove into the din and roar of Iráklion, capital of Crete. And drove out just as fast to get away from the noise and grime and traffic.

Other days they just struck out, lunching or picnicking in various little villages in the hills and along the shore.

They were not tourists. They didn't necessarily seek out particular historical sites or natural phenomena. They never set up an itinerary. They just wandered wherever whim led them. "I'm good at whims," Sam said once.

Then, one day, he announced that the meeting in Athens was set for the following day. Something to do with those security precautions they were putting in place at the airport there. He would be gone two days. That evening, he took the hotel shuttle into Iráklion, leaving Anna the Opel.

The next night, she had a dream of Paul. They had all been together. Peter and Christine were teenagers and it was some sort of backyard party. Everyone was laughing and just as she reached for Paul's hand, she woke. The sun poured through her window, laying like a blanket across her bed. But it didn't cheer her. Again, she was engulfed in a choking fog of the old wretchedness. Oh no, she thought. For the past week and a half she had been spared these bouts of despair. She hadn't even thought about the past. It seemed that the mutual grief she and Sam shared had begun to soften her own hard knot of grief, to weaken its death grip on her heart. She'd thought she was over all that.

But today she felt like that carved-out ceramic figurine again, scraped bare and empty. She felt that sense of isolation—of being cut off and lonely. The nameless dread of the future reared up again, and she buried her face in her pillow. *I am so alone,* she thought, sobs tearing from her throat. So alone.

Later, when she finally dragged herself out of bed, she berated herself for her pity party. *Good Lord,* she thought, *I'm the
world's worst ninny.* But no amount of pep talk or scolding
worked. She felt as if she had taken five giant steps backward.

She still had the image of Christine and Peter from the dream
going through her mind. *Wonder what Christine is doing.* Anna
missed the frequent phone calls with Christine talking about her
newest recipe or the book she was reading. And Peter. Was he still
wearing those baggy pants? What was she doing so far from them?

I have to get out of here, she thought. *Do something.* She fixed
herself some strong coffee and toasted some bread in the oven
and considered going into Ayios Nikolaos to see Sophia. But that
wouldn't do. Sophia would be working. She pondered going
down to the beach or, maybe, taking the car and driving east out
to Sitia. No, Sam wanted to go there. It would be better to wait
until he came back.

She took her breakfast into the sitting room. *I wish Maggie
were here,* she thought, longing for the sight of her old friend. Her
gaze wandered about the room, falling on the Demetri painting as
she ate. *Maria and Demetri.* Why hadn't she thought of them?

Since they had no phone, Anna drove to Elounda in Sam's
car, on the chance of finding them at home. She took along her
drawing materials in case they were out. At least, she thought, she
could do some sketching once she was there.

But Maria answered the door at Anna's knock. "We've
missed you," she said, brushing cheeks with Anna. "We were
afraid you had left without telling us." She herded Anna into the
sitting room, the rose-colored drapes open to the morning.

"I'd never do that," Anna said. "Actually, I've been touring
Crete." She listed the places she had been. "And I now have a
bulging portfolio to prove it."

"You've been to all these places alone?" Concern showed in
Maria's eyes.

Anna shook her head. "I've had a traveling companion, Sam
McDonald. I told you about him. He's the widower who came to
Crete to—"

"Ah, yes, to revisit places he had been with his wife." She was pouring spiced tea into clear glass cups, her graceful crippled hands moving as if consecrating both the drink and the sugar-encrusted cakes she took from a tin and arranged on a plate. "And how have you been, Anna, since we saw you last?" Maria asked in a quiet voice.

Anna looked into her dark, compassion-filled eyes. "Crete has been doing its work with me. It's been nice having a friend to talk to, to do things with." She tried to sound as chipper and filled with well-being as she had felt all week—until that morning.

Maria looked sharply at Anna, but she simply said, "That's good."

Anna stood and walked over to the window that overlooked a small forest of waist-high geraniums. "I enjoy being with Sam. He's a character, lots of fun. And he's so genuine." She laughed a little. "There's nothing fake in him. Paul would have liked him very much." She tried to tuck a loose tendril of hair back into her chignon. "But—" Damn. She was going to cry.

Crossing to the window, Maria took Anna's arm and led her to a chair. "It's sometimes best not to try to be brave, Anna."

"Oh, Maria, I don't think I'll ever recover. I mean, in these past few days I've felt so relaxed." She ran her fingers through the sides of her hair, making the combs fall out. "I thought it was over. I thought I was"—she bit her lip—"beginning to heal."

"You have begun to heal, Anna, whether you know it or not. But it takes time. You can't expect that it won't. Even years from now there will be moments when it will all rush in on you again. Life is not a straight line. Life is a spiral. We come back to things— or they come back to us."

"But these past few days have been so full." Anna turned away and cleared her throat. "Having someone to talk with, to eat with, for this little while has only pointed out to me how much I miss—" Anna buried her face in her hands.

Maria handed her a lavender-scented handkerchief and Anna used it like a towel. When she got some control back, she repeated, "I thought I was over doing this." She looked at Maria, wanting to fall into her arms. "Now I'm back to asking, 'Why did this happen to me?'"

"And the future looks bleak. I know."

Anna just stared out the window, only vaguely seeing the geraniums moving gently in a breeze.

"You know, you once talked to me about dying to things, letting go of the past, to make rebirth possible. That's what you are doing now, Anna. Dying to a past that is over. And I just want to say to you that, as painful as it is, there are all kinds of possibilities on the other side."

"Growing old alone doesn't sound like a very appealing one. I can't get used to that idea."

"Would you like to get married again, Anna?"

The question hit her like a blow. Not Maria too, she thought. "No!" she cried in disbelief and disappointment. "No one could take Paul's place," she said. "That would be unthinkable." Why couldn't people understand that?

"No one can take anyone's place. But there is more than one place, Anna. There are many places. However, that is not the point. What I'm asking you to ask yourself is"—she reached out and put her hand on Anna's arm—"are you going to spend the rest of your life feeling as if a part of you is missing because someone you loved and depended on has died, or are you going to take this opportunity, however painful, to fulfill your destiny? Great changes are opportunities, Anna, even if the changes are devastating. We don't let a building lie in ruins after an earthquake or . . . a war. We rebuild it. And sometimes, the new one is stronger and better and as beautiful as the old."

Anna had sunk into the chair, her hands pressed to her hot cheeks.

Maria went on. "You have said that you came to Crete to get away for a while and gain control of your life. And that is fine, though"—she looked at Anna sadly—"it is hard for me to understand why you didn't stay at home where you had friends and family. Why you would come, alone, to a place so far away from everything familiar."

"I had to get away from those things that were familiar. I needed . . ." Anna cast about for what it was she had needed. Could she have been wrong? "I needed new experiences. I thought if I filled my time with—"

"But no matter how you fill your time, you cannot escape the pain. So instead of running from it . . ." Anna could feel herself stiffen. "Instead of doing something every minute so you won't have time to think, why don't you embrace the pain? Sink into it."

"But I've done that, and I'm sick of it. I want to be free of all this, not embrace it," Anna said in a small, tight voice. "I've cried buckets of tears. I've remembered, relived. I've railed against God and—"

"But you haven't forgiven. If you had, you would not be feeling so lonely again. You would be feeling the sense of resurrection you spoke of before, as if you too had died and been reborn into a new world. You are very close to that, Anna."

"How do you know?" Her voice now had an edge on it that scraped her throat.

"I know. I just know. You will leave the agony—and the comfort—of grief soon, and move on. You've said that after Paul died you felt that life had no meaning. Well, the circumstances are unfortunate to be sure, but you now have the perfect opportunity to find *new* meaning in your life. Suffering opens up all those places we keep so carefully hidden, shielded from the world and from ourselves."

She was quiet for a long time. Anna could hear a clock ticking somewhere. Then Maria said, "We are all a very important part of something greater than any of us can imagine."

"How strange. That's what Sam keeps saying," Anna said.

"But our purpose is to discover who we are and then to celebrate, to rejoice in, being whatever that is. It can't depend on someone else."

"But surely Paul didn't have to die for me to realize that."

"You are right. Even if he had lived, you would have had to go through this search. It is part of life. Unfortunately, these days, it is referred to as midlife crisis and treated as a disease. But, in truth, it is an opportunity. We can never use anything, even the death of a loved one, as an excuse not to pursue our life to the fullest. If we always look back to what we consider were better times in the past, we are dragged, against our will, kicking and screaming, into the future. Life becomes a series of mournings instead of a series of adventures."

Anna didn't say anything. She sipped the hot, sweet tea and stared out the window.

"You said the other day that you are afraid. Everyone is afraid sometimes. But fear can be used. It can be turned into steel. Just follow your impulses, Anna. Take opportunity as it presents itself. You'll find, as time goes by, that enjoyment will outweigh the periods of sorrow." She reached out and poured more tea, then looked up and smiled. "Believe that the wonderful is close at hand."

The door opened, and Demetri walked into the room, smiling, all washed and brushed for the morning. "What a wonderful surprise to find you here. We've been hoping you would come."

Anna followed her impulse and jumped up to give him a hug.

Later that afternoon, she drove back to the Villas in a bemused state of mind. She felt like a child who had been chastised by a beloved aunt and then forgiven and encouraged. Something had changed, though she couldn't figure out what.

That night, she sat on her terrace above the glitter of the distant towns and villages around the gulf. A single cloud hung on the silhouetted tops of the hills, outlined from behind with a golden haze from the rising moon. Strange. Anna watched it absently.

Maria's words echoed through her thoughts. What would Paul think of Maria's counsel? At the thought of his name she waited for the crushing weight of sadness to descend again. It didn't come. In its place was a prick of tension, as if a question had been asked of her and she was supposed to give an answer.

Anna pictured Paul standing beside her, looking over the water with her. But this time it wasn't just a longing. She could feel his presence. Anna felt an urge to speak growing in her throat.

She swallowed and then said aloud, "Good-bye, Paul. I love you. I always will." *I'm so sorry you had to die,* she thought, no longer speaking out loud, but feeling the words pour from her heart. *I didn't want you to leave me so alone. But I forgive. I forgive.*

The moon rose above the top of the cloud with a burst of light, striking the water below with flecks of silver, flooding through Anna, lighting every cell. Bathed in moonlight, she knew that by forgiving, she also was forgiven.

Ten

The night Sophia came to dinner a few days after she returned from her trip, Anna decided to grill grouper—a delicious fish, common in Greece. She borrowed the hotel manager's small hibachi, had the charcoal lit, and was just tossing the salad when Sophia arrived. Anna came out to greet her, wiping her hands. "Welcome to my villa," she said. "Please come in. I'm making daiquiris." She had been delighted to find a bottle of Jamaican rum at a little American-looking quick-stop market at the edge of Ayios Nikolaos the day before, and she had ordered a bucket of crushed ice from the bar.

Sophia, as usual, looked like a misplaced Victorian lady. There was something poetical about her, and the way tendrils of her hair fell about her delicately sculptured face. But when Anna came out of the kitchenette, she found her looking very ill at ease, standing, hands clasped together.

"Make yourself at home. I won't be a minute," Anna said.

"What a delightful little place. The Demetri makes this room."

"Along with all the other things I've bought from you," Anna said. "Look around if you want to. I have no secrets."

When she came out with the tray, Sophia was peeking into the bedroom, the walls covered with Anna's drawings, haphazardly tacked up. "I see what you do with all the paper you buy from me."

"Oh, my studio. I am running out of space. I hardly have a place to sleep anymore," Anna answered. "Turn on the light if you like."

Sophia flipped the switch and went into the room to examine the drawings more closely. "When I sell art supplies, I always imagine people producing sailboats or poor renditions of flowers. But these studies are dramatic. Stiros was right. Your drawing of old Syriotis is excellent. How did you manage to capture that . . . pride, and the thick, hard texture of his hands with only a pencil?" She walked back into the sitting room. "You are a very accomplished artist," she said.

"I've been away from it for many years. But I'm having a wonderful time experimenting with different techniques." She motioned for Sophia to sit at the table outside and joined her with her own glass and a pitcher of the icy cocktail. "You have so many lovely things in your shop. You are an artist too."

"If I am," Sophia said, "it is only in the selection. I can find beautiful, well-crafted art. I can't make it myself."

"Well, that *is* an art in itself."

They talked, at first about travel, what Anna had seen in Crete, trips Sophia had taken all over Greece as well as to Turkey and Egypt on buying forays. Anna told about her lessons with Demetri Anistopolis as she poured more daiquiris. "Tell me about your shop, how you got started."

Sophia sounded reluctant as she hinted that the drop in tourism because of fear of terrorists was damaging to business, and Anna noticed that she successfully skirted questions about her recent trip.

Anna put the fish on the grill and then took the salads out of the refrigerator and the baked potatoes out of the microwave.

"One of my favorite trips was the one I took to the Lassithi Plateau, with a friend I met here," Anna said.

"During the Second World War, my family went there to hide out," Sophia said. "But that was long before I was born." She talked about other places in Crete where she had relatives.

It was a lovely evening, cool and star-studded, and by the time Anna served dinner it was the hour appropriate for a Greek. They ate on the terrace, the candles flickering in the soft breath of a breeze.

Sophia laughed when Anna told her that her tablecloth was also her shawl, and complimented the table setting with the new dishes. After the meal, Anna served Greek coffee in the small cups she found in the cabinet, but she admitted that she had bought the dessert at the Taverna. "I couldn't see myself trying to make something in the microwave," she told Sophia.

Over coffee, Sophia asked, "What brought you to Crete? Surely you didn't come here just to practice your drawing. There are many other more picturesque places in the world."

"I came here because it was one place I hadn't been with my husband," Anna said. "He died a little over a year ago."

"Oh." Sophia looked into Anna's eyes. "I'm sorry," she said simply. Anna was familiar with that look in people's eyes.

Anna smiled. "I came here to lick my wounds, really, and hope that distance and time would help heal them."

"I hope that they have . . . that that has happened."

"Are you married, Sophia?" She had noticed the gold band on her left hand.

Sophia looked up sharply. Then she realized Anna was look-ing at the ring on her left hand and smiled. "No. Americans al-ways make that mistake. This ring belonged to my mother," she said. "In Greece, women wear their wedding bands on their right hands. I have never married." She sighed. "I've been far too busy—first taking care of my father, who was ill the last few years of his life, then building up my business."

"I'm sorry for the rude question. I only thought, when I saw the ring, that I may have erred in inviting you without your husband."

"No, no husband." As if to steer the conversation away from herself she asked Anna, "Have you any children?"

They talked through two cups of coffee. At one point, Anna went in and brought out a pad and pencils. "May I?" she asked, holding up a pencil. "I'm sorry, it's one of my addictions."

Sophia smiled. "This should be interesting," she said.

Anna scratched out a couple of quick sketches as they con-tinued talking. The soft flicker of the candles made interesting light.

Suddenly Sophia looked at her watch. "Oh, my goodness, Stiros will have been waiting hours for me. I told him to pick me up at ten thirty. It's now midnight." She found her purse and thanked Anna for the evening, and the meal.

As she turned to go, Anna put her hand on Sophia's arm. "Thank you for coming. It has been lonely here for me without a woman friend to just sit and chat with. This has been especially nice for me. I hope you'll come back."

"And you must come and see me . . . in my apartment," Sophia said, and then looked surprised. As if the idea had never occurred to her and now sounded appealing, she added, looking a little baffled, "I'd like that very much."

Anna went in to clean up with a sort of bemused sense of a wonderful evening. *I don't think she really wanted to come, since she asked Stiros to pick her up after an hour and a half. But I think in the end she had a good time.* Afterward she sat out under the stars feeling content and certainly well fed. *This is starting to feel like home.*

Eleven

S am returned late in the afternoon the next day, and Anna drove his car into Iráklion to meet his plane. She had worked all day on a portrait of Sophia, using her drawings from the night before. With great reluctance, she put it away to make the hectic, harrowing drive to the airport. But when she saw Sam, head and shoulders taller than the people around him, looking across the sea of heads with that lopsided grin, she realized how much she had missed him, and she was surprised at how glad she was to see him. They got back to the hotel just at sunset.

"I need to go wash off the grime of the city," Sam said. "How about if we meet in the Taverna at nine and have a long, slow drink, then an even longer, slower dinner? Maybe they'll have that bouzouki player." He moved his hands, strumming an imaginary instrument.

Anna took her time getting ready for dinner. As she showered in the funny bathroom with no shower curtain, her almost totally brown body disappeared in the steamy mirror, the white, string-bikini strip across her buttocks and lower abdomen dividing her torso from her legs. She felt great. As she dried off, she decided that the pale bikini silhouette could serve as underpants. God, in another week she'd probably be going completely naked. She had given up bras forever.

She slipped on a sleeveless print dress with an elasticized waist made of soft Indian cotton, dark enough to need no slip, then dropped the rope of cold glass beads over her head—the ones she'd bought in Ayios Nikolaos that day that seemed so long ago. Then, tying a fringed scarf of dark red loosely around her hips, she was ready. Her feet automatically slipped into the navy thongs with velvet straps and a slight wedge heel, and she headed to the dining room.

Sam was at the bar, talking with two other men. When he saw Anna, his face rose into a slow smile as his eyebrows lifted with appreciation. "I can't tell you how good it is to be back. You look wonderful."

"It's nice to have you back too."

After dinner, they decided to sit on the deck by the pool, sipping their thick Greek coffee. The air wafted across Anna's arms like a chiffon scarf, scented with salt and the arid clarity of Crete air.

She had grown to cherish these quiet shared moments. Somehow Sam was like a bridge from the past to the future. A comfortable place where the time was simply *now* and she could rest from worries and plans. And though they certainly talked of the past, with Sam Anna didn't have the feeling of reliving the past so much as relating something that was becoming a memory. With Sam, she was able to say Paul's name without a catch in her voice and heart.

Tonight she didn't want to go back to her room. She sighed. If only time could be locked in this moment, she thought. This comfortable, comforting moment.

Sam stood and looked over the wall. "Would you like to take a walk down to the water?"

"On that trail? At night?"

"Look at the moon. It's almost like daylight. You can see the path all the way to the beach. Come on. Let's see the Aegean by moonlight."

Anna went over and looked down. He was right. She could see the path. "Why not?" she said.

The night air was pleasantly cool, and though she hadn't been cold before, she shivered. "Why don't you take that tablecloth off your waist and wrap it around your arms?" Sam suggested.

Laughing, she untied the scarf and Sam draped it around her

shoulders. Then he took her arm in a protective gesture she didn't need. She was perfectly capable of negotiating the trail on her own, but it was comforting. He was humming under his breath—some old song about the moon that Anna hadn't heard in years.

Around the last curve in the trail, they walked out on the little crescent beach. "How perfectly beautiful," she said. The swells were etched in silver, the rocks radiant white. It was a perfect night for a moonlight swim. *Why didn't I think of that?* Anna asked herself, listening to the whisper of surf. Then temptation got the best of her. Like a child, she broke away from Sam, dropped her scarf on the rocks, and waded out into the water. She intended to just step in, glad she'd worn her thongs, but the water was delicious lapping at her ankles. The moon's reflection, winking on the swells, formed a glistening pathway she couldn't resist. She waded out, farther and farther.

"Anna! Good Lord, what are you doing?" Sam shouted, incredulous. "Watch out. It drops off after only a few more feet."

"I know," she said, laughing. The water crept up to her waist as she walked, her skirt floating around her like seaweed. It was so cool, she gasped. "Oh, this is wonderful," she said, sinking into the sea up to her chin.

"You're crazy!" Sam said from the shore.

"No, you're the one who's crazy. Come on in." The moon's path came straight into her face. She felt she could drink the light. Her dress billowed around her in the wash of the soft surf, her feet barely touching the pebbles, her hair swinging in the ebb and flow. *For two cents I'd slip out of my dress,* she thought, laughing as she pictured it. Turning around, she started to say, "Sam, what would you think if I . . . Sam! My God!"

He was standing on a shelf of stone, stark naked, the print of his swimsuit around his lower body a pale pattern in the moonlight. Just as Anna shouted his name, he dived, knifelike, into the water and came up ten feet from her.

Laughing, he said, "The only way this should be experienced. Come on, I dare you."

Anna's mind still held the picture of him standing like Posei-

don, poised for the dive, the moonlight a silver patina on his skin.
"But . . . but I—"

"If you can doff your swimsuit top with such aplomb, why
not go all the way?" He was standing in front of her, his hands on
her shoulders. He shook her a little as he talked, as you would a
child you were trying to cajole into being brave.

"That sounds like a not very subtle proposition to me," Anna
said. "Should a sweet little old matron who is barely out of her
widow's weeds consider being so flagrant with a strange man?"

"I realize I'm funny looking. But I didn't think I was all that
strange."

"You know what I mean, you blackguard."

At that, he laughed, throwing his head back, his teeth gleaming in the light, droplets of water like fireflies around his head.
"Here, I'll help you," he said, taking the shoulders of her dress in
his hands to pull it down over her arms, still laughing.

Anna reached up to stop him, laughing, saying loudly, "No!
Don't—" when something shifted inside her. She was aware with
every inch of her body, of his hands touching her, of her own heart
beating in staccato.

Sam had stopped laughing too. He stood unmoving, his
hands still on her shoulders. He had turned so the moon was behind him, his face in total darkness. "Anna." He said it so softly
that it sent prickles over her skin. "God, Anna, I missed you when
I was away. I hadn't realized—"

Anna put her finger over his lips. "Shhh."

He pulled her hand aside and held it. "I just, well, I—" He
squeezed her hand, then in his normal voice he said, "If you're so
modest that you want to swim in your clothes, it's okay with me."
He was standing very close, one hand on her shoulder, the other
holding hers against his chest.

Anna could feel his heart beating through the back of her
hand and she was quite stirred, suddenly aware of his nakedness.
"You realize, I'm sure, that I am very vulnerable at this point."

"I know. I know your loss was great, and more recent than
mine, and I know that I could never fill that empty space for you."

He put his hands back on her shoulders and gently turned her so that his face was in the light again. "I wouldn't even want to try."

It was as if they were doing a slow dance. The motion of the water gently pushed them back and forth. Sam's hands pressed her shoulders, not insistent, just there. Her whole body, which only moments before had been delighting in the coolness of the water, began shivering.

"Oh, God," she said, and it was a prayer. She wasn't sure if in supplication or thanksgiving.

He pulled her to him, and she went, without protest.

His lips were much softer than she would have imagined, not urgent, not questing. They tasted of salt, warming hers . . . warming her. He held her close in an embrace that was so strong and good, she moaned from pure pleasure. Then with his hands on her shoulders again, he pushed her gently away. Anna looked up at his familiar craggy face, the great arch of his nose, his bushy eyebrows. She could feel, not see, the brown warmth of his eyes burning the question. She had no idea she had memorized his look so well. And she knew she was beyond making a choice. She reached up and slipped off the shoulders of her dress.

Completing the move, he pushed the top down and she felt the elastic waist slip over her hips and stepped out of it. With a lurch, he tossed it with a hook shot up on shore. Oh, how wonderful to be free in this lovely water . . . to be free . . . be free.

Sam hugged her close again, his lips firmer now, open, insistent. Then, leaving her mouth, he kissed her eyes, then her ear.

They danced there in the wash of the waves, turning in the moonlight, Sam's footing firm, Anna's drifting. She could feel her thongs barely hanging on; then they faded from her thoughts as Sam's mouth moved to her neck, his hand trailing first up her back, then over her shoulder, molding her with his touch. "Anna," he whispered.

She felt herself moving against him, needing him, wanting him, feeling his desire. The cool of the water and the warmth of his hands were like flashing lights against her skin. Light, inside and out. His lips moved over her neck, her ears, her shoulders.

Then gripping her waist, he lifted her, and she groaned as his mouth sought her breast. Slowly he let her down, her body sliding against his, descending, her legs automatically locking around him. One thrust and the glittering light on the waves seemed to be inside her, sparkling in surge after surge.

"Anna." He said her name once more, and time was held like a shining beam of moonlight, brighter and brighter until the moon itself burst, the shining fragments showering through every part of her body. Sobs tore from her throat, warming her cheeks with tears.

"It's okay, Anna," Sam whispered in her ear, holding her close. His fingers trailed across her back in soft, swirling patterns.

Slowly, she let her legs slide away from him, and hanging on to his neck because the water was up to her chin, she cried into his shoulder. She wondered, swaying there with the movement of the water and the still-pulsing movements of passion, if she would ever be able to walk again. Sam just held her, not talking. Finally, there were no more tears, only a deep sense of joy. It had been good. So good.

"You know what I feel like doing?" he asked. Without waiting for an answer, he went on. "I feel like swimming straight out to sea. If I died now, I'd die a happy man."

"I suppose I should consider that a compliment."

"You would be correct in doing so. If I knew how to do a back flip, I would do one." He gathered her into his arms. Then he held her at arm's length. "You are one astonishing woman."

Anna laughed. Slipping away and sliding through the water like a dolphin, she swam back to the little cove and, when she got her footing, stood up. That was when she realized she had on only one thong. "I've lost one of my shoes," she said.

"Here it is," Sam said. "It was floating over here. I ran into it."

He handed it to her, and standing on one foot, she slipped it on. Instead of feeling drained, she felt energized. She wanted to run up the hill. Naked.

"Be still a minute," Sam said softly. "I just want to look at you there, with moonlight dripping from your hair." She stood, feeling more alive than she had felt in a long, long time. "I thought my life was basically over until tonight, Anna."

"Some things are never really over, I'm told."

"I don't mean just making love to you. It's other things. It's the unexpected. You are a surprise, Anna. You continue to surprise me. Not only by what you do, but by what I find myself doing when I'm with you." He cleared his throat. "You aren't going to believe this, but I have never gone swimming in the nude before."

"You haven't?" Anna couldn't help being incredulous.

"You have given me a gift I'm barely beginning to see the value of. I loved tonight, Anna, every part of it. I thank you for being, well, for being who you are."

She turned to look at him. Of course, she and Paul had gone swimming in the nude, with all the things that could lead to, many times. She couldn't even remember the first time.

"Well," she began, "I suppose we should . . ." She looked around. "My dress!"

"Your dress?"

"You had it. You took it from me."

"I threw it onto the bank."

"Well, it's not here." The moonlight splashed the whole beach area. It was empty of the dark lump that would have been her dress. She saw only her scarf where she had dropped it.

Sam splashed around, diving, walking back and forth, feeling around with his feet. "I'm so sorry. I did throw it up here. I'm sure I saw it land."

Anna was getting cold. Reluctantly, she got out of the water. Here she was, hundreds of yards from the hotel, wearing only a string of beads and earrings. And thongs! Suddenly she felt shy and held the scarf up in front of her. Sam was diving frantically, his white derriere gleaming in the moonlight. Seeing this, Anna began to laugh so hard that she had to find a rock and sit down.

He surfaced and sputtered, "I can't find it, Anna, I'm sorry." When he realized she was laughing, he started chuckling, then let loose with wild guffaws.

"If you would wear underwear—" Sam said.

"Then I could traipse up that trail in a bra and panties? That would be lovely."

"Well, it beats stark naked." He staggered onto the shore, and weak with laughter, they tried to decide which of Sam's clothes each of them would wear, then struggled to pull them onto their wet, salty bodies.

Anna ended up in the long-tailed shirt, Sam in his now-wet slacks. He put his jacket around her, and she gave him her scarf, which he wore around his neck. They trudged up the hill, unable to talk because anything they said brought on hysterics.

"I'll be the talk of the hotel if that dress washes up tomorrow. With that print, it wouldn't be easy to forget who was wearing it last night. I'm tempted to leave and let them think I've drowned."

"Most drowned people's clothes don't just wash off," Sam said. "Besides, a lady with a reputation has a certain appeal."

"Appeal to what?" she asked.

"A tantalizing, fascinating, seductive woman who runs around naked always has appeal."

Anna tried to hit him, and he grabbed her arm and hugged her close.

At the door to Anna's villa, Sam sobered. "Anna, I don't know what to say."

She put her finger to his lips. "Don't say anything." She didn't want either of them to have to put this evening into words. Tiptoeing, she kissed him lightly and gave him his jacket. She started laughing again when he had it on. The hair on his chest looked like a sweater between the lapels. He handed her the scarf.

"Anna?"

"Good night, Sam." She closed the door. Their hysterical laughter had put the final touches on a wonderful evening.

After standing in the shower, soaking her chilled body . . . and the toilet paper she had forgotten to cover, she fell into bed. Lying there, still feeling the motion of the waves, she was rocked to sleep on their ebb and flow.

Twelve

The next morning Anna woke slowly, stretching, still immersed in the sensation of floating. Until she remembered. "Oh, my God," she said out loud, every detail of the evening before flashing through her mind. The glow of pleasure that still clung to her vanished as soon as she opened her eyes, the shaft of sunlight falling across her bed like a finger of reproach. She sat straight up, grabbing the bedclothes to cover her nudity. She went into the bathroom, where she found the toilet paper, still soaked from her shower the night before, drooping from the spindle.

Anna knew Sam would be here as soon as he thought she was awake. "Ooooh, what am I going to do?" she said out loud, clenching her fists. She grabbed the first clothes she came to. Why had she let herself get so carried away? *We had such a wonderful friendship. So comfortable. Now it's ruined. I didn't want that to happen. I didn't!* A voice inside her head said, *Of course you wanted it.* At that thought the whole scene of the night before flooded through her, making her feel light-headed.

She put on some water for tea. Maybe their friendship hadn't changed. Maybe last night was a onetime thing. A thing of the moment. They could still just be friends. Couldn't they?

The teapot whistle made Anna jump, and the cup rattled on the saucer as she lifted it from the cabinet. She knew better than that. Sex wasn't a onetime thing. Once that door was open, it was impossible to fully close it again. She knew that from the desperation she had often felt when Paul was away on trips.

Paul! Anna felt as if something crumpled inside her. And

though she knew it was unreasonable, she felt unfaithful to Paul. Unfaithful? She was a grown woman, for Christ's sake. Free to do what she liked. *After all it is not the Dark Ages.* Isn't that what Maggie had said? But free? To do what she liked? She poured the water into the china pot and rushed back into the bedroom. She had never felt less free.

What had she told Maggie? *Sex isn't just something you do. It's part of a larger whole.* Anna felt tarnished . . . shamed, as though she had broken a vow. *This is the twenty-first century!* Maggie's voice echoed in her head.

It may be the twenty-first century, but this was not right for me. Part of her knew she was being ridiculous, totally unreasonable. But she had been a virgin bride. She had made love to no one but Paul. Now she felt wanton. No amount of reasoning could convince her that her behavior last night was not merely shabby.

Anna felt herself shift into the flee mode. *I need to get away. I need some time to think.* She yanked down luggage from the top of the closet and threw it on the bed. *This is silly,* she told herself, scooping the lingerie from the drawer straight into the suitcase, frantic now to pack up and leave. She took out the garment bag and swept hangers full of clothes out of the closet. In the bathroom, she put her cosmetics bag and bathing things into a plastic sack and threw it into the suitcase. Shoes. She dumped them into the bottom of the garment bag.

"I just need a little time," she said out loud, persuading herself. *I need a trip. A trip to . . . where? Athens. Athens will do me good.*

Going back into the kitchen, she poured tea into the cup, and then scalded her tongue trying to gulp it. No time for that. She snapped shut the suitcase, zipped the garment bag, and, pulling the strap of her purse onto her shoulder, struggled out into the quiet light of early morning.

There on a chair on the terrace, spread as if a ghost were wearing it, was her dress. "Oh, God," she moaned. She turned away quickly and rushed up the highest path, well away from Sam's apartment, to the office. Trying to act normal, she told the manager's wife, who was just opening the office, that she was going to take a trip into Athens.

"How long will you be gone?"

"Probably a few days," Anna said, taking a furtive look out the open door. "I've left my things in the apartment. I won't be gone long." She dug through her purse for Stiros' number. Would she wake him? She dialed the number.

Thank heaven he answered the phone, and yes, he did sound sleepy. Anna offered him a fortune to take her to the airport in Iráklion, and then waited for him in trepidation, expecting to see Sam burst through the door at any moment. While she waited, she scribbled down a quick note to Demetri and Maria. "I'm off to Athens for a few days. I'll call when I return. Anna." She would give it to Stiros to deliver.

In Iráklion Anna had had a two-hour wait for a plane to Athens, but at last, she was here. A quick call to the Apollo Hotel from the airport had gotten her this room, two rooms, actually, with a sitting room and a bathroom with the shower in its own cubicle and a large European tub. This was where she and Paul had stayed many times. It was within walking distance to everything one wanted to see in Athens.

Anna tipped the bellhop and sat down on the couch in her little sitting room with sheepish relief. A string of hair was hanging down over her forehead, and she remembered that in her rush she had left her toothbrush on the sink at the Villas and her dress on the veranda. And her bag of art supplies. She'd left that too.

What an adolescent thing to do, she thought, leaving in such a rush. Why had she been so impulsive? She was almost half a century old. She could have talked with Sam. He would have understood what she was feeling. Maybe he felt the same way—that something was lost, that it would be better to forget the moment of ardor and go back to their easy friendship. If they both agreed, perhaps the loss could be recouped, and things could be as they had been.

Oh well, she thought, sitting on the edge of the couch, unable to relax, her hands clasped between her knees. As long as she was here, she would take a few days to visit some of the places she had enjoyed before, when she'd been here with . . . Paul. Just thinking of him made her feel vaguely uncomfortable. She recalled her vow to avoid anyplace they had been together. Here she was in Athens, one of their favorites.

She went into the bathroom to freshen up and comb her wild hair. Looking at herself in the mirror, she didn't know whether to laugh or cry. *Okay, so you're a throwback to the Puritan era. Come on, Anna.* Here she was in one of the most beautiful cities in the world. Why not enjoy? She had to have a plan.

The first thing she would do was buy art supplies. Then she'd seek out places she had never been with anyone before, she thought, raking the comb through her hair. No, she'd go and enjoy places she had been and look at them with new eyes. *It's time to grow wise, Anna. Quit feeling sorry for yourself.*

Before she left the room, she pulled back the heavy drapes in front of the French doors and walked out onto the tiny balcony that overlooked the park across the street.

Not far away was Syntagma Square, the heart of the city, its beat regulated by the changing of the Evzones, the royal body-guards, in front of the Parliament Building on the east side of the square—young men, in their tutulike uniforms with pom-poms on their shoes, beautiful, full-sleeved blouses, and stockings of re-splendent white. They marched before the Tomb of the Unknown Soldier with a slow, exaggerated precision. Anna planned to go there to sketch them soon.

Just looking out over the skyline, her pulse quickened. She had always loved Athens, even the noxious fumes and snarling clamor of the traffic. It was a paradox, the tranquillity of a noisy city. Maybe she'd end up being glad she came. She paced back across the room. Maybe it would be another hurdle in her grief process—visiting a city she and Paul had enjoyed together.

And maybe I'll rationalize myself right out of existence, she thought ruefully, turning back to close the balcony doors. Anna took the elevator to the ground floor and crossed the lobby, her heels ringing on the marble floor.

"Good afternoon, Mrs. Sandoval." She turned to find the hotel manager at her elbow. "Will Mr. Sandoval be joining you?" he asked. Then, with a smile that showed pride in his memory, he said, "I remember both of you well, from your visit two years ago at the time of the elections."

Anna didn't want to embarrass him, so she said, "How nice of you to remember. I'm sorry to have to tell you that Mr. San-doval di—passed away last year."

His face grimaced in horror. "Oh, I'm so sorry. I didn't know!"

"How could you have known?" What could she do to salvage his pride? "You can, however, do something for me."

"Anything, madam."

"Could you send someone to the flower stall across the street to get a large bouquet of whatever blossoms are in season, and have it placed in my room?" She discreetly offered some euros.

He lifted her hand and turned her fingers up to close them, leaving the money in her palm. "It will be a gift from the hotel, madam, given with pleasure." He made a curt little bow, his dignity restored. "And if I may be of other service, do not hesitate to call. My name is"—he cleared his throat—"Konstantinos."

"Thank you, Konstantinos."

It gets easier, Anna thought as she walked through the door and out into the noise of Athens traffic. She walked down the street in front of the hotel to the park by Syntagma Square, heading for the outdoor café there, under the trees. Once again, she was early for the crowds. She sat at a sun-dappled corner table and ordered a glass of iced coffee.

Some children were trying to coax a scraggly gray cat from under a table. The two waiters, with nothing to do, stood smoking and laughing by the door to the outdoor bar. She began to relax for the first time since her flight from Crete.

It was flight, all right, running away. Pure panic. Anna felt a little sheepish.

When she noticed a dowager with a carefully groomed poodle at a distant table, she knew she had to try and draw her. She dug through her purse and came up with a large tattered envelope and a felt-tip pen.

The woman was an old, sad beauty, a faded memory of what once was. Orange hair in the style of Greta Garbo in the thirties, exaggerated lipstick, large hoop earrings, jingling bracelets. Blue eyelids completed the picture. There were women like this in every city in the world.

The woman took a pull on her cigarette, smoking with gloves on as she studied the menu. The dog sat, hopefully alert, by her chair.

"Would you like more coffee?" the waiter asked. He looked at the sketch and then over at the woman. "That is very like her," he said.

Anna smiled. "Please, do bring me another," she said, her concentration on the tilt of the woman's head, as though she were expecting someone important and wanted to look cool and collected.

The next day, Anna left the hotel after lunch to walk in the National Garden, a thickly forested place in the middle of Athens not far from the hotel. Here tree-shaded paths led past playgrounds and benches for lounging in sun or shade. She enjoyed watching the people—nursemaids pushing perambulators, young mothers watching their children cavort about in the play areas, runners, older people formally dressed, the men in dark suits and ties, women in tweedy suits with calf-length skirts and often gloves and hats. Emerging on the other side of the park, she saw that she was across the street from the famous Stadion, the stadium where the first renewal of the Olympics had been held in 1896. The last time she had been in Athens with Paul he'd insisted on taking his daily run there. As he'd gone round and round the narrow oval, she had watched from the stands, thinking that, as Greek gods went, he was a pretty good specimen.

On her way back to the hotel she wandered back along Vasilissis Sophias Avenue with its rows of embassies on one side of the street and rows of flower vendors on the other. Because

Paul was in and out of the American embassy when he came to Athens, he and Anna often walked under the trees here, delighting in the bright splashes of color and the heavenly aroma. Anna had just bought a small bouquet of violets when she heard, "Anna? Anna Sandoval, is that you?"

Anna looked around to see the face of Gwen Berkley, the wife of the attaché at the U.S. Embassy. She and Paul had met Wayne and Gwen Berkley when they were in Athens for the first time several years before. They had gone with them to dinner two years ago, and because Anna was ostensibly just along for the ride on these trips, she'd had time to spend with Gwen and they had become friends.

"Anna! What are you doing in Athens? Why didn't you call? We were so sorry, shocked, really, to hear about Paul. You must be devastated. How are the children? Last I heard, one had 'flown the coop' and the other was setting the world on fire at Princeton. How long have you been here anyway?"

"I'm a tourist." Anna walked over to Gwen, who by this time was standing beside the open door of her car. They both kissed the air as they touched cheeks. Anna valued this friendship, though it was casual in the way of people who meet once every few years. This diminutive, scatterbrained blonde had been a godsend on her other visits. Gwen had been in Athens so long that she knew it better than any guide and could speak Greek as well as a native.

"Why didn't you let us know you were here?" She looked stricken. "Is there anything I can do, Anna? It must have been so awful."

At Gwen's questions, Anna felt strangely at ease and, at the same time, just as strangely concerned, as though she needed to comfort her distressed friend more than she herself needed sympathy. "Yes, it was awful . . . for a while," she said. "But I'm finding that life does go on. How are you? And how is Wayne?"

"We're fine," Gwen said. "Wayne is doing great. Listen, we're having a few people over tonight."

Anna laughed. They were always having a few people over.

"Why don't you come? Wayne would love to see you and we can get caught up on all the news—about the children . . . and everything." She looked at her watch. "Oh, my gosh, I've got to hurry. I told him I'd be home at—"

Anna didn't hear the rest of the sentence, because Gwen slammed the door on it. She waved, and Gwen blew her a kiss, then rolled down the window and shouted, "Eight thirty! Informal!"

Anna arrived at the Berkleys' at nine. The "few" people added up to about thirty, milling about the large living room of their town house off Vasilissis Sophias. Their house always gave Anna the feeling that anything could happen. She stood in the doorway to the room, looking over the collection of people chatting in small groups. She recognized at least four people. Dan Adams, an Associated Press correspondent, was talking with Sally Reinhold and her giant husband, Roger, who was an official of some kind at the embassy. Anna and Paul had first met him in the Philippines, years ago when he was head of the U.S. Information Service at the embassy in Manila. And there was Norma Greenway, looking just as friendly and frumpy as ever. Everyone liked Norma. She did something in public affairs—Anna couldn't remember what.

"How long are you going to be in Athens?" Norma asked.

"I've harbored this small fear that someone would ask me that," Anna said. "I don't know."

"It must be nice to be able to do anything you want to do."

"Well, it would be nicer if I knew *what* I wanted to do."

As Anna passed through a door, she bumped against the back of a tall man who was gesturing to someone across the room. He deftly stepped aside and laughed as he made a small bow. "Alexis Sarkis, at your service, madam." His face was as grave as his formal introduction, but his dark eyes sparkled with mirth. "I was just going to get a drink. May I bring one for you?"

Anna nodded. "Thank you. A gin and tonic would be lovely."

He turned toward the bar that had been set up in the corner when someone very fragrant gave Anna a little hug and squeezed her hand. It was Gwen. "I'm so glad you're here. I was afraid you wouldn't come, being in mourning. I mean, uh, alone." Gwen bit her lip, looking distressed.

"I wouldn't have missed this party," Anna said, returning the squeeze.

"I saw you talking with Alexis. Isn't he beautiful? Those eyelashes and curls and that square chin. I could just eat him with a spoon. He's an architect, you know—quite a famous one. He went to school in the States and then in—I think it was Sweden. They're talking with him about doing a new wing at the embassy. He's the one who's designed the whole plan for that new university out on the slopes of Mount. Hymettus. Did you ever go to the monastery out there? Kaisariani? It's a lovely place. The university is fashioned after that. He's also being consulted about changes at the airport and . . . oh, here he comes."

Alexis brought Anna her drink and, seeing Gwen, offered to get one for her.

"I can't drink at my own parties. I'd never remember people's names if I did. Oh, there's Professor Spyropoulos. I'll bring him over to meet you later, Anna. You'll find him very interesting." She floated over to join that group.

"I think she knows everyone in Athens," Alexis said. "Her parties are always the most interesting assortment of people."

"She was very kind to me and my hus—my late husband on our last visit." Anna hadn't meant to mention Paul tonight. She had memorized glib little dismissals with which to reply to people's commiserations. And yet, here she was announcing her widowhood to this person she hardly knew.

"I'm sorry about your husband," he said. "I met him only briefly and liked him. I know he was highly respected by people in Athens for his fairness and integrity in the reporting of the political situation. Please accept my condolences."

"You know who I am?"

"Of course. Gwen told me."

"Anna!" Anna's feet were suddenly dangling as she was engulfed in the arms of Roger Reinhold. "When did you blow into

Athens? It's good to see you," he boomed. He put her down so that his tall, angular wife, Sally, could also give her a hug.

"We were so sorry to hear—" Sally started to say.

"You look great," Roger said, as if determined not to speak of Paul.

Just then, Wayne Berkley came up. "I wondered what all the commotion was about in this corner. Anna, what a wonderful surprise. Gwen told me she saw you in front of the embassy. I—"

The evening went on like that—no one ever quite completing a sentence. Anna enjoyed it. How easy it was to fall into social conversation, changing the subject with each person, asking questions or making statements that gave others an opening to air their own opinions or expertise or interests.

The whole gathering was like a verbal dance. One could jump into the middle of things and perform for a while, then step to the edge and watch the others. Anna's glib side steps seemed to put people at their ease after they had said the words of sympathy that both they and she dreaded. Most looked relieved when she accepted their words, then led them on to other topics.

It was midnight when Wayne's chauffeur drove her back to the hotel. Anna filled the tub while she undressed. Sinking into the steamy water, she thought maybe she'd send for all her things in Crete and stay on in Athens. There was really no reason to go back there. And this was comfortable. She hadn't remembered what a luxury a bathtub could be. Besides, she was finding that it was easier, not harder, being here with people she already knew.

Thirteen

The next morning, Anna took her second step back into a world once inhabited by Paul. She had finally accepted the fact that if she avoided all the places they had loved and shared together, she would be confined to her rooms in Athens. If she was going to stay here for a while, she had to face the old reminders. So she started out early to conquer the one she feared most. After a Continental breakfast of hard rolls and coffee, she took a roundabout route through the National Garden to make a pilgrimage to the Acropolis.

It was a cool morning, the air invigorating in spite of the noxious smell of exhaust. Anna walked along at a fast clip. She wanted to get up there before the busloads of tourists started arriving, to have time to wander among the ruins in peace. She needed to be alone the first time she returned.

She had visited other *acropoli*. Almost every ancient Greek city of any size has one—high, fortified vantage points with vistas in every direction. They were sacred places, these temples, but they could also serve as lookouts for approaching enemies. It was easy to see how these high walled areas would be places of refuge for the people living below in times of siege.

The hillside of the Acropolis, in Athens, was green with pine and juniper trees, their scent adding a sharp tang to the air. Even though Anna had walked up this steep path many times, she never tired of it. Each time she entered the Beule Gate—the west portico in the walls surrounding the summit—was a first time. She climbed the uneven, broken marble steps leading up to the Temple of Athena Nike—Athena who brings victory—with awe and anticipation.

Coming up the last steps to the flat bare rock of the Acropolis summit, Anna stood transfixed. There, in all its glory, stood the Parthenon, dominating the hilltop with soaring Doric columns thirty-four feet high and six feet in diameter at their bases. Only one of its friezes remained, tucked in the corner of the high architrave. The others, Anna had been told, had been taken, in years past, by the British. Some were in the British Museum, and many others, at the bottom of the Mediterranean, the ships carrying them having sunk in storms. The Parthenon, built in the fifth century B.C. as a shrine to the goddess Athena, stood in ruined splendor like a crown, high above the city, a reminder of time, and a tribute to humankind.

Anna had read up on its history when she brought Peter and Christine here the first time. It had seen so many changes, so many wars. For the first nine hundred years, the Parthenon was a temple to Athena. Then, for almost one thousand years, it was a Christian church and, for two hundred years after that, a Muslim mosque. Its interior was destroyed in 1687, when either lightning or gunfire blew up explosives the Turks were storing there, and made a skeleton of the crowning glory of Athens. Anna looked at it in awe. It was beautiful even in ruin.

When she and Paul had first stood there, they had each blindly sought the other's hand, not able to bear this magnificence alone, having no words that could adequately describe their wonder. Today, Anna clasped her own hands together, then took a deep breath and walked forward, along the Sacred Way.

Occasionally, she went over to the wall to look down. The views from the Acropolis were spectacular—Athens spread at its feet all the way to the distant Aegean, seen through the haze, and, from another view, to the barren, brown hills to the north and west. Closer was the Pnyx. On another hill stood the altar of Zeus and the rock-hewn tribune from which the orators spoke in the fourth and fifth centuries B.C. But, to Anna, the most beautiful sight from the Acropolis was the Hill of the Muses with its grace-ful ruin of the monument of Philopappos. She vowed to go there someday soon, hoping the Muses would speak to her.

She walked along the path on stones worn smooth over the ages by the feet of countless visitors, and passed the rock-cut dedication to Ge, the earth mother. Were her feet also wearing away a microscopic depth of stone, Anna wondered, leaving evi-dence that she too had come here as a pilgrim paying homage to Athena?

There were few people about, and they were quiet, as though they also felt the sacredness of this place. But Anna had the sense of being with a great crowd, the ghostly spirits of the ancients moving along with her, dignified, worshipful. She was one of them as she walked on this holy ground.

Suddenly, she heard singing. It was coming from the south wall. She walked over to the wall, crossing in front of the steps leading into the Parthenon, closed to visitors with barrier ropes, and looked down at the ruined Theater of Dionysos, built into a natural hollow in the slopes of the Acropolis to her left. There the tragedies and comedies that every humanities student in the world read had first been performed.

But the singing was coming from the right. Looking down, she could see the Odeon of Herodes Atticus, a Roman theater, built in the first century A.D., which had been recently restored. Both theaters, tucked into the hill, were open to the sky.

Actors were milling around on the distant Odeon floor in re-hearsal. From the stage, at the bottom of a high half circle of tiered seats that could accommodate an audience of hundreds, came the ringing notes of a pure soprano. An aria from the opera *Aïda* poured through the morning air like sunshine, touching everything with its silvered tones.

A new group of spirits seemed to be about—the Romans, who had their place here in the sun hundreds of years after the Greeks. Anna wondered when the opera would be performed. She would ask Konstantinos to get her a ticket. No. As she listened to the lonely strains of the aria ride the pine-scented breeze to the heights of the Acropolis, Anna knew she couldn't go to *Aïda* alone. It was one of those things that had to be shared.

She made her solitary way through the growing crowd, down the rough steps of the Beule Gate and the winding pathway, against the flow of people to the street below, and back to her rooms at the hotel.

She tried to take a nap, but she wasn't sleepy. She couldn't sit still. She tried reading, got out the hotel postcards from the desk, and scratched out notes to Maggie and Peter and Christine— uninspired notes that sounded like she had copied them from a guidebook. She turned on the shower and then turned it off again, did some hand wash, sat first in the chair and then on the couch.

Maybe she should just pack up and go back to Washington. She paced around, opening curtains, closing others, looking down at the street below from her minuscule balcony.

Athens no longer felt tranquil. It was a maddening place, with the honking, screeching, buzzing, and roaring of its treacherous traffic; with jackhammers and heavy machinery screaming and pounding around pollution-blackened buildings, which always appeared to be under construction or renovation. The teeming crowds moved in irregular rivers of bobbing heads. The city streets sounded like a symphony orchestra gone awry.

No, maybe I should go back to Crete, Anna thought, a yearning for the quiet, and a longing to see Maria and Demetri rising like homesickness in her heart. Thinking of Demetri reminded her that she was going to buy drawing materials. That was what she needed, she decided. After a quick lunch in the hotel dining room, she went out in search of pads and pencils.

During the next three days, Anna settled more and more into the routine of Athens life. By day, she wandered around the city, through its parks and museums, its antiquities, the Plaka, watching people and sketching scenes. She especially loved the Plaka. This was the original old city of Athens, decaying but quaint. In early morning it was empty except for delivery people bringing in fresh groceries and shopkeepers washing down the cobblestones in front of their stores. The narrow streets were overhung with balconies edged with pots of geraniums and splashes of bougainvillea in pinks and reds and white. Rows of buildings, some dating back hundreds of years, with their scalloped, red tile roofs and peeling plaster walls, gave the Plaka a medieval atmosphere.

Anna explored narrow passageways leading off winding streets that sometimes allowed a peek through wrought-iron gates into walled flower-bedecked gardens of private flats and ancient town houses. Crooked stairs, broken and grimy, led to the upper levels. Narrow passages spilled out onto sun-flooded plazas of faded glory, studded with modern chrome and plastic tables set around trees and statues.

Anna's footfalls echoed through the empty streets in the early-morning light, past small archaeological digs and dark, domed churches, hundreds of years old, exuding the smell of incense. Sometimes she was greeted in passing by bearded priests wearing long, black cassocks and tall, flat-topped hats.

But when she went back there in the afternoon, it was like stepping into the rapids of a river. Throngs of people flowed through the streets, a myriad of languages blending with the pestering hype of the waiters, all dressed in tight black trousers and white shirts with the sleeves rolled up, trying to get people to stop at their restaurants, coffeehouses, and tavernas.

That evening, feeling time heavy on her hands, Anna wandered out about nine o'clock to go back to the Plaka. She loved going there at night, the time when Athens really came alive. The streets on the way were filled with window-shoppers, groups of laughing youths, people bustling purposefully along. Athens was noted for being a safe city with very little violent street crime. Anna felt perfectly at ease walking alone.

Though the shops on the streets leading to the Plaka were closed, the restaurants and galleries in the old city were a hive of activity, the cafés packed with tables spilling out into the narrow streets. She took out the map she had gotten from the desk at the hotel and tried to locate where she was. She wanted to go to the

Taverna Theon, a restaurant she and Paul had considered their own personal find. They had stumbled into it one afternoon when, foot-weary, unaccustomed to the constant pounding of cobblestones, they'd looked for a place to sit down and have a glass of wine.

Anna remembered that day with longing. Turning a corner off of Nikodimou Street, they'd found themselves on a street that ended after a few yards in wide, stone stairs leading up to a narrow passageway. At the top of the stairs, on a small landing, were several rough, wooden tables covered with white tablecloths, and standing in the middle of the passageway between the tables, a man in a white apron smiled down at them.

"Good afternoon," he said with a thick accent. "Please sit."

That was all the invitation they needed. They pulled back the chairs of a table located under an arbor, from which hung bunches of green grapes. After they sat down, they realized that the whole landing slanted a little to the left. They agreed that it gave the place charm. That was the day they discovered Naoussa Boutari, the light Macedonian wine with a pungent bouquet she liked so much. The proprietor brought them hard bread and cheese to go with it.

Since it was early in the afternoon, they were the only customers. After he served the wine, the proprietor surprised them by pulling up a chair and joining them, asking them about their home in America, answering questions about Athens. By the time he finally introduced himself—"I am Xenos Koutsoukellis, one of three brothers"—he had already become a friend.

Paul and Anna went back to the Taverna Theon often, and were always welcomed as part of the family. Once, they went beyond the sloping landing and up some very worn steps that hugged the building, to a roof garden with an almost straight-up view of the Acropolis and a corner of the Parthenon. Xenos stayed below to welcome his guests. After that, they always ate on the lower level, to talk with him and to marvel both at his ability to identify the nationality of the people who came up his walk and

at his proficiency in greeting and talking with them in one of the
six languages he spoke.

Wandering through the cobbled passages, Anna was remembering the hours she had spent there with Paul, talking, planning
where they would go next, assuming without conscious thought
that they had a lifetime ahead of them. She wondered, as she
made her way down Nikodimou Street past familiar landmarks, if
this was a mistake. Was it necessary to go to Xenos' when there
were so many other restaurants in the Plaka without memories?
Was it masochistic? The urge to go back to the hotel almost made
her turn in her tracks. A fleeting wish that Sam were along to give
her support warmed her for a moment, but was quickly rejected
as she remembered that he was the reason she was here in Athens.

Squaring her shoulders as she turned the corner at Lysiou
Street, she walked resolutely toward the stairs, hoping against
hope that Xenos would be there. She was not disappointed. He
was standing on the slanted landing above, his white apron fluttering with the tablecloths in the breeze. When she got closer, his
face broke into a smile of recognition and he quickly walked
down the steps with both hands out.

"Welcome, Ahnnah. It is good to see you back in Athens."
He looked behind her. "And Mr. Sandoval?"

Anna took his hands and looked into his dark eyes.

His iron gray hair had receded farther back at the temples,
but he hadn't changed much otherwise. Looking at her, his kindly
face lost its expectant smile. It was replaced by a questioning expression and then, after a close search of Anna's face, a closed-
eyed nod of understanding. He pressed her hands, looking down.

"He died, Xenos. Last year."

"I am sorry, *Kyria*." He took her arm. "Please," he said as he
led her to the table where she and Paul always sat. He left her and
went through the door into the kitchen, coming out a few moments later with a bottle of Naoussa Boutari and two glasses. He
uncorked the bottle and poured a glass for each of them. "You
came back."

Anna smiled. "How could I resist?"

"Life is not always happy. It is too bad when these things happen." He shook his head. "Too bad." He looked mournful.

"Give me something to eat, Xenos, some of that wonderful kebab of lamb and a Greek salad. That would make me happy right now."

He served her with a flourish. Between settling other customers at surrounding tables and giving orders in the kitchen, he told her that his brother was ill and that his daughter had given him another grandchild.

Later, as he served her caramel cream and coffee, he said, "You were right to come here. Not to be afraid of places you and your husband enjoyed together. It will help you to make a new life."

"How do you know this?"

"My wife, she died many years ago. I know."

Anna reached for his hand as he stood beside her, and held it against her cheek for a moment. "You are a good friend, Xenos."

"I am honored that you came."

Back in the hotel, Anna felt as if a weight had been lifted from a corner of her heart. She was too keyed up to sleep. She paced around, turning on the piped-in music and switching between the channels. But nothing satisfied. Finally she got out some sketches.

One large piece of paper was covered with several studies of a scene she had observed on a busy street not far from the hotel. She had noticed a young couple near a bus stop. They were unhappy. The boy, who could have been no older than nineteen or twenty, stood rigid, his face frozen in stoicism. The girl clung to his arm, holding back tears.

In a few minutes, a lumbering bus filled with other young men, some in military uniforms, had pulled up to a rumbling stop. The boy picked up his battered suitcase and gave the girl what began as a perfunctory hug but became a lingering kiss and tender embrace applauded by the men on the bus. Abruptly, he pushed her away and swung onto the bus, falling into a seat next to the window. As the bus pulled slowly away, he reached out for her, his hair blowing backward over his forehead. The girl ran alongside the moving bus, her hand also outstretched.

Anna had caught the action on paper. Their fingers had just slid apart. The boy was laughing for the benefit of his comrades. The girl's face, in profile, had crumpled.

Anna looked at the picture. She had later done the girl's face from several side angles, with a blur of lines and only the window in heavier detail framing the boy's false laugh. What was missing?

It was so frustrating. She knew the drawing was okay. Anyone could tell what it was. But that wasn't enough. It needed something, something to give it life.

Anna studied the drawing for a long time. Then, as if she had heard a whisper from one of the Muses of Philopappos, she picked up a white pencil, sharpened it to a pinpoint, and, in one tiny stroke, drew in the barest edge of a tear on the young man's face. She sat the drawing on a chair and stepped back from it. It was only then that she realized that she had drawn a likeness of a young Paul and that the girl's springy, dark curls had come loose from the ribbon holding them back, just as hers always did.

Anna felt as if she had a harp in her chest and someone had run their fingers across all the strings. At that moment, in her hotel room, she smelled the pungent odor of diesel fuel and hot metal. She felt the wind. And she could taste the salt of tears. She went to bed and fell sound asleep.

The next day, she was awakened by the phone. "I'm sorry to be calling so early," she heard Gwen Berkley say, "but I wanted to catch you before you went out. I remember how you're always out exploring. Tomorrow I'm having a little gathering for a few of the girls and I want you to come so they can meet you."

How like Gwen to put it that way.

"About two o'clock. Okay? Very informal. Bring your suit if you want to swim. We're going to eat out by the pool."

Anna promised to be there, and then after a long shower, she called for room service and had breakfast on her balcony. She had tried to call Christine and Peter but was able only to leave messages in both places. She wished there was some way to get them over here, but she knew they were both totally involved with their lives. Peter was so like Paul. And Christine was so like . . . so like herself. Anna poured a large cup of American-style coffee and leaned back with her feet on the railing. It would be nice to have Maggie here. She went in and found some hotel stationery. Back on the balcony she took a sip of coffee and wrote, "Dear Mags, I wish . . ." For a long time she looked out across the tile rooftops and thought about her time here in Greece. There was too much to write in a letter. Too many uncertainties, unknowns. Memories of Crete played in her mind and she knew she couldn't leave Greece without going back. She wondered if Sam was still there. What must he be thinking? She thought of Demetri and Maria and felt a longing to see them. The jangle of the phone startled her out of her reverie. She ran in to answer it, thinking it was one of the children.

"Hello!" she gasped.

"Hello, this is Alexis. Alexis Sarkis. Are you all right? You sound somewhat breathless."

Alexis? Oh, the architect. "I'm fine," Anna said. "I've been out on the balcony. It's a beautiful day."

"Yes, it is. I am calling to ask if you would like to accompany me to a performance of *Aïda* at the Odeon tomorrow evening. Several people are going together. I know this is short notice, but I have the tickets and I thought since you have just arrived in Athens . . . Well, it's being done by an Italian opera company and . . ."

A date? Was he asking her for a date? No, it was just a group of friends. He was being kind to a visitor, that's all. "How thoughtful of you to think of me. It should be wonderful. I heard them rehearsing when I went to the Parthenon a few days ago."

"Why don't I bring the car by for you at eight thirty for the nine o'clock performance? Then we will go to dinner afterward with my friends at the Themistocles Restaurant. They have wonderful shrimp there. And calamari. How does that sound to you?"

"That sounds wonderful. I'll look forward to it," Anna heard herself say. She hung up the phone in a state of bemusement. Probably, his date had canceled. But it would be a pleasure to hear that beautiful soprano with a party of people. She fell back across the bed and found herself smiling with relief. It would be a full day. Gwen's afternoon "gathering of girls," then the opera. Coming to Athens was a good move, she decided.

Fourteen

When Anna arrived at Gwen Berkley's house, there were already several women sitting around the pool. Two blue umbrellas threw circles of shade on those who wanted to avoid the sun. Three women were in the water.

"Did you bring your suit?" Gwen asked.

"With this hair?" Anna laughed. "I'm going out tonight. I'd never get it back together in time. But I do intend to soak up some sun." She patted her big straw handbag. "Shorts in here."

"You can change upstairs in our room," Gwen said. "When you come down, I'll introduce you around." She smiled. "It's so good to have you back."

Anna found the bathroom in the master bedroom and slipped into a pair of shorts and a halter top. She hung her skirt over a towel rack. A bathroom scale stared up at her from the floor with its one eye.

On impulse, she slipped out of her sandals and stepped on it, holding her breath. Then she stepped off and back on again. She had lost seven pounds! She looked up at herself in the mirror, patting her firmer behind in congratulation. All that climbing up and down the trail to the beach in Crete hadn't been for nothing.

Out on the terrace, Gwen took her from group to group, giving a little introductory speech that carefully avoided mentioning Anna's recent widowhood. Most of the women at the party were in Athens because of their husbands' jobs in the foreign service or diplomatic corps. They appeared to be women of leisure, with servants to do their housework and help with the children. Their days, to hear them talk, were filled with rounds of tennis, trips to the beach, bridge, and little luncheons like this one, and, of course, giving and appearing at cocktail parties and dinners by the score. But Anna knew different. She knew they were, in many ways, unpaid facilitators of their husbands' careers, on call twenty-four hours a day. Anna knew the demands of that job intimately. And entertaining all the time could become wearisome.

Anna was very much at ease in this atmosphere, and yet she felt, strangely, that she was standing aside watching herself, seeing the Anna of the present wearing vestiges of the past. She had forgotten how it felt to be immersed in the social whirl and politics surrounding government officials. She smiled as she listened to the light banter and chatter, but she felt somehow out of place. When she had come here two years ago with Paul, she hadn't even noticed this social-calendar way of life. It had all seemed quite natural then. Now it sounded tedious.

Gwen handed her a cool, fruity drink and, at the sound of the doorbell, left her on her own, so Anna sank into the closest chaise longue in the sun. Ripples of laughter punctuated the animated conversation. She stretched her legs out. She wondered if she could ever get used to this life again.

"Glorious weather, isn't it?" Anna turned to find a small, vivacious woman in her early thirties. "I'm Sally Hudson," she said. She explained that she was in Greece on a Fulbright Fellowship. She had just started explaining her program to Anna when Gwen came out of the house with someone else.

Anna glanced over and saw that the newcomer was a young woman looking very ill at ease. She was lovely, her skin glowing from the sun. Her shining honey-colored hair was medium length and hung in soft natural curls—no perm could get that effect. But the most distinctive thing about her was the color of her eyes. They were green, shaded by long, thick lashes. Her blouse, tucked loosely into skintight jeans, exactly matched her eyes.

"Taylor Douglas, this is Anna Sandoval," Gwen said. "Anna is from Washington, and according to her, she is a returning tourist to Greece. I've known her for years, but I haven't seen her since the last time she was here with her hus—"

Gwen bit her lip and looked at Anna apologetically.

"My late husband," Anna said gently. "And you? How do you happen to be in Athens?"

"I'm a flight attendant."

Strange that she should be here at Gwen's get-together, Anna thought. She looked at Gwen. "How did you—?"

"I met Taylor at a party at the embassy a couple of weeks ago. She was with a new friend of ours, one of the people who is working with everyone in Athens on security at the airport." Gwen added, "Then I ran into her yesterday and she said she has some time off, so"—she laughed—"the more the merrier, I always say."

How like Gwen. Athens' American hostess personified. She certainly hadn't lost her knack for picking up strays and making them feel at home, Anna observed, remembering this quality from her last visits.

Taylor smiled, adding a dimple in one cheek to her winsome good looks. She even had perfect teeth. "Glorified waitress is what I really am," she said. "But"—she gestured around—"here I am in Greece. The fringe benefits are nice." She followed Gwen to another table. The Fulbright scholar had wandered away.

Anna looked out across the pool. It had not been hard to say "my late husband" to cover Gwen's embarrassment. In fact, it came out quite naturally. But the aftermath of saying those words weighed heavily in Anna's breast. She felt on the fringes of all these married women, not quite one of them any longer. She took a sip of her drink.

"Is something wrong?" Anna looked up and she found herself staring into the green eyes of Taylor, who was settling into the chair beside her.

She forced herself to smile. "No, everything's fine."

"You looked so downcast I thought maybe you were thinking of your husband."

This girl certainly wasn't afraid to rush in where other people feared to tread. "I guess I was, in a way."

"It must be very sad to visit a place you've been to together."

"Yes. But one can't avoid everything forever." Anna smiled and asked Taylor about her home and family. Launched, Taylor, as articulate as she was beautiful, talked at length about her life.

"Is this your first visit to Athens?" Anna asked.

"I've flown here before. You know, just stayed long enough to get caught up on my sleep and eat a good Greek meal, then off to Tel Aviv or Cairo and home again." She took the glass of Perrier brought over by Gwen's maid. "This is my first vacation here."

"It's a nice place to vacation. You have everything—culture, beauty, nightlife—"

"A lot of good nightlife is doing me." Taylor turned to Anna, her eyes like cut glass behind her dark lashes. "Mrs. Sandoval, could I ask you something? Were you happily married?"

Anna smiled in relief. She liked this girl. She hadn't run into such frank, refreshing honesty since Maria. "Maybe you should call me Anna," she said, turning and leaning against the arm of her chair. "Yes, to answer your question. I was"—she swallowed—"very happily married. Not that it was perfect. No human relationship is perfect. Why do you ask?"

"How did you—how did that happen? How can you make a marriage happy? So many I've known about aren't."

"I'm not sure I can answer that to your satisfaction. The rules change over time, you know. In my family, I was taught that when you married, you followed your husband's plans. Became wife and mother first and foremost—helpmate, homemaker, darner of socks, ironer of shirts, stayer at home to be taken care of."

"That must be nice."

"Well, it was," Anna said. "To dedicate your entire life and ambitions to another person and your children. That was my job. I just accepted that and I enjoyed it." She thought for a minute. "But today, there are other pressures. Women have been liberated to not only do all that but have a career as well . . . if that can be called liberation." She looked over at Taylor. "Are you planning to get married?"

"Don't I wish." She suddenly looked shy.

"And who is this lucky man?"

"He's an old friend, really. He came over here on business so I decided to take this time to—" She looked at Anna, frowning, then said in a petulant voice, "We were having such a good time. I only have this short vacation. Then suddenly he said he had to go on a trip. Alone. Does that make sense to you?"

Picturing a dashing young man to go with this . . . this raving beauty, Anna grinned. In a way, this whole conversation had a ring of familiarity. How many times she had listened to her young daughter, with the abandoned self-centeredness of young adulthood, rattle on and on about her current passion. "How old are you, Taylor?"

"Thirty-one," Taylor wailed. "I'll be thirty-two in December and . . ." She ran her fingers through her curls and then drummed them on the table. "I just don't understand him. I've been going with him for a whole year." Taylor frowned a pretty pout. Everything this girl did made her even more beautiful. A "whole year" to a thirty-one-year-old seems an eternity, Anna remembered.

"I come all the way to Athens to be with him." Her graceful, manicured hands carved her story in the air. "But he goes off and I don't even hear from him for days."

"Maybe he wanted to think things over."

"Yeah, I guess." Taylor looked away, shaking her head. "But I'll find out what's going on tonight at—"

Gwen was calling from the porch, "Time for lunch. It's buffet, so grab a plate and dig in."

As Anna stood up, though, Taylor put her hand on Anna's arm. "Thanks for listening." Then she added shyly, "It was almost like having my mother here."

That evening before going to the opera with Alexis, Anna gave herself a once-over in the full-length bathroom mirror. She had chosen a dress that flared from a snug waist and with its almost-revealing V-neck would hardly have passed for widow's weeds. I hope I don't remind *him* of his mother, she thought.

As Anna stepped off the elevator, Alexis smiled. His eyes

swept her from head to foot in obvious approval. She held out her hand to shake his in greeting, but he bent over it, kissing the air just above it as one does royalty.

Her ego somewhat restored, she slid into the leather seat of his low Mercedes sports coupe convertible. He handed her a white scarf to put over her hair as they drove along the National Garden to the Odeon.

"I apologize again for asking you at the last moment," he said. "I had this planned before I met you and the tickets were sold out so I couldn't invite you at the party the other night. But I have a friend"—he gave her a sideways smile—"who was able to get me another, though it took some time. I'm glad you could join me . . . us."

"I'm rather impulsive myself, so I was delighted with your spur-of-the-moment invitation."

Alexis wheeled into a parking space, jumped out of the car, and came around to open Anna's door. When he took her hand to help her out, he said, "You look lovely tonight." His perfect English was rounded with his Greek accent. He looked splendid himself. He ran his fingers through his short, crisply curling hair.

They were the first of the party to arrive, and after Alexis had seated Anna, he asked to be excused to go to the entrance to greet his other guests. As she waited, she looked around at the people filing into the semicircle of steeply tiered marble seats.

The orchestra was warming up, and the air was alive with that special preperformance magic. Anna was too busy watching the activity around her to notice when Alexis returned with a group of people. When she did turn in his direction, she was staring straight at Sam McDonald, his craggy face dark as a storm-tossed sea.

Taylor was hanging on to his arm as if she would never let him go, smiling and waving at Anna with a dazzling show of her perfect teeth. Then Anna remembered the last thing Taylor had said earlier—"I'll know tonight." She meant Sam was coming back tonight. Sam!

At first Sam didn't see Anna. He was checking his ticket

stubs, looking for their seat. When he did notice her, he visibly flinched, his mournful eyes flying open.

"Anna, I didn't know you were going to be here," Taylor called out. "This is Sam, the one I was telling you about."

Sam looked at Taylor in horror and then back at Anna, his eyebrows raised in question, a rising panic in his eyes.

Anna actually felt her heart thud. Trying to maintain a cool smile, she held out her hand. "Sam, so nice to—"

"Uh, Taylor, Anna and I are, uh, friends." Anna glared. "That is, we, uh, met in Crete and—"

Taylor's lovely mouth hung open as she stared at Anna. "You never told me. I—"

"I had no idea this was who you were talking about. I don't believe you said his name."

Taylor's expression relaxed, but she kept her hold on Sam's arm. Sam had put on his half-glasses to examine his tickets. "Let's see, number twenty-four and twenty-five." He looked at the numbers marked on the front of each seat. "Here they are." They were the two seats next to Anna's right. Alexis had already claimed the seat to her left.

Sam sputtered, first guiding Taylor into the seat next to Anna, then, thinking better of it, pushing her toward the next place and seating himself beside Anna. He took a deep breath and said, "Nice evening, isn't it?"

Anna's mind raced like a time-lapse video, scenes of Crete flashing one after the other, interspersed with scenes of beautiful Taylor at the swimming party saying, *I've been going with him for a whole year!* In all their time together in Crete, Sam had never even hinted about this young woman. She remembered their quiet dinners, their long drives, their easy conversation at meals in her courtyard, afternoons at the beach down the path from . . . Anna flinched as the picture of skinny-dipping that last night reeled through her mind in living color. She cut a sidewise glance over at Sam and saw that Taylor was holding his hand tightly.

Was I just a one-night stand for him? Was his portrayal of the lonely widower a pretense? Was I just a convenient . . . a vulnera-

ble, available . . . just a girl in that particular port? Damn! It was so maddening. *Why didn't he tell me about her?* It was the deception that was so disappointing. *All that time in Crete while he was going on about his poor dead wife, he had this . . . this raving beauty waiting for him in Athens. A girl, barely past puberty. And I, the empathetic widow, let him lure me . . . let myself get sucked into this charade.*

Alexis slipped into the seat on Anna's left.

"Do you think they'll have elephants in this one?" someone asked loudly. "When I saw this opera at the Baths in Rome, they had a chariot with six horses and elephants in the 'Triumphal March.' "

"Wonder if they'll also need an ass?" Anna asked under her breath, hoping Sam heard.

"What did you say?" Alexis asked.

"I was just asking about the handling of donkeys and other beasts in this opera," she said.

"Oh. I'm not sure." Then he added, "Most of the people have arrived. I'll introduce them to you later."

Sam turned toward Anna, pulling at his tie as if to straighten the knot. "I need to talk with you," he whispered.

Just then the conductor came out, the crowd applauded, and the overture began. It was beautiful. The tenor part of Radames matched the pure, ringing voice of the soprano who played Aïda. It was an excellent performance, but Anna found it hard to concentrate on the music when she was so aware of Sam sitting next to her. Not only for his just being there. That was bad enough. But he was actually enjoying the opera, his eyes often closed, a beatific smile on his face. He swayed to the music, sometimes bumping Anna, his fingers directing the orchestra, his head nodding. Anna could have wrung his neck.

Alexis sat perfectly still, as if in deep meditation. The only indication that he was moved by the performance was a quickening of his breath in the dramatic scenes. At the intermissions, Anna stayed with Alexis and was introduced to at least a dozen people. When the opera was over and the crowd stood, as one, in ovation,

Sam yelled "Bravo! Bravo!" at the top of his lungs. Alexis applauded with dignity, more intensely as the performers took their bows.

After the last round of applause, he said to the group around him, "Let's meet at the Themistocles." He took Anna's arm and, instead of going to the main entrance with the throng, led her down onto the stage and spoke to a man in work clothes who was loudly giving orders to someone. He stopped shouting long enough to smile and, saying something in Greek, gave Alexis a single-finger salute and pointed to the stage door. Exiting through it, they were no more than twenty yards from the car.

The outer entrance to the Themistocles Restaurant Disco was a nondescript door on the street. Anna and Alexis made their way along a narrow hallway and down a flight of stairs to get to the restaurant. Just inside the door, a giant glass display counter, like one found in a butcher shop, touted dozens of attractively arranged fish and shellfish, vegetables, and fruit on crushed ice. Beside it, two spits turned a leg of lamb and a shank of beef. At the far end were desserts of every description.

Alexis spoke to the maître d', who pointed down a row of tables to a balcony overlooking the dance floor, where there was a semiprivate grouping of tables, empty and waiting. Alexis chose seats for them facing the entrance.

When the others arrived, Anna couldn't believe they included Taylor and Sam, who came in with another couple. Alexis waved and motioned them to sit down at the first table, where he and Anna were seated. "That is Kristofonos Lombardiaris and his wife, Olga. Kristofonos, once Greek ambassador to Egypt, is now on the government commission that investigates terrorist activities. The couple with them," he said, indicating Sam and Taylor, "are Sam McDonald and Taylor . . . I can't remember her last name but I believe they sat next to you at the performance."

"Yes," Anna said. "We've met."

Alexis ordered for the group—hors d'oeuvres of dolmades (grape leaves stuffed with rice) and *mesedakia*, an assortment of pickled olives and onions, cheese, and pieces of calamari. The main dish was shrimp wrapped in bacon and grilled over char-coal. They had chocolate torte for dessert.

She had just taken her last bite of the sinfully delicious torte—thin, hard chocolate laced with amaretto between many layers of cake and topped with heavy whipped cream. Before she could swallow, Alexis took her hand and pulled her onto the dance floor. Disco music throbbed.

She tried to pull back, swallowing and wiping her mouth, shaking her head. But, laughing, he got her out onto the floor and started moving to the music.

Anna loved to dance. In eighth grade, she had been required to learn ballroom dancing, and though she complained along with the rest of her friends, she had loved it. At parties, she easily mas-tered the twisting, writhing, freestyle movements of hard rock and disco. But Paul didn't dance. She could never understand it—he was such a good athlete—but after a few tries, she had to agree he was terrible on the dance floor. So Anna hadn't danced in years.

Alexis was a bold, confident dancer. Anna, feeling rusty and self-conscious, simply kept time to the beat by stepping from one foot to the other. *I can't do this,* she thought. But as Alexis kept giving her little "come on" gestures with his hands, showing her movements, she tried them and found that her body almost knew what to do. After a few tentative sways and turns, she yielded to the beat. When they sat down, she was pleasantly winded.

Alexis looked at her with admiration. "You had me fooled. I thought, at first, that you couldn't dance. But I think you are a professional."

"I was only following your lead," she answered, trying un-successfully to tuck back a lock of unruly hair. It was no use. It was all about to fall down. She excused herself to go to the ladies' room and fasten it back up.

She was just putting the combs back in when Taylor burst through the door, her earlier glow clouded by a frown. When she saw Anna, relief flooded her face. "I'm so glad you're here," she said. "I don't know what to do."

"About what?"

"Well." Taylor was holding her lipstick in her hand like a candle. "How long have you known Sam?"

Anna searched her face. *Is she angry? Does she suspect—?* "I only met him a couple of weeks ago in Crete. I really don't know him, uh, well." *The hell I don't!*

"He's acting very strange."

"Older men sometimes get like that," Anna said. "You have to humor them." She shut her purse and headed for the door.

"He's not that old."

She's right, Anna thought. *And there's no reason for me to be curt with this young woman.* She was annoyed with Sam, that old snake in the grass, not Taylor. "Listen, why don't you give him a few days to recover from his trip to Crete? Maybe he's just tired."

"That's what he said. He's too tired to even—"

"Give him a few days," Anna interrupted. She did not want to hear what he was too tired to even do.

Taylor finished her sentence anyway. "—dance."

"Well, just sit and talk. Now, come on," she said, opening the door for Taylor, "try to enjoy the rest of the evening."

Alexis beamed at her as she made her way through the tables back to her chair. "I've been thinking," he said when she sat down. "Do you like boats?"

The question took Anna by surprise. "What kind of boats?"

"I have a small cruiser," he said. "On next Thursday, my cousin and his wife, and perhaps their son, are coming with me to Hydra. Just for the day. Would you like to come along?"

"Well . . ."

"And while you think about it, how about dinner tomorrow night? I know a place in the Plaka away from the tourist area where they do Greek dances. Have you ever danced the *sirtaki*?" His direct gaze was both disturbing and flattering.

"No. I haven't."

"I'll teach you."

"That would be nice," Anna said. "I'd like that."

"I'll come for you at—" He thought for a moment. "Shall we be really Greek and say nine thirty?"

"If I can stay awake."

"You must learn to sleep late in Greece. We go by different time here."

"I've noticed."

"Well, it's settled then." He stood up. "Would you like to dance again?"

Anna smiled and nodded. It got easier. The music penetrated her whole body, becoming as much a part of her as her own pulse. With Alexis smiling at her, they gyrated through two more numbers. Then the band changed pace with a slow, crooning song. It seemed only natural to move into the circle of his arms. He was light on his feet with a powerful lead, swirling and dipping, then drawing her close and swaying.

It was almost as if her feet were not touching the floor. The texture of the shoulder of his jacket was rough under her fingers, the pressure of his hand behind her back firm and steadying. When the music stopped, they stood for a moment, suspended. Then Anna realized they were the only ones on the floor and laughed as she pulled away and walked back to the table.

They sat with coffee through the next few numbers. From time to time, Alexis excused himself and moved among his guests, making sure everything was all right. Once he said he had to make a phone call. When the music changed to a slow tempo again, Anna saw Alexis hurrying back to their table. At that moment, she heard Sam's voice from above her head, "May I have this dance?"

Anna was tempted to say no, but that would have been awkward for both of them. She caught a glimpse of Taylor's solemn face as he led her onto the floor.

As soon as Sam took her in his arms she said, "You are a fake of the first order."

"Don't you think I know that?" He cleared his throat. "Actually, I am a confused fake of the first order, that's what I am. And an ass, as you so correctly mentioned at the opera. I admit it." Anna started to turn away, but he gripped her hand and pulled her closer. "You have every right to be mad."

"Don't tell me about my rights."

"I don't blame you at all."

"Blame me? Blame me for what?"

"For being angry at me."

"For being angry at you," Anna stated deliberately in measured tones.

"You left Crete so suddenly."

"I'm convinced it wasn't sudden enough. I stayed one day too long."

"Oh, Anna."

"Don't 'Oh, Anna' me, you . . . you fraud. The poor lonely widower!" she said, looking over at Taylor.

He whirled her around, then held her away from him, looking into her eyes. "You're right. I am a fiend."

"The only reason I am not stomping off this dance floor right now is that I don't want to embarrass that poor girl over there. I don't even want to talk to you."

"Please, Anna. Don't turn me away without hearing me out. I wanted to tell you—"

"I had a very interesting conversation with your *girlfriend* this afternoon," Anna interrupted. "She is the one you need to talk to. Not me."

"You talked with Taylor?"

"Yes. She wondered why you were in Crete for so long without her."

"Anna, come to Delphi with me tomorrow."

"What?"

"I need to talk to *you*. And the only way I can get rid of Taylor is to tell her I have to go somewhere."

"Get rid of her? She thinks you two are an item." Anna was talking through her teeth.

"Shhh," Sam said, looking around to see if anyone heard.

"Well?"

"I do . . . I did . . . I don't . . . I don't know what to say. Please, just let me talk with you. Come with me, tomorrow."

"I can't."

"You can't?" Sam's eyes were filled with dismay.

"I have other plans."

Now his look was pleading, his large mouth turned down at the corners. Desperation showed in his tired, sad eyes. "Sunday?"

Anna couldn't stand it. She could feel herself giving in. *Don't do it,* she cautioned herself. "I can't go on Sunday either." Maybe if she put him off long enough, she could get out of this.

"Well, what about Monday?" He shook his head. "No, god-damn it, I have a meeting Monday."

"I think I have something . . . somewhere I have to go too."

"Have you ever been to Delphi?"

"No."

"Well, I have and I could show it to you. On Tuesday."

"Sa-am." She tried to give him a stern look.

"Please." It was the hangdog eyes that got her.

"Okay, Sam," Anna said. "Just for the day. Tuesday."

He led her back to her table. "Thanks," he said.

It was four in the morning when Alexis drove her back to the hotel and walked her into the lobby. "Thank you for coming with me," he said.

"It was lovely."

"Until tomorrow."

When Anna opened the door to her suite, she was assaulted by flowers. Four large arrangements, in a variety of colors and kinds, had been placed around the sitting room. Even on the bathroom counter a sprawling bouquet of yellow daisies stood out against the dark walls like lights. The air was spiced with their sharp scent.

There was only one card. "Welcome to Athens. Alexis," it said. When had he ordered all these? Anna wondered, filling the tub in the fragrant bathroom. She felt giddy as she slid into the hot water, thinking about the whole evening. *Ah, that phone call at the restaurant. That's when he ordered the flowers.*

She stayed in the bath until she almost fell asleep. Slipping on her white robe of watered silk, she went into the sitting room and switched on the hotel radio to a channel of soft music, then opened the curtains to the light-spattered darkness of the city, the eastern sky a deep violet with approaching dawn. A clarinet played a melody woven around a soft background of guitar music. Anna, standing at her window, could feel her body begin to move. Then, arms up, she danced, her robe flowing around her like water in the cool air. Lifted on the ebullience of her spirits, she let the music carry her still further and danced until light filled the window.

Fifteen

Anna dressed for her evening in the Plaka with Alexis with the spirit of derring-do. Feeling festive and adventurous, she wore her hair loose, something she almost never did. Alexis called up from the lobby promptly at nine thirty as he had promised. Seeing his smile as Anna stepped from the elevator lifted her spirits even higher.

They went first to a roof-garden restaurant, where they ate under the stars while a handsome man in traditional Greek dress played his bouzouki beneath a grape arbor in the corner. The clusters of grapes, still green, hung above them in the flickering candlelight.

After dinner, feeling light-headed with wine and fully satiated with food, Anna walked along the winding streets on Alexis' arm, browsing through shops and galleries. She was in a very mellow mood. She had no past, no future. Time had stopped.

In one little parklike square they passed a figure draped in flowing orange cloth dancing on six-foot stilts. The only music was the beat of a primitive drum played by an intense young man squatting on the curb. Anna and Alexis stopped to watch. Anna couldn't tell whether the person on stilts was a man or a woman. The face was painted mime white. The body was completely disguised by the robes. But whoever it was moved gracefully, with flowing motions, high above the gathering crowd, never once stumbling on the uneven cobblestones. There was something that intrigued her about the dancer with the gossamer, translucent orange costume fluttering like the wings of a strange cosmic bird.

The drumbeat filled her head. It was all she could do to keep herself from dancing to the rhythm.

"You never know what you will see here late at night," Alexis said, leading Anna away after they had watched awhile. She was reluctant to leave.

Alexis led her to a flight of stairs descending into a smoky basement, where rough wooden tables were scattered helter-skelter around a plank dance floor. As they entered, a torch singer was belting out a bluesy song in a low, gravelly voice.

They settled at a table in a far corner and Alexis ordered retsina for both of them. "If this is to be a true Greek evening, you must drink like a Greek."

To Anna, the wine was like turpentine. But after a few sips, her mouth became numb to the taste. The people in the bistro, she noticed, were mostly Greek and mostly men.

The singer sustained her last note with arms outstretched, then bowed and left the stage. Then the lights came up and a bouzouki band strummed into the room. Several young men, arms around one another's shoulders, sidestepped and leaped out onto the floor. After demonstrating their athletic prowess in a dance that was much like an old vaudeville routine, one dancer doing something complicated, the other trying to outdo him, one of the men stepped to the microphone and made an announcement in Greek.

Alexis stood. He took off his jacket and rolled up the sleeves of his shirt. "Excuse me," he said, giving Anna a curt bow. With several others, he joined the men on the stage. He could have been one of the dance troupe. They started out arms over shoulders, in a long line, swinging their legs to one side and then the other with slow dips and precise footwork. Then the music picked up tempo. All the dancers, including Alexis, were as nimble as gymnasts. With agility that defied gravity, they took turns leaping, their feet moving faster and faster.

Alexis was beautiful. His broad, muscular shoulders moved under the pure white of his shirt, open at the collar. He had tied his handkerchief of dark blue around his head as a sweatband.

The muscles of his thighs bunched as he vaulted and bounded about with the others. When he came back to the table, breathing hard, his smile was radiant with pride.

"That was wonderful," Anna said. "You must have been doing these dances all your life."

"I guess it's in my blood," he said. "My grandparents on my mother's side were peasants. And could they dance! I used to spend summers on Rhodes with them, back in the hills." He tossed down his glass of retsina and poured another from the carafe, filling Anna's glass too, over her protests.

When the band began another lively tune, Alexis pulled Anna onto the dance floor. "But I don't know these dances," she wailed.

"I'll show you. They are simple."

Anna found this to be true. The movements were repetitive and after she watched the other dancers carefully for a while, she found it had gotten into her blood too. Then later, when a light-disco group replaced the band, she and Alexis danced without stopping until Anna thought she was going to drop.

As they walked out of the taverna in the predawn light, Alexis looked for a taxi to take them back to his car parked on the far side of the Plaka. Anna said, "Let's walk back to the hotel." She was tired and footsore, but the night air was cool and delightful, and it was only a few blocks to the Apollo. She wanted to hang on to the mood of the evening a little longer. They strolled along, hand in hand, looking in the windows of the fashionable shops along the side streets, down to Ermou, the street leading to Syntagma Square.

A sleepy vendor was selling rounds of sesame-dotted bread shaped like doughnuts the size of dinner plates. Alexis bought one that was still warm from the oven for them to share as they wandered back to the hotel.

They didn't talk until they climbed the hotel steps. There, Alexis bowed over Anna's hand. Straightening up, he touched her hair lightly, lifting one long tendril that lay curled on her shoulder, and slid his fingers down its length. "You would make a good Greek, Anna Sandoval."

"Thank you," she said. "For a moment back there, I felt that I was. It was quite a wonderful evening." Beyond him, she could see the light of the coming dawn outlining the buildings. "And morning."

"The pleasure was mine," he said, placing the lock of hair back on her shoulder. "Good evening. And morning." He turned and took the steps two at a time. From the sidewalk he said in his low voice, "Go get some rest, Anna. Then, if you would like, I will come for you this afternoon. There is a restaurant in the hills that serves the best lamb in the world, and I have somewhere I would like to take you. It is a favorite place of mine, the Kaisariani Monastery."

Anna was so tired and sleepy that she heard him planning her time as if in a dream. "That sounds . . . very nice." All she wanted to do was fall into bed.

"Good." He smiled and bowed again. "I'll be by to pick you up at two. Wear something comfortable to walk in." He waved. "Rest well."

Anna nodded to the doorman and crossed the luxurious lobby of the hotel, her feet hardly touching the ground. She was going to have to be careful not to drink so much of this strong wine, she thought.

Anna was awakened by the sound of drums beating. No, it wasn't sound. It was the sensation of drums, booming behind her eyes. She rolled over in her darkened room and looked at the clock. Eleven. God, her head hurt. Her mouth tasted like she'd been drinking house paint. She dragged herself to the shower.

A perky rosebud in a glass vase and a note from Alexis that said, "I hope the retsina didn't treat you too badly" accompanied her breakfast, brought up by room service. Had he known he was giving her poison? Anna rubbed her forehead. It was still there. Though her head was no longer aching after a couple of aspirin and a long, hot shower, her thoughts labored around in it as if they had to make their way through vaporous clouds of fumes.

She threw open the curtains and opened the French doors to her fifth-floor balcony, shading her eyes from the light. Sounds of traffic from the busy intersection, muted by distance, were accompanied by the trilling coo of pigeons perched on her balcony railing. The two-note monotony of an ambulance or a fire truck got louder and louder, then, as it moved away, was swallowed up in a sudden blast of horns and the clangor of a jackhammer.

Anna went back into the sitting room and fell onto the sofa, a stack of stationery propped against the drawing pad in her lap. Sipping the hot coffee, she stared out through the open doors at the clear, blue sky over Athens. Once again she had written, "Dear Maggie."

Three cups of coffee and two croissants later, she was back in the land of the living, but she hadn't added a word to her letter to Maggie. Finally, dressed in a cool shirt and slacks, her hair pulled back in a French roll, Anna grabbed her straw handbag and went downstairs. It was exactly two o'clock.

He was waiting. He didn't kiss Anna's proffered hand but drew her close and gave her a one-armed hug. He smelled faintly aromatic, just a hint of something spicy.

"I am furious at you, you know," Anna said, sliding into the front seat of his car.

"The retsina wasn't kind to you."

"Kind? I felt like a mule had kicked me in the head."

He looked at her with such concern that she smiled.

"I've recovered—except for feeling like I've had brain surgery and the doctors left in a cotton swab or something. But I am not drinking anything for a while."

"A drive in the country is what you need," he said, expertly guiding his car through what always seemed to be rush-hour traffic in Athens. "And a good meal of—"

"Nothing exotic. Please."

"—bread and cheese and—"

"No wine."

Alexis smiled. "Tea." Reaching back, he patted a wicker basket on the seat. "A picnic."

The route out of Athens was pitted with one pothole after another. The road took them past shabby, run-down, once-white buildings streaked with soot. Then they drove through a littered industrial area lined with junkyards, the roadside dusty and scattered with trash.

"Close your eyes through this district," Alexis said. He flipped a switch and the air was filled with the rhythms of a jazz guitar. "Just listen. Soon we'll be out of the city."

Anna did as he asked, sliding down in the seat, resting her head back, the sound of the purring engine and the guitar a pleasant diversion from the smell of engine exhaust.

"Now you can open them."

They were on a road that wound through a pine woods, the sun streaming through the tall trees in golden, mote-filled rays. Alexis pulled onto a dirt road and stopped near a clearing under the broad boughs of a particularly old and stately tree. He spread a blue-checkered cloth on the ground and got the promised loaf of bread and wedge of cheese out of the basket. After laying out napkins, he set a dark blue ceramic mug in front of Anna and filled it with steaming tea from a thermos.

The tea was sweet with mint and honey. Its warmth spread through her chest and seemed to rise into her head, clearing out the fuzziness. "How did you know this was just what I needed?" she asked. She leaned back on ground cushioned with fallen needles.

"I remember when retsina attacked my brain long ago, when I was a boy."

"It doesn't affect you anymore?"

"A Greek? Greeks develop stomachs lined with marble."

"I think I got started too late in life." It was the first time she had referred to her age.

Alexis let it pass. He took out a wide sandwich made of torn bread, a slab of cheese, and slices of cold beef. They both leaned against the tree trunk and finished the tea with peaches and little oatcakes that were crumbly and just barely sweet.

The sun was warm on Anna's face. It was one of those moments that was so quiet with beauty that when Alexis took her hand it was only a natural part of the ambience of the day. Neither of them said anything for a long time.

Finally Alexis sighed and said, "I want to take you to the Monastery of Kaisariani because it is one of the most beautiful places in all of Greece. Beautiful in utter simplicity." He pressed her hand.

They packed up the picnic basket and drove a mile or so to a parking lot, then walked along crumbling, rose-colored walls of ancient stonework and through the gate of the monastery. Anna could feel the peace of the place as soon as they entered the courtyard.

Walking on the smooth, irregular paving stones, laid by some mason hundreds of years before, she drank in the beauty of the church that stood in the center of the complex. As happened so often in this ancient country, she sensed the presence of the long-dead people who had built this place, the monks and abbots who had lived and worked and worshipped and died within these walls, their lives devoted to something greater than themselves.

The buildings were set in a square around the courtyard, the church central to all. Most of the plaster on its walls, Anna noticed, had long since been washed away, leaving rough unworked sandy-pink stone. The faded terra-cotta roof tiles, battered and lifted askew by wind and rain, still shielded the old building's two domes.

The quiet of the place was only emphasized by the songs of birds fluttering around in pine trees above the buildings. Even their twittering had a sacred clarity. Anna inhaled the peace. "Is it still used at all?"

"No, unfortunately not," Alexis said quietly. "Since the eleventh century, it has been through wars and revolutions, invasions by the Turks, then an invasion of nature, trying to reclaim it."

"When did it stop being used as a monastery?"

"In the mid–eighteen hundreds, I think." He pointed to the right where stairs led up to the gaping doors of monks' cells and opened onto a graceful, stone-pillared cloister.

"I think I would have liked being one of those monks," Anna said, "living in a place like this that is so welcoming and peaceful, it makes you want to create something. Makes you want to reach beyond yourself. I don't know. To—" Anna looked around as if she could find the words she wanted in the stones themselves. "It would be easy to believe in God, living in a place like this."

"I want to create buildings that make people say just that," Alexis said in almost a whisper. "So much of modern architecture is an assault on the human soul. Sterile glass and metal cubes and monoliths piercing the sky, mirroring the ugliness of buildings around them. Hallways that are squared-off tubes, with rows of closed doors, synthetic tile floors gleaming in fluorescent lighting, rooms with windows that don't open looking out onto parking lots. Buildings have been dehumanized, built for efficiency and function. But they defeat their purpose when they inspire dread in the people who have to work or live in them. They become a prison from which people want to escape."

"I've been in buildings like that," Anna said. "But some modern architecture is beautiful."

"Yes, you are right. When it is done well, no matter what period or style, any building can have beauty. I want to go one step further. I want my buildings to join the ranks of those that have grace and charm as well—and maybe a few details that aren't efficient at all, only beautiful. Come, let me show you the Chapel of St. Anthony."

They entered the cool interior of the church. To the side of the main nave, they found a tiny, dark chapel about eight feet wide and twelve feet long. A rough stone altar against the far wall was bare. Above it, a narrow arched window of nearly opaque amber glass was recessed into the thick stone walls. Through it, Anna could see only the silhouette of the tree branches beyond.

"It's beautiful."

"Yes. That narrow golden-paned window is what some people call a Zen view. Beautiful in itself—in its simplicity. Giving a glimpse of something even more beautiful beyond it. Just enough to make one want to stop and pray. That's what I'm talking about.

A room that makes people desire to do the very function the room was designed for."

He was quiet for so long that Anna wondered if he was praying. She looked at the way the light fell softly across the stone altar and the pattern of the tree moving behind the glass, and wished she had her pencils.

They walked out of the church and across the courtyard. "When I was in the States, I had the opportunity to study under a man called Christopher Alexander. He believes that architecture should reflect the patterns of nature, should become a part of its surroundings, part of the whole—as each thing in the ecology of nature is part of something larger. He believes buildings should be designed to enhance whatever will be taking place in them."

They walked across the courtyard to a building with tall chimneys and stepped through the door into a long room, bare except for a narrow stone table with low benches designed for a half-sitting, half-kneeling position. "This was the refectory where the monks ate their meals." He pointed to a room at the far end. "That was the kitchen."

Light slanted across one section of the table through an arched window. The monastery kitchen was bare. Huge ovens yawned, cold and dark, blackened with the memory of fire. But the refectory had captured Anna's imagination. She could almost hear the chanted prayers, see the cowled figures eating rich soups from wooden bowls in silence while someone read from an illuminated manuscript under the vaulted ceiling. Were they allowed to come here between meals to have a hot drink and visit with one another? It must have smelled heavenly, bread baking in those ovens. "I could easily linger over coffee here," Anna said.

Alexis nodded. He stood in front of the window, running his hands over the grid of iron grillwork, which once held panes of glass. His face was lit. "Small-paned windows are so much more pleasant to look through than great slabs of glass, don't you think?" he asked, musing. "And if they are carefully placed, framing something beautiful, the beauty is repeated many times."

"You're right," Anna said, looking through the window. "I've always liked small-paned windows, but I never knew why."

He smiled. "Some designs uplift the human spirit. But this building is . . ."

Alexis' voice faded as Anna became entranced with the light as it fell through the grilled window across the table, creating sharp shadows on the stone. *Why didn't I throw in my pad and pencils?* She needed to draw this room—with the spirits whose presence was so real sitting at the table. "Do you suppose they would have a piece of paper and a pencil in the office at the entrance?" She wasn't looking at Alexis. "Any kind of pencil."

Alexis frowned a little impatiently, and then shrugged. "I can ask."

He came back with a pad of lined paper with three pages left and the stub of a pencil with no eraser.

Anna sat down on the edge of a bench, feeling the cold seep through the cloth of her jeans. Quickly, she did studies of the room's perspective from different angles. Choosing the one that seemed most effective, she shaded in the shadows in front of and behind the shaft of sunlight streaming through the window. Then, lightly, she drew in two men, one with the cowl of his cloak up, the other with his thrown back, the light shining on his face as it had shone on Alexis' moments before. Each had a bowl at hand. The hooded one was gesturing, as if telling a tale. The other, his tonsure catching the edge of light, had an amazed look on his face.

While Anna drew, Alexis wandered out the door. She could hear him talking with someone just outside. Then she forgot about him.

"Anna, they want to close."

Startled, she looked up to see a look of genuine appreciation on Alexis' face as he stared down at her drawing.

"That is wonderful," he said. He glanced at his watch. "But we have to move quickly if we want to drink from the fountain before they close the gates."

Anna picked up her things and followed him outside and

around back to a fountain with water gushing from a ram's head. She was thirsty. "Is this water safe to drink?" she asked.

"It definitely is."

Cupping her hands, filling them with the cool water, she drank great drafts, water running down her chin.

"This fountain cures, among other things, sterility, and makes one very fertile," Alexis said.

Anna choked and sputtered as she turned, expecting him to be laughing at her. But his expression was dead serious. As she backed away, he drank from his own hands. Only then did he smile, and give her a wink.

They drove back into Athens with the music of Stevie Wonder filling the car. Once or twice, Anna glimpsed distant views of the Acropolis, the Parthenon golden in the late-afternoon sun.

"Kaisariani Monastery is a very special place for me," Alexis said. "A place of retreat," he added. "And, as it has been for many people over the years, sometimes a place of refuge." He cleared his throat, his low voice barely audible above the music. "I go there often, by myself, early in the morning when there are few people about, to soak up the peace." He paused and then went on. "It is one place I never take other people."

"Then why did you take me?"

He gripped the steering wheel, staring straight ahead at the road. "Because I knew you would love it too."

Around the next curve, they could see, on another high hill not far from the Acropolis, the little Church of St. George gleaming white on the craggy cliff. "Let's go to the restaurant up there and have something cool to drink," he suggested.

"I think I'd better get back to the ho—"

"We can watch the sunset," he said, ignoring Anna's protests.

Oh well . . . it was easier just to go along.

The funicular, a cable car that went almost straight up through a tunnel cut out of the hillside, whisked them up to a glorious view of Athens at the top. They walked by the little church and around to outdoor tables overlooking an almost straight plunge down to the city far below. Choosing a table near the wall, Alexis said, "I know exactly what to have." He ordered in Greek, not telling Anna what it would be.

"I hope it's nothing alcoholic." She laughed a little nervously.

The waiter brought frosty glasses of sweet coffee with large scoops of ice cream floating on top. It was delicious.

"Where would you like to have dinner tonight?"

"Alexis, I don't imagine that you will be able to understand this, but I'm ready to go to bed."

His eyes widened with amazement.

"I mean it," Anna laughed, and shook her head. "Take me back to the hotel and leave me. We came in at dawn this morning, and all this fresh air and"—she grinned—"all that wine last night have taken their toll on me. I think I'll bow out of another evening."

He didn't try to hide his disappointment, but he smiled and said, "At least let me buy you a small supper. You can't go to bed on an empty stomach. There is a place near my office—"

Anna was shaking her head. "You have fed me quite enough today."

He raised his hands, palms up in defeat. "Then promise me you'll let me take you to dinner tomorrow evening. Surely you'll be hungry by then."

Anna mimicked his gesture of defeat. "As long as it doesn't include retsina."

Back at the hotel, Anna found she couldn't sleep, even though she was bone tired. The ice-cream coffee had done its work. She wandered out into the sitting room and found her aborted letter to Maggie and decided to finish it. Under the salutation, written earlier, she started, "I would never in a million years have predicted the events that have taken place in my life since I came to Greece. You won't believe all that's . . ."

Sixteen

Alexis called Anna twice the next morning, just to see how she was doing, once as she was eating her Continental breakfast in bed and again an hour later, just as she finished dressing. He had to be the most eligible bachelor in Athens. Why was he showering her with all this attention?

"Of course I'm fine," she answered. "How about you? Don't you ever work?"

"I am at work."

"Oh." She tried to picture him behind a desk. "Alexis, the flowers are beautiful."

"About dinner tonight. You must be hungry after not eating last night."

"No retsina."

"I'll be by at nine o'clock."

"Fine. That will be fine. I'll see you then." Anna hung up, shaking her head, smiling. Why would he be calling her all the time? Was he really just being nice to a visitor? Why was he even free? There must be a line of young women waiting and hoping. *This is a mystery I'd like to get to the bottom of.* She walked over to her balcony, reaching up for a long stretch, breathing in the energy of the day. She couldn't wait to get out. She scooped up her pencil box and pad and headed for the Plaka, wanting to get there while the morning light was still pure and the shadows were distinct.

Wandering aimlessly, she found herself in the Monastiraki Flea Market, narrow streets of dark shops and stalls crowding one another along the curbs. They sold everything from camping equipment to herbs. She even saw a stack of cheap Evzone shoes with pom-poms on the toes, and next to that a rack of baseball hats with propellers on top. Some shops sold dubious antiques and secondhand furniture from their shadowy depths.

Walking quickly along, she discovered a break in the mean little buildings and was surprised, as she so often was in Athens, by a stately ruin, a row of Doric columns on three sides of what was once a courtyard or square paved with marble. The paving stones, some broken with scraggly grass growing through their cracks, gleamed, smooth and polished in the sun. A group of boys nine to twelve years old were playing an abbreviated form of soccer in the flat area in front of the columns, using garbage cans for goalposts. Anna stopped to watch.

How many activities had these columns witnessed? she wondered. How many children had they watched play on that pavement, and then grow up to become philosophers, teachers, or soldiers? As she mused, a scrappy little girl she hadn't seen before stole the ball and placed a kick straight through the makeshift goal at the far end of the field. Had girls played there when the columns were new? Had lovers walked there? Had great speeches been made, or assassinations spattered the marble with blood? Had Aristotle or Plato walked here?

The ancient columns looming over the children were almost protective, shielding them from the terrors of the modern world. She sat down on a chunk of stone that must have once been part of a nearby building, and opened her drawing pad. How could she transfer the weight and age of these columns onto the paper? She noted that the slanting light marked the striations on the columns in sharp shadows against the whiteness of the marble, and that the broken corners of the marble sparkled. Then she looked at the children. How could she show their lightness of foot, their grace, their shouts?

Put on your subject, she could hear Demetri saying. *Get inside it.*

How does a laughing, sweaty boy of ten feel? She looked

around and saw that she wasn't the only one who had paused to watch. At the little store next to the ruin an arthritic old woman, filling her string bag with vegetables, had stopped to enjoy the children. Her smile revealed a gap where her two front teeth had been. A middle-aged man with the look of a stevedore, his powerful shoulders imprisoned in a tight, faded blue work shirt that strained across his ample stomach, a cloth cap pushed to the back of his head, was enthusiastically shouting advice like a football fan. Was he the father of one of the children?

A sad-looking man, stooped with age and fatigue, shuffled along, not noticing the children, his gray, bushy mustache covering a mouth that moved as he talked to himself. In one hand, he held the neck of a battered bouzouki, in the other a folding stool with a cloth seat. He passed Anna and set up his stool on the corner, spread a tattered rug at his feet, and started to play. Was he hoping only for enough money to buy his breakfast, or was this the way he made a living—playing on street corners?

He leaned his ear close to the box of the instrument to tune the strings; then, straightening up, he began to play. As he strummed the first notes, his face was transformed. Anna's throat constricted as she watched, feeling in the depths of her soul his love for the music. Was he out here in the sun, not to make money, but to play just for the pure pleasure of it, for the pleasure of having people listen to his songs? Looking at the sublime half smile that couldn't be seen on his hidden mouth but showed in the rest of his face, she let her hand put it onto the paper before her, sketching in the closed eyes, the proud set of his shoulders. His tiredness was gone.

A shout turned Anna's attention back to the soccer game. She turned a page in her pad, trying to catch the players' fleeting movements. She did rough studies of the adults who, like her, were caught up in the game. The stevedore, his enormous hands gesticulating in the air, was apparently giving nonpartisan coaching to each player who happened to get the ball. Did his shirt bind under his arms? Was it uncomfortable? Anna wondered, as she tried to still his motions on paper. Then she remembered more of

Demetri's advice. *Be economical with your strokes. Don't overwork the details.*

The little girl had gone to the sideline to tie her shoe. Her tangled hair was hanging in her eyes. One of the boys shouted at her, obviously telling her to hurry and get back in the game. How had she gained the respect of this bunch of boys?

Someone kicked the ball high, and for a moment it hung in the air, its black-and-white pattern vibrant in front of the ruined columns. Anna flipped back to the page where she had drawn the columns and sketched in the ball. Then she went back to her line drawings of people. Sometimes she drew only a hand, reaching, shielding a face. Sometimes a quick little foot at the end of a skinny leg protruding from wrinkled shorts, or a face, mouth open in a gleeful shout.

A shadow fell across her paper, and Anna looked up to find herself surrounded by several people, carefully watching as she drew. She smiled, and they nodded in approval.

She continued to draw with this audience murmuring in the background until, feeling a rumble in her stomach, she realized how hungry she was. She glanced at her watch. My God, it was after noon. How long had she been here? She stood up and stretched, feeling stiff and renewed.

Timeless hours, she thought, remembering old Syriotis in Kritsa. *Maybe I'm learning to accept this gift again. We need periods of timelessness, times when we are totally unaware of ourselves, of the world, all our aches and itches and worries.* For some reason, she thought back over her last twenty or so frantic, frenetic years, when she had filled every minute, always aware of time, trying to bend it to accommodate all she thought she had to do. She had told herself that she didn't have time to draw, much less to just sit and watch people, noting how their clothes might be binding, or wondering how it felt to be old and poor and to love the sound of your music so much that you wanted to share it with people on the street.

We cram our calendars full, she mused, *feeling guilty if we have a free moment, never allowing even an hour, much less a day, to do nothing but sit and stare.*

Children don't do that, Anna thought, noticing that most of the children were gone, probably home to lunch. But one was still there—the little girl. Totally unaware of other people around her, she was practicing her footwork with the ball, bouncing it from foot to foot, knee to foot, sending it back and forth through her feet. Did she know it was after lunchtime? Anna was sure she didn't.

And neither had Anna. She felt as if she had been on a vacation outside of herself. And now that she was back, she needed to find something to eat.

She looked over her drawings. Had she filled ten sheets? Now that time and space were once again upon her, she viewed the sketches with a critical eye, disappointed in what she found. She hadn't, after all, been able to capture the age of the ruin in contrast with the children. That nebulous sense that her hand was being guided by something outside herself had not produced any magic. In some of the sketches she could see that with a light stroke or a touch of shadow she almost had it. It was almost there. But still it eluded her.

She sighed as she closed the pad and packed up her things. No matter. It had been a wonderful morning. *It's the process that is important,* Demetri had said. *Lose yourself in the process. If you are constantly striving for perfection, it will always escape you.*

Anna walked into the Plaka to get lunch at Xenos', thinking how true Demetri's words were. *Live your life as if it were a work of art,* he once had said. If the constant desire for perfection obstructed the artist's process, Anna thought, then striving for flawlessness in life would be counterproductive as well.

That evening, after an appropriately late dinner, Alexis and Anna sat in the corner of the elegant little restaurant drinking coffee. "You're pensive tonight," he said, putting his hand over hers. "Are you still tired?"

"No, I'm not tired. Just relaxed," she sighed, "in a way I had forgotten existed."

"That's good to hear. What is responsible for this feeling?"

She laughed a little. "It has to do with time. Or rather timelessness. Being lost in something pleasant and rewarding. Not being concerned about its outcome."

"Please explain."

"Well, it's possible to be so busy at life, trying to do everything well, that we lose track of the, uh, true"—Anna floundered, trying to find words—"lose the ability to, uh, to notice. That's it, to notice the really significant happenings around us."

"What is the saying? 'Don't get too busy to stop and smell the flowers'?"

"That's part of what I'm talking about." Anna pulled her hand away gently. "Do you believe in destiny? I mean, do you feel that each of us has a mission, a talent perhaps, that we can choose to ignore?"

"What do you believe, Anna?" He was listening, looking straight into her eyes.

"I believe it's easy to lose track of what is important. To lose our vision. To finally be blind to what's really essential." She looked at her hands lying still in her lap.

"And have you ever done this?"

She raised her eyes to Alexis' face, his dark questioning eyes, his forehead creased with concern. He was beautiful. Her fingers searched through the small purse in her lap for a pen and the small tablet she always carried now and started an ink drawing of this man.

He shook his head. "What are you—?"

"No, don't move," she said, starting to sketch, leaving the white of the paper to shine through to re-create the highlights in his shining black hair. She put the lines of intentness in the broad forehead and crosshatched planes of light and dark in his beautifully formed, straight nose. With tiny lines in the corners, she brought out the concern in his eyes. The drawing grew more detailed under her hand. She sketched his smooth, wide mouth and full lips, the strong, square chin and powerful neck, the ears lying close to his head, then brought them to life with crosshatch shading again.

Holding out the drawing, she said, "For years I have not allowed myself the luxury of taking time to do things that give me pleasure. This is something I love to do."

He held the sketch between two fingers, laughing, a little embarrassed. Shaking his head, he said, "You're very good." He squinted at the small piece of paper. "You even noticed that my ears don't match."

"They do too. Give me that," Anna said, snatching the paper back. The ears matched perfectly.

He reached for her hand again, his eyes serious now. "You must promise me to keep doing the things that give you pleasure. You are very beautiful when you are happy."

Anna felt a rush of emotion she couldn't identify.

Alexis held her hand tighter, searching her face with such close scrutiny that Anna felt uncomfortable. "I have not met one like you often in my life," he said. "You notice everything. Like at the monastery yesterday. You have a deep awareness not only of the importance and beauty of a place, but an awareness of its history, its people, past events and interactions that have become a part of the walls."

Anna felt a little taken aback by this speech.

"Your drawing of the two monks in the refectory." His eyes searched her face. "I think you actually saw them."

Anna smiled and shook her head. "No, I didn't see them. But I did feel their presence. Their laughter, their words, were as much a part of the room as the carving above the door, the shape of the window. The room would have been different if they hadn't once been there."

Alexis nodded slowly, light in his eyes, his mouth open to speak. Then he hesitated, as if he was considering how to say what was on his mind. Finally he said, "You asked me, this morning, if I ever work. I am working on a new addition to the university. That is my job right now." His voice had taken on a low timbre. "But I have other work that, as you have said tonight, gives me pleasure." He cleared his throat. "I'd like to show you. Will you come with me?"

How could she refuse? As they drove through the lights of

the night city, Alexis was silent. The music on his stereo, a haunt-
ing, synthesized melody, sounded as if it came from outer space.
They left the metropolitan area and came to a part of Athens
Anna had never seen, curving roads with elegant houses set back
into wooded hills.

At one corner, they came to a large complex of modern office
buildings surrounded by carefully manicured lawns, shrubbery,
and trees illuminated by soft, indirect spotlights from the ground.
Alexis turned off onto a curved driveway that led under the lit
portico at the front of a dark office building. At the entrance, a
bleary-eyed night watchman quickly jumped up from the chair
where he had been lounging, and probably sleeping, to open the
door. He said some short greeting in Greek, ending with, "*Kyrie
Sarkis*," as they passed. He didn't seem at all surprised to see
Alexis there at midnight.

The elevator took them up five floors and Alexis unlocked a
door at the end of a hall. When he flipped on the switch, Anna
looked around in appreciation. It was obviously an office, a large
office, with a great teak desk in one corner and a matching draft-
ing table, at least four by six feet, under a dark skylight. The rest
of the room looked like an elegant living room with a huge white
flokati rug in the middle of the gleaming hardwood floor, and a
long couch and two chairs upholstered in white. Several smooth,
abstract carvings were arranged on a low table.

The wall at the end of the room had a life-sized oil painting
of a group of dancers in traditional Greek dress, a splash of movement and color in the otherwise white and wood room.

Alexis drew back the curtains, and Anna saw that the couch
and chairs were arranged so that all had a view out four narrow
cathedral windows that looked down on the city spread below.

"Come," he said, taking her arm. At the far end of the room
were several tables holding architectural models. Alexis led her to
one.

It was a topographical map showing the elevations of a large
section of land. In the center, at the end of a long drive, was a house
of such elegance and simple beauty Anna wanted to touch it.

"It is for an artist, like yourself," Alexis explained, carefully removing the simulated red tile roof. "In Greek Revival style."

"How beautiful," Anna said.

He pointed to the first rooms. "You see, a large room for entertaining, with a fireplace and French doors leading out to a veranda overlooking the sea. And here, a studio, not so large, for projects—painting, sculpture, whatever—with a northern exposure and a vaulted ceiling so that the spirit can soar. It is a room designed for creativity."

"How could one help but be creative in such a room?"

He smiled. "And here in the 'lap' of the house, through this door, which can be left open to the studio on one side, and to the living room on the other, is a solarium with many plants and a small fountain."

The floor of the solarium in the model was paved with flagstone. Bare-earth patches remained here and there. Alexis had put in tiny artificial plants and small trees.

"The fountain is a lovely idea," Anna said.

"I like the sound of water, don't you?" Alexis touched the tiered fountain that he had placed in the corner.

"That would be heavenly, to be able to take a break in a place like that, smelling the earth, hearing water."

"The ventilation will let in the sea breeze as well." He pointed back into the house. "Each indoor room has a small fireplace for warmth, but mostly for the light. Firelight and candlelight at night. Sunlight"—he showed Anna the roof—"with skylights in every room, by day." He held his hands out. "All the basic elements are present here—earth, air, fire, and water."

"A very spiritual space," Anna said. She had never seen a more beautiful plan. It wasn't large but had spacious areas combined with intimate little nooks and alcoves, places one person could hole up in with a good book. Yet one could entertain a throng of people here without feeling crowded. The guest rooms were like private apartments with fireplaces and sitting rooms.

"What is this?" she asked, pointing to a veranda with a hole in the floor.

"That's not finished yet. Here in this excavation will be a Jacuzzi, and over here a sauna. There will be no swimming pool. This path leads to the sea." He showed her a trail going down a hill to the edge of the model.

He pointed to other rooms—a kitchen with models of every appliance imaginable, a dining room designed for twenty or for two or three, depending on a careful placement of screens and the use of a sunken area in front of the fireplace. There was a play-room with a billiard table and video equipment. There were decks and verandas on all sides of the house.

Then, indicating a short flight of stairs in a wing off from the main house, Alexis said, "And here a marriage retreat. No bed-room. See, a sitting room with comfortable furniture for only two. A small fireplace. A cabinet for the sound system so there will al-ways be music." Alexis moved around the table. "And over here, spacious walk-in closets. Off there is a bathroom with a tub and a shower"—he smiled—"for two."

He had moved back around to Anna's side of the table and, pulling her over so she could have a better view, left his arm around her shoulder. His touch went through her like an electric current.

Anna tried to blank out the image of two people cavorting from bath to shower in tandem. She could feel her heartbeat in her throat. She had known as soon as they left the restaurant that he was going to show her the equivalent of his etchings. She thought she could handle that with a little offhand humor. But when they walked into this spacious but intimate office where he spent so much of his time, his presence was as much a part of the room as the furnishings. His mark was everywhere, permeating even the air. Anna felt as though she were both in and out of her body, her intellect being able to stand back and watch her person, *unable to control what that person did.*

She heard her own admiring comments. Felt her smile of ad-miration at Alexis as he presented his wonderful design. She knew what was coming. She knew the time to leave was now—if it wasn't already too late. Her mind said, "Go!" Instead, she felt herself leaning into Alexis as he explained each aspect of his design and drew her closer.

"All this"—he pointed in a circle at what he had just shown her—"clustered around the center of the retreat—the bed in its own cozy niche, within but not part of the other rooms. See the skylight above the pillows, through which can be seen stars and the moon? This place is only for night, for sleeping and"—his voice dropped to a low rumble—"for making love."

Anna felt his other arm slip around her as his lips covered hers. Softly, gently, he kissed her, his arms pressing her against his body.

She hadn't been surprised by the kiss. She had expected it with a tingling apprehension, like a young girl being walked up to her porch after a date. She just hadn't expected to be so moved by it.

She pushed gently against Alexis' chest, pulling away, mostly to get her breath. She knew, with every nerve jangling in alarm, that it would take only one intimate gesture and she would do anything he wanted. Surely that was his plan. *God, what am I doing here? I should never have come. I should have known better.*

To try to gain some composure so that she could sort out her feelings, she turned and concentrated on the model. Looking at it now, after his kiss, Anna felt a rush of feeling for Alexis that confused her. There was something mystical about this man and his work. He wasn't like anyone she had ever known. A power exuded from him that made her feel at the same time overwhelmed and exalted. A spiritual quality that inspired awe and yearning for . . . what was it about him?

Looking at his model, she realized the answer. It was what Demetri talked of so often. In Alexis she saw what she herself was seeking. He was an artist who had found his own center.

"For whom did you design this?" she asked, keeping her face turned away so he wouldn't see the tears.

Alexis put his hand on Anna's chin and turned her so that she was facing him. "It is for me," he answered. "I'll build it as soon as I have someone who will want to share it with me." His eyes searched her face.

Anna didn't know how to respond. Rising tears made her throat hurt. His hand on her face sent shock waves through her whole body. Something in her was already answering yes while her feet wanted to run, and never stop running. But before she could decide what to do, he smiled, a tender smile that touched his eyes with radiance. "Come, I'll take you home."

Seventeen

Alexis said good-bye to Anna in the lobby of the hotel with a chaste kiss on the cheek. As though in a trance, she went up to her suite. She pulled back the curtains and opened the doors to the balcony and, still holding her purse, fell into a chair. She hadn't even bothered to turn on the light.

I have just survived something—I'm not sure what. She couldn't even define her reaction. Disappointment? Relief? *My God, he could have done anything.* Surely he knew that. Why the abrupt halt? Was it out of respect for her mourning? Or because of her age? Did he kiss her and find her wanting? Lacking something? Would she ever hear from him again? Did she want to? She was still shaken by the whole encounter. Why had he . . . ?

The phone rang and Anna leaped up and ran into the bedroom, falling over a chair, then stumbling against the bed as she reached for the receiver. "Hello?" she said breathlessly, relief flooding through her. He had called back.

"Anna?" It was Sam.

"Sam."

"Where have you been?"

She picked up her luminous alarm clock. "Good Lord, Sam, it's two in the morning!"

"I know. I asked the desk to call me at my hotel as soon as you came in. I tried to get you all day."

"You what!?"

"I have the car and tomorrow's the day we go to Delphi. If we leave early—"

"To Delphi?"

"Remember, after *Aïda*? You said you'd go up there with me."

Oh no. She'd forgotten about her promise to go to Delphi. That scene at the Odeon and the restaurant afterward—Sam there with Taylor, but begging *her* to go on this trip. And, of course, creeping into her thoughts, that last night in Crete. Anna flung herself back onto the bed. Why had she agreed to go to Delphi? "I don't think—"

"Listen, I know it's late. So why don't we leave, say, hmmm, why don't you meet me down at the dining room at, uh, eight thirty and maybe a big breakfast will—"

"Sam, I can't—"

"See you tomorrow morning." Click.

Damn him! Anna called down to the desk to find out his room number. She would just call him back and refuse to go. She gave her name and asked for Sam McDonald.

"We have no one registered by that name," she was told.

"Then give me the number you called when I came in."

"Number? You must be mistaken, Mrs. Sandoval. We made no call." That con man! He must have paid someone a fortune to watch for her. Well, she just wouldn't show up. He could sit there and wait all day as far as she was concerned.

But, she thought, he'd probably steal a key to her room and she'd have him up here in her bedroom at eight thirty. She ripped off her clothes and threw them into the chair, turning it over, then fell into bed.

Sam's call had effectively doused the fire of her evening with Alexis, and Anna was suddenly exhausted. She fell asleep forgetting to set the alarm.

When the phone rang, she swam up out of sleep as if from the bottom of a blue gray cobweb ocean. "Hello."

"Just checking to make sure you're awake." Sam sounded cheerful and alert.

"Oh, God, Sam."

"Your breakfast is getting cold, so hurry."

She slammed down the phone and lay rigid in the bed, trying to think of some cruel form of revenge. Could she have her room switched without his knowing and just disappear?

Reluctantly she crawled out of bed. There was no way out. Delphi. Oh well, she had always wanted to go to Delphi. She and Paul never had time to go. He was always booked solid when they came to Athens.

"You look fresh and lively," Sam said when she slipped into the chair across from him. Anna glared at him.

"Here, drink this." He shoved a cup of coffee at her. "It does wonders for one's disposi—uh, constitution. I've ordered us a farmer's breakfast. Everything on the menu." Just see if she would eat it, Anna thought, folding her arms across her chest. She tried to look away as Sam stuffed himself with eggs, ham, rolls, his reading glasses perched on his nose so he could see to butter his bread, he said. But after being the target of the doleful looks as he offered her first one thing to eat and then another, she finally gave in. Besides, she was hungry.

"That's better," he said as she polished off a plate as full as his.

It was a challenge getting across Athens and onto the Sacred Way—the highway leading out of the city. Driving was a hazard here, Anna thought, noting the furious honking, shouting, and shaking of fists that accompanied roaring about in great bursts of speed and screeching of brakes. "I haven't figured out why Athenians, who are generally a polite people, gracious in an old-world manner, become such demons in their cars," Sam said.

But once they got out on the open road to Eleusis, which wound along the sea for a while, Anna began to feel a sense of adventure. However, she was determined not to let Sam know this.

She was sad to see that, in modern times, Eleusis had become an industrial area of ironworks and cement factories. The road along which ancient pilgrims had traveled on their way to the sacred lake to pay homage to the goddess of spring, Persephone, held no sense of the sacred. The lake was silted up with slag and garbage, and tankers filled the bay on the other side. Oil refiner-

ies belched black smoke into the powder blue sky. Anna was relieved when they finally left Eleusis.

By the time they got into the countryside of Attica, she was
glad she had come along. She needed some distance from last
night in Alexis' office. Even so, the residual undercurrents of the
evening still had her in such a strange frame of mind that she
couldn't think of anything to say.

Sam seemed to sense her mood, or perhaps he too had things
to think about. He slipped a Mozart concerto into the tape deck,
and they drove for miles without speaking. A comfortable silence.
That was one thing about Sam. One didn't have to worry about
what to say.

For an hour and a half, Sam stared straight ahead, his face
grim, gripping the wheel as if it required his full concentration,
only changing his position to switch the tape. The road turned inland, away from the shore, and climbed through undulating farmland, molded by the harsh contours of the earth. Sometimes, on a
distant hill or field, they could see flocks of sheep in the company
of an old woman or a small boy. Often they had to slow down to
pass a donkey plodding along the roadside or rough wooden carts
piled high with hay.

Children with large dark eyes watched them drive by, and
waved their thin arms in greeting. The land was bare except for
occasional carefully tended fields and stands of trees, their shade
casting feathered patterns on the red earth.

Was light in Greece brighter, Anna wondered, more lustrous
than light in other places in the world? She was sure it was. It infused the stark, spare landscape with glowing beauty, hard and
clear, playing on the glittering water, the bare bones of bright
white limestone, the dry, dusty earth. *I wonder,* Anna thought, *if
this clarity, this crystal atmosphere, was responsible for the hard, direct quality of ancient Greek thought.*

Her own thoughts meandered with the curves in the road.
What was Alexis doing today? Would he try to call her? Or was
last night the final act? He had shown her his work, given her a
good, strong look over, and then decided to take her home? He

must have guessed how old she was. After all, he knew she had a married daughter and a son in graduate school.

In the light of day she couldn't quite recall the emotional turmoil she had felt, just that she had been swept away by it. It was like a scent in the air that vanished when one tried to discover its source.

It was all ridiculous anyway. *I could have gotten myself into a real mess,* she thought, amazed and fascinated by how her body could betray her with such abandon—in spite of her high-flown morality, drilled into her since her childhood and of which she had only recently been so proud. She was confused, finally deciding that what she felt was more relief than disappointment. *I don't think I'm designed to be a merry widow on the prowl.* She determined to stop going over and over it. She gazed out across the countryside. *Stop thinking about it!*

Oh, she was flattered by Alexis' attention. There was no doubt about that. But maybe she had misread the whole thing. Maybe he was showing her his architectural models, one artist to another, and gave her the kiss just for good measure. Anna shifted in her seat.

Well, if that was so, thank God she didn't follow her inclinations after that kiss. Anna felt warmth rush to her cheeks. *Now I know firsthand what happens to women without men.* She sighed with resignation. *Insides turning wrong side out at the slightest touch of affection? Minds slipping from their heads to their—*

"Are you getting red in the face because you're hungry?"

Anna looked sharply at Sam, her hands flying to her face. "We only just ate the equivalent of a horse"—she looked at her watch—"less than two hours ago."

"I thought we'd get some ice cream." He pulled into the deserted parking lot of a café in a small hamlet. Two people—Anna guessed they were the owners—sat in broken-down chairs in the sun outside the door.

Anna stayed in the car while Sam walked up, and with gestures and a small drama showing shivering cold, then licking the air, he managed to get them to understand what he wanted. The woman nearly fell out of her chair with laughter while the man disappeared through the door and came back with two ice-cream bars on sticks.

It was delicious. Anna relaxed, looking over at Sam. His face was drawn into a frown, his eyes in some brown study.

They passed through the legendary city of Thebes, which, rather than looking legendary, appeared tired and dusty. The worst type of modern buildings—prefab, faux brick, metal door and window facings—encroached on the decaying, peeling walls and broken cobblestones of times past. The town was a collage of dented old vehicles, garish signs, gas pumps, and streets jammed with traffic. A crumbling shadow of what it must once have been.

Sam drove on, still brooding.

Well, let him. Anna watched the terrain change from rolling hills to crags and ravines with folds of mountains rising in the distance. Dry streambeds and stark outcroppings of rock gave the land the feel of a skeleton bleached dry and white in the sun.

Shades of umber, ocher, terra-cotta, sienna, and sepia flowed toward the distant hills of tawny gold. As the road climbed higher, leviathan mountains reared up on the skyline. The sense of entering the land of the gods was almost palpable. The air pouring through the open windows of the car became cooler.

"I know it was rotten, not telling you about Taylor," Sam said in a burst of words, startling Anna from her own thoughts. "I met her about a year ago. It all seemed such a good idea at the time. She was beautiful. She was a good sport. She was intelligent. She was—"

"I really don't—"

"Everyone likes her." Sam went on as if Anna hadn't interrupted. "And she . . . she says she loves me." He looked over at Anna. "Me!" he said, hitting his chest with his palm. "She loves *me*. I mean, I realize I'm exceptionally handsome and all but"— he shook his head—"it's hard to believe."

"That must be quite wonderful," she said with genuine feeling.

"Well, I thought someone young would pull me out of the

doldrums." He brushed back his thick hair. "Taylor did definitely do that." He glanced over at Anna. "She saved me from drowning. Gave me something else to think about. And"—he pursed his lips and nodded—"I loved her for it." He took a deep breath and blew it out slowly. "I decided to . . . well, I went to Crete to sort of say good-bye, I guess. To the past. But there was that problem with the hotel . . . the one that burned down. So I had to go to the Villas." He gave Anna a mournful glance. "And then I met you."

"And told me, after our romp in the sea, that you had been living in the past too long. God, Sam, I felt so sorry for you. And all the time, your *immediate past* was filled with that saucy little . . ." Anna had to remind herself again that Taylor was not to blame for any this. "How do you expect me to feel?"

"I missed my chance to tell you. Can't you see that? At first, I didn't talk about it because I went to Crete to relive the past. Then, as I got to know you better, I couldn't think of how. I mean, you don't take a nice lady you've just met and rave on about your . . . about another nice—" He drove on for a while in tight-lipped silence. "You just don't do that," he went on. "Then, that last night, I didn't know. . . . I didn't plan that. I just—"

Sam pulled the car over onto the shoulder and stopped. He faced Anna and looked directly into her eyes. "That last night was a surprise to me. A wonder-filled stunner." He took a breath and started over. "I know I didn't tell the whole truth. I didn't know how to tell you. I started out telling the truth."

"And that truth made you free. With me!"

Sam shifted into gear and drove on, scanning the road ahead of him as if looking for a place to smash the car. Then, at the first turnoff, he pulled over onto a dirt road and stopped again. He sighed and, looking into his big, gangly hands as they lay in his lap, said, "I can't tell you how sorry I am. I made an error in judgment. If I'd been flying a plane, I would have crashed." He looked over at her. "But I didn't want to offend you." He rubbed his hand over his eyes as if to blot out the memory. "That evening—no, the whole week and a half before that—changed me. I went to Crete to mourn, but when I met you, I began to realize that I was completely on the wrong track, that I had gone beyond sorrow into a serious case of self-pity, an obsessive grief that I was hanging on to, not letting go of. Just trying to sidestep it with—"

He turned to face her. "Look, I was ashamed that I had thought that by taking out someone young, who was just starting out, I could become young too. Start over myself."

Anna let him talk, feeling mixed emotions. His honesty was touching. But she still felt used. He had violated their trust by not being completely truthful, and that smarted. If she had known about Taylor, if he had told her all this, would that last evening in Crete have happened?

Sam didn't even notice the click when the Mozart tape ran out. He just continued on. "All those days we talked, down there at the beach and on our trips, it was as if the scattered pieces of my life came together. What I appreciated about it was our friendship. And to tell you the truth, at first friendship was more than enough. I considered you a lifetime friend almost from the first time we talked. I was so mixed up in all"—he rubbed his eyes again—"all that other business, revisiting the places I'd been to with Grace, that I didn't realize your effect on me until—" He looked over at Anna. "That night before you left in such a hurry."

Anna turned away, staring out the window, not really seeing anything there.

"I'm not talking only about the lovemaking, though that was, well, that was good." He cleared his throat. "It was the whole . . . our whole relationship. The talking. The laughing. The fact that I could strip down to the altogether in front of God and everyone that night."

He hesitated, then said, "I hope this is going to come out like I mean it, but if lovemaking is a consummation, then that night was the consummation of a friendship as powerful and as lifelong as . . . as any I've ever had."

He reached toward Anna. But as though he had second thoughts, he pulled back his hand. "Anna, I felt I had known you forever. It was like everything was meant to be. I didn't plan it. I swear to you I didn't."

He paused for a long time. Anna still looked away, out the window. Then he went on. "I didn't even hear the clock strike midnight, Anna. But the next morning, I got up early to go look for your dress. When I brought it by, you weren't stirring, so I left. When I rushed back later to find you, to tell you all these things— even about Taylor—you were gone. I was left standing on the steps of Crete, holding a glass slipper. Why did you run away?" His voice had grown so soft that she had to strain, sitting right beside him, to hear.

She cleared her throat. "I didn't know what else to do. You see, that was a first for me, Sam. A momentous first. Paul was the only—" She turned to look at him and saw the pain in his eyes. "I was at war with myself. Had I been disloyal to Paul? How would you feel about me after that? Had the whole thing ruined what I, also, considered a beautiful friendship? I couldn't face it. Or you."

"I'm sorry. I'm sorry you felt you had to run away."

"I'm sorry too. I've had lots of practice running away lately."

"I know I've hurt you, Anna, and I want you to know I wish I could take it back. It was unintentional. I hope you know that now. I sincerely ask your forgiveness."

"For the record, I too felt that what happened that evening was like a gift, Sam. And I don't wish it to be taken back." As she spoke, she realized it was true. "Maybe we both needed it. For that moment."

"Maybe we did. But it certainly changed things for me. What am I going to do, Anna?"

"I've been asking that question a lot lately myself. Let's go ask the oracle at Delphi."

The road, now shaded by stands of pine, rose ever up, hugging the side of Mount Parnassus, the colors of the terrain fading from dark evergreen to mist blue in the distance. The villages they passed through clung to the hills in tiers, each street level even with the faded red roofs of the row of whitewashed houses below.

To the right, the mountains bared the flinty fangs of rock-ribbed peaks, daring mortals to struggle up their boulder-strewn

shoulders. Their foothills fell in folds of olive trees, planted not
hundreds but thousands of years ago. The groves looked as
though they were pouring down the hillside into the mirrored
glint of the sea two thousand feet below, the Gulf of Corinth in
the Ionian Sea.

The car rounded the curve of a great buttress, and looking
up, Sam and Anna saw, rising above the treetops, six columns of
splotchy stone, orangey pink and white. This could only be a
monument to a god.

"The Sanctuary of Apollo," Sam said in hushed tones. He
pulled into the parking area, and the first miracle of the day happened. There was a parking space just at the entrance. "I know
you must be hungry. I am," he said. "But let's go take one short
look before we go on into Delphi and eat."

"I'm not hungry, Sam," Anna assured him.

After buying tickets at a kiosk, they started the climb from
the Roman Market up still another Sacred Way to the Temple of
Apollo.

Archaeologists were at work among the ruins with shovels
and pulleys and ropes, moving an enormous carved stone down a
makeshift track, handling it with special care, as if it were made of
dynamite.

The temple drew them up the hill. Anna watched Sam gazing
in rapt wonder at its broken columns, putting on his glasses to
consult his map and guidebook from time to time. "This present
temple," he said, "is the third built on this site. At least three
times it has been destroyed by earthquakes, fire, and rockslides."
He read on and his face brightened. "The portico used to bear the
inscriptions of the Seven Sages—listen to this—one of which was
the famous Apollonian imperative *Gnothi seauton,* 'Know thyself.' "

Sam had read the words from the glossy guidebook, but to
Anna, it was as if the god himself had spoken. "Know thyself."
How? she begged. *How does one do that?* She took a deep, satis-
fying breath of the mountain air and pondered.

She followed behind Sam, who pointed out the votive monuments to various Greek cities and the treasuries, now empty, where offerings were kept safe from weather and theft. They took turns standing on the stage of the amphitheater while the other sat up high in one of the five thousand tiered seats. Sam hummed a few bars of Mozart's Concerto in A Major for Clarinet to demonstrate the astounding acoustics of the half circle carved into the mountainside.

When it was Anna's turn to perform, Sam went to the very top of the tiers of seats. "Know thyself," she whispered.

"Are you the oracle?" Sam shouted.

"Could be," Anna answered in a soft voice, looking up at him in the distance. He smiled and bowed, and she knew he had heard.

"The spring is near here. Come on up and we'll find it."

At the top of a flight of stairs, they came upon the place that the map indicated was the Spring of Kassotis, or "Spring of the Muses." For some reason, they were the only people there. There was no evidence of water, but Anna once again had the feeling they were not alone. Too many people over thousands of years had sat on these very stones not to have left something of their presence. "How many layers of footprints do you suppose are here?" Anna asked.

"Must be millions."

"Time spirals in a place like this. I can feel myself swirling back, becoming one of the millions at the beginning as well as the end. Does that sound crazy?"

"Time *is* a spiral. Ancient people knew that. But most people today have lost touch with that knowledge." He looked at Anna in appreciation.

"I have the strangest certainty that I've been here before."

"Maybe you have," he said gently. "Maybe *we* have." He looked at his book. "It says here that the water of this spring brought women into a condition in which they could prophesy." He looked up. "You thirsty?"

"Believe me, if there were any water here, I would drink it."

"I think you have, Anna," Sam said. They sat on the stones

under the shade of a tree. "What you said back there in the theater—
'Know thyself.' That sounds pretty prophetic to me."

"Why is prophecy always shrouded in mystery?" Anna asked.
"How can we ever know ourselves?"

He thought for a moment. "I think we have to untie the
cat."

"What?"

"Untie the cat." Sam reached out and took Anna's hand,
pulling her to her feet. "Come, let's have lunch and I'll tell you the
story of the cat."

In the modern town of Delphi they found a small café with
tables on a veranda overlooking the slopes descending to the sea
and looking up at the pinnacles of Parnassus. After they had ordered their meal and the waiter had brought a carafe of wine,
Anna said, "Now tell me about the cat."

"Well, it's a story about the guru's cat. Here's how it goes."
He took a long draft of wine and settled back, trying to arrange
his face into a sage expression.

"When the guru sat down to worship each evening, the
ashram cat would roam about and distract the worshippers. So
the guru ordered that the cat be tied before the evening worship." He glared over at Anna with a serious frown. "You following so far?"

"Go on. I'm all ears."

"After the guru died, the cat continued to be tied before
evening worship. And when that cat expired, another cat was
brought to the ashram so that it could be duly tied up during
evening worship." He took a sip of his wine and looked around.
"Wonder where they are with our food?"

"Go on. Go on."

"Centuries later, learned treatises were written by the guru's
scholarly disciples on the liturgical significance of tying up a cat
while worship is performed." He leaned back in his chair and
folded his hands across his chest in satisfaction.

"That's it?"

"That's it. You once told me that not long ago you realized

you were . . . let me see, how did you say it . . . 'following a set of cultural rules that were almost genetic.' "

Anna sat forward, looking at him with awe at his remembering that.

"You're wondering how I can quote you so glibly? I wrote it down."

"You wrote down what I said?"

"It was good, and I wrote it down. Like I told you then, women aren't the only ones who are locked in cultural rules."

"I remember."

"Anyway, it seemed to fit with the story about the guru's cat." He looked up at the peaks, his mouth screwed up in thought for a long time. Then he said softly, "When are people going to do what they want, be what they want, without worrying about cultural rules? When are we going to be able to simply untie the cat?"

Just then, the waiter brought their lunch. Sam looked at his watch. "Let's see, it's three fifteen. We'll have time after lunch to go down to the temple in the Sanctuary of Athena, which is said to be far more beautiful and sacred than old Apollo's precinct."

Sam described past trips he had taken up here—trips when he had a layover in Athens long enough to get the sleep he required with a little time left over. "I came up here because the air was so clear I could think better."

"Is that why you brought me here?"

"To get some things straight? Yes. Seemed like a better place than that madhouse city."

Anna finished her wine and declined coffee. "If we're going to get back to Athens tonight, we'd better pay our call on its namesake's temple and get moving."

Anna was unprepared for the beauty of the Sanctuary of Athena. They parked and walked down a pathway between olive trees so ancient that their gnarled, deformed trunks formed hollows large enough for several people to get inside.

"Have you ever stood inside a living tree?" Sam asked.

"I probably have, I don't recall—"

He grabbed her hand and pulled her into the hollow of a tree just off the path. Inside the shady interior, the air changed. It smelled loamy and alive. "Lean back against it," Sam said, pushing her shoulders, then stepping back. "Now, close your eyes and stay where you are for a while. I'll wait for you out on the trail."

The rough wood poked Anna's shoulder blades. Dust filtered down from above her. She wondered about spiders. But the longer she stood there, the more she had a strange feeling of welcome. It was comforting, like being held.

Then she noticed the sound. No, it wasn't sound. It was like a vibration that emanated from the tree, through her back. Not sound but energy. Pure energy. Suddenly Anna was infused with the realization that she was standing within a living organism. And that it had been there, in that same spot of earth, for over a thousand years. Who else over the centuries had sought refuge in its interior as she had? She pressed her palms against the walls of the trunk, breathing the breath of the tree.

She left reluctantly, her senses purified. With heightened awareness, she listened to the twitter of birds unseen in the dense olive boughs, and almost understood their language. The air smelled of green. The burned, muted colors of the boulders were beautiful now.

Sam stood with his back to her in the trail, and with a leap of affection that almost choked her, she wanted to go up and throw her arms around him. She came up behind him, but before she could reach out, she saw what he was looking at. A *tholos* of three graceful Doric columns in mottled colors of rose, apricot, and peach stood on a rotunda along with the shattered stumps of other columns. A broken section of carved molding was balanced precariously across their tops. With the background of olive leaves, the Temple of Athena was ethereal, as if from a dream.

Anna walked past Sam and sat down on a warm stone, unable to take her eyes off the scene before her. It was only when she felt Sam's great, warm hand clasping hers that she realized she had reached back for him. She clung to his hand, tears washing through her and pouring down her cheeks.

Finally she turned to him and said, "I'm not sure I can stand any more of this."

Without saying anything, he pulled her to her feet and they walked through the ruin and back into the woods along the trail. Anna didn't even look back, but she was sure she could feel the eyes of Athena watching them leave. Shafts of light slanting through the trees pooled on the path. Then they emerged at a stone building tucked in the shade of a bluff. A few people sat at tables on the veranda. It was like a hermitage, a halfway house between antiquity and the twentieth century.

Sam, still holding her hand, led Anna to one of the tables and ordered beer for both of them. The sun was low in the west. When their drinks came, Anna didn't even move.

"You look tired, Mrs. Sandoval," he said.

She nodded, not even having the energy to reach for her drink. "People keep calling me in the middle of the night."

"Well, if you weren't out carousing around until dawn . . ." He was looking at her in mock disapproval.

Anna appreciated the fact that he hadn't asked her where she had been, but on second thought, she realized that he probably knew, if he had had spies waiting for her to come home.

"And when you do it several nights in a row, at your age—"

Anna reached for the beer, which she pretended to throw at him, then, laughing, drank a loud gulp and wiped the back of her hand across her mouth, saying, "I'm not tired. I'm not tired." Flopping back in her chair, she said, "I *am* tired. I feel old."

"If we leave in ten minutes, we can make it back to Athens before midnight. On the other hand, we could stay the night."

"Sa-am."

"I know the cutest little place in that town just down the hill there." He held up his hand to still her protest. "It's a little fishing village on a harbor called Galaxidi. The yachties on their fancy boats are the only foreign tourists. It's really off the beaten trail and we could—"

"You take the cake, Sam."

"What's that supposed to mean?"

"You have that young woman back in Athens, to whom I assume you are seriously attached, and now you want a woman in this other port . . . what did you call it? Galupseedy? Me!" She glared at him. Then she turned away.

"Is that what you think?"

"I don't know what to think."

"Anna, I'm tired too. Let's let those young people disco tonight to their hearts' content, and you and me go relax by the Ionian Sea like sedate, dignified sages of old. You notice I didn't say 'old sages.' "

For Anna, that was too close to the bone to be funny.

"Just think how nice it would be to take a twenty-minute drive down to Galaxidi. We could have dinner at a restaurant I know about down on the water." Sam went on speaking to Anna's back. "If you don't go into the kitchen, you'll think it's the most delicious food you've ever eaten."

"Sam, we'd better get on the road."

"Sit back and relax. I haven't finished my beer yet, and neither have you. Besides, look at you. You're exhausted."

"Oh, Sam, it's no good." She shook her head firmly.

"This is not a proposition, uh, in the usual sense of the word. It is just a practical suggestion which, however, could be relaxing and maybe even fun—for a couple of old friends to do together." He grinned. "That is, if your handsome young swain can do without you for one night."

This time she *did* throw something—her wadded-up napkin. "You cad," she said, but she couldn't help laughing. "Okay, you win. But we will have separate rooms, and no hanky-panky."

"Sounds dull to me, but if that's the way you want it." Sam sighed.

They spent a pleasant evening watching the "yachties," as Sam had promised, eating grilled shrimp and fried calamari and marinated *akhinos*—sea urchins—with a lovely crisp wine to wash it down. Anna was practically sleepwalking when they made their way up from the harbor to the Poseidon Hotel, a newly renovated, two-story house that had been converted into an inn.

As he had promised, Sam's call from Delphi had secured two separate rooms in the tiny hotel. Anna stumbled into hers wondering what she was going to sleep in. Her clothes? That would look pretty on the way back to Athens tomorrow. Her underwear? Too binding. She stripped, hanging her clothes on the back of a chair, and stepped into the shower for a hot sluice.

The water was icy cold no matter what she did. Instead of feeling refreshed, she just felt chilled, so she finally dried off, flipped off the light, and crawled into bed, snuggling down under the sheet and light blanket. She was asleep in an instant.

The knock on her door came from far away, and Anna ignored it until she recognized Sam's voice. "Anna, wake up," he said in a hoarse stage whisper. It couldn't be morning already.

"What do you want?"

"You've got to help me."

"What?"

"I'm being eaten alive."

"By what?" Anna had visions of dragons or crocodiles.

"Mosquitoes!" He said this loudly.

"God, Sam—"

"This is serious," he whispered. "Come in here and I'll show you."

Anna dragged herself out of bed. She draped the sheet around her togalike and unlocked the door. Sam was standing there in his slacks but no shirt.

"Just come look." In his room, the bed was a jumble of bedclothes. "See?" He pointed to splats of blood all over the walls. "I did it with a towel." He held up the weapon, also spotted with blood and squashed mosquitoes. "I tried closing the window, but they painted that one open and forgot to put on the screens. He looked at her. "Do you have screens?"

Anna just stared, trying to keep her eyes open.

Sam marched back into her room and pointed. "See, you *do* have screens. I don't."

"Why don't you simply ask the man at the desk downstairs for another room, or screens or a mosquito net?"

"Number one, there is no man, or woman, here. It's dark as a cave down there. I think they went home. I couldn't rouse anyone. I think we're the only ones here. The other rooms are locked."

"You really do have a problem."

"I probably have malaria."

"What do you propose?" It was hard to assume an indignant hands-on-hips stance in her toga getup.

He gave her his saddest, most doleful look. "Could I stay in your room?"

Anna's eyes flew open. "In my room? There is only one bed!"

"But it's a big one, a big double be—"

"Like hell!" she said, pulling the sheet closer around her. "It's a double bed, a foot wider than a single."

"Listen, I won't touch you. I promise. I just want to get some sleep." He looked at his watch. "It's midnight now. I will be anemic from loss of blood by morning if I have to stay in here slaying mosquitoes all night."

Anna didn't have the strength to argue. "Let me get some clothes on and you can come. Bring your mattress." She went back into the room and closed the door. She put on her lingerie and debated putting on her jeans, but settled for the long-tailed shirt. Opening the door again, she said, "Come on in. Be my guest."

Sam came in carrying only his bedclothes. He stood in the middle of the room looking sheepish. "The mattress is attached to the bed. I swear it won't come off." He stared mournfully at the hardwood floor.

"You can sleep next to the wall, damn it," Anna said. "Just keep this simple rule in mind. You can share my bed, but you better stay on your side."

Sam crawled in, still in his trousers, and when he was settled, Anna turned off the light and got in, so near the edge that she was practically falling off. She lay on her back, rigid. Sleep had vanished . . . apparently out her window screens.

The night dragged on and on. At first Sam was perfectly still, his breathing short and irregular. She knew he was awake. Then he turned on his side, facing the wall, bumping her with his hips.

"Hey."

"Sorry."

Anna tried to make her breathing slow and steady but got breathless in the effort and had to cough to cover up. She too turned on her side and found that they were now fanny to fanny. She slowly straightened out so they weren't touching.

She tried to blank out the visions of their last night in Crete that rose like flotsam in her mind. The ebb and flow of the swells as . . . *Think of something else!* Alexis? No, that wouldn't do either. Demetri. *Yes, think of Demetri and Maria. Demetri and Maria . . .*

Finally Anna dozed off until Sam's arm was flung across her chest. She sat straight up, startling him awake. "Stay on your side," she hissed.

He hunkered against the wall with a sigh.

Dawn crept in, through the screen, after what seemed like a millennium. Finally Anna could take it no longer. She slid off the bed and took the rest of her clothes into the bathroom to put them on. Since she didn't have a toothbrush, she washed up as best she could with cold water. Damn. Her comb was in her purse. She tiptoed out in the quiet, growing light and had just reached into the dark recesses of the bag, trying to find her comb by Braille, when Sam said loudly, "I don't know who hands out medals for valor, but—"

Anna screeched at the sound of his voice, throwing the purse against the wall.

"—I sure deserve one after last night."

Anna was holding her chest to still her heart. "You did that on purpose," she said, her breath coming in gasps.

"I just wanted you to know you didn't have to be so quiet."

Over coffee, back in Delphi, Sam said, "Anna, that was a Herculean test of will." His chin was covered with stubble and the bags under his eyes were dark smudges.

She smiled. "Don't think it was easy for me either."

"Life would be interesting with you, Anna. We could have a lot of fun."

"Is that a proposal? Or another proposition?"

"It is an observation."

"You'd take on this old worn-out mare in place of that sleek, young filly?" she teased him. "Or were you thinking of carrying out your plan to marry the filly and have the old nag for a mistress? That would be an original twist."

Sam laughed. "I'll have to give that some thought. You may have something there." Then he grew serious. "God, Anna, young women take life so seriously. They exhaust you with their musings about life and their passions."

Anna swallowed. Was that a backhanded compliment or was she to be *his* mother confessor as well as Taylor's?

"I needed this trip. I thank you for coming along with me," Sam said. "I enjoy going places with you, Anna. You make . . . you make these ruins come alive." She wasn't sure he meant the ancient ruins of Greece or his own vintage life. He smiled as if reading her thoughts. "I mean, with all your talk of spirits and time and footprints." He reached over and patted her hand. "You're a good kid."

"Thanks, pal," Anna answered. She knew he meant it, and his approval gave her a feeling of warm contentment.

"Even in your wrinkled clothes and frowsy hair."

"You're pretty cute too, you know," she said, giving his stubbly chin a gentle cuff.

They got back to Athens at noon, and Anna slept until three. She ordered a sandwich and sat in her white robe, eating as if she were starving. When she reached for the coffeepot to pour another cup, she saw the unfinished letter to Maggie. This epistle was becoming a diary. She leaned back, propping it once again on a pad of drawing paper, and set out to finish it, determined to get it in the mail the next day.

Eighteen

Anna had just signed the letter when the phone rang. Sam? She wondered, lifting the receiver with a smile. What did he want now?

"Hello, Anna?" Alexis' voice took her by surprise. "I'm glad I found you in," he said. "I was worried about you."

"Worried?" As glad as she was to hear from him, somehow it rankled that he would worry about her. What was it with these men who kept checking up on her?

"I thought you'd been called away or something."

"No, I went to Delphi."

"Alone?"

"As a matter of fact, I went with a friend." Why would he care?

"I hope you had a good time." It wasn't a question, but he paused as if waiting for a response. Then, not getting one, he said, "I missed you."

"It was only for a day and a half."

Her discomfort about this scrutiny must have shown in her voice, because Alexis changed the subject. "Are you ready for our cruise to Hydra tomorrow?"

Was it tomorrow? Life seemed to be coming at Anna in darts and arrows. "Uh, yes, that will be lovely. With your cousin and his family."

"It will be a hearty group, I assure you."

"What time will we be leaving?"

"Let's discuss that over dinner."

Anna lay back on the soft bed and thought of the big marble

bathtub where she had planned to soak for an hour before crawling back for a long night's uninterrupted sleep. After the solitude of Crete, all this constant activity over the past few days and the accompanying emotional strain were taking their toll. "I can't, Alexis. I have other plans."

"Oh." He sounded surprised and a little hurt.

To make up for what must have sounded like rudeness, Anna felt compelled to explain. "The truth is, I'm exhausted from this trip. I didn't get much sleep and . . ." God, now he would be wondering why. "I have to wash my hair," she finished lamely.

"Well, in that case, have a good rest. I'll send a car for you in the morning. The driver is called Yeorgios. Would seven thirty be too early?"

"That would be great." Feeling she had been abrupt, Anna said, "And, Alexis."

"Yes?"

"Thank you for being concerned."

His voice was low and gentle. "Until tomorrow. It will be difficult to wait. Rest well."

Listening to that deep, soothing voice, Anna regretted that she had so hastily refused his invitation to dinner. He sounded so sincere. "I will."

When Yeorgios came for her, Anna was waiting in the lobby, feeling rested and excited about this trip. Her beach basket, sitting on the floor beside her, was stuffed with a bathing suit, a caftan, shorts, and a sweater. She was ready for anything that might come up. She loved boats. She had missed the water since she'd left Crete. This was going to be a marvelous day.

Yeorgios opened the back door of a silver Mercedes sedan for Anna, then handed in her basket. When they pulled up beside an imposing-looking motor yacht, she looked around for Alexis' boat. She expected a cabin cruiser. Yeorgios held the door open for her.

"Ahoy, there," she heard Alexis shout. She looked up to see him smiling down at her from the railing of the yacht. It was a good thirty feet long, shining with polished brass, white paint, and glossy teak. The motor was already thrumming.

"Is this what you call a small boat?" Anna asked in amazement.

"Look around. There are many here that are larger."

Anna took her basket from Yeorgios and climbed the short gangplank. She would never cease being surprised. Alexis was dressed all in white. His black hair, shining in the morning sun, looked wet. She hadn't realized how tan he was. He must have spent a good deal of time on this boat.

"Anna, I'd like you to meet Nikolas Xenokles. He is my cousin's son—a cousin who has been like a brother to me. He just brought me the bad news that Theodori, his father, has fallen ill. A bad cold, I'm afraid, and the family will not be joining us today."

Anna looked at him sharply. "I'm sorry." She was sorry, not only that the man was ill. She had looked forward to a party, a relaxing day with a group of people.

"So, instead of the whole family, we have only Niko." He clapped the shoulder of his second cousin, a handsome boy who looked very much like his older cousin, except that he had let his hair grow long enough for the loose curls to frame his face and fall to his collar. He had on cutoffs and a sleeveless T-shirt with the name of the rock group Genesis scrawled in bright colors across the front.

Anna held out her hand. "I'm sorry I won't get to meet your family, but it will be nice to have you along."

Niko's even teeth gleamed white when he smiled, reminding her even more of Alexis. "I would like, madam, if I spend day with you. But I water-ski." He caressed a colorful single ski leaning against the lifeboat.

Alexis was smiling and nodding. "He has friends on Aegina, an island on the way to Hydra, so—"

"They have ski boat," Niko said.

Alexis looked at him with affection and relief. "This is a real speed demon. He is always after me to let him run the boat. We'll

be safer leaving him in Aegina." He pushed the boy's shoulder
and pretended to give him a kick to the backside. "Now, go cast
off and be quick about it."

Anna felt a prickle of apprehension and disappointment. Instead of joining a party, she would be alone with Alexis for the day,
after they got to Aegina. She wasn't sure how she felt about that.
Then she shrugged. Good Lord, how ridiculous, she thought.
Who wouldn't want to spend the day cruising the Saronic Gulf
with a handsome man? He couldn't help it if his cousin got sick.

Once they were under way, Anna went up to the bow and
stood facing the breeze as they skimmed over the wide swells of
ink blue water. It was a very fast boat. They passed several tankers
and a large cruise ship. The passengers, lining the rail, waved
madly. Anna waved back. It was going to be a wonderful day.

When they were out of the harbor, Alexis joined her. "Don't
worry," he said, pointing back at the pilothouse. "I told Nikolas I
would throw him overboard if he went faster than thirty-five
knots." He stood a little apart from her, his brown hands gripping
the railing. His dark eyes moved over her from head to foot as if
memorizing every detail. Anna's skin prickled under the sweep of
his gaze. *Now, this could get upsetting,* she thought.

She was aware of heat in her cheeks and—to her horror—felt
her nipples contract. It was probably the cool wind, she assured
herself, but she turned away so he wouldn't notice.

"You make a beautiful figurehead for my boat."

"I'm flattered." What had she gotten herself into? "It is a
beautiful boat."

"Make yourself at home. If you get tired of the sun, go to the
salon downstairs. There are cool drinks in the refrigerator and
plenty of food."

"Thank you." She smiled and looked back out over the water.

Alexis pressed her shoulder gently and said, "Enjoy your
communion with this, my sea, Anna," and trailing his fingers
briefly down her back, he left her to her own thoughts.

Anna's thoughts, however, were not on the sea. *What is happening to me?*

She could hear Niko laughing every once in a while. He and Alexis must have a very special relationship.

There were islands everywhere, some quite large, with clustered villages and single farmhouses hugging the barren hillsides. Others, obviously with their own water source, were green, and contoured with vineyards and orchards. A few rose gently from the water like great sea animals sunning themselves. Still others reared up with rocky cliffs and stone outcroppings from the vari-colored water that was every shade of blue. A few were no bigger than a house. Anna acknowledged their beauty with another part of her mind.

"We're approaching Aegina harbor now," Alexis said from just behind her, startling her out of her dreamy observation. Already? It couldn't have taken more than an hour to get here.

"I'm letting Niko impress his friends with his skill in docking. He called them on the phone a few minutes ago."

"Alexis," she said, "is it possible that he could stay with us? I mean, I would enjoy getting to know him and—"

"Take away his day of water-skiing?" He took her by both shoulders and turned her to face him. "Do you think we need a chaperone?"

Anna coughed. "I don't—" Feeling ridiculous, she couldn't think of what she wanted to say.

He was looking at her mouth as if trying to lip-read her. She could see the pulse in his throat and at his temple, slow and steady. His grip on her shoulders tightened his biceps against his shirt.

She swallowed, closing her eyes to the disturbing presence of this man. "A chaperone?" Her attempt at a laugh sounded even more ridiculous to her. "I haven't had a chaperone since my father insisted on driving me and my first date to the movies and then sat right behind us."

"I doubt that Niko would do that, even if he came along," he said, his eyebrows raised in mischief. "He's on my side. He would be no help to you."

The laugh broke the tension. She felt heady and adventure-some again. He was just teasing her.

Niko leaped over the railing and dropped to the dock below. Alexis handed down his water ski. "We will pick you up at five o'clock. That will get us into the Port of Piraeus before dark."

"I not be late," Niko said. Then with his dark eyes twinkling and a wide smile showing that dazzling display of teeth, he yelled, "Have good time."

Alexis waved him away with mock impatience and went into the pilothouse. As they sped away Anna was genuinely sorry Niko wasn't along. She had been telling Alexis the truth, that she would have enjoyed getting to know the young man.

"We'll be in Hydra in an hour and a half. Do you want to eat something now, or wait until we get there?"

"I can wait, but I'll be glad to bring you something from the kitchen."

"The galley! A beer, please. And get one for yourself if you like. There is also wine and fresh juice."

Alexis set the wheel and unfolded a deck chair for her in the sun while she went below and changed into shorts and a tank top. She brought up the beer and an orange juice for herself, then sat on a deck chair with her book. But after reading only a few sentences, she felt the book sliding off the chair as the wind and the sun and the motion took their toll on her.

She woke to silence. Alexis was standing at the rail in his swimsuit, a brief, European bikini naturally. He had his back to her.

Beyond him, across the water, was a postcard Aegean village, whitewashed clusters of block houses stacked up a rugged hillside. The town itself was built around the perimeter of rocky promontory arms, which embraced a harbor dancing with boats of all kinds. There were fishing caïques painted in bright colors, several white sailboats, and two large luxury cruise ships docked at the quay.

Alexis had anchored off a rocky Greek "beach," its shelves of rock scattered with bathers who looked, from the distance, like a herd of sunning sea lions, except for their bright towels and the paraphernalia thrown about.

Anna stood and stretched. After taking stock of the bathers

on the beach, she noted that all the women were topless. It seemed the natural Aegean thing. She remembered feeling like a conspicuous prude in Crete. *So, here's to the Greeks!* She stripped off her shorts and shirt down to her bikini bottoms just as Alexis turned around.

He didn't seem shocked. He just smiled and nodded. But before he could say anything, Anna opened the gate in the guardrail at the side of the boat and dived into the glass-clear water.

It was a total-body delight. She was sure it wasn't her imagination that the Aegean made one more buoyant. The silky coolness of the water rolled down her body as she swam powerfully toward shore. She had taken only a few strokes when she turned to breathe and found Alexis keeping pace with her. Taking a deep breath, on her next stroke she dived below the surface and swam underwater away from him.

He was too quick for her. He caught her foot and pulled her back to him as they both surfaced, laughing.

"I would have guessed you were a strong swimmer," he said.

"How could you have guessed that?" She asked, treading water with only a small effort.

"You have a swimmer's body."

"You've never seen my body before today."

He gave her such a knowing look that she knew he had probably undressed her in his mind's eye every time they were together. Ah, well, she hadn't been surprised at his physique either.

Anna turned and swam toward the shore, but Alexis headed her off and grabbed her arm. "Aren't you hungry? Let's go back and eat. Then, if you want, we can take the tender and play tourist in Hydra. We can swim again later."

Back on the boat, Alexis insisted on serving. He brought cold cuts and cheese, fresh, yeasty, hard-crusted bread, and icy white wine and spread them on a table he had set up on the deck. Anna stepped into her ankle-length striped caftan and pulled up the full-length zipper.

"You looked beautiful just as you were," Alexis protested loudly.

"The sun," she said, pointing to the sky. She knew she'd never be able to eat sitting half-naked with Alexis watching her so appreciatively.

Alexis shrugged and smiled. "Okay," he said. He attacked his lunch with gusto. He seemed to have a penchant for enthusiasm. As he ate he told her about his childhood when he'd visited these islands often with his father. "When we go ashore, I'll introduce you to some of the people who are like family to me. My father used to drop me off to stay with them sometimes, then come back for me on his way home several days later."

Anna talked about her childhood in Texas. "Would you believe I never even saw the ocean until I was twelve?"

"I think you were a deprived child," Alexis said solemnly.

"I think you're right. But I'm making up for it now."

"Tell me about your husband," Alexis said, looking straight into her face.

"What?" This was a request she hadn't expected.

"If it's too painful, don't." He shook his head. "Forget that I asked."

"No," she said when she could talk again. "It has gotten less painful. I think." She took a minute to compose herself. This was the last thing she had imagined talking about with Alexis today. "Paul was a very charismatic person. Everyone liked him. We had—"

Anna looked out at the open sea, not seeing it at all. "He would have loved this. He always wanted to sail around the world." She looked back at Alexis. "You said you had met him. If you talked to him at all, you know what kind of person he was."

"So you had a strong, fulfilling marriage." It was a statement.

"Yes," Anna whispered.

"You are fortunate." Maggie had been the first to tell her that. Then Maria, and now Alexis. "And the man you marry next will be fortunate because you will know what makes a good marriage. You can teach him."

A month ago, a presumptuous statement like that would have stirred Anna's anger. Made her defensive, protective of Paul and all that they had been together. But now she felt a new sense of acceptance of its truth. She *had* been fortunate. Been. And now her whole life was before her. "Perhaps you're right. But I have no desire to remarry."

"You are a very special person, Anna. I'm sure your husband felt this. He won't be the last to do so."

Anna looked down at her hands, not knowing how to respond to that. For some reason she noticed her ring finger. The white indentation that had glared from her finger after she'd first taken off her wedding ring hadn't been discernible for a long time.

She stood up and walked over to the rail, looking out at the beautiful little village of Hydra. How could she cross this threshold? *Know thyself?* How could she begin to evolve into whatever it was she was supposed to be?

"Would you like to go over there?" Alexis' voice was so close to her ear that she could feel his breath. She hadn't realized he had walked up behind her. "I could row us over."

Anna stared out at the village for a long time, her thoughts a jumble of confusion. "Do you know what I'd like you to do?"

"What is that?"

Anna was taking the band out of her hair, pulling at the long wet ropes of it. "I'd like you to cut my hair."

"Cut your hair? Your beautiful hair?"

"Surely you have some scissors on this boat. You have everything. Please!"

He caught her head between his hands, pushing his fingers under the wet locks, looking into her eyes. "You want me to cut your hair because your husband loved it. Is that it?"

Anna nodded, her tears distorting Alexis' face.

"Listen to me, Anna. You are who you are. You don't have to change anything to begin your life again." He leaned down and she closed her eyes. But he didn't kiss her. He pulled up the hood of her caftan and covered her wet hair, then, with his arm around her, holding her hand, led her down the narrow stairs to the lower deck and into the aft cabin.

He stood her in front of a full-length mirror on the back of a door and turned her so that she was facing it. "Look carefully, Anna Sandoval, at what you see." Reaching around from behind her, he caught the zipper pull and opened the entire length of the robe. Then he pulled it back, letting it fall from her shoulders.

Anna looked down at the heap of color at her feet. "Look up, Anna. This is the glory of you. Now. In a country far from your home." He lifted her hair from her shoulders. "Cutting your hair would not change that."

Anna glanced up. She could see the reflection of herself standing there in her bikini brief, with her hair hanging in heavy clumps over her shoulders. But instead of looking at herself, she looked at Alexis' face watching over her shoulder. She had stopped crying, and she raised her chin a little.

"You have had something wonderful. Perhaps you will never again have a relationship that is as satisfying or as beautiful. Don't ever try to, Anna. Keep the memory just as you keep the memory of a happy childhood with your parents and grandparents. It is part of you. It is part of what you are now. That is what I am trying to tell you." He spoke with such intensity that his voice shook. He turned her around. "But don't let your past rob you of a future that could also be meaningful."

Anna shivered. Alexis was trying to lead her out of a snare, she knew that. He was showing her a way out. But it was as if he were talking to her from a great distance, his deep voice echoing through her mind.

"Come, I'll help you wash your lovely hair." He took her hand and led her into the large tiled bathroom she wouldn't have believed she would find on a boat. One dim part of her mind took it all in. The toilet was in a cubicle by itself. The sink next to that. The whole end of the room was a wide shower stall behind doors of etched glass.

Alexis turned the faucets on and soon the gushing water was steamy. He gently pushed Anna through the door, stepping in right behind her.

Turning her back to the spray, he took her head in his hands and allowed the water to rinse it, then pulled her forward. From a wire rack with a hooked cover to keep its contents battened down, he took out shampoo, and pouring some into his hand, he began to massage it into Anna's hair.

Eyes closed, she stood perfectly still, feeling the hot water pepper her shoulders and back, feeling the nearness of Alexis with every atom of her body, though he touched only her head with his hands. His fingers worked the fragrant liquid into her scalp in strong, overlapping circles. Anna almost moaned. A gentle shudder moved her like an earth tremor. She wanted to reach out, draw him to her. But she couldn't.

Then, his hands around her head, Alexis started at her forehead and scooped the lather down, pulling her head back as he twisted her hair like a rope. Under the shower he rinsed it clean. Then, gathering her hair together and squeezing out the last of the water, he lifted the heavy mass and rinsed off her back with long strokes of his hand.

Untie the cat, Anna. She could hear Sam saying that in the voice of a prophet. She doubted that he had meant for her to act so soon. With someone else. *But, damn it, who makes all these rules and what keeps us bound to them?* she wondered. *A little fling never hurt anyone,* Maggie had said. Anna smiled. It was easy after all.

Pushing her a little to the side, Alexis stepped around as though in a dance. He took a turn under the shower. Quickly, he shampooed his own hair and, with a bar of soap, did a quick wash down, suit and all. Then he handed Anna the soap. Taking her by the shoulders, he changed places with her again, so the water was at her back. With a smile, he said, "Don't cut your hair," stepped out, and closed the glass doors.

Anna stood there holding the soap in her hand, staring at the steamy glass door. She felt as if she would melt and run down the drain. Her breath was coming in gasps. She reached up and touched her hair where his hands had been.

Through the glass, she could vaguely see Alexis dry off, then walk out, leaving her alone. Why had he left so abruptly?

From the bedroom, she heard some ethereal synthesized music of the kind he played in his car. She could imagine him dressing in his resplendent white ducks, combing his curls. Could he be calmly getting ready for a row into Hydra? After all that?

Anna stripped off her suit and started to wash, taking her time, letting the water carry away the feel of Alexis' hands.

Suddenly, as if by diabolical design, she was doused with icy water. "Yipes!" she yelled.

"I forgot to tell you," Alexis shouted from the next room. "There is a limited amount of hot water."

"Thanks a lot," Anna shouted, getting out quickly. *I guess I needed that,* she thought. She found a huge white towel that wrapped around her twice, and tucked the corner into the top like a sarong.

Reaching for the door handle, she hesitated. Why was he acting like this? He had had the perfect opportunity to seize the moment there in the shower just as he had at his office the other night. And yet—and yet he hadn't. Anna turned and wiped clean a little patch on the mirror and looked into her own face. Why?

The answer came slowly clear as the steam faded from the mirror. He was leaving it up to her. He would not take advantage. He would not force himself on her. Was that it? Was he giving her a graceful way out . . . or in? He had shown his intentions in more ways than one. Now he was leaving it up to her.

Untie the cat? Perhaps this would be a good time. "Alexis?" Her voice sounded strange to her as she called out.

"Yes." He sounded perfectly normal.

"I think I'd rather"—she cleared her throat—"see the town of Hydra later."

He opened the door so quickly he must have been just on the other side. Anna saw him behind her in the mirror. He was wearing a navy terry cloth robe. "You must know I wanted you to say that," he said in a low rumble. "But are you sure this is what you want?"

She turned to him. "Alexis, I lost my innocence a long time ago."

"I'm not so sure that is true."

Anna looked down. He was probably right. She had never broken the rules until just lately. Now she seemed to be breaking them all.

She looked up into his dark eyes, seeing his self-possession, knowing that he wouldn't hold it against her if she turned away. She smiled. She wanted this man. It was as simple as that. "Then I'm ready to make it true," she said.

Alexis reached out and drew Anna to him, one hand behind her head, so that her face was buried in the soft folds of his robe. Hugging her close, he rocked her in a slow dance, whispering her name. Then he led her from the misty bathroom and out into the sun. "We have all the time in the world, so relax. Let's dry your hair."

They were on the seaward side on the half deck outside the stateroom of the gently rocking boat, looking out to the open water. The unearthly music wove itself around them as Alexis brushed out Anna's hair in long strokes, spreading it and letting it fall lightly across her shoulders to catch the sun.

She did moan as she gave herself fully to the moment. When it was dry, he gathered it up in his hands and buried his face in it. Then his hands moved to her face. He kissed her gently, lifting her to her feet, then pulled her back into the stateroom.

Reaching out, he loosened the tucked corner of the towel, releasing it gently. He stood back a little and watched it slip from her body, like a sculptor unveiling his latest work.

It was the pleasure in Alexis' face that moved Anna more than the sensations as he let the towel drop. His eyes caressed every inch of her. Then he pulled her to the bed.

Eons later, Anna heard Alexis' voice as if from a distance. "The gods danced," he said softly. "Did you notice?"

Anna shook her head. "I had my eyes closed."

"Don't move. I'll bring you something wonderful to drink." He stood up and pulled on the terry cloth robe.

Anna couldn't have moved if the boat had caught on fire.

Alexis went out of the room and returned with a tray on which stood two long-stemmed glasses of amber liquid.

One sip of the orange-flavored Grand Marnier burned all the way down, awakening every cell from its somnolent state. She stretched, groaning and sighing. *If I died this moment, I would feel I had reached the ultimate,* she thought. She smiled, stretching again—a full-body smile.

"All hands on shore," he said. "The tour of Hydra, our reason for coming here, remember, is about to begin."

"Was that really why you brought me here, to see Hydra?"

He nodded. "You may not believe it, but my motives were pure when I asked you. After all, my cousin and his family were going to come." He shrugged. "But when I discovered that we were to be alone, it was as if it had been planned by fate." He started to pull the sheet off of her. "I do admit that I did, then, consider the possibilities." His face went solemn with mock seriousness. "And you? Was that really why you came?"

She threw a pillow at him. "Yes!" she said. "I was promised a family outing with new people to meet. A day of partying and exploring new sights."

He leaned over and kissed her. "I hope it hasn't been too disappointing that it didn't work out that way."

Hydra was a typical sea village with vestiges of the old life of a quiet little fishing community overlaid with tourist attractions— shops with souvenirs, outdoor cafés and vendors. It rose in a natural amphitheater above its sheltered harbor.

Alexis rowed the tender to the shore. After tying up the boat, they walked along the harbor and up the warrenlike narrow companionways and passageways to higher levels of the town. Flowers were everywhere against the white walls in each private garden they could see through wrought-iron gates. Alexis pointed out several handsome mansions high on the hill behind the village, where he had spent many happy days as a boy. They belonged to the ship-owning families who were friends of his father.

Later, they sat at an outdoor table, nursing frosty ice-cream-and-coffee drinks. Alexis stopped a flower vendor and bought several nosegays, then asked one of the waiters for envelopes and paper and wrote little notes to the friends they no longer had time to visit. "They'll know I was here—my boat is well-known—and they'll wonder why I didn't pay a call."

"What are you telling them?" Anna asked.

"That because of the storm, I must get back."

"And when they notice there was no storm?"

Alexis pointed to the north. High cirrus clouds streaked the sky.

"That doesn't look very threatening to me. It couldn't be a rainstorm."

He squinted at the clouds. "No rain until possibly later. This one will be only wind. You are in for the ride of your life." He took a long draw on his straw.

"You don't seem overly concerned."

"I enjoy storms." Then he looked at her closely. "I hope you don't get seasick?"

Anna folded her arms and lifted her chin. "Never."

Alexis called a young boy over and, with rapid-fire instructions in Greek, sent him away with a handful of coins and all the bouquets except one.

Standing up, Alexis said, "The city of Athena was the first and most important love of my life. I have dedicated my life to bringing her back to her original beauty." With a smart bow and serious face he added, "To Athena's rival for my affection." He handed her the flowers. "You are a magnificent woman, Anna."

She searched his eyes, expecting to find mischief. But she saw only tenderness. A small pain wrenched under her breastbone. She hugged the flowers to the pain. Paul used to do things like that. She had forgotten the joy of it. "Thank you, Alexis. They are lovely."

She pinched off one of the tiny pink rosebuds and reached up to put it in a buttonhole of his shirt, laying her hand along his cheek. She had no words for what she was feeling. Her gratitude was not only for the flowers. She knew she would always be grateful to him for this day.

"Thank you," she said simply.

Alexis had been right about the ride back to Athens. Anna loved it. It was the perfect ending to this tumultuous, exhilarating day. She stood, gripping the rail at the bow of the yacht, the deck under her feet dipping and slanting, the wind snatching at her hair, all the way to Aegina. They arrived at 5:47.

"You're late," Niko shouted as he climbed over the railing onto the bucking deck. He was shirtless and sunburned. He nodded to Anna with a glittering smile and shouted at Alexis, "I'm surprised to see you, cousin. I thought you would sail away across the Mediterranean with beautiful lady."

"If my sainted cousin had not saddled me with his brat, I might have done just that," Alexis shouted back. "Now get up here and earn your ride."

"Aye, aye, sir." He bowed to Anna with a twinkle in his eye and went in to steer the boat.

Alexis came out and stood on the bow with her, his arm holding her close.

When they were tied up, Anna begged off dinner. She needed some time, she told him, some space. Alexis didn't press. Saying he had to batten everything down, he left her with Yeorgios at the car after giving her a long hug, his hand caressing her hair. Brushing her cheek in a light kiss, he promised to call her the next day. He blew her a kiss as Yeorgios drove off into the dusk.

Nineteen

Anna walked into the lobby of her hotel with a new ease of movement, a sense that she had somehow crossed a threshold and had found herself in different geography. All those barriers of what she was *supposed* to do, *supposed* to be, were left behind in another life. It wasn't so much that she was physically sated, though she had to admit that was more than true. It was that *she* had made the decision. She had not been allowed . . . given permission. She had *chosen*. She had sovereignty over her future.

Strange, she now knew that she could have had this all her life, but that she had chosen then to follow someone else's lead. Even that last night in Crete with Sam—God, that seemed eons ago—she had simply allowed herself to be swept up in the tide. *To be allowed* was not the same as *to choose*.

Anna walked up to the counter smiling. She was sure that if she had turned and taken a bow, there would have been a trumpet fanfare. But she simply asked, "Do I have any mail?" She had been out only for the day, but the stack of letters made it look as if she had been gone a week. *Maybe I have,* she thought. *Maybe I have.*

Leaving a generous tip for the desk clerk, she took her mail and went up to her suite, feeling as if her feet weren't quite touching the floor. After a long, hot shower, she started to look through the accumulation of letters and phone messages, and then laid them aside. Pouring herself a glass of wine, she opened her doors and looked out across Athens, not seeing.

She reached for her sketch pad, but did not draw anything.

She wrote, in blue pencil, "In life there are many moments of decision. It matters not so much what befalls us. What matters is how we manage it. What we do with circumstances fate bestows on us." She thought for a long time about this past year and knew that she had passed through many portals. She was not the same person who came to Crete a few weeks ago. She also knew that she had had the help of many good people. Demetri and Maria, Sophia, Alexis especially, even Sam. She was not the same person. And today, she had accepted that. She *was* getting to know herself.

She picked up her pile of letters and messages. Sam had called three times. Gwen Berkley, twice. There was a friendly note from the manager of the Hotel Villas asking when they would have the pleasure of her company again, and telling her they were taking care of her rooms. They said that they had put the dress that she had left outside to dry in her closet, and hoped she was having a wonderful time in Athens. They enclosed a note from Maria Anistopolis saying she and Demetri were worried that Anna had left so suddenly and that they hoped she was having a pleasant stay on the mainland. Also enclosed was a phone message from Sophia asking Anna to return the call. There were letters from both Peter and Christine, forwarded from Crete. Anna sat down to read those, ripping each open with eagerness. Peter was in the middle of his summer courses and busy writing papers. Christine was immersed with decorating a very small apartment on very little money.

Assured that her offspring both were doing well, Anna attacked the pile again. There was an embossed invitation to a dinner party at the home of a Mrs. Kountouriotis a week from Saturday, addressed to Anna Sandoval, not to Mrs. Paul Sandoval. Anna tapped the corner of the envelope against her teeth. She had never heard of Mrs. Kountouriotis.

The treasure was a fat letter from Maggie. Anna held it in her hand, torn as to whether to just sit and stare and let the reality of this momentous day sink in, or to let go of the magic by plunging—the only way to describe reading one of Maggie's epistles—

into the down-to-earth commentary and ribald humor she knew she would find in those pages.

She called room service for a sandwich supper. While she waited, she sipped wine and watched the lights of the city twinkle on through the open doors of her balcony. The street noises from below formed a musical background to the kaleidoscope of emotions flashing through her mind . . . and anatomy. She didn't move until she heard the knock.

A waiter set the tray on her small table and filled a cup from the large pot of American coffee she had ordered. She got herself ensconced in her chair with her supper at hand and settled back to read Maggie's fat letter. Like all Maggie's letters, it was pages of haphazard paragraphs—stream-of-consciousness commentary, parenthetical remarks, and random paragraph breaks.

"I'm almost sorry I didn't pack up and go to Crete with you," it began without salutation. *"Your cards and notes sound a little forlorn."*

Wait till she receives the "book" I just sent her.

> *I hope by now you've met some fascinating people, and though you've said a thousand times you aren't interested, I hope one or two of them are men. Dallas is hot and sticky and smells of sweaty socks and cut grass, if you can imagine the combination. Everyone races from one air-conditioned enclosure to another. (Remember when we were kids and played tennis in this heat?) Last week I tried the South Beach Diet and almost starved to death for want of something sweet. I lost five pounds but then was invited to a summerhouse on Lake Dallas for the weekend and, well, I think it's downright rude to refuse food at a party. (So much for being thin. They'll never ask me to be an understudy for a fashion model, that's for sure.) It was a wild weekend of jokes and small talk, but as I sit here writing this letter I realize that that kind of schmoozing was kind of like sex with someone you*

> *don't really care about—okay while it lasts, but*
> *leaving you kind of empty feeling afterward. I need a*
> *change. Maybe I'll become a test pilot—that would be*
> *exciting. Or a brain surgeon.*

The next page was dated several days later in the style of ongoing letters Maggie and Anna had always written each other, adding to them every several days, or weeks, before they sent them.

> *I've learned never to write anything on my calendar*
> *in ink. I had this week all filled in with a commitment*
> *every night for some damn thing or other, when I got*
> *a call out of the blue from one of the men at that Lake*
> *Dallas party. I didn't take much notice of him when I*
> *was there. He is plain as a pitchfork and spent most of*
> *his time jogging or swimming or playing tennis (I*
> *stayed near the food and drink, <u>out</u> of the sun).*
> *Anyway, he invited me to go sailing on White Rock*
> *Lake one evening soon. He has a boat called a Snipe—*
> *whatever that is. (And if it turns out to be a "snipe*
> *hunt," there will be one less professor at Southern*
> *Methodist University, which is what he is. I'm still*
> *trying to think of something horrible to do to you for*
> *that back when we were fourteen.)*

Anna laughed. She had been the one to set Maggie up in her first "snipe hunt." She could still see Maggie sitting in the middle of the path that led from the high school hockey field into the woods, holding open a burlap bag to catch the snipe. Anna and two other friends, of course, were not flushing the snipe, as they had told her, but were sitting in an upstairs room watching to see how long Maggie would wait there.

Maggie's letter went on.

> *I told him it would have to be after four, since the*
> *sun doesn't agree with my lily-white skin, and he said*

*that would be fine and why didn't we have dinner on
the boat? Food again!*

She described the case she was working on:

> *A dispute over property, about as interesting as
> flossing someone else's teeth. A good homicide would
> be a relief after this. Well, give my love to Apollo if
> you see him and* have fun, *for Christ's sake.*

Her signature was an indecipherable scrawl.

It wasn't enough. Anna needed to hear her voice. She went
into the bedroom to place a transatlantic call to Dallas. But just as
she reached for the phone, it rang.

It was Gwen. "Anna, you are the hardest person in the world
to locate." She took a breath, but before Anna could offer any explanation, she rushed on. "I was just checking to see how you
are."

"Everything is . . . fine," Anna said. *An understatement if I
ever heard one.*

"Well, let us know if you need anything. I'm planning a party
next week. I'll call you with the details."

"It sounds great," Anna said, wishing she had an excuse to
decline on the spot. Anna caught a glance at her own reflection in
the mirror across the room, dim in the lamplight. She was frowning. *I used to thrive on that sort of thing. God, that seems so long
ago.*

"There is a man . . . a very nice person, new to Athens, that
I'd like you to meet. You'll like him. I'm inviting him to the party
also."

Oh, dear. Now this. "Thank you for thinking of me, Gwen."

"Well, I thought," she finished lamely, "it would be nice for
both of you to have someone to do things with. T-t-touring. That's
what I mean," Gwen stuttered. "Sightseeing. You could show him
around. You must get . . . don't you ever get lonely?"

She meant well. Anna knew that. She closed her eyes and

nodded. "Yes, I do get lonely. But that's part of the healing, Gwen. And strangely enough, I'd expected to have a lot of time on my hands here in Athens. But it hasn't turned out that way."

"Well, anyway, how would you like to come tomorrow night? For drinks with just the two of us. So we can get caught up on . . . everything. Come at seven. Then we'll have a light supper."

This might be the solution. Anna knew Gwen wanted to hear about Paul and the past year. *This will satisfy her curiosity, since we really haven't had time for a visit. Perhaps then I can gracefully bow out of the dinner where I am to meet this available man.* "That sounds perfect. I'll see you tomorrow."

After she hung up, horrified at the thought of matchmaker Gwen fixing her up with someone, the phone rang again.

"Hello, Anna?" Something fluttered in her chest when she heard Alexis' voice. "I just called to see if you made it back safely."

"It's nice hearing from you. Yes, Yeorgios got me back without disaster."

He laughed. "Not a very creative excuse to call, but the best I could do on short notice."

"I had a very wonderful time today, Alexis."

"This was a very special day for me too, Anna." How close the edge was, Anna thought, when she could be stirred by the emotion radiating from common, ordinary words. She couldn't think of anything to say.

"I know you're tired, and I won't keep you. I just wanted to ask if I might escort you to Mrs. Kountouriotis' party. I found the invitation when I returned."

"Ah, the mystery is about to be solved," she said. "Who is she, anyway?"

"An old friend of my family's. You'll like her."

Anna hesitated. The dinner tomorrow at the Berkleys', and now this? She didn't even know if she was going to stay in Athens another week. She needed to decide what to do about her things in Crete.

"We don't have to stay very long," Alexis said. "Then we could go wherever you like."

"What time?"

"Nine o'clock? And now about tomorrow. I must go to the university during the day, but where shall we go for dinner?"

"Oh, Alexis, I can't," Anna said with genuine regret. "I've been invited out with friends tomorrow."

"I must learn to call sooner."

"I'm sorry. I truly am."

"No problem. I'm glad you are finding your way about and enjoying your old friends. Besides, we have plenty of time. What about the next day?"

After she hung up, Anna thought about time. So little time. So much. She had come to Greece for time—time for herself, time to rest and reflect. Time away from the hassles of a social calendar, of having to make appearances with Paul for all those years—though for the most part she loved that—and then, now, after his death, to still feel she had to say yes to every invitation so feelings wouldn't be hurt. Here she was, back on the same merry-go-round.

But this is different, she told herself. *It's different when you're single.*

Single. The word echoed silently through her mind. It was one of those words that went down like medicine, but instead of making her feel better, it made her sick at heart. Not the sorrow of mourning. Strangely, there was no longer pain, only a feeling like that bruised, fuzzy feeling that lingers after a particularly bad headache. *Single* left an emptiness, like the word *widow.* It had the clang of loneliness about it.

The phone rang again. "Anna?" Alexis' voice was like a soothing balm. "I forgot to tell you, I found your rings."

Anna's hand flew to her chest. They were gone! "Where?"

He gave his low chuckle. "They were hanging on the faucet in the shower."

Anna lay back on the bed, listening to him talk about one

thing and then another, random comments, apparently not wanting to hang up. She had the sense of hearing a familiar tune that,
once heard, one never forgets. Maybe it wasn't so bad being single, she thought. When she got the rings back she would put them
away. She should have done it long ago.

She woke at dawn the next morning. It was an old habit she
had gotten out of these past years. When she was younger, and all
her friends slept until noon, she had felt cheated if she wasn't
awake to see the sunrise. If she slept late, it was as though the day
had crept in like stealthy members of an orchestra and was in full
concert when she arrived. She liked to be there when the instru-
ments were tuning up.

Today she stretched with pure pleasure, the memory of the
day before playing through her mind and body. *A little fling never
hurt anyone:* Maggie's advice from what seemed like years ago.
Hurt? Anna felt she could leap buildings in a single bound, lift the
heaviest weight, hit the highest note.

Yawning, she remembered that she had never called Maggie. Oh well, maybe later. She had a whole day before her, a gift,
and she was going to spend it drawing. Anxious to get started,
she flung back the sheets and tumbled out of bed, feeling
charged with creative energy. She caught sight of her naked form
and wild hair in the mirror and did a little bump and grind.
Laughing, she grabbed her robe in her hand and walked into the
sitting room.

Without turning on the lights, she pulled back the curtains
and opened the doors to the waking city. It had rained during the
night—Alexis had been wrong—and the air had a damp, city
smell of wet pavement, fumes, and ozone. The sky glowed
strangely red on the horizon.

A prickle touched the nape of Anna's neck. What was that
old saying? "Red sky at morning, sailors take warning"? She
thought of Alexis and his boat and in the predawn of morning she
had a relapse of remorse. Had she actually had sex with two men
in the space of a fortnight? She suddenly wanted to cover herself.
What was she becoming? Since the last day of her sojourn in

Crete, in the span of less than two weeks, she had been laid—
there was no delicate way to put it—not once, but twice. And now
she was having palpitations over someone younger than she was.
Robbing the cradle? Is that what her friends here in Athens would
think if she continued to see him? Gwen? The Reinholds?
Norma? Would they think it not only ludicrous but also perhaps
a little desperate and pitiful for her to "take up" with a man so
young? And was it?

Anna shivered. These morning-after questions were depress-
ing, making her want to get back in bed and pull the covers over
her head. Making her want to run away—run away like she had
from Crete.

Tying on her robe, she looked back out the window, misgivings swarming through her mind like bees. As she stared, unseeing, at the Acropolis, for some reason the specter of her Catholic
grandmother's face rose in her mind's eye, her head shaking no,
her finger pointed. Then—Anna was sure—she slowly winked.
Anna grinned and relaxed. *You've come a long way, baby,* she told
herself ruefully—from the dramatic, bereaved widow, obsessed
with her grief, to this. And what was this? To be honest, she felt
she was coming alive again.

Anna laughed just as the red glow was slashed with gold and
the sun rose from the sea, touching the Parthenon with splendor.
*For crying out loud, it's the twenty-first century! Who cares what I
do?* She looked out over Athens and took a deep breath, her apprehension vanishing with the night. She threw on her clothes and
gathered up her bag and went out into the day.

The streets had that new-washed shine. Puddles reflected
buildings and the few people who, like Anna, were out early all
carried umbrellas. She made her way toward the Plaka. When she
got there, everything was shuttered, the cobblestones slick as if
scrubbed and oiled. Anna wandered about without purpose, enjoying the morning. Vivid red clumps of geraniums crowded
wrought-iron balconies. Light fell across the courtyard of a stone
church like torn pieces of silk scattered on the pavement.
Through a wrought-iron gate, a giant tree shielded a tiny court-

yard, fragrant with the brooding sharpness of freshly trimmed rosemary.

Turning a corner, Anna glanced absently through the plate glass window of a small hotel dining room and found herself staring, almost eye to eye, at Sam McDonald. He was looking at her as if he'd seen a ghost. Standing up so abruptly that he spilled his coffee, he headed for the door, and stuck his head out.

"Good morning!" he said to Anna. "Boy, I'll bet you got the worm. Come in here, and I'll buy you a cup of coffee."

He took her elbow and practically dragged her off the street into the dining room of the little hotel, which was actually only a corner of the lobby. Anna was glad for the offer of coffee. But with him guiding her to the table, she had a moment of shyness, as if he could somehow *know*. Did he still have spies about? The thought made her wince. Best to steer far from the whole subject. "Looks like you tried to bathe in yours," Anna said, pointing to the coffee spills on the table.

"Oh, well, it was too full anyway," Sam said, mopping up around his cup with his napkin. He signaled for more to the woman coming toward their table. She nodded and disappeared through the door.

"What are you doing here?" Anna asked.

"Here at the Nefeli Hotel? I live here."

Anna looked around. It was small, but very cozy. "Why here?"

"I like it. I like the Plaka. My room has a window ledge planted with geraniums and overlooks the street so I can hear all the revelry at night. And I like the owners. What else can I say?"

"Sounds wonderful. I wish I had known about it."

"Well, you do now." His shaggy eyebrows were raised in suggestion.

Anna let that go by.

"I tried to call you all day yesterday. You must have had a heavy date," he said.

"I did," Anna said casually. "I went on a cruise to Hydra." She gave Sam a cool look. "How's Taylor?"

"Well, she's anxious, disgruntled, worried, and . . . still young and beautiful."

"Why's she so upset?"

"Seems the old codger she's been hanging out with is dragging his feet a little on *her* plans for matrimonial bliss."

Anna caught her breath. "Matrimony? I didn't know it had gone that far."

"Well, I hadn't either. She just brought that up since I came back from Crete."

"Well, is the old codger dragging his feet because he's lost the strength to pick them up? Or does he have reservations about it?"

"He'd just like things to stay as they are for a while. He wants to wait and see how the wind shifts." He looked over at Anna. "You notice that red sky this morning?"

Anna's heart skipped a beat.

"Us pilots—we're always noticing the weather." He went on without waiting for her answer. "I think it's best not to begin a long voyage in the hurricane season."

"Is this the hurricane season here?" Alexis had told her they almost never had storms this time of year.

"Could be. Could be. Well, here's your coffee. Now tell me about Hydra."

Anna told him about the beauty of the water and the islands. When the woman brought her a roll, she changed the subject. "How long do you plan to stay in Athens, Sam?"

"I've got to finish up this security stuff, and then I have a week left of my vacation. I've got some heavy decisions to make."

"I guess you do."

"Well, that too." He looked sheepish. "But I'm trying to decide whether to stay with the airline after this until I retire or . . ." He screwed up his mouth and squinted, his fist on his forehead in a caricature of *The Thinker*.

"Go on. Or . . . ?"

"Or go back to school. I have that physics degree and—"

"What physics degree?"

"Well, it was so long ago that none of what I learned is true anymore."

"You didn't tell me you had a degree in physics. When you talked in Crete about college you never mentioned . . ."

"Bachelor's degree, MIT. Master's, Cornell."

"And you've been an airline pilot all these years? Why didn't you do something in physics? Teach. Invent something."

"For the same reason that a Rhodes scholar would play professional football, I guess. It just happened. Right after I got my master's, I enlisted in the air force. That's where I learned to fly. Where better to put a physicist than in an airplane?"

"But after the service—"

"I kept on flying. I love to fly. It's as simple as that." He took a drink of his coffee. "But now it's gotten complicated and political and hectic, and I'm thinking of going back to school to learn about breeding and, maybe, settling down on a farm and raising Thoroughbreds."

"Horses?"

"Horses. Say in Maryland or West Virginia."

"Have you been drinking?"

"No. I've just been thinking." He looked at his watch. "Well, I'm due at a meeting down at Omonia Square. More about how to rid the world of terrorists." He rubbed his hand across his eyes. "I'll sure be glad when they get this all straightened out. Listen, I'll give you a call sometime, if I can ever find you home. Maybe we can go out for lunch or something."

"Bring Taylor."

Sam gave her a puzzled look.

"I like her."

After he was gone, Anna realized she hadn't asked him why he had called her the day before. *I like him too.* She smiled. *He makes me feel . . . he makes me feel at ease . . . with myself.*

A master's degree in physics. She would never in a million years have thought of him as a scholar—even if he did read books she couldn't understand.

Wandering out of the Plaka, Anna came upon the Anglican

church. She could hear organ music faintly through the doors and, on impulse, slipped in. The organist, a gray-haired, birdlike woman, played as if in prayer, oblivious to the presence of another person, though the door had scraped as Anna entered the nave. Noting the look of rapt concentration, Anna felt an immediate affinity for this woman. She was totally immersed in what she was doing, filling the church with music. Streams of light pierced the stained glass and touched objects with liquid slashes of color. The atmosphere was a true sanctuary.

At the end of the long, complex piece, the woman turned absently and discovered Anna. "May I help you?" she asked.

"You already have." Leaving the church, Anna walked through the National Garden. She stopped to look through the fence at the former palace, then meandered to Vasilissis Sophias, the street where most of the embassies stood behind wrought-iron-fences with imposing stone dignity. Taking her time, she headed toward Syntagma Square, crossing the street so her route took her by the flower stalls alongside the Parliament Building. The traffic was heavy now that the workday had begun, but it failed to daunt the birds that twittered in the trees above the sidewalk.

Suddenly, Anna heard the cadence of heavy shoes striking the pavement in marching rhythm. She turned to see a squad of Evzones, those special guards of the Greek military, bearing down on her from behind.

People stepped out of the way respectfully as they marched past, their short, fluffy skirts standing out stiffly above the white tights encasing muscular legs. The pom-poms on their heavy shoes and the tasseled black bands around their calves shook with each step.

Anna, too, moved to watch them march pass. They were beautiful, she thought, but there was nothing feminine in the skirts, or the full-sleeved white blouses, the embroidered black vests, or the floppy beretlike caps on cropped hair, adorned with long black tassels falling to the soldiers' shoulders. Members of this elite group must be chosen for their solid physiques and dark

good looks, Anna thought. Their serious bearing exuded power
and virility.

She followed the Evzones to the Tomb of the Unknown Soldier in front of the Parliament Building. With exaggerated, slow,
dancelike movements, they changed the guard, the two former
guards moving away with the escort while the new pair made their
final falling-back step, one foot in the air, into the small guard-
houses. A few minutes later the new guards stepped out and stood
in front of the doors, still as statues, not an eyelash flicking—
perfect subjects for Anna's pencil.

Twenty

The following days, Alexis sent flowers. He would have taken Anna out every evening, but she begged off, needing time to work on her drawings. Drawing had become an obsession now. She was never without her satchel of art materials when she went out alone. She wanted to capture all of this wonderful new freedom on paper. She tried to explain this, but he kept asking anyway.

"When do you work?" Anna asked Alexis one day after they had spent the afternoon in the National Archaeological Museum.

"I check in from time to time. My part of the project at the university is done. I just have to go there occasionally to see that they're following the plans." Then he laughed. "So, how would you like to go dancing tonight? I know a wonderful place out on the coastal road to Glyfada."

"What time?"

"Greek time." Anna was getting used to this.

On the way home early the next morning, after they had migrated from disco to bar, then closed the last taverna in the Plaka, Anna broached the subject of age. They were walking back to the hotel, eating sesame bread bought from a street vendor. This had become a tradition.

Anna stopped on the sidewalk and faced him. "Alexis, your energy is amazing. I can't keep up with you. Don't you know I'm an old lady? I need rest."

"Everyone needs rest. And you are not an old lady."

"Surely you have figured out that I am—"

"I know how old you are, Anna. You are six and a half years older than I am."

"That doesn't make any difference?" Anna had wanted to ask him that for a long time.

His answer, while gratifying, gave her an insight into Alexis she hadn't seen before. "Younger women don't interest me. They take themselves and life too seriously." He walked on, head down, then said, "The young women I've known try too hard to be something they are not. They lack the ability to laugh at themselves, to lean back and enjoy life. This makes them quite dull."

Anna remembered hearing the same words from Sam. Only Sam had been kinder.

"It sometimes takes years to discover who you are," Anna said.

"Perhaps for women, but not for a man. And I prefer a woman who has settled all that."

"Good luck," Anna said. His arrogant attitude was a little disconcerting.

Alexis, warming to his argument, ignored her sarcasm. "Society has its rules all wrong. Since women live longer, they should marry younger men. Then there would be far fewer widows." He caught his breath, and looked over at her, distress showing in his eyes. "Oh, I'm sorry, Anna. I wasn't referring to you. I wasn't thinking."

She took his arm and started walking up the hotel steps. "I know. Don't worry about it. However, there is one thing you are forgetting."

"What's that?"

"Older women get even older."

"So do younger men."

They stood at the top of the hotel steps. "And younger men have to slow their steps so the old biddies can keep up." She put her hands on his cheeks, still ruddy with embarrassment. "Besides, I can't be on the go all the time. I have my work to do."

"What work?"

"My drawing. It's coming back, that sense of awe and discovery. I feel—"

"Oh, that. Well, you can do that anytime."

"Not when I'm traipsing around the country from noon to dawn. I'm tired, Alexis."

He smiled. "To tell you the truth, I am too."

Anna knew he was lying, but she patted his face and turned to go in. "I had a lovely day . . . evening, and night," Anna said as she leaned into his hug.

"You are a lovely lady." He smiled, and bounded down the steps.

Alexis never accompanied Anna to her room. It was an unspoken agreement between them. He always met and left her in the lobby with tender, but dignified, affection. Anna appreciated that. She knew that in any city, there was a small-town curiosity about the comings and goings of well-known people. He had never been to her suite.

In fact, strangely, after their romantic day on the high seas, he had ended each date by bringing her straight back to the hotel. He sometimes barely kissed her, but would touch her hair and look at her as if to devour her. Both times they had been out since then, Alexis seemed to be holding back. Anna had mixed emotions about that. She was flattered by his attentions and relieved that he didn't presume on their relationship because of that one momentous afternoon. But still, she felt she was being handled as something rare and fragile. But she was having a good time . . . or was she?

With her hairbrush in her hand before turning in, Anna looked into the mirror. *Have I simply grown beyond this frenetic whirl of activity, not in age, but in interest? Is that why I feel so tired?* Anna quickly pushed that idea out of her mind. Of course she still liked to dance until dawn. Of course she wanted to see everything in Athens, cram as much into every day as possible. Of course she did.

One evening Alexis invited Anna to his apartment. "To cook you a feast," he said. His home turned out to be much as she expected—modern in design, but with an old-fashioned coziness about it with its richly colored handwoven rugs scattered about, window seats piled with cushions. Even the view added to the coziness. Windows of small, leaded-glass panes looked out onto a feathery mix of olive and pine treetops.

"Look around if you like while I finish cooking," Alexis said.

In the living room, deep, comfortable couches were arranged around thick flokati rugs. Up a spiral staircase, Anna peeked into the bedroom—a loft, an alcove that overlooked the living room, sharing the vaulted ceiling. It was furnished with a king-sized bed covered by a handwoven spread in earth tones, a long, low chest of drawers, and one chair, under a lamp that arched up from a marble base.

Anna wandered back to the kitchen and was handed a glass of Chinese wine and told that he would call her when the meal was ready. She sat in the living room listening to music. This was in every way a masculine dwelling, but at the same time, it was very welcoming and comfortable.

Like a true chef, Alexis managed to have everything ready at the same time. He served the delicious Chinese meal complete with chopsticks at a low table in front of a window. One course followed another, down to fortune cookies that Alexis admitted he had bought. When Anna found the message in hers, she knew it had been tampered with as well. It read, YOU ARE A BEAUTIFUL LADY.

Looking up from the slip of paper, Anna found Alexis' eyes gazing at her, light from the candles revealing longing in their dark intensity. Then he laughed and said, "I'll drive you home through the hills so we can enjoy the lights of Athens below."

It had been almost a week since their Thursday boat trip to Hydra. For Anna it seemed like eons. Paradoxically the old adage "Time flies when you're having fun," which didn't fit, kept coming to mind. Sam had once told her that if one traveled at the speed of light, one got younger. *I wonder if it's true,* she asked herself, feeling ancient. She knew she should make plans, get back to Crete, and then decide how much longer she would stay in Greece. But, for now, she just lived day by day and here she had stayed for almost another week without even thinking of the future.

On Wednesday Alexis said, "I once told you I thought you would like my mother."

"I'm sure I would, Alexis."

"She has invited us for dinner on Sunday, the day after the Kountouriotis party."

"That sounds lovely. And then, soon, I need to get back to Crete and get my things," she said. Musing out loud, she continued. "And I suppose I should think about going back home to the States."

Alexis made an abrupt left turn without replying. In a few minutes, they were at the entrance to his office building. "Let's go in and see if we can find something to drink."

Flipping on the lights in his office, he went over to a cabinet that contained a small refrigerator. He did something with the stereo and music of a blues clarinet started playing softly.

Anna was looking at the model. He had added another wing to the house, a large room labeled "gymnasium." And in the studio, he had added more windows. "When do you have time to work on this?" she asked.

"Oh, odd times. I sometimes come over here in the middle of the night. After I drop you off."

"That would be more like early morning most times," Anna said, smiling at him. "When on earth do you sleep?"

"Sometimes I sleep here," he said, indicating the long white couch. "Come. Relax. I'll pour us some wine."

When Anna was ensconced in the cloud of cushions on the couch, he handed her a glass of wine and pulled back the curtains for a view of the city.

"I have the feeling I'm being seduced," she said. Alexis just looked at her with a small, enigmatic smile.

Anna knew that something was expected of her, but she wasn't sure what. It was as if they were playing a game of charades, Alexis prompting her with cryptic signals, but she unable to come up with the word. She didn't know the lines she was supposed to speak. She hadn't felt this lack of confidence since her first dates, when she was terrified she wouldn't know how to talk to boys. But she had felt it several times with Alexis, especially when he looked at her this way.

"I brought you here because, as you know, it is a special place for me. It's where I am most creative. I want to tell you something." He was sitting on the far end of the couch. "Anna." His scrutiny was stripping away all her defenses. "I think I'm falling in love with you."

Anna felt as if wind were rushing through the room, roaring in her ears. Love? "But Alexis"—her voice came out an octave higher than usual—"you've known me less than three weeks." Not a very romantic rejoinder to that earthshaking confession.

"Time is of the earth. With you I am among stars and galaxies."

Anna started to smile at this grandiloquence, but he leaned over and took her glass from her, set it on the table, and pulled her into his arms. Then, as if to reassure her, he said, "I know we have only known each other a short time. But you are beginning to speak of leaving and I had to let you know that I don't want you to leave now."

"But, Alexis."

To still her words, he kissed her, gently, slowly, deeply, his hands caressing her hair. "I want you, Anna. I need you."

Alarm zigzagged through every nerve. Anna felt like running, fast and far. She wasn't sure why, just that everything seemed to be closing in. "Please, Alexis. Don't need me. I'm not ready. I don't know what to say. Please, can we go now? Please."

"I'm sorry. I didn't mean to rush." He pulled her up from the couch. "I just don't want to hear you talking about leaving. Think about staying. Tell me you will."

"I will," Anna said, ". . . think about it."

And she did. When she got back to her hotel she could think of nothing else. *Love?* Never had she even considered that this was *love! That day on the boat . . . I thought I was making a giant leap into the twenty-first century. It was an act of derring-do.* By the same token, Anna had thought that for a man like Alexis, that day was just a casual encounter. He must have the pick of the town. He must take a lot of women out on that boat.

Love? I never tried to lead him on, to make him think . . . I don't even know how. Love? Had she thought of falling in love with him at all? *Never.* In fact, now that this had come up, she realized that she was simply living one day at a time here. She couldn't even plan ahead enough to figure whether to go back to Crete or go home.

She was pacing now. *That day on the boat, it just happened.* She had let herself go, had done something that seemed right for the moment. *A little fling never hurts? Well, so much for me becoming a modern, liberated woman. I just don't know the rules.*

Then a voice from her conscience reminded her of those sanctimonious comments to Maggie. *Sex isn't something that you do. It is part of something larger.* How self-righteous that must have sounded.

Actually, she had still been in that frame of mind when she met Sam. That sex was part of something larger. Now she realized that that was why she was so disappointed in herself. Because, for her, that night with Sam *was* part of a larger relationship. And she regretted that she had let it happen so casually.

But with Alexis . . . well, she was flattered by his attention. And she had to admit that she enjoyed being with him. But she hadn't allowed herself to think beyond the now of it all.

He says he's in love with me? She felt shallow and shaken. She wondered whether after all this anything would be left standing.

What do I really feel for him? She stood on her balcony mulling this question. *This is all happening too fast,* she finally concluded. Suddenly she wanted Paul. With all her heart she wanted Paul. She went in and fell across her bed, tears of longing for Paul as fresh as when she had first come to Crete.

Alexis called the next morning to say, with regret, that he had to go to an unexpected meeting in Rome. He would be back on Saturday, the day of the Kountouriotis party. Anna received this message with a mixture of relief and a small, unexpected twinge of disappointment. "Have a good time," she said.

"I'll call as soon as I return."

"Yes," she said. She didn't add that this would give her time to think, to gather her emotions and try to sort them out. The best way for her to do this was to draw. She returned to the Acropolis and drew the Parthenon with all the people in their colorful clothes milling about. She haunted the Plaka. She sketched children in the park. She even looked into the mirror back in her room and drew self-portraits.

Like clockwork the phone rang each evening, but Alexis never mentioned love again. Maybe it had passed. He was so impetuous. Probably, like that day in Hydra, that profession of love the other night was something of the moment. How . . . in only a few days . . . could someone fall in love? Between her drawing forays, Anna was slowly packing up to go back to Crete.

The afternoon of the party, a package arrived for Anna. She was just putting the finishing touches on a drawing of a tourist asking one of the Evzones for directions. It was an old piece, done the day after she had gone to Hydra with Alexis.

Anna had stopped taking her pad and pencils on their outings since she had noticed the impatience that flitted across Alexis' face every time she wanted to stop and sketch. He never actually said anything about it. He just never knew what to do with himself while she worked. He couldn't sit still. His hovering about distracted her until she finally gave up. Alexis didn't seem to notice that she no longer even asked to stop.

Just after noon, there was a knock on the door. "A package for you, madam." Taking the package from the bellhop, Anna walked into the sitting room and set it on the table beside the vase of daisies that had arrived earlier. She slipped the ribbon from the box and slid it open. Lying in tissue paper was an intricately woven shawl with silk fringes. It was old, not new. Old and elegant. Anna lifted it from the paper and held it at arm's length—a heavy square of geometric patterns woven in silk. It was velvety as a tapestry, in rich colors that glowed against a sapphire background that matched the fringe. It smelled of cedar.

Anna buried her face in the luxury of the silk, then flung the shawl around her shoulders and went to the mirror. It looked a little ridiculous with her white slacks and red cotton pullover, but she tugged it close, tying it in a loose knot in front. Then she hurried out to look for a card in the box. There she found a card with Alexis' bold script saying, "I thought you would look wonderful in this. It belonged to my grandmother."

This is too much. I could never keep this, Anna mused as she sat down, spreading the shawl across her knees, her fingers examining the intricate weave. It had been woven with such care, the threads identical on both sides, with no evidence of loose ends. Was it part of a regional costume?

Temptation crept in slowly. What would she wear with it—if she wore it at all? Her blue floor-length dress? She went to the closet and pulled it out. Yes, the blue was the same as the fringe. On impulse she threw the dress across the bed and draped the shawl around it. It was the perfect complement—the plain dress set off the elegant mantle.

But I can't accept it, Anna thought. *I can't.*

Later, wearing the dress, but with the shawl carefully folded back in the box, Anna debated whether to carry the package down with her or leave it for Alexis to pick up later. A knock at the door interrupted her dilemma. She opened the door, expecting the maid, and stood facing Alexis himself.

"Why, hello. Come in."

"When you didn't come down, I thought I would come up and get you." He looked her over with a sweeping glance. "You look lovely, but"—he looked around the room—"where is the shawl?"

"Alexis, I can't accept such a gift."

"But I want you to have it," he said.

"It's too valuable. Too dear."

Alexis took the shawl from the box and wrapped it around Anna's shoulders from behind, his arms holding her close. "Then just wear it for me. I want to see you wear it. Maybe someday you will allow me to give it to you."

Anna took his hands in hers. How could she refuse such a warm, kind offer? "I'd be honored to wear it tonight," she said.

The Kountouriotis house was located on the side of the steep hill topped by St. George's Church in the Lycabettus area. The living room, the size of a ballroom, was lush with seventeenth-century furnishings. Anna and Alexis walked across the room over a gleaming marble floor scattered with Persian carpets. With damask-covered chairs and settees scattered about, the effect was dazzling.

A tall woman with shining black hair piled on top of her head came sweeping up to them, her gown of icy gray swinging across the floor. "Alexis. How delightful to see you." She looked him over with affectionate appreciation.

Alexis bent over her hand. "Alexandra, you get younger with each year."

"And this must be Anna," she said, eyeing Anna with an appraising look as if taking inventory.

"Alexandra, may I present Anna Sandoval. Anna, Alexandra Kountouriotis."

During Alexis' formal introduction Alexandra's eyes never left Anna's face. *She is trying to guess my age,* Anna was sure. She lifted her chin and looked straight into Alexandra's eyes. There was a moment of silence; then, the appraisal over, Alexandra smiled at Anna knowingly and, with a cocked eyebrow, seemed to congratulate her. Anna felt as if she had been slapped.

Everyone who came into the room, it seemed, knew Alexis and came up to him with great exclamations. "We haven't seen you lately. We've missed you." Admiring looks. Women falling all over themselves. They watched his every movement as he introduced Anna, then complimented each one, asking about their families or jobs or recent trips.

He is like a meteor, Anna thought. *He leaves people watching the night sky where he has been even after he is gone,* she realized, rather enjoying being the envy of every woman in the room. Paul had been like that. She had felt this same pride standing beside him at parties like this, basking in the light that seemed to emanate from him like a nimbus.

Anna stood watching Alexis, and when he saw her staring at him, he reached out and pulled her into the shelter of his arm, sharing the spotlight with her. Paul used to do that too.

Snatching two flutes of champagne from the tray of a passing waiter, Alexis took her arm and led her up curving marble stairs to a balcony that looked down on the party. "It's quieter up here," he said. It was obvious that he had been here before. He certainly knew his way around.

"Alexandra is divorced," Alexis said, handing Anna a glass. "But she always invites her husband to her parties. And he always comes. There he is over there. Costas." He pointed out a tall man with protruding eyes and receding hair who, at that moment, was talking with a group of men from the American embassy. Anna recognized several of them.

"You'll see quite a few people from the American diplomatic corps here tonight. Costas Kountouriotis is in shipping, both sea and air. He is also in Parliament. He has been very active in national security." Anna leaned against the marble balustrade and her eyes wandered around the room. Women in colorful dresses, men in black. More people were coming in. It was, again, like a dance. She was just turning back to Alexis when she saw Sam with Taylor in tow. *Well, Alexis is right. Everybody seems to be here.* Taylor looked beautiful as usual. She had a tomboy stance that lent a casual athletic grace to her appearance, enhanced by firm muscles, most likely cultivated at a fitness center. But tonight the most striking thing about Taylor was her hair. She had gotten it permed into a wild mane, so that it stood out from her head in leonine grandeur, a style few people could bring off, but which suited her well. Her dress fitted her trim form like skin.

Sam often looked fatherly with Taylor, beaming at her with parental pride. But not tonight. He looked like a statesman in his tuxedo, Anna thought, dignified. Even handsome.

For some reason, he looked straight up in Anna's direction, as if summoned. Their eyes met and held for a moment. Then Sam smiled his most hangdog smile, and Anna smiled back with a slight nod.

"Who is that?" Alexis asked. Then seeing whom she had greeted, he said, "Oh, your friend, Sam McDonald." The muscle in his jaw worked as he watched Sam and Taylor greet Alexandra. "You've never told me how you know him."

For Anna, that offhand comment, meant as a question, raised her ire with a vehemence that surprised her. She was tempted to say casually, "Oh, he's an old lover of mine." Instead she said, "He's a very good friend." And she knew that it was true.

Alexandra glided up the stairs toward them, a short, bald man with a mustache trailing behind her. She moved like oil on water, and as she passed, she gave Anna another knowing look.

Suddenly Anna was aware of the weight of the shawl. She felt heat spread from it up her neck. Even wearing it was a sham. She was a forty-five-year-old widow sporting about with a dashing young swain who, in an obvious yet surprising pique of jealousy, was questioning her choice of friends like an overbearing adolescent.

Alexandra came up to them with an ingratiating smile. "This is Athanasios Kourbelas." She introduced both Anna and Alexis. "Mr. Kourbelas is an importer."

"Oh?" Anna said with polite interest.

Kourbelas brightened, and before Anna could say anything else, Alexandra had Alexis by the arm and was leading him away. "I've been wanting to show you my new painting," she was saying as they walked off.

"I import Japanese cars," Kourbelas was saying in a thick accent.

Anna smiled her most intrigued smile and let him talk. Then, noticing Sam and Taylor coming up the stairs, she said, "It was very nice talking with you, Mr. Kourbelas. I believe I see some friends of mine over there, and I should go and greet them." She shook his hand, returned his regretful smile, and walked toward Sam and Taylor with relief as if to old friends in a sea of strangers. But as she got closer, she saw they were in animated conversation with Alexandra's ex-husband.

Feeling hot and uncomfortable, Anna made her way through

the crowd and through the open doors onto a wide veranda that stretched across the upper story of the house. The view of Athens was almost as spectacular as the one from St. George's Church from the top of the hill.

Putting her hands on the cool marble railing, Anna felt like leaning down and pressing her forehead to it. She could see the Parthenon and other monuments of the Acropolis bathed in light, and the twinkle of distant ships out on the water. She had never felt more alone.

She took off the shawl and hung it over the railing, then removed the combs from the sides of her hair and ran her fingers through its length, trying to cool her pounding temples.

This was a mistake. The whole affair. She was flattered by Alexis' attention. What woman wouldn't be? But she was acting like a teenager—going weak-kneed at the sound of his voice; fluttering around putting on six different outfits before deciding what to wear when they went out; going down to the lobby to meet him each time feeling nervous and shy. Surely this behavior wasn't becoming in a woman of her age.

These past few days had been quite wonderful. She had to admit that. It had been so long since she had felt that quickening of heart. Even with Paul in later years she had taken so many things for granted that she hadn't felt this . . . this excitement in a long time. Her love for Paul had ripened into a far richer and deeper communion, a deep love established on a foundation of trust and familiarity.

Anna sighed. *I have moved on from this game.* She looked out over the sparkling city, her hands on her temples. *I seem to be spending the whole time that I meant to spend putting my life back together ripping it into still more fragments. Oh, Paul,* she wanted to cry out, stabbing sorrow and loss tearing through her. *I need you,* she said silently, tears burning her eyes.

"Anna?"

That familiar voice was so welcome that she almost reached out. But instead, she turned away to hide her tears.

"Are you all right, Anna?" Sam was standing right beside her.

"Yes. Fine." She was dismayed to hear her voice tremble.

"Good. I always like to shed a few tears myself when everything is fine." He reached over and laid his hand on hers. "Care to talk about it?"

"I've had a relapse."

He didn't even ask for an explanation. "In my experience, that's to be expected from time to time." He cleared his throat. "Is he treating you well?"

Anna knew his concern was genuine, not prying, and that brought on even more tears, which hurt her throat when she tried to hold them back. "It's not that." She turned to him and asked, "Do you ever get tired, Sam?"

"You mean trying to keep up with these young whippersnappers? I find I have to alternate all-night disco-dancing marathons with an occasional quiet evening in my room. Taylor has a hard time understanding that."

"No, I mean with the effort."

"Now, that's something else," he said. "I try and remind myself that it's worth it."

"Why? Why is it worth it to you?"

"With Taylor? I don't know. She, well, like I said long ago, she makes me forget my mounting years. She's, ah, so unpredictable. And she needs me, or at least says she does."

"Are you going to marry her?"

He didn't answer for a long time. "Before I went to Crete, I would have said yes."

Anna jerked her head around to look at him.

"And you? What are your plans?" he asked.

"I don't have any plans. No plans at all."

"Anna?" Alexis had come out the door and was looking in the opposite direction. When he turned and saw them, he walked over purposefully. "I've looked all over for you," he said, looking not at Anna but at Sam.

"I think you'd better take Anna home," Sam said. "I saw her come out here holding her head and came out to check on her. I think she has a headache."

Alexis looked at Anna in concern. "Anna? I'm so sorry. Of course, whatever you say."

Anna could have kissed Sam. She nodded at Alexis. "It's not bad, but I would like to go back."

Alexis couldn't have been more attentive. Back at the hotel, he walked her to her suite, opened the door, and turned on the lamp. "Can I get you anything?" he asked.

"No, really, I'm fine. A long sleep is what I need. That's all." She walked him to the door.

"I'll call to see how you are."

Finally he was gone. Anna threw off her clothes and tumbled into bed. She actually did have a headache. As she drifted off, she thought of Alexis. Pleasant thoughts—the look in his eyes when he thought she was sick, his gentleness. Her lapse back into grief had been only because she hadn't felt well. Nice to see Sam. *It's all going to be all right. Isn't it?*

It was only at that moment, balancing on the edge of sleep, that she remembered she had left the shawl on Alexandra's balcony.

Twenty-one

With mixed emotions, Anna went shopping for a new dress to wear when she went to meet Mrs. Sarkis. She couldn't remember when she had been more nervous. When Alexis first brought this visit up, Anna thought he was just trying to introduce her around. He obviously adored his mother. However, since his profession of love, Anna was suspicious about the import of this little tête-à-tête. In the States she would have thought he was just introducing his mother to a friend. But Europeans might have different ideas.

What had he told his mother about her? What was this woman expecting? Had he mentioned that Anna was at the threshold of middle age? Was the old woman looking forward to the meeting or, like Anna, dreading it? And why, Anna asked herself, was she thinking of her as an old woman? Mrs. Sarkis was only ten years older than Anna! Alexis had told her she had been seventeen when he was born. Anna had been almost seven.

For hours she had shopped for this dress. She must have looked in twenty shops already that morning and was in yet one more of the fashionable shops near the hotel.

"Are you all right?" the shopkeeper asked, rolling her *r*'s.

Anna nodded.

"You don't look well."

Anna smiled and tried to keep looking through the racks as if everything were normal. One option was to flee—a recent habit of hers. She was becoming good at that. She had run to Crete to begin with. She had cleared out of there before the dust had settled on that evening with Sam. Where could she run now?

Then she saw the dress. It was red—she was perversely delighted with that—simple, V-necked, with tapered sleeves, fitted at the waist with a slim belt, the skirt gracefully full. It was made of soft suede. She handed the saleswoman her credit card. "I'll take that one."

At eight thirty that evening, Anna took the elevator down to the lobby of the Apollo to meet Alexis.

She saw him first, standing near the entrance, hands in the pockets of his cream-colored trousers, his dark jacket open, the collar turned up. He glanced at his watch, looking worried.

Anna stopped for a moment, suddenly feeling shy. Did she look all right? For reassurance, her hand automatically went up to the chain at her neck. But, of course, the rings were no longer there. Tonight she was wearing no jewelry except gold earrings.

The elevator door hissed open behind her—an escape route, a safe haven. She could get back into the elevator and be lifted out of all this. Like a runner waiting for the starting pistol, her impulses gathered for flight. But at that moment, Alexis turned. Relief flooded his face in a glorious smile, and he held out his hands to her. She heard the elevator doors slide shut behind her and slowly walked over to him.

"You look stunning," he said. His lips brushed her hair, his hands on her shoulders. He gazed into her face, his dark eyes full of admiration and boyish expectancy.

Anna turned away, pretending to check something in her purse. Feeling his hand on her waist, she let herself be guided to the waiting car at the curb.

Mrs. Alexis Sarkis Sr. was a total surprise. Anna had expected someone tall and elegant, cool and formal. Mrs. Sarkis was short and stocky, with the ageless look of the peasants Anna had seen in the country. Her dark hair, which she wore parted in the middle and wound into a braided bun on the back of her head, was less gray than Anna's. Alexis had her eyes, dark and long-lashed, now twinkling with humor and open adoration for her son. Anna liked her at once.

"Come in. Come in," she said after shaking Anna's hand and

kissing Alexis. Her smile alone would have proved that Alexis was her son. She was absolutely delighted, as if she had a secret too delicious to keep. Her good humor radiated through the muted light of the room and Anna was warmed by its glow. There were no sidelong glances or measuring-up stares, no looks of surprised scrutiny, as Anna had feared. The way Mrs. Sarkis kept straightening the collar of her blouse and pulling at her skirt made Anna realize she too was ill at ease with the situation.

The house was built into the hill, high on the Lycabettus. They sat in white wicker furniture in a solarium, with a bird's-eye view of Athens and the Acropolis, while Alexis made them drinks.

"I understand you are an artist, Anna," Mrs. Sarkis said.

"Actually, I'm just renewing an old acquaintance with something I loved doing as a young . . . a long time ago," Anna said.

"I'd like to see some of your work. Alexis tells me you can sketch a whole scene in just minutes. That must be a very satisfying hobby. Do you work with other media as well?"

Anna blinked at the word "hobby." She had never defined her love of drawing, but she had never thought of it as a hobby. Is that what Alexis had told his mother, or was that just Mrs. Sarkis' interpretation?

"Pencil drawings and pen-and-ink studies are my first love. I tried other media long ago." Why did she keep referring to her longevity? "But I always went back to pen and pencil." It was time to change the subject. "You have a wonderful view," was the only thing that came to mind. "Have you lived here long, Mrs. Sarkis?" Anna asked, meaning this wonderful house.

"Please call me Lysia, Anna." She gave Alexis a long, disappointed look. "You haven't told her, have you?" She shook her head. "Such a pity to be ashamed of your past."

Alexis smiled. "Told her that I was a child of love and that my father carried you away from Rhodes before your father could kill him? I just didn't think it was a very interesting story." His eyes were teasing. "Actually, I'm rather proud of my somewhat dubious beginnings." He smiled and reached out to press her arm.

His mother raised her eyebrows in reproach and said to

Anna, "The way he talks. Alexis' father was in shipping, and the Port of Piraeus was his headquarters. So, we have lived here, in Athens, all Alexis' life. Alexis Senior died when Alexis was ten." She looked at her son mournfully. Nothing could be sadder, Anna thought, than Greek eyes. Except, perhaps, Sam's.

A sudden mental picture of Sam, giving her the humorous, sad glance she remembered so well, startled her. What would make her think of Sam now? She turned her attention back to Alexis' mother.

"Alexis was born in this house, though it was smaller then and different. It has been renovated many times, most recently by Alexis himself." She blessed him with that smile again.

Lysia Sarkis' house was a place where the divine art of conversation flourished. Their discussions ranged from theology to literature, from science to favorite foods. They talked generally about ancient architecture and things to do in Athens, about the current political and economic problems arising from terrorist activities.

There was not one question about Anna's past. Once she ventured to say, "Of course, much of the architecture in Washington, D.C., where I live, is copied from ancient Greece—Corinthian columns, fountains, and statuary."

"And much of the modern architecture in Greece is modeled after buildings in America," Lysia countered without asking Anna about her home. Alexis described some of the successes resulting from this American influence. Were they avoiding discussion of Anna's life out of politeness, not wanting to remind her of her widowhood? Or was Lysia not very curious, waiting for her to volunteer the information?

A chime sounded from within the house. "Shall we go to dinner?" Lysia asked, leaving Anna's unspoken question unanswered.

Anna took her first sip of the hot, thick coffee after a meal so delicious and conversation so delightful that she had forgotten her earlier hesitation about this meeting. They were back in the solarium, watching the light show at the Acropolis, which, from this distance, was even more dramatic than if they had been part of the audience. Lysia had turned off the lights in the room so they could see better. Strains of Greek music from a concealed sound system provided atmosphere as Alexis gave a running commentary as each part was lit. At one point, everything was dark except the Parthenon. Bathed in golden light, it seemed to float in the dark sky in all its many-columned splendor. Finally, the whole Acropolis was blazing with light.

"What a grand heritage you have," Anna said.

"And sad. The grand part is all in the distant past. Greece is a poor, struggling country now," Alexis said. "We stand among the ruins and dream, but our dreams are all memories. We always seem to be looking back, saying, 'Look at what we were.' A past like ours is sometimes a burden. In America," he continued, "I think you dream of an even more glorious future than your short history has already produced. In Greece, we only revel in the time when our country was the center of the world."

"But isn't that the nature of things?" Anna said.

"The rise and fall of civilizations—Egypt, China, Peru, Rome. We take turns being the center of the world. In another hundred years, who knows where it will be?"

"What really matters," said Lysia, "is where the center of the world is for each of us in our own lives."

She looked over at her son. "Alexis, would you please go up to my room and bring me down that brown shawl? I think it's thrown over the back of a chair. It seems chilly in here tonight."

Alexis stood, his eyes squinted at his mother in a sidelong warning. Then he left the room.

When he was gone, Lysia turned to Anna and without preamble said, "My son is very fond of you, Anna. And I can see why. I want you to know I trust his judgment, and my desire is only to see him happy."

Anna didn't know how to respond.

"He has never been so . . . *smit-ten*—is that what you say?—with anyone before. Oh, he's had many women friends. But he's always enjoyed them by the flock." She chuckled. "Now the only one he ever speaks of is you."

Anna was beginning to feel very uncomfortable.

"I think, from what he's said, that he is thinking of finally settling down. He talks more and more of the house he plans to build." She shifted in her seat and Anna could feel her eyes in the dark. The lights on the Acropolis were vanishing one by one behind Lysia's silhouette. "And he speaks of changes he would like to make to accommodate"—she paused a moment—"your interests."

"My interests?"

"He also speaks of this house as more than just a house. He wants it to be something grand—a permanent showcase in Athens, a statement of his architectural philosophy, something his heirs will be proud to pass from generation to generation."

Heirs? Anna heard no more. She opened her mouth so Lysia couldn't hear her gasping.

Alexis came back into the room humming and draped the shawl over his mother's shoulders, then flipped on the light. Anna jumped, standing quickly, turning her back to the two of them as if looking out the wall of glass at the view, trying to calm the thud of her heart. Now it all fell into place. Now she knew why, after their day on the boat, he had not made love to her. Instead, he had put her on a pedestal—saving her for . . . now she knew why he was not interested in a casual affair.

Alexis came up behind her, holding out another sweater. "In case you're cold too," he said.

Anna shook her head. Cold? She was burning. She had to grip the back of a chair to keep from running from the room. *How can I get out of here?* she was silently shouting to herself.

"Now I think we should all go down to Bichoulas for an after-dinner drink," Alexis said in his rumbling bass. "Don't you ladies agree?"

"Go on, you two," Lysia said, as if talking to teenagers. "I'm not up to the beat of the music in those places."

Anna's impulse to run changed abruptly to a desire to cling to the furniture and stay. She wished she could be back in her own rooms. *Settle down,* she thought again. *Heirs?* The word had been like a light coming on. Alexis hadn't brought her here as his fascinating American friend. He wanted Lysia's approval of his choice of a wife! He had been serious about being *in love!*

Now Alexis wanted to trip the light fantastic at a discotheque. She was sure she had aged twenty years in this one evening as she sat, huddled in the chair, gripping the unwanted sweater around her.

Alexis grabbed her hand, helping her to her feet. "You are cold," he said as he took her icy hand. "Bring the sweater with you."

Like a sleepwalker, Anna went over to Lysia. "Thank you," she said, reaching out to shake Lysia's hand. "It was a wonderful evening."

But the older woman stood and drew her closer to brush cheeks. "You are welcome, Anna," she said. Then looking up into Anna's eyes, she added, "Tonight, and always."

Dimly Anna was aware that Alexis kissed his mother's cheek. Mrs. Sarkis stood straight as a statue, a grande dame with the bearing of a matriarch. For a moment Anna almost felt she should curtsy. She allowed herself to be herded toward the door, the thud of her own heart loud in her ears. When they were in the car, Anna said, "I think I'd better get back to my hotel. I—"

"I only told her we were going to Bichoulas so she wouldn't want to come with us," he said. "Not that I wouldn't have wanted her, but I wanted to be alone with you." He negotiated the growling Mercedes around the hairpin curves of the Lycabettus as if bent on straightening them out.

"Alexis."

He screeched to a stop in the parking lot near the funicular to Ayios Yeorgios—St. George's—on the peak. Jumping out of the car, he almost vaulted over the hood to open Anna's door. Then, taking her elbow, he led her to the ticket booth, bought tokens, and ran, pulling her by the hand, to catch a trolley car that was just leaving. It was too noisy to talk in the crowd of people they joined. At the top they all spilled out of the trolley together.

Alexis took Anna's elbow again, and steering her by the

restaurant that pulsated with Greek music and laughter, he walked her quickly around to the dark side of the terrace. The stone balustrade in front of the church was empty. From there, they had a view of all Athens.

Before Anna knew what was happening, Alexis gathered her in his arms, burying his face in the crook of her neck, saying her name over and over. "Anna," he said again, softly, raising his head. When he kissed her, he began almost shyly, with closed lips, as if he were a young boy unsure of what to do. It was tender, yearning. Then his kiss increased in intensity and she could feel herself responding as his hands moved under the sweater. Maybe Lysia had been wrong. This was all he wanted, her body, no past, no future. Maybe her fears were only in her imagination. She wanted to yield to this, to return his caresses. But she couldn't move. Everything was out of control. Her body thrummed to a familiar beat, but the rising music within her was dissonant, the tune gone awry like a song played at the wrong speed.

Alexis let her go so abruptly that she caught her breath. He turned her so she was facing out to the view, his arms around her, across her breasts.

"Look, Anna. Look at all this. It is mine. All mine." In a broad gesture, he spread Athens before her. "I spoke earlier about Greeks only looking back. Well, it is not true of me. I plan to build buildings here, in this century, in this lifetime, that will draw people to Greece. Churches, universities, public buildings, houses, that will be a tribute to mankind of this century. This is my city, Anna. And you are my goddess. With you at my side I can do all these things. You inspire me. You fulfill me."

He turned her again to face him. "I want to give you all this, Anna." Then, slowly, he knelt, his arms sliding down until he was embracing her around the hips for a moment.

He let her go then, and raising his arms as he knelt, he said quietly, "Will you marry me, Anna?"

Marry me! It seemed to echo off the hills, off the distant moonlit water of the Aegean. Anna searched herself for a reaction. She felt nothing at all. She was numb in mind and body.

Alexis was waiting for her answer, his arms still open, his beautiful face below her carved by moonlight into planes of dark and light.

Anna was caught up as if in a dream. She was Alice in a wonderland of crazy shapes and strange visions. Marry Alexis? Move through Athens on his arm? Be there when he received acclaim for his work, live in the house he had designed to accommodate her . . . her "hobbies"? Give birth to his heirs?

Again the word "heirs" shook Anna to her senses. "Alexis," she said, pulling him to his feet. "I'm . . . I'm . . . this is so, so sud—" *Run!* her every instinct shrieked.

"I know it is sudden, Anna. But you've spoken of leaving Greece. I want you to stay. I'm so sure this is your destiny. And mine. We belong together. I know this. I knew in Hydra. I know."

"But, Alexis, you need someone younger, someone who can—"

"I told you from the beginning, younger women don't interest me. You interest me, Anna. Already you seem a part of me. Age has nothing to do with it."

"And what about children, Alexis? What about the child you want to inherit the lovely home you plan to build?"

"You can have a child, can't you? Forty-five is not too old."

"Alexis, my own children are adults now. That is behind me. I don't want more children."

"You'll change your mind. They will be no trouble. You'll have servants to help take care of them."

"No. Can't you see? I couldn't go back to that. I'm free now." The word had rolled off her tongue unbidden. *Free.*

"A woman needs a man, Anna. Freedom is lonely. I know. I've been free all these years."

And I've only been free since I decided to go to Crete, when I had done all the social and legal obligations widows are faced with, when I finally could make a decision on my own.

Alexis took a deep breath. "If you could have anything you wanted in all the world, what would it be?" he asked. "Name it, and it's yours."

Anna turned back to the spangled view of Athens spread before them. "This very moment, if I could have anything I wanted, I would draw a picture that would touch the hearts of everyone who saw it." It was as if someone else were talking. "I would pour myself into a set of drawings that people would remember."

"But I meant something I could give you." He sounded petulant.

"Alexis, you are a wonderful person, and a gentle, loving man who has awakened in me feelings I thought had died when Paul died. But I came to Greece to . . ." She ran her fingers through her hair. ". . . to try to grasp what it is that gives a life meaning."

"Wouldn't loving me give you meaning?"

"You have given me a compliment of the highest order. You have loved me, expecting nothing in return, until tonight, Alexis. In many ways I would like to run into your arms and spend the rest of my life with you. But that would be like anchoring a boat in safe harbor just to avoid the storms. Letting you take care of me, as wonderful as that could be, would take something away from me."

She moved a little away and turned, trying to find the words that would make him understand. "I don't want to spend the rest of my life in safe harbor, Alexis, even with someone I've always suspected of being a Greek god in disguise. Can you understand that?"

"But, Anna."

"I've already had the opportunity to live my life as a part of someone else's, to . . . to make *his* puzzle complete. I was young and didn't realize that *my* calling was just as important. Now I am beginning to answer that call, to do what I, Anna, need to do. But I have a long way to go. I don't want to enter into a relationship with another person while I am incomplete, wanting someone else to fill in the gaps. I have to be my own person, Alexis. I have to find my own way."

She turned away, feeling as though she was emerging from a cocoon. Standing there on the parapet of the old church, she wanted to spread her still-damp wings to dry in the golden moonlight.

"I need you, Anna."

But I don't need you, she thought, taking a deep, expansive breath. *I love you in some grateful way, but I don't need you.* "You need someone, Alexis, but it is not me."

He stood leaning on his outstretched arms against the wall, his head down. Anna felt she was going to break, but she didn't go to him. Finally he turned. "Come, I'll take you home."

The drive back down the winding roads of Lycabettus and under the streetlights of Athens was electric with tension. Finally Anna said, "You are an artist, Alexis, consumed with creativity. And perhaps you do need someone by your side who can be there for you, encourage you, bask in your accomplishments." He started to say something, but she said, "No, let me finish. I've discovered something tonight, something I didn't know about myself and about life. It is this. The work of dedicated artists is the core of their being, around which all else, even marriage, revolves. I know this. I was married to an artist. But what I've discovered here in Greece is that I too am an artist."

"Anna, there is no reason why you would have to give that up. You could still do your drawings. You're very good. Your sketches of people are—"

"I don't want to only draw them, Alexis. *I want to be their soul.* It is a fervor within me. And only tonight have I realized that I came very close to letting you overshadow this . . . this—"

"Passion." He finished the sentence matter-of-factly.

"Yes. This passion. Did you notice that I had stopped . . . doing it, stopped drawing, when I'm with you? Around you, I find it impossible."

Alexis had pulled up in front of the hotel.

"For some people, Alexis, it's enough to spend themselves on another person's passion. That is their ultimate happiness." She turned and looked out the window. "For many years, that was true for me."

When there was no response, she went on. "I'm sorry if I led you to believe—" She swallowed. "What I mean is, I'm sorry if I've wasted your time."

"Nothing is a waste of time," Alexis said, "especially when it is beautiful." He took a tendril of hair that had escaped her combs again, and twisted it around his finger.

"Anna, I respect what you say, but I can't give up so easily. I love you. And I want you to be my wife. I would let you be whatever you wanted to be."

"*Let* me?" Anna looked at him in wonder. "*Let?*" She knew then that he would never understand. "Good-bye, Alexis. If we should meet again, and we most likely will, I will always consider you a very dear—" Something splintered inside her and her voice came out hoarse and tremulous. ". . . a very dear friend."

He kissed the lock of hair and then let his fingers slide to the end, laying it back on her shoulder. "Until we meet—"

But Anna was already out of the car when he finished, "—again," running up the steps to the entrance of the hotel.

Twenty-two

The next morning Anna had her hair cut. Strangely enough, instead of being frizzy, as she had imagined it would be, it curled softly all over her head. She had to agree with the hairdresser that it was becoming, even with the gray, which she refused to have rinsed out. She had earned those gray wings. They were part of her.

She had slept badly. In her confused dreams, she kept catching glimpses of Paul in crowds of people. Calling his name, she fought her way through to him. Only, when he turned, it would be Alexis saying, "I would let you. I would let you." She had finally awakened to a room full of sun, having forgotten to pull the draperies the night before. Her clothes were thrown about the furniture in heaps. She dressed carelessly in jeans and a T-shirt, ordered breakfast in her room, then left it sitting cold on the cocktail table and hurried out to find a hairdresser.

Walking back to the hotel after her haircut, Anna's head felt like a balloon floating from her neck without the weight of all that hair. But heaviness left over from last night was still on her heart.

Window-shopping aimlessly, she dreaded going back to her rooms. She felt dazed, as though she had fallen from one of the high outcroppings around Athens and was barely making her way, crushed and mangled, while people walked by chatting and going on along their way as though she were perfectly all right. Once she caught sight of herself in the plate glass of a storefront. The glass was wavy, distorting the reflection so that her form seemed to flow into the moving traffic behind her, as out of focus as her thoughts.

When she finally got back to the hotel, she found another

huge vase of flowers from Alexis sitting where she had left her un-
eaten breakfast. *Oh, God,* she thought, running her fingers
through her hair, *I can't escape.* She carried the vase into her bedroom to get it out of sight. Then, seeing it there by the bed, she
took it into the bathroom and slammed the door.

It must be late afternoon, she thought, looking at her watch.
It was only noon. The day yawned before her, empty as a ruin. She
was staring absently across the drawings she had taped to the wall
when her eyes fell on the straw bag that held her pad and pencils.
She took out the pencils and set up a new sketch to work on.

Thirty minutes later, she was still sitting, staring at the drawing,
seeing only the look on Alexis' face the night before, his disappointment . . . no, his *disbelief* that she would turn down his proposal. Anna looked down to find the pencil broken in her hand.

She went into the bathroom and looked at the rejected flowers, her hand over her stomach. He loved her. Could she find any
trace of love in herself for him? She had avoided the question
since the night in his office when he had first spoken of love.

It had been so good. It all had. Now it was over. It had to be.
She stumbled back into the sitting room. The ache had moved
from the pit of her stomach to her throat.

She knew she had hurt him deeply. She had been so caught
up in the excitement of being free, free to have an affair without
commitment, free to stop worrying about the terror of an empty
future. She had thought it was the same for him. She had taken his
profession of love lightly, assuming it was only the endearing im-
pulsiveness of a passionate young man. It had all been so flattering . . . part of the romantic ethos of the whole affair.

Affair. She felt heartless, groaning with the sorrow of it, the
pain of having hurt someone she liked so much. Maggie was
wrong. A little fling *could* hurt . . . everyone involved. The ascent
had been so spectacular these past weeks, she hadn't even thought
about her future. Now here she was, back where she started.
Anna fell onto the couch, loneliness engulfing her in a cloud.
What can I do? Where can I go?

There was a knock on the door, and when Anna opened it, a

bellhop was standing there. He handed her an envelope, "I bring you letter," he said. Anna tipped him and took the fat letter that could only be from Maggie.

How do you think I'd look in black? was the first sentence, no salutation. In relief at being distracted from her own problems, Anna read on with increasing interest. Maggie had been asked to submit her name for an appointment to the appellate court.

Maggie, a judge? Somehow the picture of that rosy pink Texas belle presiding over a courtroom was almost comical. She laughed as she read Maggie's rendition of the process.

Anna turned the pages. Then she came to one dated two weeks later with a note by the date. *As you can see by the date, this letter, like most of our correspondence, has become a serial. I've used up two pens in my haste to see that you had all the news two weeks ago and then never sent it.*

Anna read on.

> *I accepted the challenge and the wheels are in motion to gild Maggie Bradford's accomplished career. Hon, I'm here to tell you, I'm being bombarded by the press, looking into everything I have ever said or done (I hope they don't find some of it!). There are articles about me in newspapers and journals of every stripe. (You know, saying I'm an outstanding chick full of glory, laud, and honor. Looks good on your résumé to be published about, but they don't get it right half the time.) I've even been referred to as a "classy Texas broad," which I took to be a compliment. Before you know it, my name will be a household word, like Tide or Sani-Flush, after they hash me over on the local talk shows. I hope that doesn't work against me. I can stand in court and emote like a Southern Baptist preacher, but put me before a camera and I'm about as articulate as a mud fence.*
>
> *I bought an exercise tape in the hopes that I can lose twenty pounds before my first TV appearance next*

week. HOW IN HELL'S ARMPIT DID YOU LOSE
SEVEN POUNDS—AND FROM WHERE???

Anna turned the page. Maggie wrote just like she talked, in a large, free scrawl embellished with arrows pointing to footnotes in the margins.

> *Wouldn't you know, just as I've started the huge,*
> *grinding political machinations to try and get the goats*
> *(you should meet some of them) to join the sheep in*
> *support for my judgeship (many of whom, of course,*
> *would die for this opportunity), I've met a very nice*
> *man. His name is Lawrence Kennedy. I told you about*
> *him in my last letter. I wouldn't say he's God's gift to*
> *womankind, but I didn't think there were any like*
> *him left.*
> *He's a professor of economics at SMU, a widower of*
> *five years. He's such fun to be with. He has friends I*
> *enjoy and he looks for unusual things for us to do, like*
> *seeing special exhibits at the museum, and offbeat art*
> *shows in the suburbs. Something other than drinks*
> *and dinner and hope to be invited in when he brings*
> *me home. He's interesting to talk with. The thing that*
> *got me in the first place is that he doesn't let me*
> *buffalo him. He's impressed with me but not cowed,*
> *and he has his life well in hand. You'll have to admit,*
> *after Bill and Frank, that's different! And though all*
> *his parts function properly, he does not have a one-*
> *track mind. I wouldn't have believed I'd ever*
> *appreciate that in a man.*

Anna had to look for the page that followed that and finally found it on the back of page two.

> *He's not very tall. Not handsome. Rather quiet and,*
> *like I said, not at all overwhelmed by my career or*

aspirations. The only trouble is, we hardly ever see each other. I'm working sometimes sixty- to seventy-hour weeks now, and he has evening classes. Just knowing he's out there is nice, though. Oh, I forgot to tell you about the dinner *on his SAILBOAT. Do you know what size a Snipe is???? I had expected one of those boats with a little cabin . . . with a table—you know, like in the movies. A SNIPE IS SOMETHING LIKE FIFTEEN FEET LONG WITH THIS HOLE IN THE MIDDLE WHERE YOU PUT YOUR FEET! Our dinner was sandwiches and beer, which we ate at a TILT, with the boat nearly falling over every time he yelled, "Coming about." I nearly fell off the first time, because I refused to let go of the food (nothing will make me let go of food) to hang on to these cables that hold up the mast. He finally showed me that I could hook my feet under something, but I still had to bend under the sail and sit on the other side each time he changed direction, sticking my derriere practically in his face while doing so. I'm sure that view gave new definition to "classy Texas broad." It wasn't the most romantic evening I've ever spent, but it was kind of fun.*

After another search Anna found the next page.

But YOU! My God, you're being rushed like a sorority girl. Your little drawings of him are great. He's beautiful—I'm talking about the Greek—but I also think Sam is wonderful. Are you sure Sam's so enamored with that girl named Spenser or whatever? You were very mysterious about the conflict you had with him. I can't believe you slept in the same bed at that mosquito-ridden Delphi place with him without being a little flagrante delicto. God, Anna, that would take sangfroid I would have thought even you were

incapable of. And speaking of Freud—he would
dismiss you as a hopeless case. I'm absolutely dying of
curiosity about what you are up to now. Try not to
make any earth-shattering decisions before I can advise
you!

Anna clutched the pages of the letter. Oh, it would be good to see Maggie. To talk with her about this mess. To listen to her chatter on in that soft Texas drawl with her direct, down-to-earth observations. *Maybe I should go home. Maybe it's time.*

Pacing back and forth, Anna found the envelope that had come with the flowers dropped on the floor, as she'd known that they were from Alexis. "I miss you," the card said. No signature. She crumpled it in her hand, looking absently at the drawing—the reason she gave Alexis for not wanting to marry him. She repeated Maggie's question out loud to herself, "What *am* I up to?" Then answered it herself. "I'm up to my chin in bewilderment!"

She reread Maggie's letter, wishing she were here in person, then carefully laid it on the table as though it were made of glass and might break. *Why didn't I tell her about what happened with Sam in Crete? She would have thought that far more normal than that fiasco with him at the hotel in Galaxidi.*

Sam. Just thinking about his craggy face and rumbly voice gave Anna comfort. She had hurt him too. And he was a true friend who had no expectations of her.

She stood up and opened the doors to the balcony, staring out across the rooftops toward the Acropolis. Sam's hotel was just below there in the Plaka. Anna made up her mind quickly. She crossed the room and picked up the phone. Without examining her reasons, she called the Nefeli Hotel. As they rang his room she held her breath, hearing the insistent buzz on the other end of the line, praying he would answer.

"Hello." His voice was like a hand reaching out to her.

"Sam, I need . . . I'd like to see you."

"You know I can always work you into my social schedule. How about, hmmmm, a week from Thursday?"

"Sam!"

"Okay, when did you have in mind?"

"Have you had lunch?"

"For a meal yet. I thought you were all tied up with Frank Lloyd Wright."

"Not always. Listen, could you meet me somewhere?" Anna was suddenly embarrassed by the urgency she heard in her own voice. She laughed and it sounded shrill and nervous through the receiver. "I just, well—" She was sorry she had called.

"Just name the place. I love clandestine rendezvous."

To salvage at least some of her pride Anna said, trying to sound offhand, "I was coming over to the Plaka anyway to"—she searched around the room and glimpsed, through the door, her pencil box—"to do some sketches. Just thought I'd say hello."

"Why don't you come to the hotel, then, when you feel like it, and we can decide where to go from here?"

"If you're sure it's convenient." God, she sounded like a teenager.

There was a pause on the phone. Then he said, "I'll have to cancel my appointment for open-heart surgery, but maybe I can last for another day."

"I'll see you in a little while."

Anna almost ran the few blocks to Sam's hotel. She arrived breathless and stood outside the entrance for a moment, trying to calm down.

When she walked in, Sam stood up from the couch in the lobby, his finger in a thick book, his half-glasses perched precariously on his nose. "Well, look at you. I like your hairdo. I'm not sure I would have recognized you if I'd seen you on the street." Then he let his eyes rove over the rest of her. "Unless, of course, you were in your half swimsuit."

"Sam!"

He looked closely into her face. "Looks like you need some counsel," he said, eyeing her over the top of his glasses, holding up his book as if it were a pad where he was taking notes. "Would you like to step into Dr. McDonald's office upstairs, or will the couch down here do?"

Anna smiled, eyes closed. He could always cut through the fluff and get straight to the point. Maggie seemed to have known this from a distance. Hadn't she said in her letter that Sam was wonderful?

"Actually, I'm hungry," she said, realizing it was true.

"For a meal, or for something gooey and fattening?"

"Something alcoholic."

"You *are* in a bad way. But I know just the place."

They crossed the street and entered a tiny coffeehouse that smelled of cinnamon, roasted coffee beans, and fresh-baked pastry. Mismatched antique tables and chairs were scattered about at random. The tablecloths, hand embroidered in different colors, caught squares of light from an arched, leaded window with small panes of stained glass. Classical music seemed to emanate from the walls.

"My favorite place," Sam said.

Anna nodded, looking around. If she had wandered in here on her own, she would have immediately thought of Sam.

"The menu covers it all—real food, gooey desserts, any kind of liquor. I'd guess you haven't eaten today, and since I don't want to have to carry you home, why don't we start with meat pies? They make the best."

At first, Sam talked. He told her about the current book he was reading. "Did you know that fifty percent of physicists are into physics because of mysticism? In fact, the greatest mystics of our time are physicists."

"Why is that?" Anna asked, content to hear his voice but finding herself really listening.

"Science and theology—which split when Galileo had the audacity to claim that the earth was *not* the center of the universe . . . that it circled the sun when Scripture clearly states that the earth is the center—have come back together. Scientists, who in the past thought everything could eventually be explained, now stand in awe of the unexplainable. That opens, once again, the possibility for a God, or at least some mysterious creative force." He pulled on his ear. "Are you with me here?"

Anna nodded. It sounded good and it was pleasant to just let him go on, his voice a balm to her ruffled conscience.

"Time, the vast distances, both in space and within atoms—these are mystical concepts. Relative to other things, of course, as Einstein theorized. Even the structure of our cells is a mystery." He leaned forward. "Did you know that every atom in your body was once inside a star?"

"That's frightening," Anna said. "And at the same time, comforting."

Their meal came, and Sam ordered wine. They ate in silence for a while, just listening to the music, which had a tranquilizing effect on Anna. "Vivaldi," Sam said, gesturing in the air as if he knew what she was thinking. It was one of the things Anna liked most about Sam—his stillness. Then he said, "And now I want to know why you rushed down here. And don't tell me you were just passing by on your way to sketch the Parthenon. You don't have that straw suitcase with your drawing stuff."

With a shock, Anna looked down, feeling around with her hands, realizing that not only hadn't she brought her pencils and pads—her ruse—she had also forgotten her purse. Her face was burning.

"Don't worry. You won't have to do dishes. I'll tell them you'll come back later to mop up, in payment for the lunch you invited me to."

"Oh."

He gave her a long look, pursing his lips and frowning. "Now. What's bothering you?"

I will not cry, Anna said to herself. *I will not cry.*

"Okay. If you won't tell me, let me guess. You're pregnant."

In horrified relief, Anna started to laugh. "That would be the worst of all possible worlds. It's nice to be reminded that things aren't as bad as they could be." The tension broken, Anna did feel better. At least the threat of tears was gone. "I've just been offered the moon and I turned it down," she said.

"Is that right? Why?" He didn't ask for further explanation.

"Because I am in the process of redesigning myself, and I didn't care to be the person he expected, uh . . . I was expected to be."

"I rather liked the old design myself, though I must say the haircut is a nice upgrade."

"I've come a long way since Crete." Anna could hear bitterness that had crept into her voice.

"I would guess that you have." He raised his eyebrows in a knowing look.

"Sam!"

His face fell back into his serious frown. "Speaking of this moon you've been offered, one thing to remember is that when we see moonlight, what we are actually seeing is a reflection of the sun. An offering of the moon may not be all it's cracked up to be."

Anna swirled the wine in her glass, feeling the truth of this reverberating in her bones.

"I take it you are now having second thoughts, though, about turning it down."

Anna didn't reply. While Sam made his way through the beautiful meal, Anna only stirred hers in patterns on her plate. The wine, which she gladly sipped, only brought up other memories, a confusion of memories. Strange how the taste of something familiar could loosen all kinds of recollections.

Anna looked over at Sam. "Could you lend me some . . . money to pay for this lunch and just walk with me back to the hotel?" She was only getting more confused sitting here quaffing down wine, immersed in this music, with Sam reading her mind. She needed to get out in the sun and air.

Sam paid for the meal. As he pulled her hand through the crook of his arm, they walked out into the street. "I've missed you, Anna," he said.

"I've missed you too."

They walked by the square where Anna and Alexis had watched the dancer on stilts. It seemed centuries ago. In the afternoon sun, it was only a pleasant place, its magic reserved for late evening. Emerging from the Plaka, they meandered along a busy street with a narrow, broken sidewalk toward Syntagma Square.

"How is Taylor?" Anna asked, really wanting to know.

"She's on a flight to Cairo today—filling in for someone who got sick. She'll be back late this afternoon." He looked down at Anna. "How is she? Impatient. Lovely. Lithesome. Irascible sometimes. Always unpredictable. I never know when she's going to be which. Makes things interesting."

"It doesn't seem to bother you."

Sam took a deep breath and let it out with a loud sigh. "It does bother me sometimes. But at other times, it's worth it."

For no reason Anna felt her stomach sink.

"I guess what I really think makes it worth—what did you say the other night? The effort? What makes it worth enduring her moods and her insistence that I carry her off on my white charger is that she, well, she rejuvenates me."

"I rather liked the old, mature design myself." Anna smiled up at him. "Though, I guess, she had already begun her work when I met you."

"You're right. You would not have liked what I was when I first met her. I don't mean *rejuvenate* as in making young, so much as I mean *revive*. I guess, in a way, she resuscitated me when I was sure I was dead."

Hearing those words, a cold finger of envy touched Anna's heart with such iciness that it took her breath away. Like a dirge, a phrase sounded in her mind. *Too late. You were too late.* She was stunned. She had never been jealous of anyone in her life. Her walk slowed as if chains were attached to her ankles and she was dragging them through thick mud. Embarrassed tears seemed to mist her hearing as well as her vision, for the next thing she heard Sam say was, ". . . was you, though, who broke my heart. But I wouldn't have missed it for the world."

"What?"

"I'll always remember that time with you in Crete as idyllic." When he looked at her, his smile turned to alarm. "Hey, what's the matter? Don't you feel well?"

Anna had stopped walking. What had he said? She had an unaccountable sense of having missed something very important. A fleeting sensation. She couldn't even define its source. But it left her exhausted and miserable. An attempt to laugh only made her face crumple. From behind her hands, she said, "I don't know what's wrong."

Sam had flagged down a taxi and pushed Anna inside. She looked out the window unseeing, tears spilling down her cheeks. Sam didn't say anything, just held her close with one arm around her shoulders.

At the hotel, he paid the taxi driver and got her key from the desk. He then walked her to the elevator and up to her suite. He unlocked the door and took her elbow to guide her through it. "Nice flowers," he said, gesturing toward the huge bouquet on the table, which had arrived while Anna was gone. "Now, you go wash your face and come and sit down right here," he commanded, patting the back of the couch, "while I order some coffee. Then I want you to tell me what's happened to make you so unhappy."

Anna went into the bathroom and made her way past the flowers to the sink. She looked at her face in the mirror. She looked awful. Embarrassed. *He must think I'm a real ninny.* She dried her face furiously, powdered her nose, and put on lipstick. Then, lifting her chin as she walked out, she sat on the couch, wondering what kind of explanation she could give him.

Sam put down the phone and pulled the chair over so that it was facing her. But as he came around to sit down he noticed the drawings leaning along the wall. "Anna," he said with wonder. He went over, pulling out his glasses to examine them more closely. He looked at each one carefully. "These are amazing. I knew you were good, but I had no idea you were as good as this!"

He turned to her, his hangdog eyes shining. "You don't need the moon, Anna. Some people shed their own light."

"I'm afraid, Sam." She blurted it out before she knew what she was going to say.

"That is the last thing most people would expect *you* to say,"

Sam told her, falling into the chair. "You always come off so bold, so sure of yourself."

Anna shook her head. "That's a problem I've always had. My disguise is so well fashioned, I even fool myself at times. But I can't always maintain the facade."

"And you know," he said softly, "that's probably the thing I like best about you."

"You knew?"

"I know you *very* well."

"Then tell me what to do."

"Do what you really want."

"After everything that's happened, how do I know?"

"A bone, after it heals, is stronger at the place where it was broken, Anna. You have much more strength than you give your-self credit for. You couldn't do this"—he waved toward the drawings—"unless you had a very solid core. I think you're closer to the truth than you know."

He smiled. "You'll make the right decision. Just take your time. There's nothing that says you have to do anything today, is there? You don't have to make any ironclad decisions this very moment. Determined people don't give up easily." He gestured toward the bouquet on the table. "Unwilted flowers speak for a person's tenacity."

"Whose?"

"Alexis'. He's obviously not giving up easily."

Anna blinked. She had thought he was still speaking metaphor-ically when he mentioned flowers. She had forgotten all about Alexis. She took a sip of coffee, not realizing it was so hot, and it burned all the way down, leaving her coughing and sputtering.

Sam clapped her between the shoulder blades. "Good Lord, she can swim like a fish, and here she is drowning in her coffee. Are you okay?"

"I'm fine. I keep getting finer the more you talk." She laughed, the first real laugh she had enjoyed in a long time.

"Sam, let's go back to Crete." Anna hadn't planned to say that, and yet hope rose fluttering in her chest.

His face sobered, and he didn't answer for a long moment. "You can't ever go back, Anna. You can only go forward."

Smarting from his gentle rebuff of her blatant invitation, she stared into her hands. "I suppose you're right." She stood up and walked to the window, drawing back the drapes. "What are you going to do, then? Where is *forward* for you?"

"My time is up here. All that airport security business is over. I'm going back to the States. I have some heavy decisions to make too." He pursed his lips, pulling his ear. "I'm trying to listen to my heart. This time I'm going to go where it leads me. I don't intend to let anything—society or daughters or American Airlines or wind, snow, or driving rain—determine my course."

"Do you think it will include Taylor?" It was a hard question for Anna to ask and she steeled herself for the answer.

But he didn't need to say anything. The joy in his face told it all. "Could be." He stared at the floor as if considering.

It was as if a door had shut somewhere. Anna sighed, a cloud of resignation settling over her. She smiled. "I'm glad," she said.

"Why is that?"

"Because it would be hard for me to think of you spending your future with someone I didn't like."

"I feel the same way. I hope you'll let me know what you decide to do."

"I think I've decided."

He raised his eyebrows.

"I'm going back . . . no, forward, to Crete"—she smiled—"to study with Demetri for a while. Maybe I'll eventually be able to draw a picture of myself, in focus. Right now that would be impossible. And"—she nodded, eyes closed—"perhaps some distance from"—she cut her eyes at the flowers—"all this will give me a better perspective from which to make a more intelligent decision."

"Absence makes the heart grow fonder, I've heard." Anna looked over at Sam's wonderful face, its angles and lines sculpted by such a rough hand, and considered this. He still had on his half-glasses, looking over the top. Those woebegone eyes, regarding her with tenderness and sympathy, were almost more than she could bear. She nodded. He was right. But it wasn't Alexis she found herself missing.

"Are you hungry?"

Anna slapped her forehead with her palm. "Hungry. Is that all you can think about? I don't understand why you don't weigh a ton!" She reached out and pulled him to his feet. "Go and get something to eat. And then get out to the airport to meet that beautiful young woman, and give her my love."

At the door, Sam took her shoulders and looked into her face. "Give my regards to our beach," he said. He held her eyes in his gaze for a long moment. "And give my love to Anna when you find her." He ruffled her hair, as one would do a child's. "I think you have a good start."

The phone was ringing as she turned back into the room. Anna didn't answer it. She started packing.

Twenty-three

At the Iráklion airport, Anna rented a car. Driving along the familiar dusty highway to Ayios Nikolaos, with its clusters of run-down resorts littering stretches of beach like windblown newspaper, she had that rush of affection one feels when coming home after a long time.

It *had* been a long time. Perhaps not in hours and days and weeks, but certainly in moments. Anna felt infinitely older and more careworn and, at this point, not much wiser. As she neared Ayios Nikolaos, the sign to Elounda filled her with yearning. Maria and Demetri. She would contact them as soon as she got back to the hotel.

She was confused to find herself being received at the Villas like a returning celebrity. Everyone scurried to carry her luggage and packages. At her villa, the manager opened the door with a flourish. Anna could have expected there would be flowers, but not on every surface.

"They came this afternoon," the manager's wife said breathlessly, clasping her hands against her breast. "Just like in a book."

A stack of mail lay piled on the table. On the top was a telegram. After everyone had gone, Anna put some things away, threw her luggage on the bed to be unpacked later, and made herself a cup of tea. Then she lounged back in the chair and looked at her Demetri painting for a moment before opening her mail.

The telegram, as she suspected, was from Alexis. "I was distressed to find you had checked out of the hotel without letting me know where you were going."

How had he found out where? Anna wondered. Or had he only guessed? "I know you need some time, and though I want to come straight to Crete and bring you back, I will *let you . . .*" Anna didn't read further.

Letters from the children. She laughed through Christine's anecdotes, and Peter's spiky, scribbled note describing his "bone class." She looked in vain for a letter from Maggie. She had another phone message from Sophia and a note from Maria that said, "Please come to us as soon as you return. We are always here."

Anna finished her tea and, in a burst of nervous energy borne on a crest of exhaustion, threw off her clothes and wriggled into her bikini bottom, dug out of one of the suitcases. She caught sight of herself in the bathroom mirror and noted that she had lost some of her tan in her month in Athens. Tying on her beach robe, she slipped her feet into the thongs for the walk to the beach. Her bag with the mat and lotion, even the book she had been reading when she left, was in the closet. Above it hung the dress she had last seen draped on a chair on the terrace.

There was no one else at the beach. Anna unfurled her mat against the rocks and let the robe drop to the ground, all her self-consciousness gone. The luminous unreality in the air was like a blessing, not with holy water, but with the shimmering gold of late-afternoon sunlight. It was wonderful to be back. The smell of brine, the soft sound of swells running along the rib of rock, and the clean-swept sky made Anna want to raise her arms in ceremony. She did raise her arms, and dived straight off the rock into the glassy water. Forgetting her problems and decisions in a glorious moment of homecoming, she gave herself to the sea.

That evening before dinner Anna called Stiros and asked him to take a message to the Anistopolises telling them she would be there at three the next afternoon if it was convenient. Then she returned Sophia's call.

"I've missed you," Sophia said. "I didn't know you were leaving. Did you have a good time in Athens? They told me that's where you went."

"It was . . . interesting. It's nice to be back. Let's meet for lunch soon."

"That would be pleasant. I must go to Rhodes for a few days. I'll call as soon as I return."

"Please do," Anna said. "I'll look forward to it."

Later, Anna sat out on her terrace with a glass of wine, listening to the night noises. Her candle flickered in answer to the lights across the Gulf of Mirabello. She took a deep breath and stretched, trying to relax and work out the tension. But like a flock of starlings in her head, bits and pieces of old memories—poignant moments, isolated quotes from past conversations—kept intruding on the peace. The tranquillity of this pastoral island was all around her, yet it didn't touch her tonight. She had hoped Crete once again would help heal this new wretchedness and confusion as it had begun to heal her old, overriding grief before . . . before . . . *God, I've made a mess of things.* She needed to see Maria and Demetri.

Maria was waiting at the door when Anna arrived. She nodded, smiling. "Come in, come in," Maria said, holding open her arms. "Demetri said to tell you he had an appointment in Ayios Nikolaos but to beg you to stay for tea and then dinner too so he can have some time with you." She led the way into the house. "Your hair. It's lovely."

"I'm so glad to see you," Anna said, kissing Maria's cheek.

They had coffee on the shaded terrace. Anna chattered on about things she had done in Athens, especially about her trip to Delphi with Sam—without all the details.

"He was the friend you met here, at the Villas," Maria said, just to make sure.

"Yes." Anna nodded. Then, with Maria's prompting, Anna went on with descriptions of the theater parties and restaurants, the discotheques and her delight in meeting up with old friends. Maria listened eagerly. Anna needed that.

"Then Alexis took me on his yacht to Hydra and—" She paused.

"And?"

Anna was suddenly tongue-tied and stammered through, sorry she had started telling about it, editing as she spoke.

"Who is this Alexis?" Maria finally asked.

Anna raised her eyes to Maria's and said offhandedly, "Alexis Sarkis."

"Of Sarkis Shipping Lines?"

Anna nodded. "The son. He's an architect."

"Ah, yes, the younger Alexis Sarkis. I've heard he is doing wonderful things. I knew him briefly when he was a boy, back in—" A frown knit her forehead as she tried to remember what year it had been.

"Oh, Maria, I should never have gone there. I should have stayed here and faced Sam. Then I could have avoided . . . I could have avoided everything."

Maria poured her another cup of coffee. "Why don't you start back at the beginning, and tell me why you left Crete in such a hurry?"

Anna didn't know where to begin.

"I don't want to pry," Maria said, "but I think I can guess some of what happened. Of course, if you let an old woman's imagination loose, she'll probably come up with something far more scandalous than what actually took place."

"That would take some doing," Anna said with a mirthless chuckle.

"I'd guess that this Sam turned out to be a very normal man, quite taken with a lovely lady"—she indicated Anna with her hand—"at a resort on a romantic island." Anna stared into her lap. "And that the lovely lady turned out to be normal too." Anna nodded. "Then, in confusion and, possibly, unwarranted shame, the lady flies away to Athens, only to land in the clutches of a Greek—you have to watch these Greeks—who spirits her away to Hydra."

"If I didn't know better, I'd think you had been spying on me," Anna said. As always under Maria's scrutiny, the atmosphere was conducive to confession. Anna felt relief that became a flood of words. "When I first got there—Athens—I found I was once again Paul Sandoval's wife, invited hither and yon by friends who had known us before. Once again, I was an extension of Paul.

"Then, out of the blue, I was getting a marriage proposal from Alexis. I ended up hurting him and . . . I wish I had just stayed here." She glanced up briefly, crawling with misery and self-loathing. "I came to Greece to take time out to try and straighten out my life." She raised her hands palms up in a gesture of frustration. "Now I'm back where I started, only a thousand times more confused."

"You were sought after as Paul's wife? I doubt that." Maria reached over and squeezed Anna's hand. "Life goes on, Anna. We can never take time out—get off the merry-go-round, as they say. We have to keep on living, even while we are trying to find the meaning and purpose of it all. We can't let interruptions distract us in our quest. The interruptions are part of the adventure." Her smile put a spark of mischievousness in her dark, dramatic eyes. "In order to make choices, the *choices have to be available*. And to have choices available, one must be open to them. The trouble is, being open requires risk. It also means being vulnerable."

"Vulnerable and stupid. The reason I came to Crete in the first place was to find out who I really am. When I was in Washington, I didn't feel I had many viable choices. Or rather, I didn't know where to look. Now I've just spent a month screwing everything up, and here I am, knowing that all I have to do is nod and Alexis will come rescue me from all this . . . this searching."

Maria shook her head. "What you are seeking, Anna, is not out there." She waved her hand to take in the horizon. "It's in here." With one gnarled finger she touched Anna's sternum just below her collarbone. Her voice was hushed with gravity. "But consider your choices carefully. If you think you need a man to rescue you, to make you whole, you are wrong."

Anna winced.

"I don't think this was true in your first marriage, though you say so. You didn't need Paul, as much as you seem to think, to make you complete. You chose him, and chose that lifestyle with him because it made you happy. And he was happy because you were there. By the same token, he didn't need you to prove he was a whole person either. What you liked about him was that he *was* whole. And that is what he apparently loved about you, though for some strange reason you couldn't see it in yourself."

"And if he could see me now, what would he think?" Anna asked, hearing irony heavy in her voice.

"You think he would judge you for what happened in Athens?"

"I don't like to think about it at all. I'm not proud of my behavior."

"Anna, Anna. In this life many things happen in which we sometimes play a less-than-noble part. Those of us who are strong forgive ourselves and go on. There is not one of us who hasn't been in these situations. That ought to be some comfort."

Anna gazed out across the shimmering olive groves. "You spoke of forgiveness before. Well, I tried to forgive Paul and God and even myself. And I felt better, for a while. I felt liberated, optimistic. I thought I had moved on. But, Maria, it keeps coming back." She ran her fingers through her hair, still surprised at its shortness. "*I miss Paul. I want him back. I wanted it to last forever.*"

"Forgiveness. It is never done well in bits and pieces. We can't say, *I can forgive him this, but not that.* Do it all at once and never look back." She smiled out over the hillside, and Anna wondered if she was thinking back to another time—a time when she too was a widow and young and in pain. "As for something lasting forever, moments of our lives can be eternal without being everlasting. Your time with Paul was eternal. Don't brood that it didn't last forever."

Anna took a drink of her now-cold coffee and turned her eyes toward the older woman. "But, Maria, the loneliness is so hard to bear! Loneliness even when I'm with others. It's frightening." Her mind went back to Athens, days with Alexis when she had lost that fear. "It makes you desperate . . . for someone." She looked at Maria, shaking her head. "For someone who will share. For someone who is glad to be with you. For someone who will talk with you about decisions." She put her face in her hands and tried to rub the confusion away.

"I know," Maria said. Her voice shook a little. "I know." She put her hand on Anna's arm. "It is part of the delight in life, and the sadness, to need someone to share with. It is all right to need. That is the way we are created."

"I don't think I'll ever get used to it."

"No. But you can't dwell on it, sacrificing the joy of the present to a dead past, or the fear of an unborn future. If you do that, you will always be sad. I spoke of being open. Be open to the fact that there is blessing in solitude too. And that being alone doesn't always mean being lonely. Being alone is often frightful, I know. But even then there are so many possibilities for beauty and glory. It is a mystery that runs like a thread through our lives."

She paused, her hand to her head in thought, then said, "We are always becoming, Anna. Becoming a mother or a teacher or a painter or whatever. It is so complex because to *become* we need other people—their approval, care, support. And that is wonderful. But it is in solitude that we can simply *be*. Happiness does not depend on exterior circumstances. It is a state of mind. This is also true with loneliness. It too is a state of mind."

Even the shade of the ancient olive trees couldn't shield them from the heat of late afternoon. "Let's go inside," Maria said. "Demetri will be back from Ayios Nikolaos soon and he will not want to sit out."

They were settled in the cool, rosy light of the sitting room when they heard Demetri's car struggling up the hill. Anna watched the creases on Maria's face lift in pleasure and her eyes light expectantly. *How beautiful she is,* Anna thought.

Demetri took Anna's hand in both of his. "We've missed you. It is good to have you in our home again." They drank lemonade while Anna told him about her sketching forays in Athens, her frustrations, the joy of being so involved that she lost hours at a time.

"Did you bring your drawings?"

"I should be so bold," she teased. Then she said, "Of course I brought them." She went out to the car and brought in the large leather case. All her Athens drawings, even the unfinished little studies, were filed inside.

Demetri spread them all about his studio and walked from one to another, slowly, standing over each of them for a minute or more, moving to the next without comment. "What are your plans now?" he asked, looking up as if he had dismissed the drawings.

"I had hoped to continue working with you." Anna felt uncomfortable.

He walked over and looked at several of the drawings again and then turned to Anna, his face impassive. "No. I will no longer work with your drawing."

Anna was stunned with disappointment. Humiliation flamed across her face. Was her work that poor? At the same time, another thought tore through her. If he didn't work with her, she would no longer have a reason to continue to come here.

Demetri left the room. Anna could hear him rummaging around in the walk-in closet in the hall. Anna didn't want to look at Maria.

Before she could do anything, Demetri came back and handed her a wooden box. A good-bye gift? Anna opened it, apprehension fluttering in her breast. Inside was a set of watercolors— at least thirty tubes of paint, several brushes, and a palette with trays for mixing paint. "This is what I will teach you."

After a wonderful dinner, Anna took the paints home, feeling as if she had found a buried treasure. She had dismissed the medium of watercolor years before, feeling it was too unpredictable, too inexact. But to study this medium under a great master was a privilege that outweighed any of those misgivings. She was to meet Demetri the next day in Elounda for her first lesson. Maria had said, "Come early and have breakfast with me. Then you can work with Demetri and come back and have lunch."

The next morning Anna and Demetri sipped coffee at the outdoor café where they had met. Anna knew he would take his time getting started, looking at the light and shadows, watching people. Anna relaxed, waiting.

"Your drawings are very good, Anna. The ones you did in Athens. More than good. There is a mystical quality about them that borders on greatness. I see in them the gift you have carried in your body all this time, letting it mellow on a shelf for years, waiting for the day of celebration when it would be opened." He gazed out across the square. "How many gifts go unopened in a lifetime?"

"There were times in Athens," Anna said, "when I felt this surge of *celebration,* as you say. But each time, the moment I became aware of it, it evaporated."

"I would guess that it was not the awareness of the celebration, but a self-consciousness that said, *I doubt.* You must learn never to doubt yourself. It is a matter of discipline. The discipline of creation, whether it is painting or writing or composition of music or running a successful business—the act of being in touch with both the intellect and intuition—is an effort toward wholeness. It is a spiritual act that requires reverence." He shifted in his chair so he could look directly at Anna. "Many people these days have lost their sense of reverence. The result is boredom. Boredom that leads to the quest for false security and synthetic thrills.

"But when we can see," he continued, "really see beauty, in form and shape and light, and in the people around us, we are never bored. This is what you communicate in your sketches—the excitement of your discovery of life! That is why I wanted you to try this medium, because the directness of watercolor has to rely on the artist's eye and a consummate facility in sound, classical drawing. You are infinitely prepared to get into color."

He set up a folding easel and opened a large hinged box. "I've already prepared paper for you. I'll teach you how to do this in my studio one day." He clipped a drawing board, on which he had taped the paper, onto the easel. "The thing to remember about watercolor is its spontaneity. The artist does not have full control."

"That's what scares me. In drawing I can get every detail I want to emphasize exactly as I see it."

"Ah, but that is the joy of this medium. It does some of the work itself. You have to respect its capriciousness. Sometimes a water spot you didn't plan gives character to a piece that no amount of careful brushwork could accomplish. That is serendipity."

He moved from the stool to let Anna work at the easel. "Now, choose a scene or two and do simple line drawings, no details." He handed her a charcoal pencil, saying, "Charcoal washes out when you add the paint. I want you to work from real life from the beginning, because one's paintings are more alive then than working from old drawings or photographs."

Anna spent a few minutes looking around the dock and the playing field at the people wandering about. A huge woman in white running shoes stood in a line waiting for the boat that would take her to Spinalonga Island. She looked bored and moved as if her feet hurt. Beside her, bearing a faint resemblance and wearing identical shoes, a thin, birdlike woman near the same age looked about, her cheerful face and bright eyes drinking in the whole scene. The first woman, fanning herself with a guide-book, was looking at the ground. Were they sisters, one having dragged the other halfway round the world against her wishes? The boat was pulling up to the dock. Anna did a quick contour drawing of them. She tried to show the eagerness in the one, the reluctance in the other. Demetri, without speaking, lifted the paper off the easel carefully, keeping the tape intact.

Taping on a new piece of paper, Anna chose a Greek matron sitting two tables over from them—a hard, chunky person, her bosom straining at the row of buttons down the front of her flow-ered cotton dress. She was reading a paperback with a decidedly lurid cover, and the expression on her face was pure pleasure. Anna made a quick study emphasizing the book cover and the woman's eyes, glued to the pages.

She then sketched two obviously gay men wearing outlandish earrings and buzz haircuts, speaking with affected gestures and tones. Anna drew them small on the page, indicating the empty ta-bles around them, isolating them in a way that suggested the iso-lation she guessed they might feel in their lives.

Demetri said, "That is enough." He put another board with paper on the table. "Now, let's work for a while on technique. You can work directly on dry paper or you can wet the paper with a wide brush and work from wet to wet." He demonstrated this, showing her how wet paper drew the paint into small explosions of colors with feathered edges. "A method of making sky that has depth." He told her that she would not find white among her tubes of paint.

"The only white in a painting should be the white of the paper showing through the transparent color."

He reminded her how painting in watercolor was actually layering color, moving from light to dark. As she had done years ago in art classes, Anna practiced making a sphere and a cylinder look three-dimensional as the paint spread of its own accord, on the wetted surface. When she was finally working with her drawings, she first filled in broad areas with a light wash, and then let them dry before going on to the next step. Each successive layer became more detailed as she added touches of warm muted yellows and oranges to show sun on bare skin, or cool blues and grays to indicate shade. The smallest details were added last.

As Anna worked, the timeless spell of the morning was punctuated with sage comments. "You must paint often, constantly refreshing visual memories that you can bring to other paintings.

"Don't be so concerned with managing the medium that you forget what you are saying in the picture. Perfectionism inhibits human growth and saps our capacity for delighting in life. You don't want your pictures to be portraits but revelations of the inner life of the person. Try to perceive the interior of the mind of your subjects."

When Anna got frustrated and berated herself for being so unable to get it right, Demetri put his hand on her arm to calm her. "You are holding back. Blocked by the very requirement of *getting it right*. You must be like a lover, so caught up in the act that your body—in this case, your hand—knows what to do. If you let go of your compulsion to be exact, who knows what wonders you will find?"

*   *   *

Almost every morning, Anna drove her rented car through the silver air to Elounda to breakfast with Maria, then spent midmorning until the late Greek lunch hour with Demetri. Often they invited her to stay for dinner, but she rarely accepted. After mornings with Maria and sessions with Demetri, she felt suspended in a sort of hallowedness, and she wanted to be alone.

Driving back home, Anna reworked in her mind the images of the scenes she had tried to capture, reflecting at the same time on things Demetri and Maria had told her. She arrived back at the Villas each day drained and at the same time so invigorated that she often walked into her villa and went right to work—trying different perspectives, sometimes simply practicing different techniques for mixing colors or her brushwork. More and more often, she worked on paintings she had started earlier, learning patience from the capricious nature of watercolor.

When she could work no longer, she was drawn to the beach, to the golden glare of the sun and the cool mystery of the afternoon sea. She swam long distances, glorying in the power of her stroke, releasing the tension of long hours hunched over the easel.

Sometimes she didn't get down to the beach until evening, when the harsh light was muted, the soft breeze and shush of the waves making her think of times past. As she leaned against the rock watching the sun set, memories that had distressed or saddened her became first bearable, and then pleasant, like looking at snapshots in an album of times past.

It was on one of these evenings that she finally understood what it meant to let go of the past. It had to do with risk. And acceptance.

Marriage is a risk, she thought, a complex machination of give-and-take, fraught with briars and thorns. Through sickness, fatigue, absence, and maddening personal idiosyncrasies, weaknesses could be trip wires in even the best of relationships. Little moments of death. *But we, Paul and I, surmounted those moments, making the relationship stronger than before.* Her marriage to Paul had been a trust that grew through storms, getting better and bet-

ter with time. This she knew. And she knew she was indeed fortunate to have had this.

Anna closed her eyes, hearing the sea, feeling the stones
through her mat. *Life is also a risk,* she thought. *There is always
the terror,* she remembered, *however deeply buried, that the other
person will suddenly be gone. It must be every woman's fear,* Anna
thought, *and perhaps every man's as well.*

Risk and fear. It was the risk that ultimately bound two people together and made them feel secure and protected.

Two people. We were always two separate people, Paul and I,
she thought. *The old adage that "two become one" is only
metaphor. Maria is right. A good marriage is two complete people
coming together to form a unity. Each partner has to live his or her
own life. And that's what we did, only I was blind and couldn't see
it. My sense that I had become an extension of his life, his career, his
needs, was never the true reality.* With this thought Anna relaxed
and forgave herself her blindness. Having forgiven herself, she
could let loose her hold on Paul and accept the fact of his death.
At last she could love him again with pleasure.

Anna looked up and smiled. There were no tears, only the joy
of acceptance. And relief, blessed relief. A resurrection.

After that, when Anna thought of Paul, it was as if the pain of
the past year had burned away. The fire smoldering at her edges
had finally gone out, leaving only scars that were already healing.
This she accepted. *Change comes hard. It is an easy thing to decide
to change, a very difficult thing to do. We resist. We resist. We get
secure even in our miseries. . . . Even our grief becomes so familiar
that we are afraid to let it go. At least we know how that feels. The
unknown seems more threatening.*

I could have spent the rest of my life in mourning, she thought,
flooded with a sense of deliverance, a feeling that she had
emerged from that cocoon. A cocoon she had clutched at, trying
to stay inside, this whole past year.

The sea had turned a deep indigo, the top of each swell
touched with a shimmer of sunset gold. Anna dived through the
gold from a high rock as if she could fly.

*   *   *

Anna had to be careful not to speed on the narrow road each time she drove to Elounda for her lesson. She was like a child who loved school, often singing as she drove around clattering trucks and flocks of sheep and donkeys trotting along with their loads or passengers.

Demetri was encouraging and exact, tactful in his criticism, and Anna could feel her confidence growing under his careful guidance. "Believe in yourself," he told her, "and the rest will come."

Anna loved working in color. The hours she had spent scratching with pencil and charcoal paid off now in this only partially controlled flow of paint.

On the days she didn't go to Elounda, she went out on forays of her own. Sometimes she worked ten hours a day, with time out only for her daily visit to the beach or into Ayios Nikolaos every few days for groceries.

Sometimes she lunched with Sophia. At first they met at little outdoor cafés near the waterfront. But once, Sophia invited Anna up to her apartment. When she walked in, Anna saw that it was decorated in the same style as the shop downstairs.

"You certainly have a way of creating beauty," Anna said, thinking that the stained-glass window, the wicker furniture, and the muted colors of the rugs and upholstery were only extensions of the way Sophia dressed and wore her hair. Everything had been carefully chosen to carry out a theme of feminine elegance. The meal was light and delicious.

Sophia was pleasant but formal. Anna came away from these visits feeling that she had been treated as a favored guest, but knowing little more about Sophia than before.

Sam called to tell her he was leaving for the States. He asked how she was and accepted her answer that she was still looking for herself. He didn't mention Taylor. "If you ever need a mosquito slayer, do call on me," was his parting remark.

Alexis did not call. His flowers kept coming, always accompanied with the same simple message, "Love."

*   *   *

One day Anna drove to Knossos to see the ruined Minoan palace and village that she had wanted to visit with Sam. It had been built in 2000 B.C., a few miles south of present-day Iráklion. The Minoan culture was Europe's first advanced civilization and Anna was especially interested to see the frescoes, among the earliest still in existence.

It was a hot day, and Anna had to join the long line of people waiting to buy tickets to get into the ruined village. But as she stood waiting her turn, she could feel the ancient harmonies, the place haunted by abiding spirits, as were most of the ruins in Greece.

She preferred to make her own way around the ruin with a guidebook, only occasionally eavesdropping on the explanations of an English-speaking guide, who herded a group of people from one place to another. Fascinated by the contrast of modern tourists against the background of the ruin, Anna made quick line drawings, lightly penciling in important colors she would use when she painted them later.

She looked around thinking, *Why do we come here?* The answer echoed in her thoughts as if spoken by the spirit of one of the ancients. *To remember who we are.* Her pencil froze in midstroke. *Is that why I'm here in Crete? Not to find myself, as I've been saying, but to remember. To remember my dream, my destiny. To remember my name.*

Anna had lived Paul's dream. His destiny became her own. *Now, without him,* she thought, *I must remember who I am.* Maria's words rang in her head. *It's not out there. It's in here.*

Someone jostled Anna, jolting her from her reverie. Looking around, she noticed a young woman, a girl really, with heavy, orange red hair, who had stopped to sit on a bench in front of a fresco of dolphins. The girl studied the guidebook, then gazed in rapt awe at the wall, painted in the fifteenth century B.C. Because she was so still, Anna had the chance to study her. Something like the energy she felt inside the living tree so long ago at Delphi vibrated in her bones. She was drawn into the scene as if she herself were a part of it.

288

Rosanne Keller

Back at the hotel, she couldn't wait to begin to paint. It was as if she had crossed over into another dimension. In her mind's eye, Anna could see the girl with red hair, her face rapt in wonder as her eyes locked on the graceful blue dolphins in the fresco—a still frame, as when a movie film is stopped.

The girl and the great dolphins were not separate entities. They were one. One faded into the other. Anna became the red-haired girl. She became the dolphins, remembering the feel of water sliding over slippery skin. It was as though she had the thoughts, the memories, of both girl and dolphins.

Her hand was an extension of her soul, independent of mind or thought. She painted as if she were watching someone else do it from a great distance. Then, as when turning the lens of a camera and everything comes into focus, her vision cleared and she was back in her room, exhausted, her back aching, moonlight spilling through the window. It was four in the morning. The painting was finished. Suddenly the room was too small; Crete was too small; the world was too small to contain her soaring spirit.

The next day, tired and exhilarated, Anna took the painting to Demetri. She chose a time when she knew he and Maria would have finished with lunch, and prayed he would be there.

They welcomed her at the door as always. But when Demetri looked into her face and saw that she was carrying her large, flat case, he said, "Don't even stop in the sitting room. I want to see what you've done. I can tell by the look on your face that it is something extraordinary."

Anna took the painting out and Demetri placed it on an easel with slow reverence. When Maria saw it she gasped, her sharp intake of breath the only sound in the room. She reached out as if to touch it. Demetri looked at it for a long time, first from one angle and then another. So long that Anna was worried.

Finally he turned to her. "Exquisite," he whispered.

"It is as though some beautiful secret has stolen imperceptibly from the depths of your soul, Anna," Maria said in a hushed voice. She turned to Demetri. "She knows," Maria said simply. "She knows!"

"Yes, you have found what you have been looking for," Demetri said. Looking back at the painting, he smiled, shaking his head. "But you've forgotten the most important part."

Anna searched the picture. The temptation was still there, in the light of day, to touch up that highlight, to deepen this shadow. But no. She knew it was finished. "What is it I've forgotten?" she asked.

"Your name. No piece of art is complete without the signature." He took her over to his easel and handed her a thin brush.

Anna dipped the brush into a dab of burnt sienna on Demetri's palate and raised it to the painting. Her hand was trembling so that she dared not touch the painting. A nervous laugh escaped from her aching throat. Demetri took the brush from her. "Come. Let's go out in the garden and have a glass of wine."

Anna followed both of them out onto the shaded veranda. Maria hadn't said anything, but she was smiling as she poured the wine. Demetri beamed, nodding.

These are the moments we live for, Anna thought. She was so aware of her whole being that she could have painted the air she breathed, dry and fragrant with just a hint of the sea. She could have painted the heat of the sun on her back so that anyone looking at it could feel it. She knew she could do that now. She knew! She looked at her hand holding the stem of the glass. It was brown and strong. *This hand,* she thought, *can, with a few strokes of a brush, create life and hold it there on a piece of paper. All it needs is my name.*

Anna took a deep, satisfying breath and let it out slowly, smiling at Maria and Demetri. He sat smoking, his thin hair catching the evening sun like the halo one sees in paintings of saints.

"I don't know what name to sign," she finally said. "Anna Sandoval? My birth name, Anna Gentry?"

"What's wrong with simply 'Anna'?" Demetri spoke the question softly.

"But who would recognize that name? 'Anna' is so common. Who'd know that it's me?"

"You would know. That is what is important. You would

know that this could have been painted only by Anna. And from this day on, anyone who sees your work will know. It doesn't matter if they buy it or even like it. It is you, an extension of your soul. By showing it, you are making your statement." He reached over and put his hands on each side of Anna's face, saying fiercely, "Can't you see? Nothing about you is common, Anna. You have found your true self, your center. Give yourself permission to accept the gift. Name yourself!"

Anna walked back into the studio alone. On shaky legs, she stood before the easel. Picking up the brush, she dipped it again into the paint and raised it, hesitating, holding back.

"Anna! You are Anna." Demetri's voice, from the door, rumbled. It was a baptism.

Holding her breath, Anna raised the brush. *Anna. My name is Anna.* With one flourish, she signed, *Anna, Crete* . . . and she painted in the year.

Twenty-four

After what she called her *naming,* Anna stayed in Crete for another month, drawing and painting every day. The heat of her passion for creation matched the dry, hot scorch of high summer as June burned into July.

She changed her schedule to accommodate the weather and Greek time. She was up early to catch the freshness of the day, worked until a late lunch at around two o'clock, then took a nap, followed by an hour or so at the beach. She was brown and firm from these daily walks to the beach.

Each morning, she bounded out of bed, excited about the day, hungry to see what it had to offer, itching to get to her work. After breakfast, she hurried, as if racing with the strike of the noonday sun. Then, renewed and refreshed by her siesta and swim, she worked again until dinner at nine thirty or ten.

The discipline of this schedule honed her mind as well as her body. At the end of the day, after her usual solitary dinner, she sat on the veranda with her evening glass of wine. Only then did she long to have someone to talk with, to share small things, beautiful things, questions. Someone to rub her tired back, someone whose back she could rub.

But she no longer felt desperate and desolate, as she had when she had first run away to Crete. The heart-pounding dread of facing the future alone, forlorn and forsaken, had faded. She was still lonely, but even that no longer filled her with despair. Solitude was a comfort, as Maria had told her. In fact, her seclusion was necessary. She knew that. It was a luxury to be able to devote herself to her painting with no distractions.

But in the evenings, it wore thin.

One morning, Maria stopped at the Villas for a visit. She was on her way home from one of her rare shopping trips into Ayios Nikolaos. Anna was delighted with the interruption.

Maria looked around at the paintings and drawings taped and stacked everywhere. "Your work is going well?" she asked.

Anna poured them tall glasses of iced lemonade. "Very well. I now understand what it means to be a liberated woman," she said.

Maria nodded. "Yes, I can see that. But in truth, you have only been a glance away from this *liberation* all your life."

"If that is true, I wish I had discovered it sooner. Think of the gallery I could have filled by now." Anna laughed.

"We read in the Bible that 'there is a time for every season,' " Maria said. "If you believe in Providence, perhaps this was the season waiting for your renewed endeavor. No matter how we try, we can't rush these things."

"I only wish I had had more sense of my purpose those early years. It was as if I was"—Anna waved her hand back and forth— "buffeted by variable winds, and I just went where I was blown."

"Doesn't everyone? That is part of the plan, I believe. Luckily, in retrospect, we look back and see that we were exactly where we were meant to be, doing what we were meant to do, all along. It is only as we grow older, and perhaps wiser, that we seem to become aware of our alternatives." She smiled at Anna. "It was *because* of those years that you are now able to be what you are truly meant to be"—she nodded—"for this time in your life."

Her eyes twinkled. "You would have arrived here even if you hadn't lost your husband, Anna. I'm sure of it. I'm sure you are a better artist for having waited, for having lived a full life, before devoting yourself to becoming a painter."

Anna said with a grin, "You have a knack for being right every time. I'm learning to give up some of my hard and fast ideas."

"It's like owls."

"Owls?"

"There is a story about the uprising in India late in the nineteenth century, when British service families had to be evacuated suddenly. They could take only what they could carry. Later, the road they traveled was littered with such things as stuffed owls and other needless knickknacks. We want to make changes in our lives—or sometimes we are forced to make changes—but for some reason we insist that we not have to give up our stuffed owls."

"How true." Anna knew that feeling well. "Don't you have any regrets at all, Maria, anything in your life that you would change if you had it to do over again?"

"I'm too old for regrets. Besides, they are a waste of time. Best to learn from our misfortunes or mistakes and get on with life."

Since she had left a driver waiting at the entrance, Maria didn't stay long. After Anna walked her to the car, she couldn't get back into her work. Restless, she walked up to the office, hoping the mail had come, hoping she had a big, fat letter from Maggie. When she didn't, she decided on impulse to call her from the phone in the office, just to hear the sound of her voice.

"Hello?" The line sounded blank. "Hello? Maggie?" Anna was shouting.

"Stop yelling. I can hear you fine. Is everything all right?" She sounded worried.

"Everything is fine. I just missed you, so I—"

"Well, how the hell are you? Still up to your ears in men?"

"I've given them up."

"Given up men? Oh, God, Anna, you're impossible."

"I've become a painter."

"What of? Houses? Billboards? At least you didn't say you had become a painted lady."

"Well, I tried that too, after a fashion. I'm no good at it."

"I'm picking myself up off the floor. Is this the Anna Sandoval I once knew?"

"Actually not. Tell me about yourself. Are you a woman in black yet?"

"Didn't you get my telegram? I sent it to that hotel in Athens where you're staying."

"No! I didn't. I've moved back to Crete, and they haven't forwarded my mail in a few days. Tell me. Tell me. Are you a judge?"

Maggie was silent for a humming moment. "I guess the only thing worse than not getting what you want is getting it. Yes, I'm a judge." Her voice was flat. "I got the appointment."

"Congratulations! Aren't you excited?"

"It was a grand moment, I'm here to tell you. And, if I do say so myself, I am stunning in black! At least those flowing robes hide where I'm not so stunning. But—"

"But? But what?" Anna was shouting again.

"Like everything else, there was a price."

"Isn't there always? What was it?"

"Larry. You know, the one with the 'luxurious' sailboat that tips over all the time? He leaves for England in August. Sans Maggie."

"You wanted to go?"

"I would have given anything to go except . . . oh, God, Anna. If he had come along before this judgeship appointment, I would have been willing, I think, to give it all up and just be someone's wife."

"Are you sure?" Anna asked in measured tones.

"Well, maybe I wouldn't have," Maggie finally said. "I frankly can't see myself sitting around doing nothing, I guess. And I don't think they would let me practice as a barrister in jolly old England." She sighed. "It probably would have been like going to Oz and finding out you preferred Kansas. But it sounded nice. It would have been fun to try."

"How did Larry feel about it?"

"He was wonderful, saying he was kind of flattered to be runner-up to a judgeship. In fact, he was one of the most enthusiastic revelers at the celebration party after the ceremony. I'm going to miss him, Anna."

"Sounds like a great guy. Isn't his visiting professorship in England a temporary position? I thought you told me two years."

"Two years is a long time, hon. He's a real jewel."

"Why don't you come over here for a while? We're due, aren't we, for a long visit?"

"No time. No time. I'm busier than ever. Anyway, when are you coming home? Or have you emigrated?"

"I don't know. I'm enjoying just living day to day with no plans."

"At the moment that sounds great to me. And tempting. You sound . . . different. I'd like to meet the new you."

"You might be surprised."

"I wish I could come, but—I forgot to tell you—I'm having the house redone again."

"From Japanese? I thought this was the year of the dragon or monkey or something, and you were going all out for it."

"Now that I'm a lordly judge, Oriental is too spare for me. Besides, my friends don't like sitting on the floor. So I'm going Southwest all the way. Western—you know, Navajo rugs, wagon wheels, comfortable furniture."

"Sounds good. I think I concur with your friends."

"Oh, and another thing. I've started going to church—an Episcopal church with windows like splintered glass, St. Michael and All Angels."

"Good Lord, that must have rocked the heavenly hosts back on their heels! What brought this on?" Anna was the one to be surprised.

"Looking for something, I'm not sure what. I guess I'd like to ask for something and get bread, for a change, instead of stones." Maggie sighed. "Or something like that. Have you found what you were looking for, Anna?"

"Yes. Yes, I have," she answered. There was a long pause; then she continued. "I know my name."

"You what?"

"Someday, when we have a long evening with nothing to do, I'll tell you about it."

"Tell me now," Maggie said. "I can't wait."

"It's hard to put into words, Mags. I've let go of so many things that I thought defined me. It's taken a while, and a few wrong turns, but I've had some help. I've met some wonderful people here. With their encouragement, I've been able to strip off several layers to get down to who I really am." Anna was silent for a moment. "I've become a painter. A serious painter." Then she added, "I've rediscovered that *state of grace*."

There was silence on the line.

"Are you still there?" Anna asked.

"Yes, I'm still here," Maggie said. "Nothing could be truer than that. I've stayed in the same place and tried to change everything around myself. You went far away, and are yourself changed. What do you mean, you know your name?"

"I've found out who I am," Anna said.

"I envy you, Anna."

"No, you don't, Mags. It's taken me this long to find myself. You've known who you are all your life. Now all you need to do is celebrate what you are, not what you think you ought to be."

"Thank you for saying that. And I think I finally am feeling a little pride about all this judge stuff. I guess I got lost there for a while in mourning my losses rather than rejoicing in what I have gained." She cleared her throat. "This judgeship was what I wanted all along. You've helped me see that." This last was said with a quavery voice. Then she laughed. "Do you think it would look strange to have a Japanese tea garden with a Southwest-style home? I love it. It is my place of solace. My sanctuary."

"I think it would be a unique Maggie innovation. It will probably become the rage in Dallas."

"I wish we could get together, Anna."

"I do too, Maggie. Soon. I'll be home soon."

Anna was surprised to hear herself say that. She hung up, feeling more lonely than before. Talking with Maggie had only whetted her appetite for company. Who could she call? The last time she saw Sophia, she was leaving for two weeks on a buying trip.

Sophia. When Anna had stopped by the Blue Dolphin a few

days ago, she had found a young man there who told her Sophia was still away. He didn't know when she'd return. Anna picked up the phone again.

Sophia answered on the first ring.

"I'm glad to find you back," Anna said. "Did you have a good trip?"

"Yes, but it is good to be home." She sounded tentative. "I arrived only yesterday. I was first on Mykonos and Rhodes, then in Athens for a few days."

"I'd like to hear about it. Why don't you come have dinner with me?" *Please,* Anna thought. It was a prayer.

"I'd like that very much."

Anna laughed in relief. "I warn you it will be a cold meal and very informal. Come whenever you like."

"I must stay in the shop until eight thirty. I could be there by nine o'clock."

"That'll be fine," Anna said, disappointed. "I'll see you then."

Anna could hear the click of heels coming down the hill at exactly nine o'clock. Sophia arrived dressed in that careful abandon she wore so well. "Welcome home. I've missed you," Anna said as Sophia came in.

Sophia smiled as she looked around at the paintings all over the room. "My, you have been very busy." She walked around, carefully examining each sketch and watercolor, finally stopping in front of the girl and the dolphin fresco from Knossos. She looked up at Anna, her eyes wide. "You did this?"

Anna nodded. "I've been working under the tutelage of Demetri Anistopolis. He talked me into using color."

"I'm glad he did."

Anna handed Sophia a daiquiri. "Shall we take our drinks out on the terrace? It's a beautiful night." They settled themselves at the table, where Anna had laid out a spread of cold cuts and cheeses, fruits and vegetables, breads and condiments. Candles provided the only light.

"Now tell me about your trip."

"Well, I went to—" She paused, then looked straight at Anna. "Have you ever noticed how a work of art that has been hanging unrespected and unloved in some dark corner of, let us say, a dusty old estate glows with new meaning when it is brought out and hung in a sanctuary for which it was made?"

"Yes, I have noticed that."

"Do you think this is also true of people? That when they get to the place in which they are meant to be, they come . . . come more alive?"

Anna thought about that, and then nodded. "Definitely."

Sophia looked into her lap.

"Is something bothering you?"

Sophia looked into Anna's eyes. "I am thirty-seven years old, and except for my father, whom I cared for until he died, I have never loved a man."

"And now you are in love with someone? Someone you met on this trip?"

"Yes. I mean no. He's someone I've known for a long time." She took a sip of her drink. "I mean, I don't know. I think so. He . . . his name is Myko. . . . He wants me to sell my shop and move to the mainland. He says I have been in this dark, dusty corner of Crete too long, that I belong in Athens."

"He is the one who spoke of a work of art needing a sanctuary? He sounds quite special. Do you want to do this?"

Sophia gazed out to the lights of Ayios Nikolaos. "I'm afraid. Afraid to be tied to someone. To be responsible for someone. I'm afraid I'll feel trapped."

Anna's heart contracted as she pictured a beautiful little girl caring for an old invalid while her friends enjoyed a normal life. A little girl who wouldn't allow herself to resent being so tied down by him, but whose soul remembers now how it felt.

"A very wise woman told me something interesting today." She repeated the story of the owls. "The past is past, Sophia. That's what I've learned during my stay here in Greece. I thought my life was over. Now I feel a very important part of it is only beginning. Life is full of beginnings."

"But how can we be sure that the decisions we make in our lives are the right ones?"

"Ah, the devil's whisper, making us doubt, making us lose faith in ourselves. The truth is, Sophia, you can't be sure. Choosing is always a risk. Changing takes risk. But risk is what makes life interesting."

"And if you make a bad mistake? Choose the wrong thing?"

"Part of it is believing. Believing in yourself. Believing that you are doing the right thing. We have to keep believing, because the moment we stop, doubts close the circle and then we are, indeed, trapped."

"How will I know what to do?" Sophia's voice wavered a little.

"The only thing I can say is that you can't let fear be your guide. I've only just learned that. If your heart leads you to certain conclusions, don't hesitate to draw them." She smiled at Sophia and gave her hand a squeeze. "You'll know what to do when the time comes. Count on it."

After Sophia left, Anna thought, *We hand on the wisdom we receive. That's how it works. Thank you, Maria.*

At the end of the month, Demetri left a message for Anna to come to Elounda the next day. When she arrived, he wore a smile that rivaled the Cretan sun. "I have friends who have a small gallery in Georgetown. That is very near where you live, I believe."

"Yes, it is."

"I have told them about you, and if you will allow it, I would like to let them see a portfolio of your work."

Four days later, Anna received an "urgent" message from Demetri to hurry to Elounda for some very interesting news. He met her on the steps, waving a telegram in the air.

"I sent the sample of your work, and an accompanying letter, by air express. And today I received a telegram that the paintings and drawings had indeed arrived, and that the gallery would, very definitely, like to show this work! In fact," he said, "they have an unexpected opening in only two weeks." He glanced at the telegram. "The artist slated for that showing has been ill. If possible, they would like to have the entire collection immediately." He gave her both the telegram and a copy of the letter he had sent, in which he praised the series he had called *Watercolors by Anna—Aegean Illuminations*. Anna noticed that he never mentioned that she was Paul Sandoval's wife.

Maria grabbed Anna's hand in both of hers. "I knew something like this would happen," she said.

They went into the sitting room, and after they had discussed all the things that needed to be done in the next few days, Demetri made his announcement. "It is time for Maria and me to make our yearly visit to Switzerland. August in Crete is just too hot for us," he said. They were drinking wine to celebrate Anna's show. "We will be closing this house at the end of the week. We have only to pack our clothes. Everything else stays here for us."

Panic rose in Anna's throat. She had gotten used to this routine, these dear friends, the bare brown crags, and the breath of the sea of Crete, and she loved her little villa.

She looked around the room of rose-colored light, not wanting this time to come to an end. So much had happened here. She had learned so much. But it was time to leave. She knew that. Her thoughts turned to Washington. And suddenly she felt a quickening of excitement. It would be good to get home.

"I wish I could give you a gift," Anna said, looking at Maria and Demetri.

"But you have," Demetri answered. "Your voice and your breath have infused these walls. Your spirit will remain here, waiting for us when we return. Many times over the coming years we will remember things you said, the way you looked. And we will look forward to your visits."

Demetri, holding Maria's hand, blurred before Anna's vision. "Thank you," she whispered. "Thank you."

Twenty-five

The day Anna arrived back at her house in Washington, everything looked different. As she entered the driveway, the house
seemed smaller than she remembered. She had taken a taxi from
the airport, not wanting anyone with her for this homecoming.
Turning the key in the lock, she hesitated. Then, with a determined twist, she held the door open for the cab driver to bring in
her luggage.

She stood in the stillness of the empty house, waiting to see
how she felt here now. Leaving everything in the entrance hall, she
went from room to room touching the furniture, looking out at familiar views from the windows. The light spot was still on the rug
in the dining room where she had dropped the full bottle of Chi-
anti and couldn't ever quite get it out; the marks on the door
made by the collie puppy years before were still there; Paul's
sweater still hung on the rack in his study. But something had
changed. The voices that had permeated these walls were faint
now. There were no longer ghosts of little children becoming
adults in every corner. It was just a nice house.

In the bedroom, Anna took Paul's picture from the mantel
and smiled. Her heart wrenched. She had to admit that. But she
was no longer devastated by the pain.

Walking through the familiar rooms and out onto the wide
porches, she wondered what it was that felt so peculiar. Then,
passing by the full-length mirror in the entrance hall, she caught a
glimpse of herself. Her short hair curled softly around a face
browned by the sun. Her eyes looked large in her lean face. She

brought her hands to her cheeks, then held them out and looked at them. No long fingernails here. These hands too were brown, and they had a new power in them. She knew what they were capable of doing.

Looking up at herself again, she thought, *That's what it is. I know what I am capable of.* That was what was different. "Anna," she whispered. And in her mind she heard an echo of Demetri's voice.

Now I can sell the house. She waited for the sinking fear to rise and the niggling pros and cons to begin their battle, but she felt only a sense of finality. Out loud she whispered, "To every thing there is a season."

She fixed herself a cup of tea and called both of the children to tell them she was home, and to come as soon as they could. Peter promised to be there for the art show. "If Grandma Moses could do it, I suppose you can too," he teased.

"You have no respect for your aging mother," Anna answered. "And please don't wear your smelly old tennis shoes."

"Oh, I have a new pair. High-tops. Plaid."

Christine couldn't take off from her job on such short notice, but she promised to come later, before the show was taken down. "Mom," she said, "you sound different. Are you all right?"

"All right with sparkles." It was a phrase Christine had coined when she was five.

"I can't wait to see you. And your show. Did you really go swimming topless?"

"And have a tan to prove it!"

Maggie was coming. "You couldn't keep me away," she said after whooping with joy when Anna called her from Washington. "I can't get away the day of the opening, but I'll be there with bells on the next day. So stock up on the wine, and don't plan to sleep for at least thirty-six hours."

Anna hesitated to call her Washington friends. She felt strange, as though she had a new skin she needed to get used to. She would just wait and see if she ran into them. With delight, she had given the gallery, at their request, a list of all her friends' names and addresses for the announcement and invitation to her one-woman show. Of course, they would have no idea that "Anna" was none other than the prodigal daughter of Washington. And even if they suspected, it would be fun if some of them came.

Sitting on her veranda, Anna watched the stream flow by behind her house. She had just spent the day helping hang her exhibit in the lovely Georgetown gallery. Before dressing for the opening that evening, she was relaxing with a drink, made by Peter, who had arrived the day before for the grand event.

It was good to be home. She had forgotten the greenness—the smell of cut grass. She smiled. Tomorrow Maggie would be here. There was so much to tell her.

Sipping her drink, Anna gazed absently down the path that led between landscaped flower beds to the stream, watching a cream-colored butterfly flit from bush to bush. From the depths of the house she heard the phone ring.

"You have a phone call, Mother," shouted Peter. "From Athens."

"Hello?" Anna's pulse throbbed in her ears as she answered. Athens? Through the transatlantic hum, she could hear a voice saying, "I have your party on the line, sir."

"Anna, Alexis here. How are you?"

"I'm—" She cleared her throat. "I'm . . . I'm just fine. And you?"

"I miss you. I hadn't realized that you had returned to the States. I would have liked to have seen you again."

"Please, Alexis. I told you—"

"I know. I have accepted what you told me. But I have something to say to you. You must listen to me."

Anna listened for a moment and heard only crackling on the line. Then he went on. "I have loved you, Anna, and I think you had some feeling for me. That's why I called. If it's true that we continue to be shaped throughout our lives as we grow, we each have had a hand in the other's creation, you and I. I will be forever different because we met. I wanted to tell you that."

The catch in Anna's throat didn't allow her to respond.

"You told me good-bye that last night in Athens, but I didn't answer you. I couldn't then. That is why I called."

"To say good-bye?"

"Yes. But I hope if you are ever in Athens again, you will call. 'Good-bye'—if my English lessons taught me correctly—only means 'God be with you.' And I value your friendship, even if it"—he paused for a moment—"couldn't be more. I will always be glad to see you."

"Thank you, Alexis."

"Good-bye, Anna."

"God be with you, Alexis." Anna hung up, feeling that she had been given a gift of great value. She dressed for the show in a bemused state, her body light and airy, barely touching the floor, a glow somewhere near her heart.

Late that evening, Anna looked out across the almost-empty gallery. Peter was talking with a young couple near the entrance, laughing. His features were getting more angular. Every move he made reminded her of Paul. The caterers were picking up the empty glasses and cleaning the long table, littered with tired fragments of the fabulous food.

The French doors leading to a balcony at the other end of the narrow room stood open, letting in the fragrance of the warm summer evening. Anna could see the silhouettes of trees against the soft, charcoal sky that, in the city, was never truly dark.

She hunched her shoulders and rolled her head around to release the tension. The whole evening had been one grand moment after another—as Maggie would say. There were few things more satisfying than to have people exclaim over something you created, whether it was a house, a baby, or a painting. She smiled, looking down the length of the gallery at her work lining the walls and at her son. *Especially pleasing,* she added, *if it has been gratifying to create.*

She stood and stretched, then wandered slowly down the length of the room. The owners of the gallery had displayed her pencil drawings as well as the paintings. The drawings that she had later done over in watercolor were hung next to their paintings.

Each piece was a memoir, an essay on a memorable occasion, a statement of her frame of mind at the time. The boys and single girl playing soccer in front of the ruined columns, the old man playing his bouzouki on the corner. The white florid face of the old vendor who offered her chocolate in "payment" for the drawing of her little kiosk in Syntagma Square.

Anna had included a portrait of Sam, his "half-assed" glasses perched on his craggy nose, his attention on a potsherd he was holding so that it caught a shaft of light coming through the hole in the roof of that house in Lato. It was a composite, some of it painted from memory. Anna smiled again. *Wonder if he ever caught that little filly—or rather, if she caught him.*

The series of boat pictures she had done on the trip with Alexis were her least favorite, because they were like all boat pictures, she thought—white boat and blue water. She did have some nice angles of Alexis at the wheel and a good scene sketched of the beach at Hydra.

Her favorite piece was of Demetri at his easel, his face a study of concentration. Her practice drawings were hung around the final painting, which was a composite of all of them.

On an easel in the middle of the room was a painting Anna had added at the last minute. It was unnamed, another beach scene on a rock-ribbed shore. It was a back view of a woman sitting on a beach mat, her face in profile looking out to sea as if she were searching for something. She had red hair, but it was thick and long with wiry curls at her temples. Her nose had a distinct arch. Clutched in the hand she leaned on, was the top to her bikini. In the distance were several other women bathers, also topless, portrayed without detail.

"I'd say that was a very good likeness," said a voice from behind her.

Sam! Anna whirled around, and there he was, in shirtsleeves, his tie loosened, his light summer jacket hanging from one finger, an enigmatic smile on his comical face.

"But her hair is the wrong color."

"Where did you—? How did you—?"

He ignored Anna's stammering and walked by her nonchalantly, checking his guide to the titles as he looked at each piece. "These are good, don't you think?"

Anna fell in beside him. "I'm not sure the artist will be a legend in her own time, but all things considered, they're not bad." She was so glad to see him. He looked at her over the top of his glasses.

"The artist isn't so bad either," he said, nodding in approval, his mouth screwed up in that familiar scowl.

"Where's Taylor?"

"Oh, somewhere out in the wild blue yonder. She transferred to San Francisco."

"Who left whom at the altar?"

"We didn't get that far."

"Oh?"

"I discovered something. You know, I told you she made me feel . . ."

"*Young,* I think you said. *Renewed,* I think, was the way you put it."

"Well, it wasn't true. Or rather"—he cleared his throat—"it was true, in a way. But what I discovered was that I had never stopped feeling like that. I just thought I had."

"Oh."

"I had fallen into such a comfortable routine with Grace. Then, when she died, I thought I was old—finished. In a panic, I went out and kicked up my heels a little." He cut his eyes sideways at Anna.

"I remember."

"No," he said, exasperated. *"Before Crete."*

"It must have been satisfying. You—"

"It wasn't." He pulled at his ear and took a deep breath. "Strangely enough, it was boring. It took me a while to figure that out. Plus an enlightening experience with that lady." He pointed to the easel. He walked on to the next painting and examined it.

Then he said offhandedly, "When I told Taylor, in the end, that I probably wasn't the man she needed, I think she was relieved."

They were walking by the group of drawings Anna had done early in her Crete days, when Sam stopped. "When did you do that?" It was the sketch of Sam as he looked out over the Lassithi Plateau.

"On one of our little excursions."

"I think you exaggerated the nose."

"How do you happen to be in Washington?" Anna asked.

"I bought a spread up in Maryland. I am now what is known as a country gentleman. Thought I'd come into the city for some culture. I've been to the symphony and the opera. And"—he looked around—"I thought I'd take in a little art show, especially since the artist's name had a familiar ring to it."

"Did you buy the horses?"

"Yes. I have a pasture full of fillies and a stallion pawing down the door to his stall. I've even got a stereo system in the barn. They like Scarlatti."

"Sounds like a nice setup."

"Except for one thing."

"And what's that?"

"No nag."

"What?"

"I figure every farm should have at least one old nag around. You know, to add atmosphere to the place." He pulled his ear again. "See, I rattle around in this barn of a house." He looked at Anna, screwing up his mouth as if cogitating over his next words. Then, like a real estate agent, he said, "It has good light. Lots of windows. And it even has a pond out back where nobody would notice if a person went swimming"—he cocked an eyebrow—"in whatever dress or lack of dress . . ."

"And you figure an old nag would want to do that?"

"I was thinking it might be interesting to find out."

Anna shook her head, imagining him standing with one foot on the rung of a fence looking at horses, a piece of straw in his mouth. She didn't say anything.

"Ah, well, just an idea I had." He folded the guide and put it in his pocket. "Listen, why don't you get your kid over there—I could have picked him out as your son from a crowd in Grand Central Station—something about the nose," he mused. "Go get him, and I'll buy us all a drink, and maybe a steak, if you're hungry."

"Hungry! God, Sam, do you do anything without thinking of food?"

He took her arm and walked her back toward the entrance. "I forgot to tell you about Esmerelda."

"Oh?" Alarm shot through Anna as a picture flashed through her mind of another young Taylor. Oh well. She looked up at him with a smile of resignation. "How wonderful. Are congratulations in order?" she asked.

Sam was giving her a knowing look over his glasses. "She's my cat."

"Ahh." Anna took a deep breath, calming the pulse she could hear beating in her ears. She swallowed. "Do you really have a cat?" she asked.

"I do."

She gave him a long look. "And do you ever tie her?"

He shook his head, a grin lifting the lines of his craggy face, love glowing from his sad eyes.

"Never."

A Summer All Her Own

Rosanne Keller

This Conversation Guide is intended to enrich the
individual reading experience, as well as encourage us
to explore these topics together—because books,
and life, are meant for sharing.

A CONVERSATION WITH ROSANNE KELLER

Q. *What was your inspiration for* A Summer All Her Own?

A. I was in Athens with a group of people when one of the women, a recent widow, asked me to take her to a certain shop in the Plaka. I got us so lost that we finally just sat down in an outdoor café and ordered Greek coffee. She turned to me and began talking about being a widow—how people treated her; her fear of facing the future alone; the ridiculous and discouraging things people did, even out of love; the encouraging, thoughtful support of honest, true friends.

Later that summer, after spending three weeks with my family in Crete, I couldn't get my conversation with that woman out of my mind. I began reading about death and dying, widowhood, mourning and the stages of grief. It was a comment made by another widow I knew, whose husband had died from a sudden heart attack, that tugged at my heart: "He didn't even say good-bye."

Q. *What did you hope to achieve in writing this novel?*

A. I would like readers to come away with a renewed sense of self. I hope the novel will inspire people to stop and ponder their own potential, which may have been buried by societal expectations, busyness (the hallmark of our times), and the humdrum of daily life. There are certainly times when our obligations to other people must take precedence. But these times don't last forever. We must be careful not to let them take over our lives so that our own identity is smothered. I hope readers will see that change, even drastic change, can be the catalyst for something good if they have the courage to take a few risks and follow their dreams, even when they are advised against it by well-meaning loved ones, people's expectations, or the status quo.

Anna *chose* marriage over pursuing her own fledgling career. She *chose* to stay home with her children. She *chose* to support her husband's profession by entertaining, accompanying him on his frequent travels, being there for him. There is nothing wrong with these choices unless they become totally consuming. Even if Paul had not died, I hope Anna would have had the courage to go in search of herself, follow her own passion for art . . . and eventually take control of her own fate. It was time.

Q. What is the most important message you would like to convey in this book?

A. That true self-knowledge is essential in living a fulfilling and satisfying life. If we are always trying to *be* something expected—by another person, by society, or by myths that have been instilled in us—we can never reach our full potential. I would hope that people reading this book would take time to reflect on their deepest desires and needs, and begin to find ways to fulfill them.

Q. When did you know that you were a writer?

A. When I was a child, I had a very lively imagination. Sometimes the stories I told were deemed lies, worthy of a good switching. But my mother, also a writer, encouraged me to write things down. Hundreds of stories, essays and poems fill my files. Every morning, I get up early, put on music, light candles, and write in my journal. The entries might consist of a letter to a friend or a scene from a book I am working on. My journal is part diary, part to-do lists, and part Book of Commonplace. (If I hear a good phrase, saying, idea, or line from a song or poem, I write it down with the source. Then later, I can adapt these entries and incorporate them into my writing.) In the late eighties, I quit my job as a teacher of English at both Arizona State University and Cook School of Theology with the intention of becoming a gainfully *un*employed rich and famous writer of novels. When I made this move, I was raising three sons and continued, as I had for many years, doing literacy and ESL projects. I wrote dozens of short stories, manuals, and workbooks for new adult readers (all on a low reading level), and articles for magazines. Then I moved to Minnesota and got *another* master's degree, from Saint John's School of Theology/Seminary—just for the pure joy of learning—and worked as an adviser to foreign students. During that time, I wrote—what else?—academic papers. And bad poetry, as well as long, short, and true stories—which I never submitted for publication. Then my new "hobby" of doing sculpture took off in unexpected ways, and I was getting commissions, including one for Exeter Cathedral in England and a Buddha for the private meditation room of His Holiness the Dalai Lama. *Selling* what I wrote came much harder for me than writing, and I haven't gotten to the rich and famous part yet either.

Q. How does it feel to have written a novel?

A. I have borne three sons, run five marathons, walked five hundred miles across Spain. I have three university degrees. I created a life-size bronze sculpture that's situated on the campus of Texas Woman's University, and my art is displayed throughout the world. Getting a novel published is right up there with these accomplishments—I feel euphoric!

All of my stories start with an idea, a theme. Sometimes with a sentence or two, such as: "I had just buried Rachel. She was the last. In my seventy-two years I'd known many interesting people, had a multitude of fascinating acquaintances. But I'd only had five friends." I was forty-two when that statement resonated through my brain. It became a book I have never sold, called "A Handful of Friends." I then had to figure out who this seventy-two-year-old woman was and create a world for her to live in.

In writing a novel, a writer creates a world and then peoples it with characters who appear like apparitions, begging to be given voice. These characters begin to relate to each other. They do and say things I myself would never think of in the circumstances I conceive. I observe them from afar. Then they become me . . . or I become them. I see through their eyes, remember with their memories, rejoice at their discoveries. I am surprised by the turns they take and revel in what they learn from one another.

Novels are often more real than real life. The challenge is to write this ultrarealness so that the reader doesn't have the sense that it is *ultra* because by craft (or craftiness) the author weaves a semblance of life, for which there is no vocabulary, into an invisible web of words without revealing the intricate loops and knots and symmetry that provide the enabling strength. The reader sees only the drops of dew caught by the web . . . if it's done well. To borrow from the Book of Genesis, the characters become clay in my hands. And after I fashion them, I try to blow into them the breath of life. The result can be astounding! For when they begin to live and relate in the world I have created for them, they act as if they have free will.

Writing a novel is, for me, the ultimate of playing God.

Q. How do you happen to know so much about Greece?

A. My father worked in the Foreign Service, so since I was a child I've traveled all over the world, including six trips to Eastern Europe and the Middle East that included Greece. In my journal I write detailed descriptions of the places I visit—although *finding* those descriptions later is another matter! When I am at a site where known history has taken place, I can visualize how it must have been. Fanciful, that's me. Also, I am a student of philosophy and have read widely about Greece at the dawn of civilization. It is a magical place and always somewhere within me is the yearning to return. I did go topless when I was there, by the way. My teenage sons were a little startled, but they got used to it. It's the only way to swim in the Aegean!

Q. Where did you get the ideas for the men in your story?

A. I have had many wonderful men in my life—a loving father, two great brothers, a kind, generous, and devoted husband, three delightful sons—all responsible, thinking adults—and numerous friends. I like men and find them fascinating. Alexis is a composite character for me, taken from men I have known. I like him, but like Anna, I wouldn't want to marry him. Sam is the man of my dreams, I guess. He wouldn't think of holding Anna back from her desire for fulfillment. He is a whole person who isn't needy and who *likes* Anna as much as he apparently loves her. He does not need her to be complete.

This book is about the evolving roles of women and men in our society, as is my next book. It is unprecedented that people should have twenty to thirty years of healthy living after parenting and career days are over. It is unprecedented that housework takes so little effort that wives at home have so much free time. It is unprecedented that women and men are so well educated, that travel is so easy, that we are aware of so many possibilities and options in our lives. I want to write stories in which my characters address these changes with grace and dignity and a little humor. Sam is one of those wise characters.

Q. Why did it take you so long to get published?

A. First, I have to admit that patience is not one of my virtues. After I wrote some novels in the eighties, I tried to sell them on my own and became frustrated by the length of time it took to get a rejection. For a while, I did have a New York agent who believed in my work but was unable to place it. And I was very busy. Only last year did I have time to dust off my novels and try again. One of the first agents to ask to see *A Summer All Her Own* was Helen Breitwieser, who became my agent. She was my angel in the City of Angels.

Until five years ago, I was married (for thirty-five years)

and I always worked. Now I am semiretired. It is pure luxury to be able to plan my time any way I like.

I write because I am compelled to do it. I love being published. But when I write a story, novel, essay, or even a bad poem, something in me is satisfied. I dread the details of sending my material out into the world, so I put it off. And if I put it off long enough, I'm on to something else.

Q. What are you working on now?

A. My newest book, now in its final stages, is the story of four American women, all at turning points in their lives, who have come to Wales as a "place apart" to seek renewed possibilities, to rediscover their purpose and identity as they deal with radical, moving and sometimes disturbing changes that have recently taken place for each of them.

They meet and finally all four become friends over pints in pubs, long walks, trips into town for concerts, shopping, and the best custard tarts. To celebrate their friendship they decide to hike together a portion of an ancient path along the border between Wales and England.

Each woman has a hand in aiding the others in discovering her faith in a future filled with possibilities, adding their stories to the multilayered history of the land, their footsteps to the centuries deep footprints on that timeless path, which leads them all out of chaos and confusion into their own clearly defined destinies. Perhaps one day this book, too, will be published and available for you to read.

QUESTIONS FOR DISCUSSION

1. Did the book make you feel you were on a vacation in Greece? What do you like, or possibly not like, about the author's descriptions of the places that Anna sees during her summer there?

2. Expectations of a wife's role in marriage have been evolving in our society over the past three to four decades. Women often want to "have it all": marriage, children, and a demanding, satisfying career. Does Anna's identity crisis ring true in these days when many women often follow their careers and make sure to take care of themselves and fulfill their dreams? If Anna had chosen to continue working, put the children in day care, and not go with Paul on his world travels, how would their marriage and her life been affected?

3. Many women face the second half of their lives solo. Often they have made such a habit of putting other people's needs before their own, and they don't know what to do with the freedom, the solitude. Sometimes this can happen within a marriage when the demands of children are no longer so urgent or when new opportunities present themselves. How can changes in one's circumstances, even if they

are not as drastic as death or divorce, be a catalyst for self-discovery?

4. The reason Anna gives herself for her irrational running away after becoming physically intimate with Sam is that she fears the sex will ruin their comfortable, deeply nurturing friendship. But we don't always tell ourselves the real reasons for our actions. What else might have motivated her to flee in such haste? Do you find Anna's sexual relationship with Alexis believable? Discuss some of the joys and pitfalls of resuming a sex life in midlife, in our society, after a long, faithful marriage or relationship.

5. Maria is the woman many of us would like to be "when we grow up"—wise, beautiful, calm, and still in a good marriage. She never mentions having children of her own, and she is always there for Anna. Could she be fulfilling her own needs as well as Anna's by counseling this unhappy younger woman?

6. Have you known successful and sophisticated men like Alexis who idolize woman but also feel entitled and superior to them? Could Anna be happy with him . . . with a little compromise? Or are you glad that, at the end of the novel, she seems poised to pursue a relationship with Sam, who treats her with respect and equality but also keeps her off balance because he's confused about what he wants?

7. Demetri is old school in his relationship with Maria. He plans his day; she plans hers around it. She seems to be content with this arrangement. Does this kind of marriage exist today successfully, with both people happy and at ease?

8. Anna rediscovers her talent for drawing and painting during her summer in Greece, but not everyone is so richly talented. How do you feel about her artistic gifts and how do they make her typical, or not typical, of other women in her circumstances? If you had "a summer all your own," what dream would you pursue?

9. Anna has the financial freedom to indulge herself for an entire summer. Few women are so lucky. Discuss how a woman's financial situation might limit her chances to rediscover herself as a single woman in midlife. How might some of those limitations be self-imposed?

10. Have you ever sunbathed topless on a public beach? Care to share your experience?

About the Author

Photo by Kay Nell Bates

Rosanne Keller, a world traveler, writer, teacher, and sculptor, has enjoyed many visits to Greece. In 1999, Keller walked five hundred miles, from the Spanish Pyrenees to Santiago, on the Pilgrims' Way of *El Camino de Compostela*—featured in her book *Pilgrim in Time*. She lives in the woods of the Texas Hill Country.